Wallfloweresque

A Novel

Alan Devey

Published 2005 by The London Press

ISBN: 1-905006-01-2

Cover design by Chris Perry (csperry_75@yahoo.co.uk).

"*I have to admit we are locked in the most exquisite mysterious muck. This muck heaves and palpitates. It is multi-directional and has a mayor. To describe it takes many hundreds of thousands of words. Our muck is only part of a much greater muck - the nation-state - which is itself the creation of that muck of mucks, human consciousness. Of course all these things also have a touch of sub-limity...*"

- Donald Barthelme, City Life

Part One:
No Mouth,
No Trousers

Chapter One

There are a great many more available women in London than there are available men, although it's easy to forget this when none of them want to sleep with you. I shifted my weight on the uncomfortable wooden furniture, hand-whittled by natives the proprietor's son had met during his gap year, and glanced around the West London bar. It was early evening in *U-Pon-Sea*, the brightly-lit establishment where we'd arranged to meet, a place where the fashionable congregate and a light snack costs more than a DVD. The only saving graces were the beautiful women who frequented this kind of place but sadly they hadn't turned up yet. Instead moneyed thirtysomethings scattered themselves around, enjoying strangely-named cocktails this Saturday night, soon moving on to dinner parties, gallery openings, exclusive clubs. Unexpected flashes of movement caused me to look more closely and I noticed many of the laughing women held ornamental dogs in their laps. Shitzus, chihuahuas, toy poodles, all burrowed their noses into designer skirts and sniffed at fingers holding bright, spirit-laced drinks. I recalled one of the girls at the office talk about getting a *doggy* to carry round with her so I guess this must be another recent craze. The canines were sported like accessories, beside handbags or glittering jewellery, and given about as much attention as those objects of style.

Talking of style, here came Si. Back from the bar with our pints, clothes rumpled carefully, hair ferociously gelled but all over the place, like he didn't care how it looked. Simon exuded a considered bohemianism and instantly struck even the smartest girl as desirable. That is, until she struck up a conversation and discovered he was shallow as the ruts in a hand-ploughed field. Si was a good mate though, and a gifted guitarist who'd had precious little luck with the ladies of late, pulling only girls who proved to be annoying or obsessive the next morning. Which was why we'd endeavoured to get Simon here tonight and set him up with someone equally pleasant and superficial.

"Cheers." We clanked glasses. "So Monty, you go out last night?"

"Nah, couldn't be bothered." I waited for Si to tell me what he'd been up to.

"I checked out the goth night at that club down my road, met this girl who seemed really sweet so I went back to her place." From the other side of the room there came a frenzied yapping as one of the canines made its presence known. "Jesus, what's with this place?"

"I think ornamental dogs are part of the new season."

"Well anyway, she was making coffee, so I went into her room and there's all these posters on the walls of Animal from *The Muppet Show*."

"Animal?"

"I swear, there must have been two dozen, not to mention toys and dolls. So I asked her about the pictures and she said there was something about Animal that really turned her on."

"Um."

"That was my response. From that point I was making excuses to get away. I eventually told her I had to be up for band practice but I'd give her a call and maybe introduce her to some drummers." Si put down his pint and fiddled with a drooping spike of hair. "I had to get night buses across London, it was five o'clock by the time I got in."

"I've got to hand it to you mate, that's one hell of a losing streak if the best you can do is some girl who's sexually obsessed with feral puppets."

"Tell me about it."

Behind us a couple of groups gathered up their belongings and left, the women clutching struggling pets to modest breasts as they approached the exit. That was when the sizeable frame of Fergal flew in, almost barging into one twittery lady holding a Mexican hairless. Dressed, as usual, in some middle-aged art teacher's idea of casual, my flatmate acknowledged our presence and went to get a drink.

"Raises an interesting question though." Si was unfazed. "It got me thinking today, what *would* be the best muppet to have sex with?"

"Piggy, obviously."

"You say that, but I think she'd just give you shit." He checked his hair in the mirrored wall opposite. "Look at Kermit, he's a broken man."

"Frog."

"Frog. Anyway, the more I got to thinking, the more I ended up with Janice. *The Muppet Show* was like real life in a lot of ways, and in real life you should never go for the most glamorous woman."

"Pig."

"Pig. Never go for the one dressed like a tart. Always date the hippychick instead. She's far more likely to do whatever you want her to, just make sure you've got plenty of joss sticks to burn. They like that."

"Thanks. If I ever find myself seducing Janice out of the Muppets I'll remember your advice."

At this point Fergal joined us, a great erudite figure in corduroy and tweed he possessed the vague remnants of an Irish accent and seemed much older than his twenty eight years.

"So, which earthshaking topics are you gentlemen setting to rights this evening?"

"If you could choose any of them, which Muppet would you have sex with?"

"Hmm, highbrow as ever." Fergal sipped his gin. "You know, I always found Beaureguard compelling."

"Beaureguard? What the hell was he? Apart from the janitor."

"No idea, but he had a lovely distinctive voice. You know how I like a bit of rough Simon."

"Huh."

"Although what's more likely is I'd find myself attracted to whichever fellow was working the anthropomorphic pooch."

Si groaned. "I knew it, the moment you get here the conversation turns gay."

"Well Simon, what else do you expect from a big ol' puff like myself?" Fergal winked at him. "Other heterosexuals will arrive soon laddo, don't trouble yourself." He beckoned at someone who was stood behind me. "In the meantime I hope you'll welcome my new boy."

A thoroughly tanned man, much younger than us, approached the table. He wore a sleeveless white t-shirt exposing toned biceps and an absence of underarm hair. There was a blank expression on his clean-shaven face.

"Ah, Roland my boy. Good to see you're still denying a beard." Fergal kissed the gay on his lips. I scanned the bar for homophobes who might take offence, small-town habits die hard. "Welcome, welcome. Be seated."

We greeted this newcomer who appeared to have no obvious character traits and he settled down beside Fergal, a man with enough personality for both of them. Fergal launched into a train of conversation making stops at the worldwide political situation, Jane Fonda's donations to liberal causes, the English class system and his feelings about having an Irish heritage. I rose to get a round in, knocking over Roland's empty bottle as I went.

While I took up a position at the bar, beside a cluster of thickset men in rugby shirts, the lights went low and dance music was turned on in preparation for the evening. The darkly attractive barmaid took my order with a smile and when she returned I concentrated on holding the quartet of drinks rather than looking where I was going. I came within inches of walking into Simon's chair but he'd anticipated this turn of events and assisted me, placing the bevvies before members of our group.

"Don't get me wrong, I find straightforward men charming." Fergal continued talking as Roland looked on, either awestruck or bored, the natural mien of his face was difficult to read. "Give me a strapping proletarian gaylord over the effete upper class whoopsie any day, I just have a problem with the working classes when it comes to their lack of imagination."

"I don't agree with that." I said.

"I know you don't my friend, and perhaps you're the exception that proves the rule. But look at how most of your people spend their leisure time; it's pub or TV, or pub *and* TV, or football followed by a trip to the off licence and then some TV. Culturally that's it, as far as I can tell."

I didn't feel the need to argue with him, my diplomacy possibly inspired by the knowledge I always lost. Hell, it wasn't like I really felt a part of the working classes. Maybe compared to Irish landowners I was a peasant, but I'd never subsisted on a diet of bread and dripping, and my parents had always aspired to more than council tenancy.

Si nudged me out of the reverie. "What time are Justin and his bird getting here?"

I looked at my watch. "Any minute now."

"I wouldn't expect young Just-in any time soon." Announced Fergal. "He was going to Harley Street this afternoon to get the nerve endings in his neck clipped."

"I've heard about that." Roland looked at him. "Isn't that supposed to stop you blushing?"

"Indeed it does my boy, unfortunately for Just-in they miscalculated slightly and went all the way through his jugular vein."

Si turned to me. "Is that true?"

"No it's not. Fergal just doesn't approve of Justin."

"He's a big John Thomas."

With admirable timing Justin chose that moment to make his entrance, flanked on either side by a blonde girl and wearing what appeared to be a trilby. The trio came over to our table and offered to buy us drinks, the blondes pulling up chairs. Justin's girl-friend (Yohanna) greeted me with a hug and seated herself to my right, a deliberate attempt to manoeuvre her friend next to Simon. Saying hello to this other blonde, a girl called Lettice who worked with me at the agency, I hoped Fergal wouldn't treat us to his views on people who wore hats indoors. She showed no sign of removing the beret which partially covered her bleached locks.

At the bar Justin had taken off his trilby and held the felt apparel in one hand while prising his way through the hulking students. Justin was finding it difficult, being only five foot four. Cowboy boots added another inch and a half, but that still left him a good foot shorter than the college rugby team. Eventually he found a way in and thrust that carefully presented face, with its tiny beard and sideburns meticulously shaven to points, at the bar staff.

To my right Yohanna was telling Lettice, her housemate in a horribly sought-after area off Sloane Square, all about Si's band. As soon as Lettice appeared impressed by her descriptions Yohanna left the two of them talking about Simon's musical endeavours and turned to me.

"Well, that should go okay, hopefully."

"I think they're well suited."

"So do I, I'm glad we did that." She gave an enthusiastic smile and touched my arm. A weakness, but I tend to think of Yohanna as just another of Justin's appendages, they've been together so long. It comes as something of a jolt, on the irregular occasions we meet up, to be reminded how attractive she is. The force of Yohanna's appearance always gives me a shock, my heart leaping at the warm smile, full lips and pool-deep green eyes. She was Justin's though, always had been, and I needed more than looks.

"So Monty." Said Yohanna. "What's new in the world of bears?"

"I've been learning a lot about Ceausescu lately. You know, that dictator guy who used to run Romania?"

"Umm-humm." Justin appeared with the drinks and seated himself between Lettice, who'd lapsed deep into conversation with an enthralled Si, and his girl.

"Nicolae Ceausescu used to be this big hunter and there's photos of him with huge bears he'd supposedly killed. Actually aides shot them and he just posed with the bodies afterwards, it was all false images. Ceausescu marketed himself to his people like some kind of saviour; a heroic conqueror of the ursine world. It made me think about what we do at the agency."

"I like panda bears best." Asserted Yohanna with a giggle, sipping her sparkling yellow drink.

While I was busy being nonplussed Justin cut in. "Pandas can eat forty per cent of their body weight a day."

"Didn't you once date a girl like that?"

"Shut it Fergal."

"No, but seriously." The gin was clearly hitting my flatmate, he had one arm draped over Roland's broad shoulders. "The odd thing about ol' Ceausescu was how animal lovers around the

7

world should really have supported him. Even though his people starved to death he built bear numbers right up. Didn't he Monty?"

"By the thousand, but only because he wanted to shoot them."

"That can be dangerous, all that. My father had a hunting accident last year."

Fergal turned to Roland with a quizzical expression. "You told me your father lived in Carshalton! What was he hunting, squirrels?"

"I only know what my mother told me, alright?"

In response to the pouty defensiveness Fergal whispered something conciliatory into Roland's ear. Across the table I heard Lettice telling Si her favourite type of music was "anything really". Beside me Yohanna watched the gays to my left with that fascination slightly-cosseted girls have for unfamiliar subcultures.

"How long have those two been together?" She asked.

"Since last night."

And didn't I know it. Struggling to sleep, as I often do on a Friday night without the wind-down of alcohol, I'd just drifted off, when I was awoken by the moans of man-on-man sex emanating from the next room in our too-bijou flat. Tonight I'd vowed to get home and pass out before the squelching noises could keep me awake again.

I shuddered at the memory and looked across at Fergal who appeared to have convinced Roland not to be offended. The younger man was formally introduced to Lettice, the curvaceous blonde in her beret explained by Simon in the manner of someone proud to be associated with her. A good sign. Clearly our conspiracy was working.

"From the middle of nowhere, out near the west coast. Good farming stock." Fergal pulled a face. "You understand why I got out."

"Absolutely." Lettice shifted to hear better, a move which left her breast resting against Si. "Erm, do you get many people telling you Irish jokes?"

Fergal grinned. "Something that idiotic doesn't bother a renaissance man like myself *Lettuce*. The way I see it, all that's partly our own fault. Us Irish complain about the ridiculing and the stereotypes, but when you look at my country and the way we continue to indulge in fighting and sectarianism and fecking marching bands, it makes sense. Growing up with that, you start to realise why the rest of the world sees us as the butt of their jokes. As luck would have it I can usually outwit anyone foolish enough to mock my nationality. Or my sexual orientation for that matter."

"I'm sure you can." She turned to Yohanna. "He's very smart isn't he?"

"Indeed I am dear. So smart in fact I often think my seed should be bottled and passed to fertile young women such as yourselves." Fergal finished his gin. "It would be an act of charity, so it would. None of your fine gender should have a child by a foolish or less physically magnificent specimen, not when my sperm is available for you to utilise, albeit surreptitiously."

"Eugh." Said the girls in unison.

More rounds followed and the hours rolled by. There was one tricky moment when Justin asked me whether I knew which of his acquaintances was telling people he'd died. Apparently it had gone "beyond a joke" earlier in the week when an old school friend phoned up offering to say something at the memorial service. I studied Justin's entreating face, the silly facial hair, those gelled eyebrows and shining, exfoliated skin, and for a moment I was almost tempted to tell him the truth. For the sake of harmony I managed to restrain myself. I should have a word with Fergal about that sometime soon, but it wouldn't have done any good while he was several gin and tonics down the line. So far gone in fact, Fergal actually accepted Roland's invitation to get up and dance, the male couple occupying that section of floor ruled by a DJ playing funk and soul classics. As I watched the pair were joined by Justin who dragged Yohanna along, then Si and Lettice.

I remained at the table for two reasons. Ostensibly I was reserving the area and making sure our belongings were safe, but really I stayed because I've always been more comfortable on the periphery. There was no one for me to dance with, and I never pushed myself upon strangers in situations like this. Fergal shuffled,

9

cigarette in hand, like someone's uncle at a wedding party, while Roland apparently auditioned for the role of caged man-floozy at G.A.Y. I was content to observe partying females who sidled onto the dance area in short skirts and low-cut tops. They shook and twisted while Si and Lettice grew closer, the girl allowing him to lift her up, twirl them both amidst the revelry.

The pretty barmaid collected glasses from our table and I wished I had the confidence to ask her what she was doing afterwards. To brush off the rejection if her answer wasn't positive. Forgetting this refusal I would leave my seat behind, get up there and strut gloriously through the throng. But rebuffs don't bounce off a guy like me. I wasn't capable of forgetting myself and sharing in the unthinking good time happening all around. Afflicted with the disease of the wallflower, I felt like one of the self-excluded, forever letting others get on with the dance, that high-stakes game of flirtatious interaction. If I got up there now my movements would be stilted, my demeanour uncertain, past occasions had confirmed this beyond any doubt. Nervously dancing, I came to believe the whole room stared at my jerking movements, that less than assured presence. Inevitably I'd spill my drink on some poor girl, slip on a pool of liquid or whack some guy in the face with a gesticulating limb. It always happened.

Maybe this was a disease peculiar to certain English males, the repressed and uptight. Or maybe it was the curse of an only child to be always unsettled around the opposite sex. Whatever the reason it seemed impossible to overcome. I was twenty six years down the road, and however much alcohol I consumed I never felt bold enough to go out there, out where the lights flash and the music blares, where the young folks move unselfconsciously. Even at the most bacchanalian of orgies I'd be stuck at the side, red and abashed, maybe doing a crossword.

Simon had his arms around the waist of Lettice, the two of them like upright spoons, his face in her hair, her beret on his head for some reason. Now there was a guy who didn't care what he looked like. Yohanna gazed at them approvingly while Justin continued his signature dance, arms flailing up and down, face contorted, body swaying strangely, like a slalom skier with heartburn. I watched Si spin Lettice around and kiss her, briefly but with feeling. In that instant I felt all the emptiness of a single man on a Saturday night, all the envy engulfing a lonely guy when his mate pulls. It was envy a better man than me would never feel after helping a friend find something good.

These thoughts were upsetting. Despite having nothing myself I shouldn't begrudge others. But for all the positives of intoxication, drink often left me depressive rather than euphoric and I'd had enough. Fergal extricated himself from the crowd, perspiring like an unfit man in heavy clothes on a dance floor, and squeezed into the chair beside me. He nodded when I told him I was leaving.

Outside the autumn air hit me in the face and I checked my watch. Well after midnight, so the tubes wouldn't be running. I'd have to walk to a bus stop and continue my journey west from there. Setting off at pace, my annoyance evaporated as I got further away from that scene. I was merrily drunk, a bit cold, not too out of pocket, and the evening had been an unqualified success; we'd set Si up with Lettice. To find a girl for myself this Saturday was asking too much. She could wait, I was nothing if not patient.

Walking fast, I caught up with the four stocky men who must have left the bar before me. I watched them turn down a side street and crouch around a parked car about forty yards up the turning. Emboldened by the alcohol, I paused to see what they were doing. The vehicle looked smaller than its neighbours and I realised it was a Smart Car, one of those two seater German contraptions, kind of like half a normal automobile. Positioning themselves under one corner of the car each the students gripped tyres and a portion of the chassis with their tree trunk arms. One of the guys counted: "*1! 2! 3!*" and on the third number they rose together, the weight of the vehicle held by four beefy shoulders. Before my astounded gaze they gingerly sidestepped into the road, made unintelligible cries, then jogged off towards Shepherd's Bush. Into the darkness they went, carrying the car like pallbearers at a vehicular funeral, the disappearing shape resembling what might happen if a giant tortoise mated with a dune buggy.

That was certainly an innovative method of stealing a car I thought as the ten foot monster disappeared into the distance. I wondered how far they would be able to carry it, and if they did manage to get the car back to their digs whether they'd attempt to get it through the front door.

Turning on my heels, I walked along the main road and spotted a night bus to take me home within minutes.

Chapter Two

I woke up feeling surprisingly good, no headache or fuzziness, just the regular Sunday lethargy. It seems to me that our internal clocks always know when the week reaches its end, removing all motivation from our bodies to fulfil that God-given edict of the rest day. Mind you, it probably didn't help that I never scheduled anything for Sunday so I'd no reason to get up.

Checking the clock, I saw it was after noon. I'd successfully slept off the beer, and drinking water for a couple of hours late last night probably helped. After I got in I'd correctly guessed the group would go on to a club. Feeling another slight twinge of jealousy, I drunkenly decided to convince myself I wasn't missing out on anything.

During one of those occasions when I'd been out until 4am last year I made a record of the adventure. It was this tape I slotted into the video in the small hours, the recording of a drink-fuelled idea which actually came off. I'd borrowed Fergal's handheld camera and captured several hours of footage in a bad club from the view of a drunkard. Pretty much by accident, since I didn't know what the hell I was doing, my tape recreated the experience of an inebriated clubgoer stumbling around the cramped and noisy space, his gaze lingering on attractive women as the faint sound of chart music reverberates through the backdrop.

After a while spent watching the film most people tend to long for something more professional and tightly-edited, but the point of this recording wasn't its entertainment value. My tape served as a kind of aversion therapy, capturing that unpleasant combination of seizure-inducing lights, staff giving you funny looks and punters in tightly ironed shirts spilling drink on your trousers which seems so enticing after an evening in the pub. Then there were the extended sequences of hotties moving their bodies as nature and the Lord intended, sections which satisfied some drunken masculine urge to see foxy women, but without having to spend forty quid for the privilege or endure a clubgoer's frustration as they refuse to give you *the eye*.

Having seen the footage all the way through several times much of it I can take or leave. The point is made after about half an hour and then I tend to pass out, but one section makes me go back and watch again. There was a girl I filmed for a while that night, drawn to her vibe and natural happiness. She wasn't checking out the talent, just enjoying herself, sporting a big smile which was unforced and purely carefree. The girl looked perfect to me, twisting her body in time with the popular sounds, and it was only after a couple of minutes spent observing her grace and beauty that I noticed she only moved one arm. The other ended in a useless stump an inch or two above the elbow. At the time this realisation shocked me into turning the camera away, scared it might appear I'd singled her out for filming. Now I watched that clip more than the rest, and each time I see the sequence she grows in power and beauty. The girl doesn't care, she doesn't want my attention or sympathy, she only wants to dance. And dance she does, better than I could even if I tried, even with four limbs. Better, in my eyes, than anyone there. The sight overwhelms me.

Reluctant to leave the image behind, I pulled the duvet up to my nose and took the important decision not to get up just yet. Alone in my bed I thought about Sunday, how it was another of those times a single man misses a lover by his side. The karmic value of someone to wake up with seemed immeasurable right now, some smiling girl to help decide what we would do for breakfast, discuss the previous night's socialising and maybe make love with once more. It's not the same somehow, going into the kitchen to be greeted by a big gay man.

My mind spooled back to previous lovers, women I'd encountered over the last two years of living with Fergal. When we first moved in I was unused to the single life everyone who didn't know me very well assumed the two of us were living in some kind of homo sin. Spurred on by this misconception, I cast my line everywhere for a decent match. I undertook volunteer work, attended human rights meetings and leafleted supermarkets, hoping a shared mindset might give me something in common with the girls I met, a potential way into the hearts of liberal chicks who worked for the cause.

That was how I met Jill, we wrote letters to murderous dictatorships together and organised sit-ins for all kinds of obscure causes. A frizzy-haired redhead with freckles and a Frank Sinatra obsession, in hindsight Jill was a bit too serious, almost po-faced about living a life of which she could be proud. We had fun nevertheless, for the most part, although my abiding memory of our months together is the unfortunate occasion when the two of us visited some of her relations in the Midlands. Inspired by my desire to see a sloth bear, and thereby impress the boss with my extra-curricular research, Jill took the group of us to their local zoo, kids, grandparents and all.

I should have taken it as a bad omen when we walked past the bird enclosure and one of the parrots squawked: *"You cunt!"* at me. We were going to register a complaint about that, but such avian obscenity paled in comparison to what happened in the monkey house.

My girlfriend was eating an ice cream and happily pointing out chimpanzees for her cousins when one of the larger apes spotted Jill and began to clamber toward us, grunting loudly. Now, I'll admit Jill had quite a unique look, and if you were a fan of pretty ginger types with big hair you might even have been instantly excited by her, but there was no call for what that monkey did next. Within seconds my amusement turned to horror as the ape reached his bars and clung there with one hand while pleasuring himself furiously with the other. By the time we realised what was happening it was too late. Within seconds Jill, Jill's family, her ice cream, and a great deal of the surrounding area was showered with great splashes of hot monkey jism. I'm sure she must have washed her hair five or six times when we got home.

Unpleasant as that incident was it didn't break us up. No, Jill did that all by herself without the need for primate intervention. My supposed girlfriend announced one day she was moving to Canada. Why Canada I asked? I've got a friend there she replied, and apparently it's nice. One of your friends is dead I said, letting anger get the better of me, and everyone says heaven is nice, but you're not going to top yourself are you? That didn't go down too well and nothing I said could change her mind. It was made up, she was going to live there and plot how best to help further the Fair Trade movement, Jill and her friend moving on to South America or Africa or somewhere like that when the chance arose to *make a difference*. I wasn't part of her plans, what we had was just some interim distraction. So she left and I told all my friends she was too sombre for me so I had to let her go.

Alright, I admit it, we weren't exactly what you'd call *in love*, but Jill brightened up my day, and it pissed me off when she just upped and left. That's always been one of my problems, I find myself attracted to fearless or independent women, so strong and self-contained that one day they decided they don't need me or this country anymore and go off to live in Venezuela or France or somewhere equally backward. There was Paige, the oversexed Aussie who admitted she only went home with me at the end of the night because the batteries in her vibrator were dead and she hadn't found time to replace them. I thought she was joking, but after a few weeks of frenzied coupling with little or no accompanying conversation, it became clear she wasn't. I do look back on that month fondly though, a time when I was permanently on call to meet her bounteous physical needs. She went back to Perth in the end.

Then there was Barbara, the Sussex ice maiden who came on strong when we met but tested my self-esteem by getting all defensive and monosyllabic each time I phoned her. She refused potential dates for the two of us, cited spurious excuses, and only ever called me back at ridiculous times of the night. The phone would ring at 1 or 2am and Barbara's tone of voice at the other end suggested she was in a darkened street with a worryingly large guy lurking nearby and needed to be talking with someone. And I was the person on her phone she cared least about annoying. Barbara did that several times, and after the shock of being woken up subsided, her generic questions ("How are you?", "What have you been up to?", "How's the family?") soon bored me. That girl taught me to switch my mobile off before I went to bed every night, but if she renewed contact tomorrow I know I'd still try to set something up, such was her glacial beauty.

Then there were the girls I didn't even want to remember, the hope-diminishing rejections, the failed one-date wonders, the awkward flirtations, the hesitant seductions which petered out, on and on goes the list.....

I threw the duvet off. These memories were leaving me downbeat before the day had even begun. I had to retain my optimism for the female multitudes who needed me in their lives but just didn't know it yet. Fergal always said young people like us should be single every so often, how there was no point thinking you had to be part of a couple at all times whether you were in love or not. If I wasted time with one girl just to salve my loneliness I could miss a shot at someone foxier. The potential love of my life might pass by unnoticed, a real chance for happiness lost because I stuck with a steady partner for the sake of security and support and a united front at social events. Then again, you couldn't just stay with a girl until a better one came along (or one you thought was better anyway). Dumping people at random made your friends and family think you were a bit of a dirtbag.

The whole tapestry of relationships was my ongoing dilemma. Fortunately it was also a moot point at the moment. As I believe I've already mentioned, nobody in this city of several million eligible women was currently interested in me.

Wearing his crimson dressing gown, Fergal sat at the table munching on marmalade toast and reading supplement fourteen of the Sunday broadsheet. I hobbled into the dining area and collapsed at the table, examining the damage done to my toe a few moments ago when I'd come out into the hallway and whacked it against his dalek, the four-foot prop having apparently shifted at some point during the night. When we moved in Fergal was vague about where he'd got the legendary bad guy, although I've come to suspect he was a bit of a *Dr. Who* anorak during his younger years. What I am certain of is that the overgrown pepper pot was made from very hard metal, the kind which could inflict a nasty bruise on your flatmate's foot.

"Good morning Montgomery, care for some coffee?"

"Cheers."

Fergal moved around the kitchen, boiling water and tidying up. This room was an extension of our lounge with the two

17

bedrooms and bathroom nearby. Apart from my room pretty much all of the flat was spotless, one of the positives of living with a gay man. It doesn't half impress the lasses when you invite them back and every surface is crud-free. Believe me, I've been to enough shared houses, I know what women usually have to deal with when they visit twentysomething males. Plus Fergal would never hit on a girl while I was out of the room, something several of my hetero-sexual 'friends' had attempted in the past, coming on to women I'd spent hours coaxing into our house.

I sipped my mug of bitter, steaming fluid. "You're up early today."

"Indeed, laddo had to be back in Carshalton. He works on a Sunday, I can't remember as what, something vapid."

"Hmmm, did he move the dalek on his way out?"

"Young Roland was quite fascinated by that particular pos-session of mine." Fergal watched me rub my foot. "Apologies my friend, he may have. Is it badly bruised?"

"I'll live."

"I attempted to doze off after Roland's departure but I suf-fered the most terrible nightmare. In it I was chased o'er hill and dale by a veritable posse of gay bishops."

"Gay bishops?"

"Gay bishops, yes. They were about to catch up and forci-bly indoctrinate my poor quivering form into their religion when I woke up in a frightful cold sweat." Fergal picked up a section of newspaper. "After that vision of hell sleep was quite impossible."

"I can imagine."

He leafed through the broadsheet, locating a sub-heading previously circled in felt pen. Fergal liked to select odd news stories and read them to me at weekends, he said it was a charitable act, intended to broaden my outlook, but I think he just wanted an au-dience every now and again.

"Did you see this Montgomery? Apparently Japan has a fully ordained robot priest. It's been saying Buddhist prayers at fu-nerals for more than ten years."

"A robopriest? Is that dignified? What if it rains?"

"More to the point, what if it gets one of those computer virus thingies I've heard so much about?" He folded the paper with a flourish. "Do other robot priests have to conduct an exorcism on it? The mind boggles."

"Um, yes. It does, yes." I slurped my coffee. "How did it end up last night?"

"Fine I suppose. Toast?" I nodded, Fergal went to make some. "Those two you marked out for each other were an item by the close of business."

"Cool."

"Although I don't trust that Lettuce girl. Did you hear her response when asked what music she likes? 'Anything really'! Anything? *Anything?* Are you sure dear? Lift music? Ukrainian marching bands? Atonal psychedelia with blasts of untreated white noise?"

"This is because she wore a hat indoors isn't it?"

He turned to me. "You know my views on indoor headgear Montgomery, I've expressed them often enough in the past."

"You certainly have, many times."

Fergal didn't take the hint. "Anyone who refuses to remove their hat once inside a building is clearly lacking some vital facet of humanity. Here they are, under cover and in the warm, retaining an item on their noggin. The only explanation I can think of is that these fools are trying to compensate for some absence of personality. The hat is on, so they look interesting in the eyes of strangers. Unfortunately what they actually reveal, to anyone with any kind of nous, is the exact opposite."

"I didn't have a hangover a minute ago."

Fergal pointed in my direction. "I'm not talking about fancy dress or the uniform of a professional, or even something worn to cover the indignities of alopecia or the horrendous side-effects of chemotherapy. That's entirely understandable."

"Glad to hear it."

"What I can't stand is apparel deliberately employed for illusory purposes, worn whatever the weather and kept on under a roof. I can always tell if people aren't my type, they're the ones who wear hats indoors." He passed my toast across. "A case in point. What on earth did Just-in have on last night? Was that a trilby?"

"They're probably very *in* this week. He's starting to get suspicious someone's spreading rumours about him by the way."

"He'll never figure it out."

"It isn't polite to tell people he's died."

Fergal dismissed the notion with a flick of his wrist. "Fine, you've made your point, let's talk about something else."

"Okay, give me some queer gossip. What's the low-down on you and Roland."

"Oh him." Another flick. "I don't know if I'll be seeing *him* again. Young Roland wants me to go to the opera with him."

"Don't you like opera?"

Fergal looked at me sceptically. "You know Montgomery, I can take most things in order to spend time with an attractive lad, but opera is where I draw the line. The singing induces in me a strange neurological condition somewhat akin to narcolepsy. I took my mother to the Royal Opera House once and suffered a mild seizure for the last three hours of the performance."

"Sorry I asked."

"Besides, I'm not convinced I give two hoots about young Roland when all's said and done. If Carshalton's so damn horrid be quiet about it and move out, and if I hear one more mincer going on about *unresolved issues* with his father, I think I'm going to scream."

"That bad, huh?"

"It's not just that." Fergal sighed. "From discussions last night it appears his favourite film is *Caddyshack*."

"That is a good one." Remembering, I spluttered with laughter. "Those gophers, and that turd in the pool and....."

"Will you be quiet? The upshot is I don't know whether Roland and I are compatible, even if he does shave under his arms especially for me." He stood. "Now, if you'll excuse me, I must prepare myself to face the day."

My flatmate sauntered off to his room and I went into the lounge, flicking through TV channels in a futile attempt to discover something worth watching. Failing that I'd settle for a female pre-senter in a short skirt. After a while Fergal came back, dressed in a variation on his usual clobber and fiddling with a video camera as I admired the braces and cravat.

"I'm off to find more groundbreaking footage, I shall return anon."

"If you see Mrs. Winterbottom tell her I'm not gay."

"What, apropos of nothing?" Fergal tucked the camera under his arm. "Don't you think that sounds a mite suspicious?"

"All our neighbours think we're a couple."

"That's just as offensive to me as it is you Montgomery. Not wishing to insult, but I like to think I could do slightly better." Before I could respond he was out the door with a parting shot: "And try not to break anything *too* valuable while I'm away."

Fergal called himself a *conscientious objector* to the world of work and he possessed both the resourcefulness and savvy to get away with not holding down a job. Instead my flatmate stayed solvent through the segments of comic footage he sold to a prime-time clip show. He'd be out there now, taping scenes which had the potential to break into hilarity at any moment; families in the park, skateboarders doing their thing, wedding parties leaving church. Perhaps he'd call up a friend who was proficient at pratfalls if no footage came organically. Sadly I had no such inspired scheme to keep me in funds and would have to spend the afternoon preparing for another week at work.

Eventually the mesmeric hum of the television relaxed its grip and I got bored of staring at the framed poster of Jane Fonda in *Barefoot In The Park* above our set. I decided to change into some clothes which might enable me to leave the flat should such a need arise. While getting dressed I looked down at my torso. That stomach was far from flat nowadays, and if I ever got round to eating more than one meal a day I'm sure I'd have a gut to contend with. As it was I remained average height, average build, nothing special or upsetting to look at. A guy without the kind of physique which encouraged preening, but not energetic enough to overhaul an exercise regime that currently consisted of walks to the station and the occasional detour into a shop.

Were all young men like me? Did everyone go straight from being uncertain in newly-grown adult bodies, suffering through spots and inhibitions and gawkiness in the late teens and early twenties, to obsessing over rolls of flab and potential hair loss at the age I was now. I'd be thirty in three and a bit years and I'd never felt confident enough to take my top off in public. Not at the beach, not in the park, not even lounging around my parents' garden where the odds of anyone looking at me were exceptionally low. Then again, if I found my body that unpleasant I guess I would have joined a gym or something, but I was no narcissist. Why then this mild depression every time I combed my hair? Had it thinned out over the previous year, or was that just my imagination? Forget about it Monty. I had bigger problems than a receding hairline, or not being able to run up a flight of steps without falling out of breath.

I returned to the kitchen and grabbed a tea towel to dry the remaining dishes. Soon everything was cleared except for one last saucer which slipped from my right hand, evaded the desperate grasp of my left, and landed heavily in the sink, breaking neatly in two. Standing there, looking at my handiwork, I was forced to admit my preternatural clumsiness. Everyone has failings; maybe they're selfish, possess bad personal hygiene or a need for women in high heels to tread on their genitalia. My major flaw was a heavy-handed tendency to damage objects or myself. Fergal once told me that someone said of the author George Orwell *the inanimate was always against him.* That was how the world felt to me, as if every possession which came my way goaded me into ruining it. Such absence of coordination and unintentional lack of care doesn't tend to win people over, however much I apologise or debase myself afterwards. Some, like my mother, tend to place an unhealthy importance on material objects. If I accidentally smashed a commemorative plate or ornamental Alsatian mum would always go ballistic. Yell and holler and never shut up about it, no matter how many hours I spent trying to glue the damned thing back together.

I wrapped the pieces of china in kitchen towel and put them in the bin. Some see the glass as half empty, others see it as half full, I only see a fragile receptacle at some point in the evening

I'm going to end up breaking. Gingerly I lifted the ironing board down from the cupboard to begin the least rewarding of weekend tasks, pressing a shirt for Monday.

Running the hot metal over creased material, I thought about how I'd always been awkward and ham-fisted. Rare was the woman who didn't tire of me forever destroying her belongings or injuring myself. This clumsiness never bothered Shirley though, the dark and friendly half-Chinese girl I met during my final year of studies. We clicked and became an item, moving in together shortly after we graduated when it became apparent neither of us could cope with the idea of going back to our parents. I got myself domesticated for the first time and we both found jobs doing the things we were qualified in. Everyone thought it was meant to be, but after a couple of years the lovemaking just stopped. Our interest in each other as sexual beings flickered for a while then was extinguished altogether. I've learnt since it happens to many couples, but at the time sex disappearing from our home seemed like the weirdest thing. We became like two best friends living together, and while the absence of a physical element might not have been a problem were the two of us in our seventies and retired, at twenty two our connection was always going to break. And so it did, in a way that was utterly painful for us both. Recriminations, torn photographs, promises made to all and sundry we were forced to renege upon. I was certain one of us was heartbroken at least, but a few years down the line I look back and can't even be sure I was that much in love.

After hanging up my poorly-ironed clothes the rest of my day was spent in a hurricane like miasma of nothing much. My mother rang to make sure I was still visiting next weekend, then I cooked pasta for one and finished some other chores. Our flat could easily have become cramped were it filled with possessions but I'd never accumulated that much. Following the break up with Shirley I stayed in a succession of problematic shared houses, each for six months at a time. All of them screwed with my head for one reason or another until finally I was introduced to Fergal. At first I treated the offer of a room among the more obscure stops at the western end of the District Line with some scepticism. But I was desperate, ground-down, soon to be homeless, and the Irish gay provided a way out of my peripatetic existence. No longer would I have to endure dad moving me to a different part of the city twice a year. Those uncomfortable silences in the family car, packing and unloading the vehicle with the minimum of eye contact, him begrudging the incursion into valuable leisure time, me apologetic, wishing I could afford removal men.

Dad raised an eyebrow when he met Fergal Cofaigh, that was inevitable. A flaming pansy from the wilds of the Irish republic, the Cofaigh family farm is located somewhere west of Cork, within cycling distance of the coast. By his own account my flatmate had grown up in a repressed agricultural community without even a television to show him how the world could be. At what point during his nascent years Fergal metamorphosed into the uninhibited dandy with the air of aristocratic exuberance I knew today is a mystery. Although at a guess I'd say it was probably college.

Our arrangement turned out really well, despite my parents' concerns I'd be knitting pink jumpers within a month. I learnt a great deal from Fergal, and I've come to rely on him for calm advice, good humour, and an unparalleled ability to put the Hoover round twice a week. Okay, there's that occasional confusion about orientation, and he does tend to bang on a bit about my heterosexuality being "compulsory" and "society-inflicted". Come to think of it, I'm sure I don't make anything like that much noise when I'm rogering a girl. But overall we make it work, that's the important thing.

Dusk had come and gone, leaving night in its place, and I was in the bathroom attempting to shave. This was something I did every night, ensuring extra time in bed come the morning. I use an old-fashioned razor, holding the great metal blade tightly while I incline my head to catch every emerging hair. Such an antiquated device suggests to me a certain Victorian rigour and professionalism; here is a man who makes an effort to care about his appearance. Checking the mirror, I noticed three spots of blood on my face. Three wasn't bad, considering. I washed the mixture of white and red from my skin and dried off.

In the bedroom I checked my scalp again. I've spent a long time trying to understand my hair but never really succeeded, it kind of goes everywhere all at once. The dark mass was looking particularly unkempt today, clearly I needed a haircut and soon. That was something to look forward to, a foxy hairdresser running her fingers through my follicles for twenty minutes might be just the tonic I needed. That kind of feminine contact hadn't happened for a while. Ever since I called a dating hiatus after one too many assignations went awry. If I was going to be relaxed on a date it had to be someone with the self-confidence to make positive feelings known, but who wasn't so aggressive and ballsy I got scared off. I didn't realise what a fine balance that was until my bad run through Spring, during that season every girl either made me want to escape through the restaurant kitchen or acted so withdrawn I felt like checking for a pulse.

I looked at the clock, making sure I was in time for the semi-regular Sunday night bear documentary. It hadn't started yet so I switched to one of the other channels, a reality show called *Lesbian Brother*. This format had a well-endowed black man locked in a house for half a year with twenty eight amateur lesbians, two of whom were up for eviction every week. In many ways the series was refreshingly idiotic, but I still turned over when the zoo-based programme came on.

The familiar sound of Fergal's key, followed by my flatmate jouncing into the room like a children's entertainer.

"Any luck?"

"One or two sections which might be usable Montgomery. Derek came along and completed a very convincing trip into a large puddle, the producers will cough up for that one no doubt." He studied the TV screen. "What on earth are you watching?"

"*When Bears Attack Penguins*. I thought it might be useful for work but the show's a bit trashy so far."

"You don't say." Fergal took the other armchair. "I didn't think those creatures lived in the same part of the world."

"They don't. All the clips have come from zoos so far." On the screen a grizzly bear chased several waddling birds around a cage. "I reckon the producers have been throwing penguins into bear enclosures for the sake of conflict." We watched an emperor penguin hop up onto a rock and look down at its frustrated pursuer.

"All very edifying I'm sure."

"Switch over if you want. There's a drunk woman arguing with her reflection on the other side."

"No, no. You carry on."

And so, with that typically soporific Sunday, another unspectacular weekend came to a close. There I was, relaxing at home against a backdrop of ordinariness, ready to tackle whatever the coming week had to offer, sort of. Everything seemed routine and predictable and there was certainly no indication, as I sat watching a polar bear stare down a king penguin, that the next seven days would bring on the most momentous time in my life.

Chapter Three

I have to be careful on my daily walk to the tube station. Usually I'm drowsy and confused from recently waking and that puts me off guard as pigeons glide down, soaring along the avenue about five and a half feet up. Or head height, as I prefer to call it. Beside trees and benches the concrete is splattered by droppings the birds deposit on their airborne forays. More than once I've walked down this busy street, between conversing mothers or hurrying workers, and had to pause and duck, crouching as if from sniper fire or wayward Frisbees as a beak soars toward my face. I always swerve first.

Today the dumb birds were absent. Perhaps sleeping off the over-indulgences of their weekend this drizzly October morning. There was no need for me to dodge as I mingled with the onrush of Monday morning commuters. Although I felt sure the pigeons were lurking somewhere in the branches above me, just waiting for their chance.

Scores of us stomped through the station entrance and to the escalators, navigating automated ticket machines in seconds with our daily, weekly, monthly passes. Experience choreographed our movements in a way that kept everyone flowing. Down on the platform the LED display told me a train was due in two minutes. This gave me enough time to make my daily decision as I walked left, along the rear half of the platform, waiting men and women three deep to my right. What would I choose today? To stay near the most attractive female, squeezing myself through in the hope of remaining in close proximity with her, thereby brightening up my journey no end. Or would I continue walking and board the last carriage, a section which always seemed to have more space and perhaps that priceless commodity, a seat?

Scanning the pensive faces, I found one pleasing young professional in a figure-hugging outfit which revealed a sliver of pert cleavage, but she stood beside a middle-aged man emptying the contents of his sinuses into a large handkerchief so I moved on. I didn't need another strain of flu or unidentifiable lurgee laying me up for a week or more.

The train pulled in and I was fifth inside, rewarded with six empty seats. I sat down and checked those around me for signs of infection. This might sound obsessive-compulsive, but only to those who don't travel on a transport system with several millions other passengers every day, a generous percentage of whom will always suffer from some kind of illness. My journey takes me on four tubes every day, sometimes eight if the system has problems or I'm out again in the evening. There's nothing worse than catching a virus from some fellow commuter who can't help hacking and sneezing over the whole vicinity, all of us standing in the packed carriage, pretending not to notice.

Thankfully no one appeared to have a cold and there weren't any pregnant or frail passengers standing so I relaxed into the worn seat and waited out my journey to Embankment. With each stop the train became more cramped, fewer people getting off than boarding. That is, until we pulled into Victoria, whereupon half the passengers departed and approximately three times that many attempted to get on. Two stops later I tried to stand where there wasn't any room, forcing myself into the seething mass of bodies while desperately gripping a rail to stop myself overbalancing. I couldn't fall back into the seat because there was now an Indian woman occupying it. How on earth had she managed to sneak behind me? No time to worry about that now, the doors were opening. Those who wanted to stay on board tried to make themselves small as commuters made to disembark. I had difficulty getting through until I located a man in a suit charging through and followed his slipstream, the both of us sprawling out for the interchange.

The Northern Line was even worse but I'll leave the particularities of that to your imagination. My mind seems to have blocked it out, the way someone might forget shellshock or a mediocre movie. Eventually I came upon Oxford Street and navigated my way through the back streets to Soho Square.

Fifty five minutes after leaving my flat I reached the agency headquarters, a five storey building on Carlisle Street, just off the square. Our offices occupied the ground floor. Like the plaque said, *Bears!Bears!Bears!* were first, beneath *Princess* Advertising and *Emancipation Inc.* who rented the upper levels and dealt in feminine hygiene products I preferred not to even think about, let alone work out ways of marketing. I was buzzed in and walked past reception, greeting Lettice and five other blondes who manned the phones and were called things like *Pammy* or *Roweena*.

Arriving at the dim corner where our boss, Martin, liked to say, 'the donkey work got done', the desk beside mine was occupied by a diminutive figure whose hat and coat hung by the side of his workstation. I greeted Justin as cordially as I could manage and switched my PC on.

"Morning Monty. Can I ask you a question?"

"Not before I've had coffee."

"What's your favourite font?"

I logged on. "Did you hear what I just said?"

"Mine's *Bazooka*, look." He twisted the screen to show me our agency's latest promotional blurb.

"You don't have to worry about typing in upper or lower case with *Bazooka* and it makes words more fun, see?"

BEARS! BEARS! BEARS!
THE ONE AGENCY CATERING FOR ALL YOUR URSINE ADVERTISE-MENT NEEDS. MARKET ANY PRODUCT MORE EFFECTIVELY WITH OUR WORLD-FAMOUS SERVICES AND AWARD-WINNING CON-TACTS. FROM ANIMATED BEARS TO CGI BEARS, FROM FLESH & BLOOD BEARS TO BEAR-RELATED MERCHANDISE, WHATEVER YOUR NEEDS - WE CAN HELP! OUR HIGHLY-EXPERIENCED EX-PERTS WILL MAKE YOUR PRODUCT A WORLD LEADER USING NOTHING MORE THAN BEARS AND A LITTLE IMAGINATION. FOR MORE DETAILS VISIT OUR WEBSITE AT WWW.BEARSBEARSBEARS.COM OR CONTACT THE WORLD'S GREATEST AGENCY SOLELY DEVOTED TO THE URSINE WORLD ON THE ABOVE NUMBER.

The world's *only* industry solely devoted to the ursine world.

"I'm making coffee." I said. "Did you want one?"

"No thanks."

In our tiny kitchen I mixed an extra-strong measure and was joined by Lettice, profuse in her thanks for introducing Si to her world. Apparently he'd gone down very well, as it were. I asked Lettice not to be quite so graphic and cheekily told her to be on her way, watching her behind move in that tight skirt as she went back to the phones.

While I sipped coffee and waited for the urge to punch Justin to subside, Martin came in. Although he was in charge I felt no urge to busy myself for his benefit, we'd known each other too long. A dapper whirlwind of a man, Mart was my age but successful and he always took care to cultivate the appearance of being in demand. People believed that here was a man who had irons in the fire and little time on his hands. I suppose it was true to an extent, partially.

Mart invited me into his office, the only sectioned-off part of our open-plan area, for our regular update. Martin Landry had been a go-getter ever since I first met him, fizzing with ideas, but less keen to put in the hours required to turn every unrealised venture into reality. Which was where I came in. We'd been peers at university, both studying for a bog-standard media degree, and while I saw the course as a way of avoiding real work for another three years, to Mart it became a stepping stone, a jumping off point for loftier ambitions. Back then his energy exhausted me; there was networking and projects, societies and meetings, the connections and experience leading to a career in commercials. After all this Mart found little time to do any work so I rejigged four of my essays to pass off as his during that final year, ending up as uncredited co-writer on his dissertation as well. Taking time out to accomplish this wasn't something I begrudged, Martin's family were minted, and it was obvious he'd make it big one day too. You only had to look at the entrepreneurial zeal with which he conducted the (failed) campaign to have pole dancing introduced to our student union to know that.

After the graduation ceremony sad news came through; Martin's dad had died. I wasn't surprised when it was followed by the rather less sad news Mart had been left a huge inheritance. He immediately set about fulfilling that promise to take me along on whatever scheme he planned. Mart's dream turned out to be an agency in the centre of London, a company which would keep its focus narrow and work in some specialised area, an untapped niche where we might become world leaders. I believed he could do it, after three years in the same world as Mart I believed he could do anything, but he didn't have the faintest idea which area of the industry cried out for our capital. We spent weeks brainstorming, pouring over recent trends in popular print and screen campaigns. I suggested targeting a certain type of consumable or particular style of approach, all to no avail until, one evening, I was at home watching a natural history programme on frolicking cubs, when it hit me.

Bears.

Bears were being used to sell everything in those days, everything from confectionery to electrical goods. The ad industry employed furry fellas to scare kids, amuse adults, and make housewives go *aaaah*. They were everywhere, yet there was no service to advise confused factory owners how black bears could shift rolls of carpet or to inform Saatchi & Saatchi where they might get a koala from on a Wednesday afternoon at short notice.

There was now.

Those early days were terrific fun for all of us. Martin was only twenty two, but it felt like he had the world at his feet. We rented office space and set about filling it with equipment, hiring female *account executives* to answer the phones on the basis of how attractive they were, as per the official industry guidelines. I was installed as Martin's right-hand man and chief copywriter, charged with everything from fact checking to historical research. Meanwhile Mart himself took care of the schmoozing, a faux-sincere *shake and fake* as he visited every zoo in the country and made appointments with London's top advertising men. Soon they knew exactly what we were doing, the boss using that bottomless charm and gift of the gab to get our name out there. Another old pal, Justin, was brought in as website designer, technical consultant, and person who I dumped the more irritating jobs on. We were optimistic as first-time buyers, it was the late nineties and the bear business was booming. With the banks behind us we built up the kind of brand recognition appropriate for high-flyers like ourselves.

But interest in bears can go down as well as up.

It was Mart who first showed signs of disillusionment. Landry's the sort of person who loses interest in an endeavour after taking it as far as the idea will go. Even if the world at large is only starting to hear about his venture, even if the boredom and repetition are exceptionally lucrative, Mart's feet start to itch. While the rest of us saw the millennium in celebrating unparalleled growth, fuelled by our interactive online services, exhaustive bear archive and growing list of clients, Mart was already plotting his next move.

We saw less and less of the boss as the twenty first century got underway. He'd take a month off to "explore bear opportunities" in the US, then spend time in Scandinavia to observe how the medicine prescribed for a polar bear's laryngitis had turned it purple. Business bubbled along without him, sort of. Actually, Justin and I found ourselves ill-equipped to deal with some of the things we came up against, things like the intricacies of the British legal system. In the end we enlisted the services of a lawyer to make other companies think twice about swiping our ideas, and defend us in those instances when a personal bear appearance caused trouble.

Despite the occasional out of court settlement, *Bears!Bears!Bears!* continued to stay in the black, but there was precious little growth and those overseas opportunities Mart explored on a generous expense budget didn't seem to bear fruit, if you'll excuse the pun.

Then came TWAT.

The war against terror turned our industry upside down. Advertising budgets were slashed, the global economy began to impersonate a land-stuck turbot, and bears fell down the list of priorities for the human race, number one on which was *not dying*. To make matters worse, no one in the office seemed to notice the steady drop off in business except me, although Justin and the girls rarely concerned themselves with much beyond the way that the light hit their hair prior to 9/11, so it was churlish of me to expect them to obsess over *WMDs* afterwards.

Without an excess of capital Mart was forced to stick around with us, and he must have seen the ship needed steadying, he did all the accounting for one thing. But if I was hoping for positive action I'd be waiting a long time. Lately the boss had been more preoccupied with some nebulous fancy he called a *personal creative project* than fixing what was wrong with our business. Although I didn't know it at the time, it was this vague undertaking at the top of our agenda as he offered me the seat before his desk.

"Sit down Monty, I've something important to share with you." Martin pushed those round-frame spectacles up his nose and leant forward.

"Oh God, we're not being sued again are we?" One of the brown bears we used for functions was becoming erratic and ornery. Word had it our insurers grew nervous of the creature's unpredictability.

"No, no. Nothing like that." Martin laced his hands together and stared at the thumbs for a long while. "Monty, do you believe the act of creation is holy?"

Oh no. "You're talking to the wrong person Mart. I write copy. You know, stuff for the site with headings like: 'What a sloth bear can do for your small business'."

"Well, I believe it is." He pinned me to the chair with an intense gaze. All the drive in Martin was still there, but apparently it was no longer directed towards selling things. "For the first time I feel like I've found some kind of spirituality in my life, and it's all because of this."

He reached for the desk drawer and pulled out a manuscript. The title pronounced it; 'Too Beautiful - A Play by Martin Landry'.

"I finished it over the weekend. What you see there is almost three years work." Emotion in the voice. "I'd like you to read it."

I flicked through the pages. "Mart, I don't know what to say." It was awfully long. "I'm not a playwright, you know? The last time I went to the theatre Christopher Biggins played Mother Goose."

"I ask you as a friend, and because I value everyone's opinion on this." A self-satisfied smile. "This baby's going to be produced anyway, we're finalising arrangements right now."

"Okay, no problem." I picked up the manuscript, its weight made me tired. "Was there anything else?"

"No, I don't think so." Mart clicked his mouse a few times. "Ah, just the one thing. We've a request for Poppy to appear at some society wedding next week." Poppy was Chester Zoo's brown bear, the one who'd led us close to litigation. We used her irregularly since that good nature became flecked by bouts of illtemperedness.

"You know what she's been like Monty, I'm not sure one's enough to handle her." I knew what was coming. "If you and Just could get your tuxes on and keep an eye on the bear, maybe we can avoid complaints."

"No problem."

I trudged back to my desk and gave Justin the good news. It didn't seem to register, he was busy watching some footage which appeared to show a man being penetrated by a donkey. I gave up and spent a while answering legitimate emails ("Do you have a brochure?", "I need a dancing bear for the Christmas party.") or deleting crank ones ("You people are all sick. My husband was hospitalised by a bear." "I am a forty three year old bear coming to your country and in need of work."). Beside me Justin turned his keyboard upside down and shook it, whereupon a cavalcade of breadcrumbs and dust flooded the desk. After about five minutes of this Justin inverted his head and peered between the keys. I'd had enough. It wasn't yet lunchtime, and I couldn't really disappear with Mart around, so I was left with only one possibility.

Time to visit the smoking room.

I didn't actually want a cigarette, nicotine had never really done it for me. No, that enclosed space by the stairs was more of a sanctuary at times like these, an enclave where a man could relax, talk and maybe gamble away his hard earned cash.

Inside the smoking room two blondes from the third floor sat on the sofa enjoying Marlboro Lights. The main action went on at the centre, halfway between the entrance and a door to the yard around a circular table where three men played out a hand of five card stud.

I pulled up a chair and waited for someone to win, the dealer wore a green visor and chewed on a toothpick. Leon had worked in the building a long time ago, but an astuteness with investments and several contacts in the horse racing game combined to render him a thirtysomething man of leisure. Now he devoted himself to this neverending game of revolving players, old friends and poker buddies, people who came from around the square to play a few hands during their breaks. The other two I vaguely recognised, one worked in the fifth floor post room while the other, a long haired guy with wallet chains, was employed at the bodega-ish vinyl and memorabilia shop around the corner. I'd visited this emporium a few times, it was owned by a famous style guru from the punk era who made his fortune in the days of green hair and flying phlegm by leading hopefuls to chart success. An innovative manager always ready with sure-fire tactics, his riches derived from techniques like making sure his bands swore on television or advising the lead singer to dress up like a pirate.

"Looks like my ladies do it gentlemen, very bad luck there." Leon showed his pair of queens and raked in the pot. "Monty my man, up for some action?"

"Five pounds." I passed Leon my blue note, the dealer dished out plastic discs and shuffled his deck.

"Make 'em good ones this time." The long haired guy sounded bitter. "Those cards are really screwing me today."

By the time I'd lost my chips I was hungry, collecting my coat to escape the office. Beneath the iron latticework connecting steps to our building I noticed Bernard in his regular spot, sheltered by the metal and kept warm by his extensive stockpile of cardboard.

"How's it going Bernard?" I flipped him a silver coin.

The homeless man caught it with a gloved hand. "You know how it is my boy; women want me, men want to be me." Bernard chuckled to himself then started to cough, a harsh, choking roar from long years exposed to the elements. If this violent sound afflicted someone in a movie that character would be dead within a few scenes. Here in real life Bernard remained exactly the same, always wrapped in layers of ragged clothing and irrepressibly cheerful, only leaving his spot to explore the immediate surroundings or visit a soup kitchen during wintertime.

I gave Bernard a thumbs up, then lost my footing on the bottom step and fell onto the pavement. Rubbing my left knee, I continued on my way, into a sandwich shop before walking back to Soho Square. This greenery at the centre of London was bordered by fifty benches and there were no shortage of places to sit this sunny October day. I walked past the graffiti-disfigured statue of King Charles the second and found a spot sheltered from the wind against the gardener's shed.

While I munched a BLT I thought about how stymied I was by that script Mart had given me. From a cursory glance it looked like some kind of three act meditation on the disappearance of Richey Edwards, late of Welsh rockers *The Manic Street Preachers*. Although Martin rarely expressed admiration for artistic types he felt some affinity for Richey. I remembered how Landry halted in his tracks when the guitarist disappeared, briefly upset and inconsolable. Mart even wrote a short tribute for the college magazine which made it clear he'd been touched by that troubled young man and what he had to say. Now he was trying to take that rhetoric to the people, give something of Richey's memory to the world. A courageous move, the only problem being that a brief glance at the play instantly told you it was ill-conceived, if not downright rubbish. But I couldn't tell my boss and friend what he'd toiled over for the past three years wasn't any good. As Mart pointed out, such was his determination it was going to be performed anyway. Which left me without a clue what to do. I could only hope a proper examination of the manuscript would reveal hidden treasures, otherwise I'd have to lie.

Nearby a weather-beaten man with a ponytail was ejected from the square for drinking a can of lager. I deposited my rubbish in one of the bins and made my way back to the agency. At my desk nothing much had changed except that Justin was now wearing his trilby.

"Take that off mate, you're supposed to be at work."

"I'm getting used to it being on. People think more of a chap when he wears a hat."

"In which one of your style mags did it say that?" Behind us Lettice drew the attention of her blonde colleagues to Justin. "People are pointing."

"Let them, we'll have the last laugh." Why did I doubt that? "I'm going to make herbal tea, would you like anything Monty?"

"Coffee could be good."

Justin stood up. "Hey, you'll never guess what I did yesterday."

"Found God? Met Jane Fonda? Discovered a previously undreamt of creativity in your soul?"

"No, I melted our kettle."

"Of course you did."

"It was bust anyway, so mum said to boil water on the stove instead." He grinned foolishly. "So I lit the gas and watched it heat up."

"Let me guess, the water was still in the plastic kettle. Which was on the hob."

Justin laughed. "Is there any worse smell than burning plastic?"

"I. Don't. Know."

He left for the kitchen, chuckling away. Once again I brought to mind the image which gave me solace at times like these. Justin was at school, minding his own business during playtime, when four big boys grabbed a limb each, spread Justin's legs and ran him, groin-first, into a small tree. Imagining this sequence of events he'd once described in detail always served to calm me down.

I passed the afternoon doing 'research', scanning a 1970 book called *Soldier Bear*. It told the story of Wojtek, a bear who helped the Allied forces win the second world war by carrying the Polish army ammunition on his back and being generally useful. After tours of duty through Egypt and Italy, Wojtek was smuggled into Scotland disguised as an infantryman and spent the rest of his years living a life of quiet contemplation in Edinburgh zoo. Quite apart from how useless customs must have been then, failing to spot that soldier was actually a six hundred pound brown bear, the story raised a niggling issue. This bear would forever be remembered for aiding the downfall of evil, Wojtek meant something in Warsaw and there was even a statue of him looking magnificent inside a

South Kensington Polish club. His courage and gallantry would not be forgotten, and he was just a bear. I was a man, I had the power to reason, a sense of morality and opposable thumbs, and what had I ever done for the world, for my country, for anyone? So far the list of notable achievements for Monty Sanderson included an ability to bore for Britain on all matters ursine and a few cleverly-phrased band reviews in the alternative music press. That was it.

When I started at *Bears!Bears!Bears!* the generous wage and limitless potential meant I threw myself into this new role with a much remarked upon zeal. I learnt the locations of mainland Europe's remaining grizzlies, read an unhealthy amount on koala mating habits and studied the tortuous process by which pandas were granted official bear status (and there was some serious celebrating in the giant panda community when that validation finally came through, let me tell you). My enthusiasm had diminished over the years in parallel with the workload, but I had still poured resources into this agency, and between the cost of living and that perpetual poker game I saved nothing. Now Martin was more interested in finding his inner artiste than making the business work and I was beginning to get worried about the long-term picture for *Bears!Bears!Bears!*

On the other hand, it was four o'clock. My working day, such as it was, could now end. I clapped Justin on the back, let Mart know I was off early (a departure he interpreted as eagerness to read his play), and hurried off to South London in time for band rehearsal. I possessed no musical ability of my own, no, Monty's role was that of an observer, sitting in on the practice session of a group featuring my friends Brett, Si, Giles and Tosspot, collectively known as *The Airborne Toxic Event.*

Chapter Four

"I'm not singing this. Look, it says here 'the night was cold and flesh-coloured'!" Tosspot pointed at the threadlike writing. "What sort of a line is that? How can a night be *flesh-coloured?* Flesh is pink!"

"I think you're being a touch prejudiced there." Giles swept a stray dreadlock behind his ear.

"Prejudiced? Prejudiced?" Tosspot O'Reilly was not staying calm. "I'm half Irish for fuck's sake, we're the blacks of Europe!"

"I thought that was the Welsh?" Queried Si, regretting it after the look Tosspot gave him.

"I'm sorry Giles, but it's a widely accepted fact among songwriters that 'flesh-coloured' means pink. When we say *flesh-coloured* we don't mean brown or black or yellow...." The singer counted on his fingers. "...or red or even fake tan."

"Well maybe it's time me and my strong brothers changed all that."

"You're not going to change anything by writing words that don't scan properly and playing drums in an indie band."

Giles turned away and crossed his arms. "Look mate, there's no need to be like that." Conciliatory now, Tosspot undoubtedly realised they weren't even going to get started if this carried on. "I know we've had trouble with the lyrics on that one and I appreciate your suggestions, really I do. They were certainly no worse than Simon's story about the boy who builds the really big sandcastle." Si and Tosspot exchanged an unfriendly glance. "But I think we're going to have to keep our thinking caps on, okay? Now, can we run through the songs, please?"

At last. I'd been inside that cramped practice room for half an hour, pen poised above paper, ready to record the working practices of this band, glean numerous insights from their methods. So far all they'd done was set their equipment up and drink several cans of lager each. But now it looked like the rehearsal was about to get underway.

Simon conducted a final tune with all the care of a guitar artisan while beside him Brett fiddled with the dials on his amp.

Brett was the bassist, a skinny fellow whose entire wardrobe seemed to consist of t-shirts with holes in them. In my experience the bass player tends to be the least effusive member of a band, and Brett was no exception. Here was a man so reticent it was difficult for the other musicians to know if he liked what they were doing, but the fact he turned up on time ultimately proved enthusiasm enough.

Behind the bassist Giles made sure his cymbals were firmly secured and waited for Tosspot to sort himself out, one foot hitting a pedal absentmindedly. Part of the growing trend for black drummers in guitar bands, presumably because white boys with rhythm weren't exactly plentiful around here, Giles was a third generation Jamaican whose background and accent belied his Rastafarian appearance. Born and raised in Shepperton by a self-made man and an interior designer, the drummer was actually the product of one of England's most reputable public schools. Not that this was readily apparent from his behaviour. The first time I met Giles was on Brixton High Street, headbanging like a metaller and giving devil hand signals to a bunch of smart Caribbean zealots speaking of their faith to passers-by. We got him away in the end, but not before he'd drunkenly shanghaied their attempts to enlist recruits with his inappropriate dancing. Later I found out Giles hated heavy metal music and was actually quite devout in his Heile Salassie-worshipping faith. None of which explained why he stood amidst that multiracial swarm throwing his dreads everywhere. I knew then this man wasn't easily categorised, and it didn't surprise me when he joined the band.

Tosspot indicated he was ready to go and Giles counted them in for the first song, a jagged number with no vocals except for the word *WELL-FED!* hollered at key moments. I wrote down phrases like "loping guitar riff" and "incandescent fury", notes for an article I'd been persuaded to write about the allegedly *unstoppable* rise of *The Airborne Toxic Event*. This band about to take the record industry by storm with their unique mixture of classic melodies and irresistible fury. Or something. There was a demo tape and gigs coming up anyway, so I'd been hauled on board to help generate 'a buzz'. I think the quartet saw me as a middle man, a bridge between their music and the A&R types who could realise this dream. But they were mistaken to think I could convince anyone *The A.T.E.* were worth signing without incredible live shows to back up my claims.

That first song shuddered to a halt with the consensus it sounded 'alright', so let's plough on with another, a more traditional verse-chorus-verse affair this time. Again I struggled to make out what Tosspot was singing above the distortion and unexpected reverb confusing their sound. It didn't necessarily matter, experience had taught me not to trust the noise a band makes in their practice room, a place where dodgy acoustics and the lack of a soundman can render even stadium rockers muddy. Once *The A.T.E.* were playing through a decent P.A. their sound would be completely different from what I heard now, spilling out of that tiny room above a Peckham cafe. This particular space was rented to the group on the understanding they clean up any spillages and vacate by early evening, before any neighbours could get upset, and it was rudimentary to say the least. As the band continued to play various manly odours filled the space, sweat appearing to run down its thin walls.

I jotted a few sentences about the "commercial potential" of their sound before focussing on the frontman. Tosspot's coruscating voice and varied intonation might have dominated their sound had I been able to make it out, but what he definitely had was presence. A gangling, angular figure, physically reminiscent of Bowie or Nick Cave but topped with a shock of red hair, O'Reilly jerked and shook, twisting the mike lead around himself like a man feeling the music somewhere deep in the brainstem. In fact Tosspot was classic lead singer material, possessed of a self-belief rare in these times of unprepossessing milquetoasts fronting acts who inadvertently provide evidence of masculinity in crisis. That said, if you'd seen as many strutting, poncing, vaguely ridiculous lead singers as I have maybe you wouldn't think self-belief was such a rare commodity after all.

Tosspot shouted then crooned, screamed and whispered, his power evident despite the technical difficulties. I wrote down words like "mercurial", "unstoppable" and "figurehead". The real deal, O'Reilly was an exception among these guys. His bandmates all came from the moneyed world of the upper middle classes, with allowances or trust funds to fall back on while they worked at low-paying, flexible jobs which could be abandoned to pursue the music. The formative years of Giles, Brett and Si were a world away from their singer who'd been raised with several boisterous siblings in the East End. The nickname came from Robert O'Reilly's parents who'd called him 'Tosspot' for as long as anyone could remember, seeing nothing offensive it. Just another strange endearment salt of the earth types gave to loved ones, like 'Buster' or 'Spud'.

The sobriquet followed O'Reilly through the playgrounds of Bethnal Green, on into his adult life and decades after the habit began his inner circle of friends continued to call him 'Tosspot'. It was a name some might consider unfortunate, but O'Reilly wore the epithet with a lightness and good humour. He knew we meant it fondly. Besides, it suited him.

They ran through a third song then took a break, passing round more beers.

"Do you think that last one was a bit near the knuckle?" Tosspot asked me.

"Um." I hadn't made out a single word. "Which was that again?"

"We're calling the track *It's Okay, I'm The Pope.*" Simon looked to his bandmates. "Aren't we?"

O'Reilly explained. "It's about the Catholic church. We talk about the main man taking responsibility for what happened to all those kids. Everyone's responsible, and I say you should start at the top."

"Right." I took a note then crossed it out. "I'm not sure you need to court controversy at this point in your career Tosspot. It might be better to leave the fans to work your lyrics out for themselves. All the greatest songs have a kind of ambiguity about them."

"I don't think we should avoid controversy." The singer was taken aback. "That's what gets you attention."

Giles wiped the sweat from his brow with a towel. "Anyone who tries to enlighten the masses gets persecuted don't they? Look at Peter Stringfellow."

"Peter Stringfellow?"

"No, not Peter Stringfellow." The drummer thought about it. "What was that guy's name? Socrates."

We stared at Giles for a few seconds, I was the first to snap out of it. "I just think the initial impact gets made by the quality of what you do rather than scandal chasing. It's all very well to be esoteric...."

"Is it?"

"What's that mean?"

"...but the songs are what get your feet in the door. I'll write you 'work from a broader lyrical palette that the average indie band' and leave it at that."

"Fine. Cheers for your help on this Monty." Tosspot drained his can and stood up. "Are we ready to go again?"

"Can I take a piss first?" These were Brett's first words of the night.

"You know the rules." O'Reilly wagged a finger. "First one to piss gets the round in later."

"..."

"Come on, let's do *Mensa Bimbo*."

The band retook their positions, Brett grimacing in pain at what I suspected were bad bladder cramps. One of Tosspot's working methods was to demand no one left the room until the practice was over. He'd brought it in after one particularly frustrating meet when the band lost ninety minutes with members repeatedly going downstairs to relieve themselves. Annoyed at this weakness, Tosspot invoked the scheme at their next rehearsal. Musicians would be allowed to visit the toilet before and after, but not during. Of course, thanks to the amount of beer they consumed while playing it led to whingeing, but at least this rule helped them get things done. The innovative *diuretic test* also gauged bandmates' loyalty to their project. Would they go beyond the call of duty and exercise an ascetic's control over the ache in their loins? I was all in favour of self-discipline, but it sometimes seemed a little harsh. Surprising too that I hadn't heard any stories of Si wetting himself during a middle eight.

I wrote "willing to suffer for their art" on the pad and turned my attention to the song in progress, a quiet-loud-quiet composition with drums crashing in as the chorus hit. This structure allowed me to hear some of the words wherein a promiscuous girl with an abnormally high IQ had broken the singer's heart. Scribbling down "a fresh take on relationship issues" I watched Tosspot yowl like a man in existential torment which, after three beers and no possibility of going to the toilet for another hour, may well have been the case.

O'Reilly was an interesting guy all round, his surname came from Irish relations on the father's side including one uncle who was a bit of a literary type, having published several volumes of poetry since the seventies. It was he who turned Tosspot on to the contemporary American fiction from which the band derived their name and some of their more recherché song titles, tunes called things like *Copacetic* and *Contrail*. As well as aligning The *Airborne Toxic Event* with the Americana which was such an influence to their sound these touchstones created the illusion of culture amongst the ranks. This illusion of sophistication meant I could plausibly write about the group "putting the intelligence back into rock" or "not being afraid of frightening people with their knowledge". The feature was only for a cultily obscure, if well-respected, fanzine. It was unlikely anyone reading the piece would know the band members well enough to be peeved by my elastic attitude to the facts.

During the final few numbers I scribbled down profiles of the foursome, stressing their 'cultural diversity' and 'intense mien'. As soon as the drawn-out drone of that last song died away Brett tore off his bass guitar and fled the room, Tosspot uttering a supportive yell of: "Ha! You lose!" at the scampering figure.

Si was pleased. "Brilliant. I'll have a double J.D. when we get to the gig." He high-fived Tosspot. "But first I'm after Brett in the lav."

Giles ignored their cheeriness and began dismantling his drum kit while I fiddled with my notes, attempting to give some kind of structure to the piece.

"Plenty of myth-making in there Monty." Tosspot specified. "Don't be afraid to expand the truth a little, if you know what I mean."

"Yeah, that's right." Giles carried out his snare drum. "Like when you say he's a competent singer."

"Oi! I tell the jokes, and they'll all be about drummers if you don't watch it."

Brett and Si returned, the latter having apparently visited a food shop. Their percussionist squeezed past to get to his equipment.

"Cheese slice Giles?"

"Cheese is for wankers."

"Right, okay." Simon turned to me. "Monty?"

"Thanks."

Tosspot eyed Giles suspiciously. "Don't tell me you've gone back to the vegans?"

"No, I only eat Genetically Modified food now. I'm thinking it might give me superpowers."

"Heh."

"You ought to eat meat and nothing else." Si munched a yellow square. "The more primitive a drummer the better, have you ever thought about moving into the woods?"

"I live in Shepperton. That's wild enough." Tosspot laughed at him. "What's up with you O'Reilly? Questioning my street credibility?"

"Well, yes."

"Why?"

"Well, you call it *credibility* for one thing."

Si sat down and offered me another processed slice. "Here Monty, I never thanked you for setting me up with that Lettice girl. She's quite the goer."

"You like her?"

"Fuck yeah. She was all over me like an expensive smock." Si grinned. "I'm meeting up with her tomorrow night, we're going to some kind of chick-flick she wants to see."

"You ought to be careful mate." Tosspot grabbed the final beer for himself. "They won't mention it to your face, but even in their twenties girls are only interested in guys who can help them get the three Ms."

"The three Ms?"

"Marriage, mortgage and motherhood."

"Oh Christ." Si pretended to be horrified. "I'm not ready for motherhood."

"Laugh all you want, but just because it's subtle doesn't mean it's not there. Don't say I didn't warn you."

I packed my notes away. The feeling that nothing more was going to be accomplished here had become impossible to ignore. "I wouldn't listen Si." I said. "You and Lettice are well-suited, everyone thinks so. Have some fun."

"Don't worry mate, I will."

Giles came back and began discussing recent female conquests with Tosspot, Simon joining in with the coarse laughter at tales of weekend misadventures, casual flings with seventeen year olds and the conscienceless manipulation of pretty girls. I listened to O'Reilly describe how he and a mate had picked up a willing secretary in Canary Wharf, enjoying a threesome at her Docklands apartment before going back out to continue their bender. That wasn't the end of it, the other bloke had a digital camera, and this morning action shots of the girl enjoying the dual attentions were sent to her boss from an anonymous email address.

I had no comments to add, wishing to avoid the lapse into laddism. Embellishing stories didn't interest me, I wasn't drunk enough to push personal matters out into the open for the entertainment of all. Whenever I'd joined in before, regaling the band with bawdy moments from my carnal past, I always regretted it after sobering up, had been disappointed with myself the following morning.

But there was no point coming on like a prude either, it was the way of the world for guys to act like this. Apart from Si the band were all a few years younger than myself and I wasn't about to come on like a schoolteacher, spoiling their fun. It was when they regressed I really felt old, like the time Tosspot suffered from a particularly violent bout of flatulence. I was reading a music paper at the time, and the first thing I saw was a gush of orange flame in the corner of my eye. They never got the fire lasting long enough to achieve their stated aim of toasting the marshmallows they'd impaled on drumsticks, but lighting O'Reilly's gas gave the band a chance to gather round and giggle stupidly for about an hour.

Now the conversation turned from one night stands to groupies, then on to the possibility of attractive girlie fans at their forthcoming gig, a set supporting some faded nineties star in Kentish Town. Tiring of these fantasies, Simon guided the conversation to what they needed to achieve for this show, his bandmates admitting work needed to be done before the date rolled around. Everyone concurred solemnly, they had to be technically competent on the night and spread the word beforehand.

I said I'd help wherever possible. Maybe friendship had fooled me, but I honestly believed *The Airborne Toxic Event* possessed something special. Promise, talent, enough varied elements to impress the most jaded artiste and repertoire men who, like me, were fed up with hauling their weary arses around London's nastiest venues. Nowadays all I saw were derivative idiots doing bad impersonations of other bands, at least these guys tried to throw off the weight of their influences and make something new. That was the best a young guitar band could hope for.

Our collective thoughtfulness ended and suddenly we were on our feet. I helped them shift the remaining equipment to their storage area below the rehearsal room, getting my feet caught up in the microphone stand halfway down the stairs then falling against a wall. Si stuck out his hand to keep me upright and I got through the rest of the tidy up without ruining any of their gear. The patter now was anticipatory, about the gig we were attending that evening, another much-hyped group of youngsters I'd nabbed free tickets to see. I think the guys were hoping this band would be terrible rather than providing quality entertainment, indeed Si quoted some of The *Pop Shots*' more ill-advised press statements on our walk to the station while Tosspot dictated the exact content of that monumental round of drinks to the hapless Brett.

Chapter Five

The train journey to Victoria was overshadowed by Tosspot and Giles arguing whether rice or potatoes was the better foodstuff at a gradually increasing volume.

"I go with the Irish." O'Reilly - predictably enough.

"Chinese beats Irish, there's more of them." Countered the drummer with impeccable logic. "Rice is more reliable too. Whoever heard of a rice famine?" He directed this question to the rest of us, but we kept quiet.

"Maybe, but you can make vodka from potatoes."

"And you can make wine from rice! Wine beats vodka!"

"No fucking way does wine beat vodka."

"It does."

"NO IT DOESN'T!"

At which point the three of us had to step in as Tosspot grabbed Giles by the lapels and angrily brought the black face to his. The men glared at each other until Simon and Brett managed to release O'Reilly's grip while I made apologetic 'what can you do?' faces to the other passengers on our carriage. Fortunately we avoided further embarrassment by reaching our destination, whereupon those of us who remained too sober for this kind of confrontation purchased more alcohol. A wise decision as it turned out, since our northbound train was stuck at the Victoria line platform.

The uniformed station worker, a man somewhere in his thirties, spoke into a handheld device and his announcement came over the speakers. "Customer information. We apologise for the delay. This train is currently being held at the platform indefinitely."

We walked past him, searching for a sparsely-populated carriage. Inside every section passengers showed signs of weary restlessness, shifting in discomfort or peering out the open doors.

"As soon as I've more information it will be relayed to you. Meanwhile, allow me to entertain for a few moments with something I've been working on."

The statement caused us to turn and watch this attendant, whereupon he launched into a kind of human beatbox routine.

"Shuka-shuka-shuka, pat-pat-pat sssssssssh, chicka-chicka, boosh bam-bam, tcccch boom boom boom."

Compelling. We set our beer down and began to clap along. The guy expressed himself well, flailing with his free arm while making rhythmic spluttering sounds. He was pretty good, and it reminded me of the eighties rap records I'd grown up with. All in all we were disappointed when a stout female colleague in a peaked cap curtailed his act, the woman conversing briefly with the attendant before he was escorted away, the man acknowledging our applause with a peace sign.

"That was fairly unusual." We boarded the train, everyone inside apparently nonplussed by what they'd heard.

"Everyone's a frustrated performer in this city." Tosspot grabbed a beer. "Although I've never seen anyone lose it and think he was a drum machine before."

The doors closed with their customary beeping noise and we were on our way, changing at Embankment as we headed into the hub of tourist London, sat together while we tried to get through as much beer as possible.

For the hundredth time, or maybe even the thousandth, I read the messages scrolling from right to left above our heads.

The next station is Charing Cross. Change here for the Bakerloo Line and mainline rail services.

Beside me Tosspot conducted a quick inventory of our remaining drink, offloading what he could to the rest of us but keeping one for himself. There was a can left so O'Reilly got up and walked along the carriage, offering it to a couple of girls who looked about sixteen (much to the consternation of their father).

The next station is Leicester Square. Change here for the Piccadilly Line. Tonight could see big changes in your life Monty Sanderson.

Left agog, I blinked several times and looked around. No one was watching the screen and after a blank space the message continued.

Fate is on your side Monty. Grasp every opportunity with both hands and happiness can be yours.

No, this wasn't happening. I grabbed Si's arm and pointed at the display.

"What? No smoking on any London Underground train? I know this Monty, you don't have to worry."

"No, not that. Never mind." Only generic phrases passed my eyes now so I drank more beer. Too pissed, that's what it was. I'd imagined something weird. Odd though, one thing my brain definitely hadn't done on previous drunks was invent electronic messages. If I had imagined it, how come I felt so unnerved all of a sudden? I ended up very glad when the doors slid open for our stop, Giles escorting Tosspot away from the girls' mother who'd been getting quite cosy with him.

At ground level we merged with the dizzying mixture of nationalities moving along Charing Cross Road in search of night-time fun. Past the tourist-targeted merchandise stalls and touts selling tickets for larger venues lay the *5 Easy Pieces* club, set back from instrument shops in a kind of yard off the sideroad. I was still spaced out by what I'd seen and almost walked into the forthcoming attraction board. Then it took Si to remind me we already had tickets and could bypass the queue. Against the strains of a support act we hurried downstairs, Giles stopping to study the framed lists, past luminaries who'd played here down the years. The posters containing the names of legends, the dead before their time, some of the biggest rockers in the world and *Spinal Tap*.

Inside the venue a guy in thick glasses wielded an acoustic guitar and sang in a strangulated manner about the difficulties he had with girls. I joined Brett and Tosspot at the bar, the other two spotting a table to colonise at the back of the room. Up front the singer-songwriter's friends clustered around the stage, taking up a third or so of the standing section. Tosspot instructed Brett to buy two jugs of lager, a couple of whisky based shorts and some kind of transparent cocktail with a greenish tinge. A hefty brunette with a brown bob watched the drinks mount up.

"That's quite a round you're getting there boys."

"He's buying." Tosspot jerked a thumb in Brett's direction. "Want one?"

The brunette smiled, inclining her head towards the emaciated bassist. "Is that okay?"

"..."

"Alright then I'll have a vodka and coke. Thanks."

"And a vodka and coke for the lady." Yelled Tosspot above the music, passing glasses and a jug to me. With the utmost precision I placed them on the table before Giles and Si. I don't know how much our round cost, but the two twenties Brett handed over weren't enough and he had to go rooting through his change. A big price to pay for having to pass water. Maybe there was a moral there, but I couldn't find it. If you child has a weak bladder don't let him join a band? Possibly. Tosspot poured Brett a pint and left him at the bar with the girl who seemed happy to do the talking.

"Why did you do that?" I wondered. "Look at the way he's behaving, it's painful to watch."

From our vantage point we could see Brett converse with her through a variety of tics and the occasional nod of agreement. He would rub his cheek, run a hand over his hair, fiddle with a hole in that ragged t-shirt, scratch his nose, shake his head, then pass his fingers through his hair again, all the time taking care to avoid the girl's eyes as she nattered on.

"I was just trying to help. God knows how long its been since a bird paid attention to him." O'Reilly watched Brett withdraw both of his veiny arms into the top. It made him look as if he was wearing a straitjacket. "She gave me a way in and I took it on his behalf. That's what friends are for."

Onstage the guitarist finished his last song to much clapping from people he knew. The four of us continued to observe Brett squirming uncomfortably.

"He doesn't have any confidence around chicks does he?" Si was amused. "Not even when he's drunk."

Tosspot nodded. "It's not even as if she's a stunner." The girl was clad entirely in black which somehow served to both conceal and accentuate her dowdiness. "I wonder how he got so fucked up."

"We can only guess."

"Look, did you see it?" Giles became animated. "His lips moved then, I'm sure they did."

Laughing, we left them to it and worked our way through the various drinks. The sheer volume of liquid and receptacles worried me. I let Si refill my glass and tried to avoid gesturing or inching close to the jugs. By now the club was about two thirds full, the DJ warming us up for the headliners with a series of ominously unmemorable singles from long-split Britpop also-rans. The likes of *Menswear*, *Powder* and *Northern Uproar* brought back terrible memories for me, then *The Pop Shots'* equipment came out and people began to congregate on the lower level, between tables and stage. Our whiskies were gone and one of the jugs was dead so I moved the empties away to create some room. Beside me Tosspot was telling Giles and Si about the time he arranged a bed-in as tribute to John and Yoko but neither of the girls he was seeing at the time turned up. World peace didn't happen, but at least he caught up on some sleep.

A guy in his early twenties wearing designer sunglasses walked from the wings and plugged in his guitar. There were a few excited *whoos* from the audience. The three members of *The A.T.E.* filled their pint glasses and walked towards the raised area while *The Pop Shots* took their places. I brought out my pen and paper and began writing under the table, a habit I'd adopted at gigs. I'm the guy with his name at the bottom of the column, so if I get branded a journo prior to the appearance of a less than complimentary review band members could well be nursing a grudge the next time we meet. Best to stay unrecognised and incommunicado

The Pop Shots looked like a melange of styles copied from New York bands of the past thirty-five years, all faded thrift store clothes and sallow complexions. But when their singer announced: "We're *The Pop Shots* and this is *She Knows Me*, ah-one-two-three-four..." it became clear this visual style was a red herring. Over a staccato guitar riff stolen from *The Kinks* their frontman, who I knew was called Ken, intoned meaningless lyrics in the Mockney style. The DJ knew what he was doing, evoking memories of mid-nineties has-beens. By the end of that first song I realised this band were very far from being good, and nothing they subsequently played changed my opinion. The test now was whether I could sit through the entire set without losing my marbles. On the positive side I wouldn't be short of things to write about in that rectangle of text *Plectrum Abuser* were giving this performance. While the singer batted his lashes, flicked eyes upwards and moved his head in a manner reminiscent of the brief craze for *vogueing*, I jotted down phrases like "adequate punk-pop if they played faster", "don't understand what makes a proper tune" and "gobshites".

After pouring more bile into my notepad I left it in my lap and glanced back at the spectacle. *The Pop Shots'* live show seemed to include some kind of rehearsed choreography. At various points the band would raise their guitars, drumsticks and fingers to the stars. Visually diverting it may have been, but for the watching public, desperate to enjoy themselves in spite of the main act, the band's practice time could have been better spent writing a few half-decent songs.

I drank more beer and soon enough my irritation was replaced with weariness. For a number of years I'd written paragraphs on up and coming bands for the weekly music national *Plectrum Abuser* in return for free entry to gigs and beer money. Back when I started it was easy to get caught up in the whole carnival of rock and roll. I used to impress dates by getting them onto guest lists, hobnob with musicians, spend evenings in buoyant dressing rooms with acts I enjoyed, sharing their rider and discussing influences. Once it was a great feeling, but the buzz had dissipated, and tonight my passion was completely gone. Maybe it was the paucity of decent acts playing the toilet circuit that did it. Every rising group of youngbloods who got the magazine excited lately sounded like they were stealing from better bands of five, ten, twenty years before. I find it difficult to hype those who pilfer from music I love. More often than not my recent reviews were full of anger and negativity, upsetting the youngsters and their parents who bought all the equipment.

Or perhaps the fault lay with me. I'd grown embittered and disillusioned by an industry which invariably chose the safe option, churning out acts reminiscent of those who've shifted units in the past. The record companies blamed declining sales on downloads rather than unwillingness to seek out new talent. Not to mention those bloated groups of muso fortysomethings who made a practice of exploiting, alienating and sometimes even suing their own fans. I couldn't remember the last time I'd written an encouraging piece about a band, and I was finding it harder to drum up enthusiasm for gigs like this one.

My thoughts turned to that war bear from earlier. Some of Wojtek's army colleagues visited him in Edinburgh zoo after the Nazis were vanquished. When the veterans got to the bear's cage they started whistling the Polish national anthem and Wojtek exploded with memories, shaking the bars ferociously. The bear wouldn't stop until his keeper got into the cage and hugged Wojtek, holding the huge animal in his arms until all was calmness once more. The thought of that scene, man and animal locked in an embrace which spoke of everything the world felt after World War II, it made me want to cry.

She must have seen me staring into space, a direction which meant I couldn't be watching the headliners and that was what accounted for the tap on my shoulder.

"Are you alright?"

I turned, seeing a girl dressed in the dark t-shirt and black trousers which formed the club's uniform. She had a tower of pint glasses in one hand, and a strange expression; half-concerned, half-amused, on her face. Backlit by the lights of the bar, the girl looked familiar somehow.

"I'm okay." I muttered unconvincingly and checked my face for tears. Fumbling to gather the notepad and pen with my other hand, both items fell to the floor.

The girl looked at me for a moment, then placed her empties on a table, picked up my possessions and passed them across. The end of another undistinguished number left the venue in silence for a strange second. Within that nothingness I watched the girl sit down beside me. Then the crowd gave out a smattering of applause, over which a voice I recognised yelled *"You're shit!"*

"Thanks, thank you very much." Responded the singer, who may well have been drugged up. "This one's called *Pocket Rocket.*"

The girl offered me her hand. "Kathleen." She said.

We shook. "Monty."

Kathleen smiled revealing a pink gum above her upper set of teeth. I normally hated that in a girl, but this time it wasn't too disagreeable.

"What are you writing?"

I explained my sideline in gig reviewing while checking her out. That feeling of familiarity I experienced must have been an illusion, some weird kind of deja vu moment, because I'd never met this girl before. She was slimmer than the women I usually go for, blonde with dark roots and too-thin lips. But Kathleen had these brown eyes. Had they belonged to a deer, those big brown eyes could have convinced a hunter to let it go.

"Okay, I get why you're not into it now, this is work right?"

"Kind of."

"But why on earth are you sat here with such a long face?" She looked to the bar. "Kevin pointed you out and I couldn't help but come over, you looked so sad."

I found this irksome, the way she made me sound like an abandoned puppy. Looking at Kathleen, I realised again this wasn't the sort of girl I fell for, however seductive those exceptional eyes.

"I'm just a little sick of it, that's all. You work here, yeah?" She nodded. "Then you must see it too. All these supposedly brilliant new bands who get endless column inches, they're *rubbish*. And I'm contributing to it. Whatever comes out of this evening will just become more promotional crap for talentless idiots." Before us *The Pop Shots* failed to execute scissor kicks, poor coordination letting them down.

"They aren't great, I'll admit." Kathleen leaned in so we didn't have to shout. "Sounds to me like you've been doing this too long."

The girl was perceptive, I'll give her that. There was definitely something passing between us, through the airwaves, but it wasn't the usual male-female stirring. Kathleen felt easy to talk to and appeared interested in me. Then again, she was just a girl collecting glasses in a dingy club. To hell with it, I was drunk, might as well keep up the conversation.

"The guy I live with has this fascination with Jane Fonda, he's a big fan. She's up on our walls and there's a kind of shrine to her in his room. The weird part is that he's as gay as a Morris dancer. I didn't realise she was a gay icon until I met him."

Kathleen looked behind her again. Some of the audience were growing tired of the band's uselessness and drifting to the bar. "I might have to go and help Kev in a minute."

"Okay, the point is this. My flatmate's always finding parallels between the lives of his friends and Jane's experiences, and what he'd say to me right now is that I'm in the same position as Jane around nineteen-ninety. What turned out to be her last movie had just come out, no one really liked it, she'd done, like, forty films by then, and there was so much else going on she didn't need the Hollywood bullshit anymore. So she left behind the directors who pushed her around and the cranky co-stars and the critics who savaged her whenever she worked because they bore grudges and just stopped. Thirteen years later and Jane still hasn't gone back to acting."

The girl stroked my arm, consoling. "Maybe that's true. It's not easy to stop, but sometimes you have to accept a part of your life is over and move on." That thin-lipped smile below high cheekbones. "People carry on doing stuff they've always done out of fear, it's our nature. If you can make the break it might be really good for you. You could start devoting time to other things." Did I imagine a glint in her eye just then? "Like Jane did."

"I don't know any workout routines."

Kathleen laughed, a surprisingly big noise for one so demure. The way she cracked up made me feel she'd actually got the joke and wasn't just being polite.

"Take that plunge Monty! You might be glad you did." She paused and checked the bar once more, Kevin appeared to be coping manfully. "But I don't think that's the real reason for your misery." She turned to the band, the headliners' big finish seemed to consist of them jumping from one side of the stage to the other.

"Okay, they're pretty awful, but that can't be why an interesting guy like you looks so sad."

Then Kathleen took my pen and paper and scribbled some digits. "Don't call after eight, that's when it gets busy here." She handed her phone number to me and stood up. "But do call me Monty, I'd like to know how it's going." A hand reached out and tousled my hair.

Then she was gone, leaving me shocked and surprised and staring at the number in my hand stupidly. Did it all tie together? The message I saw on the train, a girl hoping to inspire me, that strange connection I felt to her, like nothing I'd experienced before.

Someone sat down on my left, opposite the seat Kathleen had just vacated. I looked up and found Brett helping himself to the communal beer. The girl was nowhere to be seen.

"Did you catch any of that?" I asked Brett, stunned by the oddity of this evening. The bassist shrugged and drank some of the flat amber fluid while *The Pop Shots* ended their final song, the lights going down to some clapping and a few loud boos. I saw Tosspot and Giles leading the chorus, hands cupped around mouths to get their point across. Recorded music kicked in and the crowd dispersed, Si first back, followed by the other two.

"Well, they were shit." Tosspot shared out the remaining drink. "What happened to that fat bird Brett? I thought you were in there." The bassist blushed, a shade of red visible even in this darkened club. He rose to leave.

Tosspot barked out an order. "See you Sunday, two o'clock." The departing figure nodded and raised a hand, bidding the rest of us farewell.

"That was uncalled for." Si observed after he'd gone.

"Yeah well, I'm pissed off. Brett's too shy to say anything and too drunk to be coherent if he did. Hanging around girls is just asking for the kind of rejection he can't deal with, and that bunch of arse we've just seen pisses me off even more."

Giles concurred. "I'm with you Tosser, what the fuck were they doing? How can those losers be signed to V3, of all the fucking places?"

"Look at it this way." Si acted as peacemaker. "If they can get a deal we've got to be shoo-ins."

The three of them carried on like this for a while, complaining about chancers who got signed to big labels more through connections than talent. I tuned out their talk, it had all been said before, and I'd more important things on my mind. At last I'd worked out that chemistry which passed between Kathleen and myself, distracting me so acutely. What I felt wasn't the epinephrine rush of initial attraction, or even that familiar itch which comes with sexual desire. Instead the girl brought with her a certainty, unprecedented and welcome. It took me a while, but I'd finally figured out the feelings pulsing through my heart, impossible to ignore. They told me Kathleen belonged in my life.

Chapter Six

Trudging up the stairs to our flat I came upon the sight of Mrs. Winterbottom knocking on her own front door.

"Hello? Hellooo?" She called.

I paused, wondering whether I should ignore her and continue on my way. I'd had another difficult day at work, and any pleasure experienced by the week ending was undermined by the upcoming visit to my parents. What I wanted more than anything was to bypass this daffy old girl and slump in front of the television for five or six hours. Stopping me were the sounds which came from above, the mewls of a baby joining adult voices which floated down from my flat. I didn't need to deal with any of that right now. The confused woman tapping her door hadn't noticed me so I cleared my throat.

"Oh, hello dearie. Can you help? They won't let me in." The forlorn expression of my white-haired neighbour made me want to assist her. I resolved to get this poor soul into her home, even if it meant breaking the door down.

"Won't they? That's not very nice of them is it? Let's see what we can do."

I tried the handle. The door opened. We walked inside, me calling out to whoever Mrs. Winterbottom believed was inside. No one there.

"Can I offer you a cup of tea dear?"

"Thanks. Milk, no sugar."

She shuffled to the kitchen while I sat in an antiquated chair. Pictures of her closest relations, all passed on now, lined the mantelpiece. By all accounts Mrs. Winterbottom had been good company and sharp as a tack until a few years back. But one balmy Sunday her overweight son, who'd remained with her ever since his father died many years before, suffered an enormous heart attack. Nothing the ambulance workers could do revived him, this bulbous man in his early forties, a human healthcare campaign against the dangers of a sedentary lifestyle. The loss must have hit Mrs. Winterbottom hard, without a son to base her life around she began to lose touch with the real world. The old lady started turning up in

59

the homes of strangers on the block, making Ovaltine and trying to persuade them to bake her a fruitcake. Up until now these unwitting hosts had shown great understanding, managing to uncover the old lady's address and escort her back without informing social services. Hopefully the authorities wouldn't find out about her for a while, I didn't like to think of Mrs. W in a care home. She was still active and independent minded, her bouts of bewilderment in the minority compared to those times when she knew exactly what was going on. Like now.

"There you go dearie." She passed me a milky tea and eased herself onto the dust cover-adorned sofa. "Been at work today have you?"

"Yes, but it's the weekend now. Thank God."

"Is it?" She squinted at the cat themed calendar on her wall. "Yes, I suppose it is. I saw that big poofter of yours earlier."

"Fergal."

"Yes, Fergie." The old woman paused, lost in thought. "He was carrying a baby. You haven't adopted have you?"

"No Mrs. W, we haven't adopted."

"They let your type do that sort of thing now you know." She sipped her tea. "I can't see why the two of you don't get a one bedroom place. You'd save a fortune in rent."

I sighed. Here were two of Mrs. Winterbottom's favourite themes, the extortionate cost of living here and why us 'poofters' were throwing money down the drain by having a two bedroom flat.

"I've told you before, he's *not* my lover." My voice was mild but firm. "I'm not even gay, we just live in the same house."

"Yes, yes." She flicked the television on with her remote control. "But a smaller place would save you money. Prices are ridiculous these days. When I was growing up the three of us shared a bed that couldn't have been more than three feet across."

We watched the country's leading husband and wife presenting team interview a soap heart-throb for a while. Then I heard steps on the stairs so I thanked the old lady and excused myself.

Fergal led a young couple down the staircase, the man carrying a high chair while his girl clutched a gurgling infant.

"Greetings Monty." Cofaigh called from below. "We're going to get some outdoor shots, I'm afraid it's a bit of a mess up there."

"Okay."

Inside the flat I found myself confronted with the aftermath of a food fight. Grey mush, probably baby food, was splattered around kitchen cupboards and ceiling, while an unidentifiable green gunk streaked the walls and floor. This foodstuff impressionism was one of the downsides to Fergal's work. Every so often he'd need clips of some adorably anarchic child or gunk-covered kid, and I'd come home from a hard day keeping the agency afloat to find some borrowed baby turning our flat into a food mixer.

I moved to my bedroom, grumbling to myself. Most of the time my flatmate's trade had little impact on me so I wasn't really entitled to complain. Usually Fergal would work out a visual trick in his mind, set it up, film quickly and reap the benefits. At £250 a clip one minute of screen time on *The Camera Never Lies* equalled a month of living it up. People at the production company sold rights all around the world so Fergal's past excerpts ensured he had a steady income from the work if inspiration failed to strike. Previous sleights of hand included a toy dinosaur appearing to eat a little girl, the normal-size teenager using an enormous sponge to clean what was soon revealed as a toy car, an elderly lady going about her housework, oblivious to the flames licking at her back, and a veritable cornucopia of staged slips, trips, stumbles and dives. As long as the slapstick made viewers laugh the producers didn't care if it was staged. Fergal helped supply the show with home-grown hilarity, mixed with imported clips of Americans falling off snow-covered roofs or 'accidentally' letting their car roll over a cliff. Physical comedy was easy money, but Fergal's specialty was perspective and magic, comic stunts with mirrors, lenses and props, which fitted neatly into light entertainment. Images appeared and flashed away before an audience realised they were being duped, no one understanding until later that this was a conjuror's footage, full of falsity and misdirection.

When creativity dried up there was no shortage of other possibilities. I myself had ended up as the star of several clips when

Fergal had a camera trained my way and I'd accidentally done something televisual. In these sections I was transformed from Monty Sanderson into 'man hitting head', 'man falling over' or 'man breaking decanter' for the viewing public at home. But what they adored more than anything were excerpts of animals or kids. From the cat entering through a letterbox, to the toddler pulling a stupid face and falling over. With no pets or offspring himself, Fergal gave acquaintances a share of the profits in return for access to their domesticated moggy or newborn baby. He filmed a kid until something *cute* happened or else arranged some stunt involving his stock props; balloon animals, bowls of baby food, confusing kiddie toys, enormous cream buns. Everyone came out on top; the family got a nice cash bonus and the child certainly had a good time, although some parents got a little peeved when their darling continued its food-throwing antics at the dinner table.

I admired Fergal's industry and skill, that determination to avoid being sucked into a spirit-crushing day job. We all profited, from the local gentlemen's' outfitters he patronised, right down to a chortling studio audience. But sometimes, just occasionally, I'd come back from a long week in the office to find a brat wreaking havoc and wish Fergal was stuck behind a desk somewhere, like me.

Deciding to exploit my flatmate's absence, I had a nose around his bedroom, away from the dripping fixtures and familiar areas. The first thing which strikes a visitor to Fergal's *boudoir* is the six foot hamster beside his bed. He'd picked 'Dennis' up cheap at that auction where the contents of the now-defunct millennium dome were sold off. I faced the fat-cheeked rodent for a while, two black beady eyes staring down at me, then I touched Dennis with my forehead and moved on.

There were a number of reproduction paintings around the walls of this room, from Munch to Dali, while one side decorated by a full-size Jackson Pollock. The premeditated chaos of the piece reflected Fergal's own system of organisation. Books were piled everywhere, clothes spilled out of his overstuffed wardrobe, and while everything was shiny and clean there were too many heaps for the room to be considered neat. A myriad of items, purchased offhandedly because they caught Fergal's eye, cluttered up this space. Objects continued to be brought here by a man with plenty of spending power to indulge his consumerist whims.

Amid these explosions of culture the Chippendales calendar on Fergal's wall stuck out like a glamour model at a literary festival. This monthly display of beefcake was about the only item which explicitly alluded to his homosexuality. In fact there was plenty of evidence to contradict gayness; that shrine on the chest of drawers for instance. Fergal stored his collection of Jane Fonda merchandise there, including framed photographs, publicity stills from Jane's films or moments in her personal life. There she was, in dozens of guises; topless with a finger to her lips, addressing a meeting of demonstrators, wielding a pistol as the world's hottest cowgirl, fist raised in support of secretaries' rights. Beside pictures sat articles describing Jane's achievements, from a headline on her recent spiritual conversion to youthful rebellions around film sets. The love of Roger Vadim, then Tom Hayden, then Ted Turner. A willingness to admit her misguidedness in Vietnam and fifteen years of bulimia. The success and heartbreak, Oscars and enemies and obsessive fans who built strange monuments to her, just like this one.

My eyes explored the many facets of Fonda's beauty. That sultriness in the starlet, the spirited activist, talented actor, domesticated wife and mother, the woman caught as she stirred the contents of a saucepan between takes, still clad in the outlandish garb of erotic sci-fi. All the while this lambent actress entranced all around her, a confident stance, lustrous skin, that compelling gaze.

I checked my watch. Well into Friday evening and I still hadn't phoned Kathleen. That morning after the *Pop Shots* gig I'd woken up terribly hung-over and it was as much as I could do just to get through my working day. With the benefit of distance and sober logic I began to wonder why I'd been so taken with someone who wasn't my kind of girl. I was thinking about phoning her on Wednesday but then my father rang up, an occurrence both rare and problematic.

Dad's phone manner is non-existent. He finds it difficult to get to the point, opting instead for vagueness and long pauses. I find him impossible to talk to, even when I'm doing the calling and

I've carefully mapped out the conversation beforehand, so when my father rings me exchanges tend to become frustrating very quickly.

After about ten minutes of polite inquiries and dead air longueurs I got sucked into filling, burbling on about the temperature or low pressure fronts, dad finally got to the point. This turned out to be a request for an extension lead if I'd a spare one. He knew I did, so I said I'd bring it with me on Saturday. Then we engaged in the traditional call end dodge, the verbal equivalent of two people in the street who keep moving into each other's way as they try to pass. The gaps between statements left me reluctant to put the phone down until I heard a dialling tone, he might have been mid-statement for all I knew. But dad never hung up as soon as he'd finished what he had to say. The end of Wednesday's conversation went something like this:

Him: "So..." *(interminable pause)* "You'll bring it with you then?"

Me: "Yes, you don't have to worry dad, I'll have it. See you Saturday."

Him: "Right, good...." *(another pause, me hoping he was about to put the receiver down)* "And will you need picking up from the station?"

Me *(quickly)*: "I'll give you a call when I know what time my train gets in, should be about mid-afternoon."

Him: "Right." *(a further pause, during which several as-yet-undiscovered rainforest-dwelling species were rendered extinct)* "That'll be fine.... I think."

Me: "Right, goodbye then."

Him: "....."

Me: "Bye?"

Him: "....goodbye son."

Me *(waiting for the tone)*: "...."

Him: "You still there son?"

Me *(tiny voice)*: "yes."

Him: "Well, cheerio then."

Me: "Cheerio."

Him: "...."

Me *(praying to God he's about to put the phone down)*: "..."

Him: "....."*<mmmmmmmmm>*

Me: "Thank you Jesus." *(hangs up, emits huge sigh of relief, considers taking up smoking).*

After twenty minutes of this torture I didn't even consider picking up the phone again, and at work the next day I realised I hadn't turned in my review of *The Pop Shots* with the deadline looming. I spent most of Thursday evening fiddling with the grammar of my insults and now it was Friday. Kathleen might well be working at the club and my chance of speaking to her had vanished.

Not that I'd just let it slide. During two lunch hours this week I went into the *5 Easy Pieces*, both yesterday and today. In the daytime the venue served as a kind of alternative coffee house, and when she wasn't there on either occasion I ended up buying an overpriced baguette and watching the regulars, one of whom, a fiftysomething man in a duffel coat, purchased his coffee and drink it outside in the rain.

Worry spread like an ink blot through my mind. I ought to call Kathleen, I ought to call her right now, otherwise she'd think I'd forgotten. Despite the lack of physical attraction it wasn't as if I was overburdened with women yearning for my company. Then again, did I really want the hassle? Life was so much less stressful without a girl's needs to consider as well as my own. I hadn't stopped dating without good reason, it was a resolution intended to simplify my life until that special someone came along, a babe whose sexuality would hit me with the force of a prop forward; great jiggling breasts, that J-Lo arse and a filthy gleam in her eye.

Who was I kidding? I'd lost my touch, that's why I wasn't pursuing women. For a long time the only girls I scored with were the ones who quickly found some way to turn me off, be it through timidity or abhorrent moodswings.. Now one who might be really sorted had come along and just the thought of speaking to her on the phone made me nervous. That flicker of terror in the brain and churning in the stomach I used to experience all the time as a spotty adolescent, and it couldn't be put down to the cheap hamburgers I'd eaten on the way home from work.

You see, most girls couldn't care less how handsome you are or what you've got in the way of worldly goods. I mean, obviously they prefer someone solvent and good looking as opposed to a penniless mutant, but what it really comes down to is confidence. That's what sparks the interest and creates the chemistry, a man who can maintain the illusion, who appears to know what he's doing, this Romeo might take her in his arms any moment, send shivers down the girl's spine. I'd been so worn out by months of women who didn't intrigue me or screwing it up when they did that my self-assurance was baritone low. It's hard to keep up the pretence of suavity when you've just dragged the cloth off the restaurant table, taking several condiments with it. But that happened a long time ago, the fear was all in my head now and Kathleen didn't know I was anything other than some in-demand guy with several women on the go. Come on Monty, faint heart never won fair lady and all that crap.

I took one last look at Jane, lying there on her front, those come-to-bed eyes unwilling to relinquish their grip, and I prayed to her for courage. Then I sparred for a while with the six foot hamster, made boxer noises and landed a few right hooks to his gut. Finally I got my mobile and Kathleen's number.

A recorded message. I knew it, her phone was switched off. Okay, don't let that bother you, leave an explanation instead. Oh Christ, what did I want to say? I should have prepared something. Calm down. And don't hang up. You're not a coward, a wuss, yellow...... Oh shit, here comes the beep.

"Hello, Kathleen? It's Monty here. We met at the club on Monday night, I don't know if you remember?"

That's right, it was only five days ago, suggest she's a forgetful imbecile or has Alzheimer's or something.

"Actually, I'm sure you do remember because you cheered me up, and I meant to phone you before but, um...."

An excuse please, one that doesn't make her sound like a low priority.

"I've had a few catastrophes this week, you know how it is."

Excellent, except it makes your life sound disastrous.

"You're probably working at the moment so I guess I've called too late, but maybe you'd like to meet up sometime, if that's possible. You might have a lot on..."

Forceful, direct, possessed of a compelling magnetism. If only that were me.

"I've got to visit my parents this weekend but I'll call you again Sunday, earlier this time."

Will I? Apparently so. Right.

"So, yes. Thanks for the pep talk on Monday, it was really nice."

Nice?

"And don't go thinking I haven't called because I didn't want to, that's not true. And I haven't been caught up in some crazy social whirl either."

Where exactly are you going with this?

"That's not really me, I'm more like the panda bear, you know? I mean I'm a bit of a solitary guy, not that I eat bamboo and rub my gland up against trees."

Put the phone down.

"But you probably didn't need to know that so...."

Shut up about bears and hang up.

"Anyway, if you could leave your phone on Sunday afternoon that'd be good and I look forward to maybe seeing you again, erm....."

Enough of this Casanova.

"Bye Kathleen, bye."

My God, I was sweaty as an obese sunbather. But I'd done alright *(really?)*. Well, at least I'd done something. I looked at the clock on my phone and slipped it into my pocket. Nearly nine. Back in the kitchen Fergal was stood on a chair cleaning gunk off the ceiling.

"Ah Montgomery, good to see you." He stepped down and checked the area for baby food. "Almost done here. I can only apologise again, the little one got very eager with the old chicken and fruity vegetables."

"As long as you clean it up." I flicked through the TV guide. "Not going out tonight?"

"No, I think not." Fergal held the gack-spattered cloth under a tap. "You know who I saw on the way up? Mrs. Winterbottom. She said you're a hero for getting her back into her house. I said we were all very proud of you."

"All I did was open the door."

"Ah, so our dear neighbour was discombobulated again?" He wrung the cloth out and joined me in the lounge. "Perhaps I should have realised that when she asked me if I'd finished baking her pie. I told her there was a nationwide shortage of pastry and she seemed to accept that. Strange old bird."

"Stop changing the subject." He was very good at evasion. "I can't remember the last time you didn't have a bloke waiting on Friday night. Or some potential conquest. I want to know why."

Fergal exhaled theatrically. "You make me sound like such a wanton thing." I could tell he was piqued at being made to explain. "The truth is I seem to have caught your disease my friend. For whatever reason I've become quite jaded with the parties and the young fellows. At times promiscuity only reinforces my belief everyone is basically the same. So why meet new boys? Why not choose a fellow and stay with him? If only they didn't bore me so."

"Plenty of greased-up botty sex not enough?"

"I'll thank you not to mock, I've spent a great deal of time pondering this. I'm sure you're aware how we grow up expecting there to be some kind of emotional or intellectual logic inspiring the sexual etiquette of human beings. Then we become adults and learn there is not. However evolved the participants and sophisticated their rituals, all it comes down to is grunting and thrusting and a sense of waste." I turned from the TV to my despondent flatmate, rarely had I seen him this melancholy. "Am I getting too complicated for you?"

"Not at all, I'm quite enjoying this insight into the world of bent."

"Harumph." Fergal stretched and thrust his pot belly outwards. "I might be offended if I didn't think you felt similarly regarding the fairer sex."

"Whatever you say."

"So here we are, two strapping young men in the prime of our bodies, inside on a Friday night watching *Will and Grace*. What on earth will become of us?"

"You're not going to hit on me are you?"

"I said I was fed up with it all, not that I was lowering my standards."

"Thanks."

"Well, you did ask."

And so on, until I'd almost forgotten the family I had to face the next day. Those freedoms of my weekend curtailed by mum and dad, a return to the domain I'd long since left behind for the set of circumstances I liked to call my life. Basingstoke here I come.

Chapter Seven

The further my train progressed out of Waterloo, carriages clanking along unsteady rails, the deeper I descended into a cloud of gloom. It was always like this, returning to the town, the house, the people I grew up with. My father was waiting for me when I arrived in Basingstoke, his car positioned between taxis at the station entrance, the aggrieved-looking drivers upset I wasn't adding to their profits.

We greeted each other in the usual cursory manner and I slung my shoulder bag into his back seat. It was years since my father had been exuberant in my presence and he wasn't starting now. The wipers went on to clear this ongoing drizzle, Brian Sanderson turned the key and shifted the car into gear. I glanced at him, dad's once dark hair now an even shade of grey, his lined face looking more drained each time I saw him. This was no longer the imposing figure of my childhood, I'd outgrown him, both in stature and life experience. Next year he'd turn sixty, and after that it was a cruise to the finish, to the end of his career at the coach company, dad's place of employment for the past twenty three years. Impending retirement was one of the two subjects about which I could eke more than a few words out of him, the weather being the other.

"Doesn't look like easing off." My father observed, switching his headlights on. "I've got a leak in the shed, have to fix that when we get back."

I mumbled agreement as he drove on, over roundabouts which grew smaller as we approached our suburban destination. Veering away from the town centre, I instinctively looked to the blocks of Montgomery Road flashing past on our right. Inside one of those buildings I'd been conceived and raised to the age of twelve, a boy christened after the street in which he was born and keeping his head down in that tricky neighbourhood. I wasn't named to retain some of the spirit and exoticism of that place, my parents weren't celebrities, evoking memories each time they looked at their child. No, I was called Montgomery because mum and dad couldn't think of anything better. How long they spent agonising over that one I didn't know, I'm sure it was a busy time.

We pulled into the driveway, the end of a terrace where my father bought a modest house when he was promoted, back in the late eighties. He was still paying off the mortgage now. I got out of the car and stared down our road. This area was all-too familiar for me, I'd explored every step of the neighbourhood back in my teens, this place where I passed my driving test, stumbled home drunk for the first time, lost my virginity, brought back a maiden girlfriend, experienced millions of sensations; some joyous, some horrible, mainly variations on tedium. Now I felt as if no part of this town held any mystery, an illusion which kept me away as much as possible.

My father locked up and glanced at me, confused, then hunched over to walk indoors. I realised I was standing in the rain and followed him inside.

"Don't bring those wet feet in here!" Shouted my mother in the same tone she used for ordering the dogs around. Dad changed from shoes to boots, swapped his jacket for a plastic mackintosh and hurried through our kitchen to the garden. I watched my father scurry off silently, a shamed public figure avoiding the attention of the press. Then my mother materialised to hug me, closely followed by the two collies who yelped with pleasure and circled us both.

"Hello darling." She shooed Betty and Sheba towards the living room. "Can I get you something to drink?"

"Thanks." We retired to the kitchen and she poured orange juice. From the window I could see dad at the other end of the lawn. The shed door was open and he was standing on a stepladder, examining the roof.

"You look well. How have you been?"

"Fine, fine."

"Any young ladies I should know about?" That was her way of asking me whether Fergal had turned me gay yet. My mother still believed homosexuality was some kind of unpleasant disorder passed along through exposure to improvident lifestyles. Like casual drug use, or joining a golf club.

"No girl at the moment mum but I'll keep you posted."

"Make sure you do." She moved to the oven, a compact, dominating woman with a mass of greying curls, artificially coloured whenever the mood took her. "Steak and kidney pie tonight."

"Great." I'd pick out the kidney and feed it to the dogs later. Outside a banging noise announced dad fixing the shed, despite the rain coming in on him. According to my mother the old man spent more and more time out there now, even rigging up a camp bed for those nights he didn't feel like coming back into the house. They never spoke about it of course, I hadn't seen my parents conduct a conversation in years.

Mum prepared the accoutrements of dinner, humming to herself as she filled the house with odours of beef stock and boiled vegetables. I leafed through local newspapers she kept on the worktop, a recent edition of the *Basingstoke Advertiser* leading on a man who suffered the obscure fate of distastefully garish ties stuffed through his letterbox in the middle of the night. Police were baffled at this obsessive action by person or persons unknown which had been going on for six months. They could only speculate these items of neckwear were inflicted on the victim as some kind of obscure revenge, but for what no one knew. Meanwhile the culprit escaped every time, local authorities loath to monitor a man's house and arrest someone for malicious tie delivery. Besides, the action was erratic, sometimes no visit for months, then a week with nasty neckties delivered every night.

Food was ready so I hustled the collies into the garden and signalled at my father to come in. We ate at the dining room table in silence, a tensionless absence of sound broken only by the scrape of cutlery and squishing mastication noises. The food was reasonably appetising by my mother's standards, she had a tendency to render the tastiest foodstuffs inedible by microwaving them because it was "easier". I suppose she'd put in more effort today because of my appearance, and there was little she could do wrong with a shop-bought pie and greens. Mum had always believed a meal did you no good unless it caused some kind of pain or discomfort and throughout my childhood she encouraged me to eat steaming hot food that burnt my tongue, poured too much spice into curries and left objects lurking which could have broken my molars. It wasn't just coins in the pudding at Christmas, half the desserts she served had stones or pips of some kind inside. During my early years her main courses tried to destroy my taste buds, before sweet launched a follow-up assault on the teeth. By rights my mouth should have been a disaster zone by now, but her tendencies had only toughened me up and whatever we were served in the Russian roulette of my mother's cooking, at least it was never bland.

I cleaned the gravy from chunks of kidney and took my plate away, depositing the foul meat into the bowls of Betty and Sheba. Then I stepped outside and called to the cheerful pets, adopted shortly after I moved out. Back with my parents we had our next course, a suspicious-looking plum duff I eviscerated with a pathologist's care. My father was soon done, disappearing without a word. I eventually excused myself, having resolved to get through Mart's play by Monday after putting him off all week, claiming it was "nearly finished" when in fact I'd barely begun.

Upstairs I extracted the manuscript from my rucksack in that bedroom which remained 'mine', even though I'd left more than half a decade before. Relics from my youth stayed untouched, boxes of comics and antiquated computer games, plastic toys and top trumps stuffed into my wardrobe. Returning to this space was handy for visits, but it didn't make a whole lot of sense in the wider scheme of things. Mum kept it for me when there was only one other bedroom in the house so my father preferred to endure a dusty shed rather than sleep with my mother. But I guess if you were after sense my parents' marriage was the wrong place to look. Following almost three decades of wedlock they'd descended into some kind of non-verbal war of attrition and it was a point of principle to avoid expressing emotion. Maybe my mother wouldn't give up this room for dad's use because that could accede vital ground in the ongoing marital conflict.

Downstairs my mother had settled into her Saturday evening television extravaganza. She held a dialogue with game shows, guessed answers or berated contestants for failures of knowledge. I joined the dogs on the sofa, scratching Sheba behind the ear as I delved into *Too Beautiful*. The play was divided into three acts, the first tracking Richey's childhood in the Welsh town of Gwent, up to his mental and physical deterioration, followed by a lengthy scene at the final gig he ever played with *The Manic Street Preachers*. A second part dealt with what was officially known of Edwards' final days, exploring the media speculation around his disappearance and imagined reaction from those left behind. The final third, and by far the worst, consisted of Mart's speculations on Richey's current whereabouts. My boss concluded that the musician lived in some remote corner of the world, content in his isolation but haunted by figures from the past who appeared to him in oddly conventional dreams. The problem with this ending was obvious. Most of those familiar with the case believed Edwards to have taken his own life, he was even declared officially dead a while back. Mart preferred to dismiss this notion and engage in some quixotic fantasy of a troubled young man disguising himself amongst Goa backpackers. These final scenes seemed wholly at odds with the dark and discordant style which ought to have been maintained throughout.

Beyond the implausibility of the ending there were more fundamental problems with the script. Mart's pacing was all over the place, and he appeared to have no real storyline. Scenes were juxtaposed haphazardly and with little regard for narrative propulsion. One minute Richey was exploring sex tourism on tour in Thailand and a couple of pages later he'd be taking laundry to his mother's house when he couldn't get the washing machine to work. And all the time there was no way of connecting the fragments into a whole which made any kind of point. Much was made of the protagonist's tormented personality and metaphysical terror with scenes in which Edwards addressed the audience, delivering clumsy exposition on alcoholism, eating disorders and his confused attitude to love. These sections abounded in the first two acts, intercut with ill-advised attempts at levity, as if Mart was uncomfortable taking us too far into the darkness. So Richey refuses to appear nude in a women's magazine because his manhood isn't big enough, Richey gets into a fight with a rival band and accidentally breaks one of Norman Cook's gold discs, Richey goes to a strip club and has great fun doing the moonwalk with some naked ladies. I drew big crosses against each of these scenes, they'd be the first to go.

Nearby my mother verbally appraised each of the advertisements in a commercial break. 'I don't understand this' she would say or 'stupid advert!'. Mum wasn't talking to me so I continued working my way through *Too Beautiful*. Who knew what I was going to tell my boss about it? There was no way I wanted to see this production go ahead as it stood, but if Martin demanded an honest opinion my thoughts could be seen as a kind of disloyalty that might drive a wedge between us. Mart had toiled over this project for years, the last thing he needed was me denting his confidence, and maybe I could get myself the sack into the bargain. Because his life's artistic work, as encapsulated by this play, was nonsense.

So, in conclusion, I didn't have the faintest idea how to respond to Martin's request. I'd just have to go on playing it by ear. The frustrating aspect was that somewhere inside Landry's two hundred pages of drivel there was a good little story trying to get out. A slight meditation on one terribly lost man, the irreconcilability of creative rebellion and commercial imperatives, the human cost of rock and roll and how four mates took on the world and tragically became three. What it needed was a tight, hard treatment, not this expansive draft which read like Mart had taken everything interesting he could find about Richey's life and thrown it together at random.

Rubbing my eyes, I checked the time and discovered I had been reading for hours. My mother made hot chocolate and turned on the football highlights for me. While we drank she told me about one of her friends, a social worker who'd been assigned to visit an incapacitated man at home, helping him to shower and shave. That is, until it came to light that the council had given her the wrong address. The man she was tending to, and who'd accepted her care without a word for several months, was entirely able-bodied. Apparently the authorities were currently debating whether to press charges or not. I muttered my amusement and filed the tale away to tell Fergal later.

On the television teams from around England scored goals with little effort. My mother went to bed and I pondered how we hadn't seen dad all evening. In fact I didn't set eyes on him until the next day when mum sent me out to see if he wanted breakfast. It was around eleven as I picked my way across the damp lawn, the extension lead he'd asked for in one hand. I reached the six by ten construction and knocked on its door.

Dad appeared, dishevelled but smiling. "Hello son, thanks for that." He took the lead and nodded toward the shed's interior. "What do you think?"

"It's, er... great." Inside the windowless hut there was little to relieve the murk, the only light provided by some kind of ancient lamp. I picked out two rows of shelves, set about four and six feet up the sides and cluttered with paint pots, tools, jars of nails and cracked mugs. On the ground before us lay the mattress and bedding where my father slept, his clothes piled up in a heap before us, while above plasterboard and tarpaulin served to block out what must have been the leak. A half full bucket of water sat in the corner while spades and forks rested against the walls. How my father moved around this confined space without it all crashing down I'd no idea. I would have scattered the contents within seconds of going in there.

"Mum wanted to know if you were coming in."

"Yes, right, will do. See how I've got myself set up here? That heater keeps me nice and warm." He indicated the gas-powered contraption. "I come out here and get away from it all, a man needs his own space."

I glanced around that interior again, it was like a prison cell without the amenities. That makeshift home made my heart heavy and for the first time I could remember I felt sorry for my father. This was the best he could do, shut out here between his office and a cold welcome in a house he was still paying for. Behind us Betty and Sheba ran up to investigate, sniffing my ankles before they turned, chasing each other round the garden.

"You know, I envy those dogs sometimes." My father was thoughtful. "They don't have to plan for the future, they don't feel the need to carry it all on somehow." He looked at me, sizing up his son. "Your mother, well, she likes her television. I've never liked television."

"No."

"You're her only hope for a grandchild Montgomery. She'd like a grandchild."

"Erm..."

"You shouldn't let anyone force it on you son." He went into the shed and sat down on his cot. "If you end up raising a little one with the wrong woman, well, it's a recipe for disaster. Even when you can see it'd be wrong, they've ways of talking you into it. That's what happened to me, learn from my mistakes son."

My compassion abruptly vanished. Mistakes? The grey haired individual put on a pair of shoes in the gloom.

"Your mother was different then. You should have seen us before you came along, you wouldn't have believed it." I'd come across a few photos, they were different people in those days; happy and loving. "Round about the time you appeared on the scene everything changed."

Then something unfamiliar to me, a note of apology in his voice. "Not that I'm blaming you of course, it's just the way things went." My father joined me and we walked toward the house. "Don't look back at my age and have regrets son. There's a lot of things I'd do differently if it happened again, but you can't dwell on that sort of thing."

"No, right."

We got to the kitchen, both of us silent now. The shock of his talk must have shown on my face because mum saw me and shot my father a dirty look, a look which bounced off him. I sat down to eat feeling numb and confused. It was years since my father had spoken to me about anything in that much depth and even then it was only general guidance; get a pension, put your money away, think about buying property, that sort of thing. Never before had dad sounded quite so defeated as he did during that guided tour of his shed.

I continued thinking about those words over bacon and eggs. Then, round about a third cup of coffee, my mind turned to Kathleen and I vowed then to get her into my life. After this decision I felt much better, had no objection to assisting mum with some tasks around the house. Evidently it was easier to wait months for me than ask her husband to help. I hefted a variety of boxes and objects into the attic while she stayed below, holding the ladder and advising me to "watch out up there" and "be careful". I'm sure if I'd been allowed to concentrate rather than listening for instructions I wouldn't have come back down with quite so many bruises.

In the kitchen I looked at my watch again, a couple of hours until freedom. Mum basted a chicken for Sunday roast while I changed the plug on a kettle for her. Each time I came back here it was the same, the hassles of an only child returning to haunt me. When I was growing up mum used to treat me as if I were some kind of rare object, her precious son who needed protecting from the world. Rarely was I allowed out to play and she never let me walk home from school during winter's darkness until I was about fifteen. As a result I became nervous of other kids and had to amuse myself with solitary pursuits while longing for playmates. Eventually this lonely child became an adult and I managed to get over my introversion, only for a new set of problems arise.

You see, without siblings there was no one to share the burden of my parents and now they were starting to drift apart I became more conflicted with each passing year. It felt impossible to stay devoted to each of them equally, listening to both as they described the failings of the other, not without driving me crazy. As well as feeling torn between them the problem with being an only child, as dad already mentioned and my mother was about to prove, is that you have to satisfy any hankering for grandchildren.

"Old Mrs. Frobisher down the charity shop was saying her daughter had a little girl." My mother stirred a pot of gravy into which she'd placed a variety of seasonings. "It's only her first child and she's almost forty! That can't be healthy, but it's the fashion now. Girls want to have their life, they don't think about children 'til later." She lowered her voice. "I hope that doesn't happen to me."

The screwdriver came away and scratched my index finger. I muttered swear words under my breath as the blood appeared.

"Still, at least she's got a granddaughter. Edie must be well into her seventies, but you should see her eyes light up when she talks about little Melinda."

I sucked my bloody hand. "That's nice. Have you got a plaster?"

She took the first aid box out from under the sink. "Mrs. Frobisher asked about you. I told her, 'I shouldn't expect anything from my Montgomery' I said, 'he's living with a swish now'".

I covered my cut with a protective strip. "Great, now she'll be telling the whole of Basingstoke I'm gay."

"Well, what else could I say?" My mother checked her saucepans. "I had to tell her something."

"Really? You had to tell her that? Think back mum, when exactly have I brought home anybody who wasn't a girl? Remember any?"

She snorted. "I don't know what influences you've got now, do I? That boy could be leading you to anything for all I know."

I sighed. "Your plug's done."

"Thank you. Now go and get your father, and don't be so long this time, I'm about to dish it up. If you're not at the table in two minutes it'll get cold."

We ate in silence again, me burning the roof of my mouth as I forced down the molten food. The spiciness of this dish caused dad to sneeze, my mother casting a disgusted glance at him from across the table. He faced away and blew his nose before carrying on.

When mum went off to deal with the dirty plates and my father came into the lounge. "You'll be wanting a lift to the station soon." He noted, stroking the head of a sleeping dog.

"If we go in about half an hour that'd be good."

"Fine, fine." All was quiet save for the sound of my mother humming to herself in the kitchen. "Remember what I told you son, it's...."

At that point mum came into the room so my father stopped mid-sentence. She scanned the room for more washing up then left. When the man felt sure his wife was out of earshot he continued.

"It's easy to end up like me if you don't think much about the future. There's...."

He stopped, she was on her way in once more.

"Coffee anyone?" I responded positively, dad grunted. She left.

"There's no way to see what's coming, but you've got a head on your shoulders Monty. You must realise there's more to life than just getting by. I'm not much of a role model, I know, but I've been around longer than you. I've seen what happens when things break down. Look after yourself and consider what you want in everything you do. Especially when it comes women."

"Okay."

My mother brought me coffee and settled herself down causing my father to react as if an insect had bitten his rear end. He rushed to escape her presence, confirming the time we'd be leaving on his way out. Until then dad would be in the shed.

Just as it had descended before, the cloud lifted as my train wound its way back to London. I was returning to the life I liked, away from my parents' petty skirmishes and the dullness of Basingstoke. This weekend had not been without its deviations from the norm though. The old man hadn't spoken to me like that before, he even told me to "take care" as I left the car. Sincerity always seemed beyond my father in the past and I didn't realise he could admit to wrong decisions. I knew of no evidence my parents had been unfaithful to each other during those twenty eight years of wedlock, but I was certain their love eroded after I was born. The passage of time, those everyday regrets of their lives, it gradually leached all affection from the relationship. What kept them together was a mixture of habit, debt and bloody-mindedness. I'd been forced to confront that fact in recent years. My father was right, I'd be a fool to end up like him.

I took my phone out and switched it on. No texts, no voicemails, no calls; no distractions. Okay, that was good, even if it implied no one was interested enough to get in touch with me. Best not to think like that. Right, I'd already programmed the number in so there weren't any problems. Except, what was I going to say? Just "can we meet up?" I suppose. What had I said to her on Friday? Oh Jesus, why did I start going on about the glands of bears? Idiot. She must think I've got a screw loose.

Turning the mobile off, I put it in my rucksack. Then my thoughts went back to the situation I'd left, how my parents were about to confront another week of drudgery and loveless cohabitation. How long was it since I'd found a girl I really liked? Could I risk the embarrassment and try to hook up with Kathleen, or was I happy to spend my life on the fringes, jealously watching happy couples? And what was it I had to lose anyway? Apart from self-respect if she didn't want to hear from me. Possibly followed by my will to live if she got shirty. Don't dwell on that Monty.

I retrieved the phone again and selected Kathleen's name from the list. Before I could change my mind a third time it was ringing.

"Hello?"

"Hi Kathleen, it's Monty here."

"Hey Monty, how you getting on?" Excellent, she remembered who was.

"Not bad, I'm recovering from my family."

"Know the feeling."

"Listen, sorry about the message Friday, I think my point kind of got left behind." A pause at the other end.

"Don't worry yourself, I thought it was pretty funny." What, funny ha-ha? Apparently so. "You make me smile."

"Well, good."

"So what was your point anyway?" Her tone of voice made it feel like she was teasing me, now or never.

"The point was er, um..." Fuck, I was turning into Hugh Grant. Get a grip. "I think we should meet up and do, erm, something." Hmmm, I don't like the way that sounded.

"Tomorrow night's good for me."

"Me too." Fantastic. Easy as that.

"Do you like sushi? I haven't had sushi in too long."

"Sushi, sure. Sushi's fine." Jesus, raw fish. "Where's good?"

"There's this place in Chinatown I really like." The pips went on my phone, one minute's credit left, I'd have to speed this up. "It's called *The Kalamazoo* on Modal Street, round the corner from Leicester Square."

"Sounds good, eightish?"

"Make it seven thirty and you've got a deal." Kathleen sounded upbeat. Was it possible she'd been without a date as long as me? Surely not.

"Excellent, see you there. Seven thirty."

"Seven thirty."

"Seven thirty." I declared, meaninglessly. "See you tomorrow, have fun now."

"You t........" I was out of credit. It didn't matter, we were settled. I didn't even care about the people who'd been observing some nervous guy trying to arrange a rendezvous on the train. Even now the passengers confided to one another, talked of his hesitation and that noisy excitement as the conversation wore on.

They could snigger as much as they liked, Monty Sanderson had done it. He was going out with a fine girl. We would have a good time and see if there was anything worth pursuing between us. As we pulled into Waterloo I realised I was back in the game. Out to discover whether that feeling for Kathleen was a drunken illusion or not. All I had to worry about now was every aspect of the date.

Chapter Eight

We threw in our chips and discarded useless cards, snapping up new ones in their place.

"Come on Justin, we haven't got all day." Leon urged. "This is poker, you know? Rat-a-tat-tat? Bing-bang-boom? How many d'you want?"

"Let's see those rules again."

Groans from the other players. I passed Justin the sheet which defined each hand. He studied explanations of the best combinations, from Royal Flush down to Ace High, and after long seconds requested two cards.

"A pair of fresh ones for the novice." Leon threw them over. "Dealer takes three and...." He glanced at his cards. "...starts the betting at fifty new pence."

"Too rich for my blood." The long haired guy from the vinyl emporium threw his hand away. Now it was time for Justin to bet or fold.

"Monty." He whispered. "I'm going to need your help."

Leon slapped a palm against his forehead. "For Christ's sake Justin, there's no point showing Monty your cards and asking how good they are. He's still in the hand for one thing. If you start consulting people you'll destroy the game."

"Right, okay." Justin sat up straight, looked at his cards once and attempted to pull a poker face. It made him look like he was chewing a chilli pepper. "Let's just say, for the sake of argument, that I've got a friend with three jacks. Do you think he should raise or not?"

Muttering obscenities to themselves, everyone folded. I threw my two pair away and pointed at the pot. "It's yours."

"Really? Cool."

I was beginning to regret offering to teach Justin the game. In half an hour of playing five card stud he'd failed to grasp even the most basic elements, yet he kept getting the best hands. Beginner's luck was overpowering Justin's uselessness, a state of affairs which landmined our dealer's belief, indeed the faith on which

83

Leon based his whole existence; that good players won out whatever their cards.

I'd extended an invitation to Justin after finding it impossible to concentrate on my job this morning. With Mart out, holding auditions for the lead role in *Too Beautiful*, there wasn't much incentive to get on with any work, or any work to get on with. None that wasn't exasperating anyway. One of the animation studios *Bears!Bears!Bears!* dealt with had finally sent through the sample drawings we asked for, but they were well below par. I didn't feel like pointing it out to the artists, I wasn't about to get into an argument today, but the stills for this future campaign by a European multinational simply weren't up to scratch. We intended using a wisecracking bear to sell a new type of confectionery, rolled up strips of fruit-based candy supposedly filled with vitamins. Unfortunately the cartoon grizzly those animators sent us looked like he was suffering from leprosy. There the bear went, walking through the forest, plucking apples and pears from trees along the way, one of his legs hanging off and claws different in every drawing. If the company went ahead with the commercial like this it was going to terrify kids and upset the Broadcasting Standards Association. Deciding to delegate upwards, I'd left the whole sorry package on Mart's desk. Now it was my boss' problem.

Apart from deleting another prank message ("*I have appeared as a bear in the United States many times and can fax you a resume if required.*") I'd wasted much of my time today digesting a long email about a confidence trick being perpetrated around London's commuter belt. Apparently a respectable looking woman would talk her way into middle class homes to make an 'emergency' call, but the number she rang was set at such a high rate it cost each household several hundred pounds.

The rest of the morning was spent staring blankly at my computer screen, thinking about the upcoming date. I ran through possible topics of conversation in my head, tried to think of compliments I could give Kathleen, wondered whether the clothes I wore were suitable and worried about every eventuality.

Realising I needed to take my mind off the evening ahead, I'd dragged Justin along to the smoking room. I'd love to say I let him take part out of magnanimous motives, a willingness to open my colleague to new experience. In actual fact Justin was allowed entry to our game because I figured we could win easy money off him. My colleague was one of those guys who didn't mind being fleeced and he always seemed to have plenty of cash because his parents didn't charge him rent. Maybe it would turn out to be good for him in the long run. Any money we took off Justin was money he couldn't spend on ridiculous trousers.

Sadly the cards didn't work out that way. After yet another hand which Justin won by fluke, this time with the help of a straight, I decided to go for lunch, ignoring Leon's pleas to take Justin with me and leave him somewhere. Outside there was a wintry chill to the air and Bernard was looking a bit forlorn, huddled up there under the steps. I asked the tramp to join me and bought two portions of soup with bread which we took into the square.

The tramp slurped his meaty broth and chewed on the soft roll, apparently deep in thought. I was in my own world too. Kathleen kept appearing in my mind's eye, the girl expecting me to sweep her off her feet, waiting to be entertained and enraptured. She was asking a lot.

"Can I ask you a question Bernard?"

"Go ahead my boy." His voice was gruff but friendly, like always.

"You've been around, right?" The man next to me wore several frayed jumpers and fingerless gloves. "Knowing what you know now, is there any advice you can give to a confused young man about women?"

Bernard began to laugh, pieces of bread falling to the ground from his mouth. Soon enough the guffaws turned to coughing and Bernard clutched his stomach until the noise subsided.

"You alright?"

"Fine, yes." There were crumbs in his beard. "If you want to know what girls today are thinking you're asking the wrong man. What's brought this on?"

"It's just...." I took a sip from my cup and watched pedestrians cut across the square. "I'm seeing this girl for the first time tonight, seeing her *properly* if you know what I mean, and I want it to go really well."

"Has it not been going well?"

"To be honest with you Bernard I'm a bit out of practice. The girls haven't been interested lately. I don't know what it is, I'm clean, and I've got all my own teeth."

The tramp wiped his mouth with a sleeve, leaning back on the bench for a moment of quiet contemplation. Leaves fluttered to the ground around us, dislodged by the abrasive wind. I pulled my coat tighter around me.

"Did you ever hear the joke about the beautiful woman and the tramp?"

"Don't think I caught that one."

Bernard grinned at me, revealing blackened incisors. "A sexy career woman is walking down Oxford Street and a homeless man comes up to her and says: 'Spare some change love? I haven't eaten all day'."

"And what does the woman say?"

"She says, 'My God, I wish I had your will-power!'."

He laughed again, wheezing beside me. "Okay Bernard, I get it. What's the point?"

"Well my boy, the point is, all those girls you're so worried about are just as worried. I've seen them you know, all covered in make-up, going on about how fat they are. These are beautiful girls Monty, but they don't think they've got what the models and movie stars have. Do you understand what it is I'm saying?"

"I think I do, yes."

"I bet you this young lady is telling someone how nervous she is right now." He chuckled. "Though probably not a smelly old tramp like me."

"You're not smelly Bernard, no more than the average out-doorsman."

"Thank you my boy, and thanks for the meal."

So, according to this vagrant, girls like Kathleen had bad self-images after a life of exposure to stick-thin perfection on maga-zine covers and TV. Every girl out there rounded on the flaws which made her unique, doubting her seductive capabilities because of human imperfections. Maybe Bernard was right, maybe not. He made me feel better anyway, so I gave him some money for dinner and returned to the agency where Justin was eating a sandwich containing what looked like the contents of a weed patch while watching a clip of some Americans accidentally setting light to themselves.

Back to business, I typed in a URL and looked up the location of that faux-country pub where this afternoon's reception was to be held. Printing a copy of the resultant map, I advised Justin that it was time to leave. My colleague said he 'definitely owed me one' for introducing him to the poker game in which he'd won 'big money', but I ignored his thanks as we walked to Tottenham Court Road, stepping into the lunchtime flow of workers who merged with visitors on a looser timetable.

We rode the tube for a while then switched lines, onto a train where the driver spoke to his passengers so condescendingly I felt like a naughty child.

"*Come on now. Who hasn't stood clear of the doors?*" Chided a voice from the ceiling speaker. "*Who was it?*"

"He's funny." Said Justin idiotically, his smaller frame crushed up against me. If I looked down now I was in danger of getting hair gel on my face.

"Right. Listen carefully Justin, here's how we're going to play it." I withdrew as far as I could, standing against the glass partition as he looked up at me. "First off, no drinking. These people have paid through the nose for a bear, God knows why, but it means they're definitely flush enough to offer booze so we need to stay off it. More importantly, we need to keep Barry off it as well." Barry was the keeper who dealt with bears and other large animals at Chester zoo. An ingratiating northerner, he had a reputation for getting in a round of drinks and consuming them all himself.

Justin nodded. "No problem Monty, you can rely on me." Famous last words but he'd have to do. My colleague couldn't be trusted to fulfil the role I'd assigned myself.

The doors slid open. "What are you going to do?" He wondered as we left the train.

"I'm taking care of the meet and greet. I'll make sure *Bears!Bears!Bears!* comes out of this event with a reputation for the highest standards of service."

"Reputation for service, right."

The restaurant-slash-public house was set back from the road in an affluent area of north-west London. We walked round the side to a spacious garden where workers in black and white uniforms hurried through the enormous marquee, setting out tables. Away from this activity a porky figure sprawled on the ground, drinking from a bottle of ale. On the grass behind Barry sat a bear. Poppy was tethered to a metal pole, watching the comings and goings, her digging hump protrusive behind that big furry head. As the two of us approached she stood up. Even on all fours this bear was tall enough to scare a weightlifter.

"Alright fellas?" Barry wore a puffa jacket and swigged from his bottle with a grin.

I muttered. "Okay, forget about him not drinking, Just keep a lid on it as much as you can."

"No probs." Justin walked up to the bear. "Hello Poppy! How's my favourite girl today?"

"RAAAARGH!" The animal reared up on its hind legs and bared sharp teeth. Justin abandoned his attempt to stroke her while behind Poppy the metal pole bent out of shape as she pulled against it.

"Better be careful there!" Laughed the man, whose job title this afternoon was *Bear Wrangler*. "She didn't want to come today, by rights the old girl ought to be 'ibernating."

"You'll have to tie her up somewhere safer than that." I said with as much authority as I could muster. I've always been better at receiving orders than giving them, but in the interests of my livelihood, not to mention the safety of those arriving now in a bevy of ribbon-adorned limousines, I felt it was important to get the message across. Grunting with effort, Barry got to his feet.

"I see 'em comin' through, I'll deal with 'er, don't you worry." He undid the bear's chain as Justin cowered nearby. "I only 'ope they don't want 'er to dance or nuffin', she ain't in the mood."

The fat man led a growling Poppy over to the marquee where arrivals could see her. I followed them, shoving Justin onwards.

"Don't let anyone touch that bear, or I'll feed you to her myself!" Justin looked terrified but assumed his post. I walked over to guests who'd appeared in the garden, an insincere smile plastered on my face.

"Congratulations. Why not go and see the real live bear while you're here?" I shook the hand of a patriarchal figure in his sixties. "I'm your representative from *Bears!Bears!Bears!*, the world's number one supplier of ursines to the rich and famous. We're here to ensure you enjoy our bear on this special day, but we would ask you not to touch her."

"I'll do whatever I want." Snorted the man. "I paid for the damned thing." Ah, the father of the bride. I watched him strut over and inspect Poppy, a combination of Justin and her large fangs keeping him out of the animal's personal space.

"Enjoying yourselves?" I inquired of three pre-pubescent bridesmaids, resplendent in pink taffeta dresses. The trio nodded shyly as I knelt down. "Don't get too close now, 'cause she might bite your head off, but there's a bear here if you want to say hello."

Following my finger, the three girls stared at the creature open-mouthed. With cries of *Baloo!*, and *Yogi!*, they threw their bouquets to the floor and raced over.

I carried on like this for a while, my enthusiasm fading as elderly relatives and young lads in tuxedos walked past followed by the bride's female friends, all clad in extravagant outfits and foxy as a vulpine lair.

"Bear. There's a bear over there. Oh yes. Go and have a look. Then get good and drunk. Don't antagonise the bear, she'll rip your face clean off. Bear. Everybody look at the bear."

People milled around the covered area, a four-tiered wedding cake dominating the spread, everything from vol-au-vents to profiteroles. Plastic figurines of the bride and groom, arm in arm, adorned this feat of baking architecture.

Outside waiters carried champagne flutes on glimmering trays. One of the men offered me a glass of the sparkling liquid but I refused and asked him not to go near Barry.

"I wasn't about to sir, I'm not particularly fond of bears. But I can't say the same for my colleagues." He nodded to a teenage waitress cooing over Poppy, that creature who snoozed peacefully on the grass. Justin and Barry chatted to the girl offering them drinks, the wrangler taking one immediately. My colleague remonstrated with him, they discussed the matter for a while, then Justin took a flute of champagne and thanked the waitress. I stormed over. Barry saw me first, downing the contents of his glass in a single gulp.

"Give me that." I snatched the drink from Justin's hand. "Jesus."

"Sorry Monty, I was..."

A spluttering noise as Barry choked. "Bloody bubbles, get right up yer nose they do."

"Serves you right. What did I tell you Justin?"

"She was really nice, it seemed rude not to...." I cuffed him on the back of the head. "Ow!"

"Ah, give the lad a break." Barry gasped and dried his eyes. "They lost interest in the old girl ages ago, can't I tie 'er up somewhere and take a piss?"

I looked over at the revellers, the novelty did appear to have worn off. Wedding guests were more absorbed by the buffet and their conversations than the presence of a big furry mammal. Poppy opened one eye to look at us then shut it again, unimpressed.

"I suppose you can, but keep her in view. We haven't finished plugging the agency yet." Grumbling, the bear was coaxed to her feet. "Stay with him Justin, don't let them out of your sight."

"You 'olding me todger then?" Asked Barry as they wandered off. I took a deep breath and went back into the melee. The groom found me and we shook hands, chatting for a while about our respective jobs. Then I handed out business cards and pitched agency services to posh ladies who showed a polite interest. At one point the bridesmaids surrounded me, still breathless, and I made up a story about Poppy being an orphan from Alaska we'd brought over to raise as our own. My techniques were unlikely to drum up immediate business, but at least I was spreading the word, implanting *Bears!Bears!Bears!* into more minds. Should any of these people need an ursine in the future, ours would be the first name they looked for in the phone book or entered into a search engine.

The staff cleared tablecloths and edible remnants away, lifting several of the tables into a corner of the marquee. Next to the uncut cake a DJ positioned his speakers and crates of CDs. The father of the bride walked over and spoke in his ear, presumably instructing this man about the rest of the afternoon's schedule. A few minutes later an eighties novelty hit kicked in and the interior of that great white tent transformed into a dancefloor. The more exultant or intoxicated gave their bodies free reign to move while those who were more reticent, like myself, escaped to the edges, away from the merrymaking.

I was just discussing the vagaries of my role at the agency with one of the bride's friends who, despite a certain dizziness from the champagne, was making a decent show of pretending to be interested, when I spotted a red-faced fat man nearby, a man rendered even wider by the puffa jacket he was wearing. Barry jiggled his bulk while Justin matched this exuberance but flailed in a way that was all his own. They must have taken Poppy back to the van. That was alright, her work here was over for the day, but what did annoy me was the sight of that beer in Barry's hand. He must have been close to the driving limit by now if not over it, plus these two idiots were effectively gatecrashing the celebrations. We didn't know anyone at this party, and just because I was working the guests didn't mean they could fraternise with our employers or treat the rest of the day as leisure time. I couldn't see the bride's father in our immediate vicinity, but I doubted the unindulgent figure would welcome a fat northerner and someone apparently in the throes of an aneurysm dominating his daughter's big day.

Deciding to have a quiet word, maybe escort these two malcontents away from the celebrations, I picked my way through the gathering. That was when something big and brown lolloped past at chest height. Before I could make it out I heard a number of shrill cries, swiftly followed by movement. There came a stuttering dash out of the covered area, men escorting their women who struggled to move quickly. The music stopped mid-song, leaving Justin and Barry staring at each other as the panicking crowd fled and the DJ abandoned his equipment. The man squirmed away from those tables where Poppy had her paws up on the wooden surface, scarfing down a collapsed wedding cake. That metal post I'd explicitly told Barry not to use was attached to the bear's chain and dangled behind her uselessly.

Later I would wonder exactly what it was that persuaded me to try and restrain a brown bear single-handed, assigning myself complex and variegated motives. The truth was that my attempt to prevent further damage was entirely instinctive. And stupid. Very, very stupid.

"Fook." Bellowed Barry as I ran over and grabbed the post, trying to pull the bear away from that edible totem of marital bliss. I wrenched wildly and Poppy got off the table, turning to confront this irritation, the anger in this animal's eyes clear above the icing which covered its snout and that plastic groom's head which poked out from between her teeth.

"That's it Monty." Barry coached me from a safe distance. "You don't 'ave to worry, this ain't 'er territory. Poppy don't feel safe to attack you 'ere." I pulled at the pole once more, struggling to keep my grip on the metal shaft. The bear responded by rearing up as if readying herself for the kill. "Well, she might if you do that."

Poppy aimed a swipe at me with her claws so I let go of the pole and jumped backwards, managing to avoid being sliced open by the slimmest of margins. Landing heavily on my arse, I watched the animal turn back to her meal and shot the tubby zookeeper a hateful look.

"Aren't you supposed to be the bear wrangler? Get in there and wrangle for Christ's sake."

The fat man fiddled with the pocket of his massive coat. "I can't mate, who's going to knock 'er out but me? Lucky I always keep this in case the old girl gets out of control." He produced a syringe and checked the fluid inside. "Ought to be enough there."

Poppy was down to the last tier of wedding cake now, munching her way through fondant and vanilla crème. I got to my feet to see male members of the wedding party observing my travails.

"Should we call the fire brigade?" Yelled the best man.

"No, that's alright." The thought of newspapers printing more bad publicity nullified my desire for help. Besides, what could firemen do? Spray water at her?

"Nothing to worry about." I lied. "All under control."

Barry brandished the needle before Justin who'd gone white as a macaroon. "Right. I need the two of you to distract 'er while I find a nice bit of flesh to stick this in."

"Distract her?" I pointed to the creature, still gobbling away. "The only way we're going to distract that bear now is if we offer it cheese and biscuits. What the fuck are you talking about?"

The wrangler remained calm. "Just do what you did before, only don't try and restrain 'er. You ain't got the weight advantage."

"Not like you fat boy." I muttered

"I can't do this, keep her away from me." Justin pleaded. I glared at him before turning back to the danger.

Alone, I crept up on the feasting bear, cursing to myself now. *"Motherfucking, son of a wussie fuck and useless fat twat. Going to kill you with my bare hands you fat motherfucker. You too, you whimpering little twerp."*

I grabbed the bear's chain and gave it a sharp tug.

"That's it, that's it. Come on old girl." To my left Barry waddled closer. I dug both heels into the ground and pulled again. This time the bear flopped down onto the grass looking muddled and vaguely sick. Poppy spotted me and began to snarl so I let the chain slip a little and backed off, keeping my grip on the pole. Circling round to the right, I encouraged Poppy to go on facing me, holding her attention with a series of sharp jerks.

Barry came up behind the bear. "Nearly there my darlin', 'ere we go."

Retaining eye contact with Poppy, all the while praying she wasn't about to make a move, I used my free hand to gather a pile of the dessert which littered the tables, rolling the sticky mess into a ball with my shaky fingers.

"You want this you bloated bitch? Want more cake, eh? I'll bet you do."

I sensed Poppy was about to come at me, either tempted by the food or because she'd had enough, so I tossed the ball of cake down by her paws. She fell on the food and Barry launched himself at her, that needle sinking into the pelt of Poppy's shoulder. The bear uttered a roar of pain and I dropped the pole, jumping toward the fat guy as he tried to get out of range. We connected and rolled over on the grass, Poppy clawing wildly behind us, the syringe protruding from her shoulder.

The bear reared up and stated her intentions with a thunderous howl. I clutched the fat man and waited to be torn limb from limb. But that deep cry changed to a confused whimper, the bear's eyes glazing over. She staggered forward on her hind legs for a step then collapsed backwards, landing in slow motion. Poppy fell onto the tables with a crash, smashing them to smithereens and sending a shower of goo several feet into the air.

Chapter Nine

I trod warily down the curving stone steps, greeted at the entrance by a cheery Japanese girl in a cream kimono with green obi. After some discussion she concluded there was no girl waiting and led me to an alcove which contained a bench for two people, set back from the main part of the restaurant with a view of its interior. Metropolitan types talked and ate nearby, manipulating chopsticks as if the implements were a natural extension of their limbs.

The *Kalamazoo* was a curious mishmash of content, a Japanese restaurant with the appropriate decor; symbols and photos evoking the Far East up on its walls. But for whatever reason the place had been named after an American town and both the Union Jack and Stars & Stripes could also be seen, alongside that red target on a white background from Japan. It was almost as if the owners felt a need to align themselves with their country of business and the prevalent global culture, just in case.

They also served English and American beers so I ordered a bottle of the latter and slid into my seat, wincing in pain as I did so. Today's incident had left me with several fresh bruises from my heavy landings and now it hurt to sit down. Also my arms ached from carrying a twenty-five stone mammal to Barry's van. We got away as quickly as we could for three men with an unconscious bear, me instructing Justin to hand our details over to the landlord and tell him to bill *Bears!Bears!Bears!* for the damage. Barry offered to drive us back to the agency, convincing me the bear's rampage had sobered him up "pretty fookin' quick". I believed the wrangler, but I made him walk in a straight line for a bit anyway, just to get my own back. If I had my way this man and his unreliable ursine would never again be part of our set-up, not after this debacle. Inside the van I phoned Martin with a brief description of events while Barry drove in silence and Justin called his girlfriend, trying to convince her he'd performed most of the heroics.

Yohanna was waiting for us in Soho Square, impressed by Justin's supposed bravery while I trudged into Martin's office and gave him my side of the story. The boss listened patiently, made noises of agreement when I requested Barry be 'let go', then changed the subject, explaining how the theatre group had "found their Richey". I told him that was really great and slunk out, wondering exactly how big a crisis it would take to return Mart's attention to the business.

The time was approaching seven by then and I was going to be late for my date with Kathleen. Catching me on the way out, Justin wittered on about how grateful he was. I hadn't told Yohanna the truth you see, although this was more due to exhaustion than any desire for Justin's girlfriend to see him as the big hero. More plausible than his story to the blondes was Justin's belief that if I hadn't been there Poppy would be chewing on his bones right now. My colleague resolved to pay me back in a big way, and soon. I told him I didn't do it for him and he shouldn't buy me any hats because of it.

When I finally got away from the office, travelling that one stop on the tube and finding *Kalamazoo*, I ended up being so efficient that I was fifteen minutes early. The beer went down well, invigorating me a little, but what effect that rampaging bear had on my mental state was difficult to judge. On the way here I'd glanced up at the Tottenham Court Road LED board to find out the length of my wait and beneath the number of minutes came a message reading something like:

Delays possible to all destinations due to an earlier signal failure at Archway. Play it right tonight Monty Sanderson, and the girl is yours. But if you.....

I'd looked away at that point. My stress-swathed mind was playing tricks again and I didn't need supernatural messages inflicting extra pressure. I'd deliberately kept this date a secret from everyone except Fergal who, as ever, managed to find out every detail. He went off on one of his flights of fancy then, likening the way I'd overcome my apprehension about asking Kathleen out to the petrifying fear Jane Fonda felt at acting with her father for the first time. A fear Jane eventually redirected into the performance, enabling her character to cry at will. His parallel was unclear to me, but I let Fergal indulge the obsession. My flatmate hadn't been particularly gregarious on Sunday night and only brightened up when he heard of my latest date, details giving him a chance to introduce Fonda into the conversation.

The bottle was empty so I craned my neck, hoping to catch the kimono girl's eye for another. I was about to step out and look around when she arrived at my table, Kathleen by her side. We greeted each other and the Japanese waitress dispensed a couple of menus, then wrote down my request for a drink.

"So, how are you?"

"Good, I'm good." Kathleen studied me. "What's that in your hair?"

I reached up and extracted a lump of pink fondant. "Wedding cake."

"Wedding cake?" She laughed, that raucous noise. "How does someone get *wedding cake* in their hair?"

"I'd prefer not to talk about it." The events of this afternoon were too traumatic to look back on. I wasn't up to embellishing some hilarious anecdote about rogue bears and telling the story straight only depicted my working life as filled with incompetents. "Maybe when you're older."

"Still some there." The girl raised herself and plucked more crumbs out of the black mass on my head. Kathleen wore a red silk top bearing oriental insignias, a scaly dragon snaking up from waist to shoulder. The outfit was tight in all the right places, this girl wasn't at all flat-chested as I'd thought, her breasts were simply in modest proportion to the rest of that slender frame. I shot a glance at her brown eyes as they concentrated on finding more fragments, still alluring but with a little kohl applied to the edges now. Apart from this blackness Kathleen wore only touches of make-up, a subtle shade of lipstick, no perfume as far as I could tell. She smelt clean, the closeness of her body and those long fingers enough to remind me of the natural power women have over me. It was a strange moment in some ways, the act of a concerned relative rather than a potential lover, but the heat from her body stirred in me feelings very far from fraternal. Once again I was drinking, she was sober, and we'd clicked instantly. Comfortable in each other's presence.

The grooming was interrupted by our waitress who set another bottle down. Kathleen relaxed into her side of the bench with a sheepish smile.

"Ready to ord-ah?"

"Five minutes." My date advised.

With a jolt I remembered why we were here. To eat raw fish, right. I opened the menu and studied the descriptions beside photographs of colourful morsels. Sushi wasn't something I'd ever felt a hankering for previously, in fact my parents hadn't even acknowledged the existence of such a thing while I was growing up. Like steaks or tofu, the Sandersons thought of this as a foodstuff only other people ate. Still, I'd always enjoyed crabsticks as a lad, during our visits to seaside towns, this shouldn't be all that different. Best to go for something fairly straightforward though, I didn't want to end up with food that was slimy and inedible, not at these prices. Flounder? Nope. Fatty tuna belly? Jesus, definitely not. Rice balls with fish and vinegar on top? That sounded fairly safe. I could get most anything into my stomach if I put enough vinegar on it, and my taste buds wouldn't resist this acrid recipe. They were tougher than that.

"I'll have the Norimaki." Kathleen specified, the waitress scribbling the word on her pad before looking to me expectantly.

"Ni...., niggey....., um." Oh dear, I wasn't sounding very cultured. "That one." I pointed to the picture, my face turning red.

"Nigiri."

"Yes." Our menus were removed. "And another beer."

"So." My date turned her attention to me, apparently unembarrassed by the confusion. "What line of work are you in Monty?"

A sudden impulse to falsify came over me. Kathleen knew no better, I could say something close to my career, like journalist or businessman. Or perhaps one of those meaningless titles Fergal used to dismiss people he considered beneath him. Cultural analyst, contemporary researcher, producer even.

"I work for an advertising agency, we specialise in bears." She took the card I offered. "It's a small field but varied work, never dull."

Kathleen read the blurb. "Bears, huh?" My drink arrived and our waitress took the empties. "I used to totally dig grizzlies when I was little."

"Really?"

"Oh yeah, none of those soppy teddy bears for me, I wanted *scary* toys." She smiled, white teeth and that pink gum.

"Grizzly bears aren't particularly aggressive you know, not compared to polar bears anyway." I drank from my bottle. "They've had a bad press, the name actually comes from the *grizzling* of their fur. The hair's a lighter colour at the tips."

"A bit like mine." Kathleen pulled a lock round and studied it, briefly becoming cross-eyed. "I never seem to get round to sorting it out."

"It's fine, I like your hair." What else did I know about her favourite bears? Come on Monty, you hadn't spent years in the world of ursines to lack facts when someone was genuinely interested. "Erm, did you know that when female grizzlies are fertile they can mate with several different male bears. Five months later there's this litter of cubs who've all got different fathers."

"That's interesting." Kathleen silently tucked the hair behind her ear, maybe she didn't need to hear about the mating habits of grizzlies. "I liked using toys to frighten my sister, she used to hate them."

"You have a sister? How old is she?"

"Twenty one, two years younger than me. Bit of a madam she is too."

"It's a difficult age." What the hell did that mean? Sort it out Monty. "You still live with her?"

"Yeah, we share a house with mum, out in the wilds of Purley."

Hmmm. "Your mother easy to live with?"

"Sometimes she lets it all get on top of her, if you know what I mean." Those eyes flicked away, then came back to my face. "What's your set up?"

"I flatshare with this guy I know." The girl nodded. "My folks live in Basingstoke."

"Still together?"

"Just about."

"That's nice." If only she knew. "Get on well with them?"

"You know how it is, everybody holds grievances against their mum and dad, I'm no different." How much to tell her? We'd only just met after all, best to cloak my bitterness in humour. "My father's not a git by any means, he's just difficult to get through to. On a different wavelength you might say."

"That's a generational thing."

"Not really, he's on a different wavelength from people his own age too, including my mother." I thought of Brian's present existence, holed up in that leaky shed. "*Especially* my mother."

"What about her? What's she like?" If this girl wasn't interested in me she certainly feigned it well. If only my head didn't hurt so much. And my hair felt sticky, and I was hungry and sore, and I hadn't come here to discuss the people I'd got away from only yesterday.

"She's okay. Mum talks to me in the same tone she uses for her dogs, sometimes I wonder if there's any difference to her."

"You're making this up."

"I'm not, I swear. When I was four years old she tried to have me neutered." Kathleen laughed. This was my chance to turn talk away from the tiresome. "I guess it isn't your ambition to work at *5 Easy Pieces* for the rest of your life?"

"Not really, I've just finished an M.A. in business management." The thought left her somewhat solemn. "My results are out later this month, then it'll be time for all the stuff I've been putting off. You know, career, place in the city, that sort of thing."

Cool. "You want to move up here?"

"Yea-eah!" The girl looked around, as if this cavity carved out of the rock represented the whole of England's capital. "This is the place for me. I might have really dull qualifications, but that doesn't mean I don't need excitement Monty. I've always wanted to have a go at acting, theatre or something. I'd love to get up there and lose myself by becoming someone else, I think it's fantastic. This is the only place in the country that inspires me to try something like that, I love London." She was really into her stride now, bubbling with confidence. It was a pleasure to watch. "I love the way this place offers up new experiences and possibilities every single day. You can lose yourself in the crowd or hop a tube and be alone somewhere, get close to a person one day, then never have to see them again. Whatever I turn out to be I'll find like-minded people here, people whose souls have the same texture as mine. Maybe it'll be some artist who lives minutes away from all those famous monuments and galleries and landmarks I grew up hearing about. Who knows? But yeah, I'm coming to this city for all that and anything else it wants to throw at me. Because I know I can handle it." Kathleen paused, her determination melting away. "I'm rambling, sorry."

"No, I like it when you ramble." Truth be told I was impressed, even overawed. "Is that why all the drop-dead gorgeous women flock here?"

"Nope. *They* come to London 'cause it's the best place to shop."

Kathleen left me stunned, the girl was funny and intelligent, ambitious and compelling. And here I was, embodying what felt like the opposite, a man injured and beaten down, with dirt stains on his clothes. I'd been turned around, from believing she was some service sector know-nothing, to becoming unnerved by the hidden depths. Now instinct said Kathleen was out of my league, all these exotic restaurants, talk of the theatre and artistic impulses, that wasn't me. I came from a proletarian background. Even at the start of the twenty-first century my bloodline risked being wiped out by bears.

With no idea what to say the general hubbub of *Kalamazoo* rose into my perception, that clatter of dishes and susurrus of murmurings from other customers.

"God I hate that." I followed the direction of Kathleen's gaze, to where a young couple used chopsticks, playing with the food on each other's plates. "Don't get me wrong Monty, I don't have a problem with displays of affection. Even canoodling in public doesn't have to be sick-making, not necessarily."

"Canoodling, right."

"But when couples feed each other in full view of everyone, people are trying to enjoy their food, you know? It's just... ugh!"

She pulled a face. The guy opened his mouth to take a modicum of seaweed offered by the girl, juice running down his chin. "Why they have to inflict *that* on the rest of us I'll never know, I'm old enough to feed myself thank you very much. A man can show a girl how much he cares in ways that don't involve her digestive system."

The pair leaned across the table, each holding a piece of fish between their sticks. Before the guy could reach her willing mouth his fragment of food slipped away and fell down the girl's front. She began to giggle and dropped her fish as well, the morsel hitting his arm before landing on the table. The couple burst into laughter and began brushing each other with napkins, the guy taking special care to ensure all remnants were removed from his date's chest.

"I think I agree with you." I turned away from the sight as our waitress arrived with the food. Kathleen unwrapped her chopsticks and tucked in eagerly while I sat there, staring at the dainty packages of fish and rice.

"Yum." She said. I stabbed at the food with a wooden utensil for a while, then tried to manipulate some of the dish into my mouth. This whole rigmarole felt unfamiliar and slightly disturbing. I decided that I didn't really have a problem with couples feeding each other. If someone had been there to feed me it would have made dinner a whole lot easier.

Eventually I got some of the fish into my mouth. It was salty and unpleasant and I hurried to scoop in vinegary rice afterwards, hoping to take away the crude sensation. The mixture sat in my mouth for a while as I tried to swallow. Opposite me Kathleen was engrossed in her meal, mixing the green and white ingredients into tiny piles she transported to her lips with the minimum of fuss. A swig of beer finally got the combination down my throat and I drenched what remained in vinegar before repeating the process, managing to keep down several bites of this food I found utterly revolting. The waitress came to check on us and Kathleen nodded her assent as I passed my quarter-eaten dish back to the Japanese girl and requested another beer. I could have complained there was something wrong with my meal I guess, pretended I was a gourmet and *Kalamazoo*'s sushi was entirely wrong, wrong beyond the fact that normal people like me found it inedible. But my appetite had waned, and they'd only replace the Nigiri with something even more exotically disgusting, like live shrimp or fish eggs.

While Kathleen cleared her plate I drank and watched the clientele enjoy themselves. I needed to dispel this despondency, the girl would expect me to restart the conversation soon, but I couldn't think of anything to interest her. Silly, because this girl was younger than me, and she still lived with her mother. Despite her big ideas and voluptuous dreams, Kathleen hadn't mentioned any connections which might realise these goals. She needed older people, people who saw how the world worked, knew the cogs operating the engineering. That's if she wanted to get close to the creativity she craved. Wait a minute.

"My boss is putting on a play soon, I might be able to put in a word for you."

"Wow, really?" She flopped back melodramatically. "God, I'm stuffed."

"He's already cast the lead, but I reckon he'll be willing to consider suggestions for the smaller roles, we've known each other a long time." The only female presence in *Too Beautiful* was the underwritten role of Richey's girlfriend, a rock chick he'd fallen in love with before disappearing. With an appropriately sleazy wardrobe I felt certain Kathleen could look the part.

"Are you sure? I'm not very experienced." All that conviction and certainty of a few minutes ago had gone. Now she was confronted with the opportunity of achieving her aims Kathleen sounded unsure, full of self-doubt. Girls and their facades.

"I wouldn't worry. The director isn't what you'd call *proven*, and there's no money behind it." I wondered where Mart *was* getting his investment from. "I'll put in a word for you anyway, see what he says."

"Thank you." She smiled, still nervous at the thought of it. "You're very sweet."

I shrugged. "You help people you like, nothing special about that."

The waitress removed Kathleen's empty plate. "This is nice." She decided. "I really dig getting to know people this way,

103

you know? Even if nothing comes of it, a good meal is so much more civilized. You should see what some of my girlfriends go through to meet blokes."

"I can guess. We live in an age where techniques of seduction have degenerated to an exceptionally low level." I was parroting Fergal here, hopefully it sounded impressive. "Is rubbing up against someone in a crowded club while singing *let me see that thong* really the best we can do?"

"Absolutely!" She rubbed her cheek, an act I found myself unconsciously copying. "And what about *touch my bum, this is life?* Isn't that just an invitation to indecent assault? No wonder you guys are confused."

"We are, we are." I picked up my fresh bottle. "The rules used to be so clear. Back in my parents' day you'd meet a girl, court for a bit, get a kiss..." The words were coming out slightly slurred, I tried to clarify. "Then gradually keep going further, until one day you woke up and were married."

"Um, I think you're generalising there."

"Now, *nooow*, it's pot luck. Some girls are so chaste they won't do anything before marriage, while others are even hungrier for a one night stand than the guys. I don't know whether I'm coming or going sometimes."

"I would never shag someone after one date, it's dangerous and stupid."

"Well, I guess it can be." Ostensibly I was agreeing with her, keeping the alcohol-fuelled disappointment hidden. "But I wouldn't condemn those who do it, each to their own and all that."

"As you say, each to their own, but it's not me. I don't think you should give your body away lightly. It's the most important thing."

Talk flagged again. I didn't agree with her, this view of the world wasn't the liberated one I needed in a potential lover. But I'd spent enough time with girls who said one thing then did the opposite to realise Kathleen might not practice the lifestyle she preached. That abstemious approach was one few men would endorse. I continued sipping from my bottle, despite already being drunk enough. The consumption was a kind of nervous tic, somehow I'd become less at ease with this girl as the evening wore on. It was as if we clicked on some primitive level, but as soon as the trappings of civilization came along we pushed each other away.

The bill arrived, my booze coming to more than either of our meals. If we shared the expense evenly Kathleen would be well out of pocket. I tuned my faculties back to my date and realised she'd been talking for a while about some arthouse film she enjoyed.

"....I think he's a poet of the screen you know? Some of the compositions are breathtaking, it's the kind of filmmaking that makes you cry."

"Yeah, right." This probably wasn't the best time to mention my love of cheerleader movies. What had I ever seen that was culturally enriching? "I watched that French film when I was young, *The Phantom Of Liberty.*"

"Bunuel."

"Fine, thanks." I took another gulp. "It must have had a big impression on me. Ever since then I've felt slightly embarrassed at eating in front of other people."

"Is this your way of telling me you poo in public?"

"Not normally, no." There was mockery in her eyes. "Oh, you're joking, right. Yeah, I remember that bit." God, I was coming off like some kind of idiot. Whose work was I familiar with from the highbrow world? "Did you know Roland Barthes had his last meal near here? Just round the corner."

"Who?"

"Barthes. He invented this science to recognise what signs mean. Very brilliant man."

"What happened?"

"He came out of the restaurant and got run over by a laundry truck."

"Sometimes I hate this city." Kathleen glanced at the bill. "Do you want to go Dutch?"

"Sure." I'd save some money, excellent. Let chivalry lie dormant for a while. If I hadn't been drunk I'm sure this evening would have gone worse for both of us. By that logic it was only fair she paid for half my beer. Although a sober Monty might not have felt quite so vexed right now. About what I wasn't sure, maybe those elements lacking in Kathleen combined with the negative points I'd come to see in myself. "Let's get out of here." I said.

We settled up and moved to leave, me caroming between alcove walls as I tried to gain my balance. Steadying myself I followed her, past the blurry shapes of other diners and up those stone steps. We were confronted by heavy rain so Kathleen pulled out an umbrella, but her efforts to cover me with one side were thwarted by the wind. In the end I was going to be soaked whatever we tried, drops hitting my face as rivulets formed down the back of my neck. Walking side by side wherever possible the two of us made our way through the drenched crowd. Water surged along gutters and I tried to avoid puddles without straying into the street where cars waited to send me flying. Approaching Leicester Square, I noticed a beggar huddled in a doorway to our left and decided to salvage Kathleen's impression of me by acting generously. The beggar took one look at the coins I proffered and told me to *"fuck off"*. In my inebriated state I was impressed by this novel approach to his profession. A true original like this man ought to be rewarded. I attempted to give the beggar a five pound note which he then proceeded to tell me where to shove. Looking around for support, I saw Kathleen's pleading with me to *come on*. I left the crotchety vagrant and approached the station entrance, scores of people sheltering off the pavement as we approached.

I gestured to a crossroads up the road. "I think I'm going to hop a bus."

"Okay." She checked the time. "I'd better get a move on if I want to catch my train. Thanks Monty, see you later."

Then Kathleen had vanished, into packs of travellers who dripped water onto the smooth flooring. I stepped back into the rain, jogging a few yards up the road to a takeaway where I bought chips to quieten my stomach. Munching the salty potato chunks, I went into the station through a different entrance. The coast would be clear now, that girl long gone. Her generic goodbye, that disappearance without even a hint of further contact, it put a downer on our night. I hadn't charmed Kathleen into my life this evening, my

106

presence in her future wasn't suddenly longed-for or necessary. In fact I felt sure I'd blown it.

Chapter Ten

I walked out from the great arches of the station entrance and turned right, into Canary Wharf. My path took me away from that river, snaking off toward the distant quayside, and under clock faces set ten feet up on black metal poles which confirmed I was late for my meeting with Justin. Workers based in the great towers overwhelming the skyline spilled out of the shining bars to either side. I plodded up the steps, walking through the colonnade and wondering exactly what my colleague had in store for me. During the three days since I foolishly restrained that bear Justin had hardly shut up about the incident, going on about how he'd treat me to something "a bit special" in return for saving his skin. I clearly hadn't been unpleasant enough to Justin, I should have explicitly told him not to bother, but instead I unenthusiastically agreed to my reward and continued brooding. Justin subsequently came in to work this morning, the kind of cold November Thursday where being forced out of bed seems like a humanitarian issue, and made me promise to meet him in a docklands bar come evening. Whatever was going on Justin found it very exciting, and he clearly wasn't going to take no for an answer. I eventually admitted I didn't have any plans for tonight, whereupon his silly face lit up with such happiness that failure to turn up would have crushed the little pleb.

Hell, I needed to escape Fergal anyway. The atmosphere in our flat was becoming oppressive. Cofaigh made no attempt to work, expressing instead an intention to make his living as a short-con artist, some master of the grift who'd inhabit the fringes of polite society and live on his wits. Phase one of this plan seemed to involve sitting around in his dressing gown, watching bodybuilding videos and smoking cigarettes, the latter habit lending a stale smell to our flat and even risking eviction. Our landlord had lost several family members to the cancer stick and unannounced visits were his trademark. If any of his tenants were caught having a fag he took it as a personal affront to the memory of those relatives.

I wasn't helping the vibe either, dwelling on my failure with Kathleen. Monday night at *Kalamazoo* showed me how future dates would go. I'd be hopeless and unsuccessful, giving girls an impression full of flaws and off-putting quirks. Laying awake these past nights, I dwelt on that drunken behaviour, my lack of interest in the things she loved, wondering if offhand remarks offended her or whether I'd come across as needy and blasé. Then my mind raced on, through the ways she'd turned me off; that superiority over other diners, her desire to act but a fear of actually doing it, talk of sexual unwillingness no guy wants to hear. Despite my left brain repeatedly saying *give it up, forget about her,* it all rankled with me, particularly that last stance which seemed foolish in the extreme. If Kathleen really cared for someone then withholding her body was a sure way of making them lose interest and look elsewhere. Years ago friends told me of their frustration with Christian girls who wouldn't put out, how they'd give up when the God-botherer confirmed sex came after marriage or not at all. Confused by the disingenuousness of Kathleen's claims to chastity, I'd raised the subject with Fergal during one of those moments when he wasn't being surly or unapproachable.

"It may not be what you think Montgomery." Fergal advised. "That sort of talk is often a safety net. A girl gives the appearance of chasteness to those who might get the wrong idea, it's a typical tactic of your modern woman. Despite what glossy TV shows and handbag magazines say, it still isn't the done thing for a girl to admit she's promiscuous, or even that she'd have sex with certain guys and probably enjoy it. People would be shocked and disapprove, that's the way the world is. This Kathleen might not be telling you the whole truth, I wouldn't be too concerned about it. Didn't you strike out anyway?" Then he started going on about Jane Fonda, how she was one of the few women to approach sex with honesty, a trail-blazer leading the way for sixties America to overcome the sickness of its repressed society which lied to itself about innate carnality. Something like that, I'd pretty much switched off by then.

So I suffered through the week with frustration and insomnia, futilely attempting to get inside the female mind. I wondered how badly Kathleen thought I'd behaved during our time together, if there was any hope at all for something between us.

Every night I concluded there definitely wasn't and, after a state of dejection which lasted through the small hours, finally dozed off.

The lack of sleep was destroying my attention span, left me slow-witted and goofy. I walked straight past the bar where we'd arranged to meet. Going back, I saw *Parvenu* was in a row of exclusive restaurants and bars, set back from the walkway bordered by a great water fountain set into a stone plateau. In warmer times people must have sat out on the nasty metal furniture, enjoying drinks and talking of sophisticated matters. Tonight everyone was inside, so I moved toward the darkened interior, wondering if I really wanted to venture within. A poster advertised the delights of something called *speed dating*. The drawing showed two figures; a square-jawed man and upright woman, gazing into each other's eyes. Below this picture was the date of the event. Tonight. An instinct came then, to turn and run, but I made the mistake of looking past the poster and into the bar. On the other side of that glass, no more than inches away, I saw the face of a grinning idiot with a stupid little beard. Justin beckoned to me.

"This is great isn't it Monty? You want a drink?"

"Yes I do." He went to the bar. "But not necessarily here."

I stood beside Justin while a few women and several men who appeared to have recently taken off their ties made stilted conversation. To our left a line of tables had been cordoned off, cards, pens and timers on the varnished surfaces.

Justin handed me my pint. "Do me a favour mate, don't tell Yohanna about this. I'm only supporting you really, I know you've not had much success with the ladies recently so I thought I'd pay for us to come here. That's my way of saying thank you, tonight we're gonna turn your luck around."

"Great, that's absolutely terrific Justin. You could have got me a CD or something, but no. You bring me to a *speed dating* evening." I tried to convey my limitless anger but tiredness won the battle. He was checking out everybody else anyway, Justin hadn't brought us here out of the goodness of his heart, this fad-swallowing numbskull wanted an excuse to explore this latest craze, discussed at length in *Shoreditch Tart* or *Monkey Teats* or whatever the fashion magazines were called. A tightening knot tickled my stomach lining, combined with that sense of impending doom in my mind "Not that I really want to know Justin, but how does this work?"

"We get three minutes to chat up each of the girls, I think there's gonna be about a dozen here tonight." He handed me a booklet. "Read this, I got it with the tickets."

The pamphlet was a *Guide To Speed Dating* but it didn't explain much of what was involved. Instead there was the usual marketing bullshit about a "revolutionary approach to an age-old problem" and tips on how to be successful with the opposite sex. For guys the sure-fire trick was to stand with your feet six to ten inches apart while socialising (I adjusted my stance accordingly) dress yourself entirely in blue (I glanced ruefully at the black clothes that had matched my mood this morning) and, most importantly, keep coming to speed dating events. In terms of a fragrance girls should use cinnamon perfumes while guys needed to douse themselves in extract of liquorice. I raised an arm and sniffed underneath. The faint odour of sweat and nothing more. Well, I hadn't had chance to read this guide in advance, that wasn't my fault. Fortunately not every hint required preparation. According to the text one foolproof way to be desired was to make yourself the centre of attention. I tried to think of ways guaranteed to achieve this. For women exhibitionism and bursting into tears would probably do the trick, while experience told me men got noticed through arguing or the expulsion of loud farts. None of these methods seemed appropriate in the circumstances.

I left the booklet on the bar and thought about how I might sneak out. In the meantime the best course of action seemed to be getting drunk at Justin's expense. He got another round as a twentysomething bloke with mousy hair sticking up like a shark's fin came over and introduced himself.

"All-right fellas, y'here for the speed dating?"

"Yeah, yeah." Said Justin.

"Good work, you'll love it." This guy looked like he ought to be presenting some youth-oriented programme on digital TV. "We're gonna be starting any minute. Give us your names and I'll write you out a badge."

"Justin."

"Montague Lembett Sanderson-Smythe." He wrote it down, filling half his card with the first three letters before looking up. I enjoyed his lost expression. "Monty'll do."

"Right, there you go." We pinned the name badges to our shirts. "Listen out for me on the mic, we're gonna be starting any minute."

"Yes, you said." But he was gone, that pointed line of hair moving to the next group of hopefuls. "Justin, what the fuck have you got me into?"

"Relax." The dopey grin was back on his face. "Look at all the girls you're about to meet." I scanned the area, most of them *were* quite attractive. Surely there wasn't a shortage of dating possibilities in their lives? "Any of these ladies could be yours Monty. What have we got to lose?"

"Do you know how much I hate it when people say that? *What have you got to lose?* Oh, I don't know, my dignity, my self-esteem, the ability to hold suicidal impulses at bay." I drained my glass and turned to Justin. "You've got far more to lose than me though. One mention of what we're doing tonight and that lovely girlfriend of yours will be off before you can say *what the fuck have I done?* And to someone like him probably." I pointed to a buffed bloke in jacket and jeans, a good foot taller than Justin.

"You wouldn't tell her."

"Get more drinks."

Taking advantage of the blackmail opportunity might prove fun, but it didn't change the fact that the pipsqueak's plan made me profoundly nervous. I thought about how badly my date with Kathleen had gone. And that wasn't even against the clock. But three minutes wasn't very long, at least if I made a fool out of myself I could move quickly on. Whatever happened would be forgotten in seconds. Then again, that exit looked terrifically inviting. I got through my third pint even faster than the second one and was just ordering a fourth when that smarmy voice came over the P.A.

"Okay girls and boys, if you could move to the tables and sit by your designated numbers we'll get this extravaganza started."

112

Shark fin watched people find their seats from his corner at the back. Dates excused themselves or apologised for having to squeeze past as eleven women, all flushed with excitement and anticipation, sat against the wall. They faced men whose stern faces masked their apprehension, as if this were a serious business in which they wanted to achieve, to compete and succeed. All except Justin that is, he continued to grin away happily. I carried my drink across and took the space next to him.

"All-right, a brief run through of the rules for those new to this." The guy smiled, exposing bleached white teeth. I could see him compering the bingo in thirty years, a vision which somehow failed to quell my animosity. "The clocks on your tables have been set for three minutes. Ladies, when I say 'go', I want you to start them running. You're in charge of this girls, give me a *hooray* if you understand."

"Rayyy."

Jesus.

"And boys, when the three minutes are up, I'll be asking you to move one place to your right, taking your scorecards and pencils with you. Do we understand?" Various incomprehensible affirmatives. "Now, these are very important." Shark fin held up a card. "Photos of the people you'll be meeting tonight are set out here next to their names. All you have to do is place a cross in one of the two boxes when your time's up. Either yes or no, depending on whether you want to see a bit more of this person, if you know what I mean. D'you get it?"

"Rayyy!" Said the girls.

"Nyuh." Said the boys.

"Wanker." Said I under my breath, then took a deep draw from my pint. My picture on the scorecard had been badly photo-copied from the files of *Bears!Bears!Bears!* and made me look like a sullen adolescent with chicken pox.

"We'll be having a short break five dates in, but for any of you who can't wait that long the staff at *Parvenu* will be available to take orders between dates." He winked at the twenty two faces looking up at him, only one of which exuded hatred. "So, let's not waste any more time. Hands on the clock please girls, and when I give the signal your first date will begin." He gestured with one arm, a race official lowering his flag. "Go!"

My mind wandered. Behind me a few resolutely cool barflies were hanging out, pretending not to watch the cabaret, this low-rent show of which I was a part. I should have got out while I had the chance, I'd be mingling with them right now, away from it all, looking down on these singles in their organised dance of desperation. To my right pairs of people fired questions in a scattershot manner, trying to find out as much as they could in the limited time, dialogue flying back and forth like warring lovers in a screwball comedy. It was exhausting to observe, something I did while slouched down in my chair with a beer in one hand. Gradually my head moved round so I was facing forwards. Turned out a girl was there and she was waiting for me to date her. Oh yeah, I remember.

"Hello." She said tentatively.

"Hello." I threw back at her.

"So what do you do?"

"Bears."

"Pardon?"

"Uh, I'm in advertising."

"Right, that's great." She looked to the couples either side of us, jabbering away effortlessly.

"Erm, okay, yeah." I'd have to make an attempt. "What about you?"

"Still studying."

"Terrific, well done." She was definitely younger than me, quite pretty in a freckled kind of way with two striking blue eyes. I leaned in. "Listen, you seem quite normal and stuff. What in the world persuaded you to come here? I mean, this is a bit of a last resort isn't it?"

"I thought it might be fun." My first date was nice, an amiable one. "What are you anyway, some kind of journalist?"

"Not really no." I thought about that for a second, it was a good question. "Well, actually I am, yeah. But not here, I tend to write about shit bands...."

At this point the alarms went off and eleven sets of painted fingernails descended onto their timers, quietening the sound.

"Okay, good. Yes or no? You decide. Now boys, collect up your cards and move one place to the right. If the boy at the end could come down to me. All-right then, everybody ready?"

"Nyearh." Said everybody.

"Right, go!"

I came face to face with an elfin girl whose badge read *Betsy*. Time to atone for that last date. I'd missed one chance already, it would be silly to repeat my mistake. Although something about Betsy immediately screamed, *not your type*. Maybe it was the superior air about her, or the fact that she smelt of lavender. More likely I was put off by the horrid bandanna tied around her cropped hair.

"Hi there, how are you?" I offered a hand which Betsy shook, her skin cold to the touch.

"I'm fine..." She peered at my badge. "Monty. What line of work are you in Monty?"

"I'm in the music industry." The half-truth freed me somehow. "What about you?"

"Choreographer."

"Really, how interesting." A what? "You mean like, dancing and things?"

"At the moment I'm training a cast of thirty for a major production in the West End. It starts next year."

"That's great, really great." I took a *great* gulp of beer. "You certainly look fit." Betsy gave me a look as icy as her touch. "I mean, toned. I mean....."

"And *you* look like you could do with some exercise."

I stared down at my modest gut. "You're right about that, maybe you'd like to help me train?"

"I don't think so."

"I couldn't pay you of course, you'd have to do it out of love." Silence. "Erm, a love for aiding fat knackers like me. I suppose it'd be more like charity really." Betsy's pallid eyes gave no response. "Do you like bears at all?"

"What?"

Buzzzzzzzzzz.

Thank you God. I gathered up my bits and pieces and tried to avoid looking at Betsy ever again. To the left Justin pulled his coat from the chair and began to rummage in its pockets.

"How you getting on?" He whispered.

"Not great, what are you saying to them?"

"You know, the usual." Justin pulled out a plastic carton containing a sandwich. "We've been talking about clothes, electronica, styling products, normal stuff. Want some?" He offered me a limp triangle of ham salad.

"We're supposed to be in the middle of a dating session."

"I'm famished." I took my new seat as Justin gobbled his food. "What's this one like?"

"Fucking weird, don't even bother with her." Once it came out I wondered if Betsy had heard, she was only a few feet away after all.

"Annnnd, *go!*"

"That's not fair!" Complained my third date, apropos of nothing. A straight-haired brunette with sunglasses perched on top of her head, she was pointing to the previous guy. "We totally clicked, I want to go on talking with him."

The muscled bloke to our right with the suit jacket sleeves rolled up was too absorbed by his latest date to hear. "Really?" I looked at the great biceps. "I think he looks a bit retarded to be honest."

The girl's face became thundery. "That's not funny, one of my brothers has learning difficulties." Her t-shirt had a diagonal slash on it, across which she folded her arms while pulling the face of a sulky six year old. "You're not as nice as Leonard."

"*Leonard?* God." I got to my feet. "Excuse me a moment, I forgot my drink." Reaching over to collect my pint glass, I heard Justin tell Betsy about his favourite places to buy shoes in Camden, spitting globules of bread at her with each sentence. To her credit Betsy wiped the chewed sandwich off her face without a word and continued listening. I retook my seat, this third date still staring at Leonard with lust in her eyes.

"So, you like that guy then?" I jerked a thumb to my right.

"He's *dreamy.*"

"You should go for it." I advised her. "I'm sure he'd be more than happy to give you a good seeing to."

"Don't say that." Offended. "I just want a nice man to hug and kiss."

"Bloody hell, really?" The girl nodded. "You wouldn't even beat him off?"

"Euuuu!! No!"

At this point Leonard paused in his conversation and looked at us questioningly. "Everything's fine mate." I assured him. "You carry on." The guy went back to his date and I returned my attention to this girl.

"I'll let you into a secret babe, men need relief. If you want to win Leonard's heart you'll have to manipulate other bits of him, it's part of a girlfriend's responsibility to get a man off...."

Buzzzzzz.

She'd have to beg me for more of this wisdom afterwards. I moved along, signalling to one of the bar staff and mouthing the word *Stella* as I went. By the time Shark Fin gave word to begin again I'd gratefully accepted another pint. My fourth date was a diminutive blonde with a high-pitched voice whose name badge read *Abigail.*

"Are you drunk?" She demanded.

"Did you prepare that question in advance?" I replied, charmingly.

"Don't you come the smartarse with me!" Jesus. Fifteen seconds in and she was already busting my balls. "Eight dates to go, and you're pissed."

What was that line? "I may be pissed my dear, but I'm also very beautiful. You'll be ugly in the morning."

"What?"

"Erm, you'll be sober in the morning?"

"I'm sober now, moron."

"Look, what does it matter?" I was starting to get annoyed with this hostility. "A little alcohol loosens the tongue, smoothes out social interaction. We get to know each other better and see what happens, I don't see the problem."

"You men, you're all the same." She whinnied. "Out for what you can get. I should have known better than to come here." Abigail looked around *Parvenu.* "They say women have it easy, that we're all equal. Well, fuck them. Look at us, we go unrecognised, we earn less money, we don't get respect.."

"I'm willing to respect you, anally."

"What did you say?"

"I said you're absolutely right, *really.*"

"Yes, I am." That sharp voice really grated. "You're faced with a strong woman and you can't handle it, all of you *men.*" She spat the word out. "We're branded lesbians, or worse."

"Thank Christ I don't have to spend the whole evening with you. This is probably the worst date I've ever been on."

"The night's young Monty." She laughed. I looked Abigail up and down; the confrontational bearing, that superior twist to her mouth, a symmetry of the features which might have made her pretty if she weren't so intent on confrontation.

"However did you turn out like this? I bet your father wanted a boy."

That shocked her. "Fuck you." She said.

"No please, fuck you."

Buzzzzzzz.

A big black cross in the 'no' box against Abigail's inappropriately smiley photo, then I hurried to the next chair, so keen to get away I didn't look where I was going and trod heavily on my fifth date's foot.

"Ow!" She yelped as Shark Fin told us to begin for a fifth time.

"Damn it. I'm really sorry." I hit the timer while the girl withdrew a long leg and rubbed it. "I didn't expect you to reach that far."

"I'll live... Monty." Her name was Lisa-Marie. A mixed race hottie, olive-skinned and Amazonian.

"How tall are you anyway?" I asked.

"Six-two."

"Blimey, that's six inches more than me. I bet you'd never go out with someone my height."

"Probably not." A reassuring smile, wide and full of teeth. "But I don't rule guys out just 'cause of how they look."

"That's good." This was better, Lisa-Marie was buying into the spirit of this evening. A little flirting would get me back on course, even if she was far too beautiful. I drank Lisa-Marie in, she was definitely the kind of girl who'd never usually speak to me in social situations, and here I was, injuring her.

"Are you okay?" She asked. "You seemed a bit upset when you sat down."

"It's her." I glared at Abigail, currently berating a terrified Justin for something the male gender had once done. "She's a bit... scary."

Lisa-Marie watched the scene. "God, I see what you mean."

"It's not just that." Drinking more lager, I decided to give myself up to the charity of this striking girl. "I was lured here tonight under false pretences. I can't talk to women, not this way, and I'm damn sure I can't make them want me. I've succeeded before, don't get me wrong, but I was with this really cool girl the other day and I don't know what happened but it all went horribly to cock. When that happens I always think I ought to not even try because I end up wanting to slit my throat out of embarrassment. So why the fuck would I come to a place like this? It's inevitably going to end in disappointment. What am I going to talk about with girls like you, girls who wouldn't look at me twice in the real world? My shit job? My depressing family? My miserable flatmate? My boring hobbies? I'm sorry Lisa-Marie, but when you get right down to it, life sucks. You live alone and you die alone, and all this crap isn't going to make one iota of difference. The chance of finding someone to love here has got to be a thousand to one, so we might as well stop right now and go home, watch TV and wait for death." For some reason the adjacent conversations had stopped. Both Justin with Abigail and Leonard opposite some plain girl were looking at me strangely. I ignored them and focussed on Lisa-Marie.

"Okay." I said to her. "Now you go."

Buzzzzzz.....

During the half-time interval I moved away from the other daters. Justin joined me in the far corner of *Parvenu* and agreed that the evening could probably have gone better. For his fifth date Justin had been blasted out of the water by that militant feminist, but he was keen to keep trying. Eager to secure a cross in the 'yes' box from his remaining six dates.

"Well I wouldn't count on getting anywhere with Lisa-Marie." I pointed at the next photograph on his list. "You'd need platform shoes just to kiss her on the cheek."

"You're not giving me the boost I need Monty."

"No, sorry." Before us the girl who had a retarded brother honed in on Leonard. "This whole set-up is so exhausting, we need to give ourselves some kind of pep if we're going to get through the rest of these women."

"I've a suggestion." He moved past me to the bar. "Why don't I get a tray of shots? That'll perk us up, and we can offer them to the girls."

I stared at him, shocked. "You know Justin, I think that's the best idea you've ever had." He grinned and caught the barman's eye. "Different colours if you can, chicks love multicoloured drinks."

"Right. How many?"

"Better get ten. Actually no, make it twelve."

We carried the silver tray to our place, plinked two of the miniature tumblers together and downed the fluid inside. He was right, I perked up immediately. That lethargy disappeared as our fellow contestants joined us. My new date was called Dawn and willingly accepted a drink. Answering my polite questions, the girl told me about living with an eighty year old woman (her grand-mother) and a deep love of animals. I listened and prompted, re-freshed by a female who was cheerful and eager to please. I guess this was mainly because she wasn't very good looking, Dawn had a jowly double chin and patches of red on her face, but I was grateful for a few minutes of normal conversation. She went on about train-ing to be a nurse and her recent holiday on Kos, smiling at me all the while. Then the buzzer went and I put a cross against her name.

Shallow, I'll admit, but I wouldn't want to lead the girl on. A good visual aspect is very important to us guys.

Talking of which. "Hello."

"Hi Monty." Responded the thirtysomething blonde in the low cut dress. "Shall we get down to it?"

"Won't you have a drink first?" She leaned forward and chose a clear liquid from the tray. I glanced at her name badge, then got a good look at those huge breasts. "I'd better take one too." I gulped a vial of green fluid. "So Julie, how are things?"

"Not bad." She looked me over. "What's a boy like you do for a living?"

"I run a pub." I lied.

"Really? I used to be a barmaid."

"I'm sure you were excellent." My eyes automatically fell to her chest. Incredible. "You have the right equipment."

Julie looked at her cleavage. "Do you like them?"

"They're brilliant." I sounded like a schoolboy, but they were.

"And natural." Julie pushed the great turrets outwards. "I'm very proud of my boobs."

"So you should be, those are terrific hooters. It's good of you to talk so openly about them."

"Nah, it's not. I know men're fascinated." She lit a cigarette. "I find 'em fascinating too." Julie chuckled hoarsely and cast a hand over the competition. "I bet this is more honest than what you got from the others."

"It sure is." To my left Justin had lost interest in Dawn and was stealing glances at Julie every chance he got. "What bra size do you take, if you don't mind me asking?"

She exhaled a cloud of smoke. "Thirty-four double-D."

"Bloody hell, that's fantastic. Really fantastic." I forced myself to take in the rest of her, Julie was probably ten years older than me, fleshy with yellowing teeth. Not that it mattered. "Don't you get back problems from jubblies that size?"

"Not really lover, my body can cope with them." That was more than mine ever could I'd wager.

"Well, thanks for this." I shook her hand, getting a good look at that cleavage one last time.

"My pleasure."

Buzzzzz.

The next date was a skinny girl with glasses who looked askance at me. It seemed everything that had passed between myself and Julie reached her ears too. I downed another shot and moved rightwards, collapsing into the chair before her hateful face. The smoothly inane tones of Shark Fin invited us to start.

"Hello." I ventured. This girl was called Hanna and looked like a librarian, one whose expression suggested I'd been caught burning books. Keeping her look of animosity locked on me, Hanna noiselessly picked up a pencil. Then, very slowly and deliberately, she drew a cross for 'no' against my picture. I got the message. She didn't approve of my honest fascination with bajoomies. Well, so what? It was only three minutes until I could move on. Ho hum. I looked at the clock and brushed some saliva from the corner of my mouth. Two and a half minutes to go. Jesus, those seconds could drag. I decided to look in on Justin's technique for a bit.

"So Justin." The buxom blonde wiggled forwards in her seat. "What are you after in a woman?"

"A shag."

Julie slapped his face. "Watch your mouth around a lady!"

I reached over and cuffed Justin on the head. "Yeah, stop being so rude."

"Ow! Get off!"

Julie and I shared a chuckle while an aggrieved Justin knocked back another shot. I decided to update my scorecard. That first one was okay. The next three? Definitely not. Lisa-Marie? Well, yes, like she was going to tick me. Julie? Too violent and tarty I'm afraid. A man could not live by titties alone. And Hanna could go fuck herself. Right, overall that didn't look too promising.

I returned to my latest date but she continued to regard me with contempt. One minute to go so I scrawled a variety of shapes around the edge of my scorecard to kill the boredom.

Buzzzzz.

About time, I slid along and finished my doodling, completing the shading on my perfect replication of a swastika. Looking up, I saw a pale redhead squinting at me suspiciously. I dropped the pencil and tried to cover the Nazi insignia with my hand.

"Hi, erm, yes. I'm Monty."

"Susan."

"So, how are you?"

"I don't really want to answer that right now."

"Okay." Hmmm, out of solitary confinement and into the igloo. I decided to give my genuine side an airing. "What do you like to do? I mean, what do you really love Susan?"

"I'm not prepared to discuss that with you."

Damn, talk about putting up walls. I looked into her aquamarine eyes, but there was no hint of emollience. "Got any brothers or sisters?"

"That's none of your business."

"No, I guess not."

I ticked Susan's box, she intrigued me. Then I observed her for a while longer as she tapped a text message into her phone. Down the row Justin was working his way through the remaining shots, apparently Hanna hadn't taken a shine to him either.

Buzzzzzz.

These alarms were speeding up. I moved to the last seat on the line for my penultimate date, feeling groggy and not a little drunk. Luckily the welcome was pleasant, a big smile from a woman a few years older than me with a long, equine nose and chestnut hair falling down her back.

"Annnnnd, *go!*"

"Good evening to you." The woman was called Kelly and spoke with an American accent.

"You're from the States?"

"Colorado, but I've lived here for five years."

The two of us passed a very pleasant three minutes discussing Kelly and why she called London home, what she thought of her current President and why American girls believed English guys were more gentlemanly that their US counterparts. Kelly retained eye contact with me all the way, occasionally twirling one of those lengthy curls with a finger, a gesture I found beguiling. She didn't ask anything about me, but that was fine. I wasn't feeling particularly coherent by this stage of the evening. To my left Justin offered our final shot to Susan, drinking it himself when she refused. Enjoying the American's company, I was about to mention my ambition to visit her country, maybe ask about the best places to see, when we were interrupted.

Buzzzzz.

The look of disappointment on Kelly's face worsened when she saw who was next.

"Listen," she whispered. "That's your friend, right?"

"Acquaintance."

"Well, I'd like to have a few more minutes with you. Stay here and make him skip a place."

I glanced at Justin, he was goggle-eyed and swayed slightly. "You don't want to speak to him?"

"Look at his beard, the guy's a dork." I couldn't contradict her.

Shark Fin came over the microphone. "Would all the boys move along for the last time?"

Justin tried to stand but tripped on a chair leg I caught him under the arms and turned the short guy around.

"Go on mate, you're at the end."

"Oh, okay." Justin's head went down and he walked to the back. When I was certain my colleague had reached the spare seat I sat, ready to continue with Kelly.

"For the very last time girls and boys... *GO!*"

"Where were we Monty?" She asked with a smile.

"Oh balls." Shark Fin had responded to a call from the girl opposite Justin. "Sorry Kelly, I'll have to make sure he's alright."

I strode up to the discussion involving a girl who claimed she'd already dated Justin while a stocky barman looked on and Leonard blessed everyone with his opinion, having apparently abandoned his final date. In the middle of it all my colleague looked panicked and unwell, whimpering in confusion as people rounded on him.

"He's breaking the rules," stated Leonard piously. "And he brought food in!"

"I don't need to speak to this bloke again, he was crap the first time."

Shark Fin looked agitated. "Can everyone just calm down?"

"It's okay." I interjected. "There's been a mistake, but we can swap back. Get up Justin."

"Not sure I can." He gazed at the unfriendly faces, the barman in particular was studying Justin with some resentment.

"He's your friend is he?" The stocky employee inquired of me. "I think you should take him home."

"My friend, yes." Justin gibbered. "I ONLY DID THIS FOR MONTY - I'VE ALREADY GOT A GIRLFRIEND!"

Silence in the bar. Everyone was glaring at us, conversations on hold while they cast stony looks at Justin who giggled to himself after the loud outburst, utterly oblivious to them all. That lie he confessed was obviously a serious one in the world of speed dating; the sin of being in a relationship. Even Shark Fin regarded my acquaintance with disgust.

"Right, that's it sonny." The barman grabbed hold of Justin, lifting him away from the table.

"Wheeee!" Chortled Justin as he was carried out of the bar. I ticked the remaining boxes on our scorecards and handed them to the host. Then I apologised to Kelly and hurried out, passing the barman on his way back in as he brushed his hands together. Outside Justin lay face down on the pavement, moaning. I crouched beside him.

"Here you go mate, put this on." I got Justin's arms into the coat and rolled him over. There was a drowsy smile on my colleague's face and gravel in his hair.

"Mother?"

"No, it's not. Come on now." Huffing with the effort I brought this undersized figure to his feet. "We're going to the station."

Justin gazed at Parvenu and became momentarily lucid. "I wonder how we did?"

Much later we would receive emails with our results. Mine said: *Thank you for taking part in Speed Dating. You have 0 matches. We wish you every good fortune in contacting those who expressed an interest.*

Justin's said: *Thank you for taking part in Speed Dating. We regret to say that you have been banned from all future events. Your details and photograph will be circulated to organisers around the country. Please do not attempt to attend one of these evenings again.*

The messages would come as a salutary reminder of our failure during this unfortunate night, a night which could have ended for me then and there, carrying a violently ill man through Canary Wharf. Every hundred yards or so Justin would make a noise like a nervous turkey, whereupon I let him go and backed away. The end tally of our journey amounted to three flowerbeds, a bus shelter and two shop doorways desecrated by Justin's vomit, by which time I was convinced he had nothing more to give. After some retching outside the arched entranceway he agreed, so we went down the station steps and caught the Jubilee Line.

At London Bridge I looked for the time of Justin's train and escorted him to the appropriate platform, giving explicit instructions regarding the rest of his journey. Then I strolled back to the underground, feeling capably inebriated but plagued by thoughts of those girls I'd met, what might have been. I rode two stops westbound before changing at Waterloo to head north. My experience of speed dating had been pretty dire overall, although that American seemed nice, and I certainly enjoyed the blonde's cleavage. The problem was that those women weren't keen to learn about me, revelling in the chime of their own voices too much. I'd no rapport with any of them, and maybe it was down to the tight time limit, but if a girl wasn't going to evince interest in me I was never going to become attracted to her.

I boarded a Northern Line train, intending to get off at Embankment as usual. It was all a sham anyway. Two people couldn't find an affinity in a hundred and eighty seconds, it took a whole evening for that at least. Through the course of a night two people found out what they had in common and uncovered curiosity-sparking differences, like Kathleen and I did on Monday. I wondered what she was up to right now, probably serving overpriced drinks to geeky music fans. I looked up at the LED display and noticed that the train wasn't going to the end of the line, terminating instead at Golders Green. Following this statement came the words:

Monty - Go To Her!

Then it was gone and we pulled into my stop. I was cracking up, didn't hallucinating in a public place get you locked up? But those strange scrolling announcements had been right before. To hell with it, I stayed on board.

Three stations later I disembarked and found my way to the club, paying twelve pounds to be allowed inside. Tonight the *5 Easy Pieces* played host to a selection of bluegrass acts from around Britain, but I was less interested in the music than who was behind the bar. Several staff were working but I couldn't see Kathleen so I waited until Kevin was free, ordered a coke from him to help sober up, and asked if she was around.

He pointed to the area in front of the stage. "Over there, collecting glasses."

A blonde head bobbed along, the girl picking up empties from the floor. "Thanks."

I took up a position where I could watch her movement between glances at the band. The men with guitars wore faded denim while women sang harmony parts and wielded fiddles or banjos. Kathleen climbed the steps, sleek in the black uniform of the club, her hair mussed. The girl was beautiful, I wished I smelt of liquorice for her.

"Hello." She said demurely, handing the glasses to Kevin. "What are you doing here?"

"I wanted to see you."

"I've been waiting for your call since Monday." Admonishing. "Why didn't you get in touch?"

I looked down. "I don't know, I thought I'd messed up. I want to apologise."

"Don't worry about it, I'm more tolerant than that." Those striking eyes, they understood. "It wasn't difficult to work out you were under a lot of strain, you had wedding cake in your hair for God's sake."

We laughed, she was standing quite close to me. "I'll tell you all about it." I promised.

"See that you do." Kathleen smiled. "So, what have you been up to tonight?"

"Oh God, it was horrible."

"What was."

"Speed dating. It brought out the worst in me."

"Speed dating? You poor thing!" The girl hugged me, her whole body leaning in. As Kathleen withdrew she kept her hands on my hips. "No wonder you look so harassed!"

One of my hands moved to stroke her hair, an involuntary motion. "Everything's better now."

The girl smiled coquettishly and looked into my eyes, one of her hands moving to cup the back of my neck. Then Kathleen brought my head forwards until our lips touched.

Part Two:
With Hilarious
Consequences

Chapter Eleven

Kathleen snuffled in her sleep, the sound of some burrowing animal, then curled back into her question mark shape. I watched the girl from my position, perched up on one elbow, at ease with this peaceful form. An array of scorched hair on my pillow, the soft satin of her skin, she looked lovely to me. Not your typical film star, that was true, but with the right stylist she could be magazine cover material. Besides, none of the greatest actresses were conventionally beautiful. Kathleen would make her mark, I was sure of it. Ably assisted by Monty Sanderson, showbusiness talent spotter extraordinaire. My boss had cast Kathleen in the main female role after the briefest of readings. As I looked at her now I pictured myself creating a career arc for Kathleen Tibbits that showed off every side of her abilities. The Roger Vadim to her Jane Fonda. She would do drama, like Jane playing Bree Daniels in *Klute*, or comedy, like Corrie Bratter in *Barefoot In The Park*, then the vulnerability of Gloria Beatty in *They Shoot Horses Don't They?* the eroticism of Barbarella in *Barbarella*. Actually, maybe not the sexy stuff. I might draw the line there.

Martin let me rewrite *Too Beautiful*, although he wasn't too pleased at my stated desire to rip it apart. He'd probably be stunned by my version, finished late last night, it was very different to his final draft. Well, my boss would just have to accept the changes. I'd told him the piece wouldn't be a success in its present form, so he'd better let me have free reign to do what I wanted. As producer he could do what he liked with the results anyway.

Implicit in my ultimatum was the frustration I felt at his dwindling agency. We'd been losing clients on a regular basis, should I leave the bear-crammed ship they'd be rudderless. I think Martin knew that and so he let me do what I wanted with the script. This involved removing those scenes that didn't seem to have a point and reworking others. My play existed as a sequence of fragments from Richey's life, cohering into an ambiguous ending which, I hoped, reflected the spirit of the man. And yes, I'd beefed up Kathleen's part, writing more lines for 'Jo' and skewing her influence toward the end of our hero's life. I spent hours reading Edwards' philosophy, listening to his music, studying the photographs, my toil ought to be rewarded somehow. And what I wanted, more than anything else, was a chance for my girlfriend to show what she could do.

My girlfriend. It felt strange, thinking of someone like that. Strange and right. I eased myself off the bed and left her sleeping. In the bathroom our replica public lice sat beside the bowl and reminded me of the first time she'd stayed over. It happened a few weeks after we became an item, I heard a scream and rushed in to find Kathleen demanding to know what exactly those *things* were. She'd become accustomed to finding weird stuff around our flat since then, but at the time I had to explain how I'd bought these monstrosities, both the size of cats and lurking malevolently by our toilet. They were quite horrible actually, six pairs of spindly legs protruding from the domed bodies, but at the auction owning them had seemed like a good idea. I didn't attend with the intention of bidding for items, but after Fergal picked up his six foot hamster (*"His what?"* - Kathleen) I was feeling a little jealous. Then the pair of pubic lice, former stars of the Millennium Dome's *Body Zone*, came up for sale. There wasn't one offer and I felt sorry for the little fellas. (*"You felt sorry for them? A pair of plastic parasites?"*) They'd guarded our bathroom ever since.

Back in bed I snuggled up to Kathleen, feeling the warmth through her t-shirt, that steady rise and fall from her breath. Our first kiss led to a late-Autumn happiness for me. I discovered the girl wasn't superior or affected but empathic, forgiving and totally lovely. When she wasn't working we'd meet up every night to eat and go to the cinema, laughing through the nonsensical action movies I enjoyed or taking in an arthouse flick at her urging. To my surprise I usually found something redeeming in these obscure tales, some actor or idea, a plot twist or chemistry between the lead players which paralleled our own. Holding her hand in that pious darkness, we let the images wash over us.

The two of us took advantage of all the big city possibilities, found new experiences on the cheap where we could. I knew about the free gigs and arts centre all-dayers, while Kathleen suggested book readings and discounted theatrical shows. Then there were the more unusual experiences, like the climax to an *Opera on Waterskis* season we watched from the bank of the Thames, a fat soprano in a corset letting out an ear-splitting cry of remorse before losing his grip on the rope and plunging into that polluted river.

Sometimes we'd visit an estate agent, pose as an upwardly mobile couple keen to look round properties in the upper six figure bracket. The pair of us met our guide outside the house, invariably an oleaginous, ingratiating bloke who would conduct a running commentary. We got an insight into how the moneyed classes lived, lying through our teeth as we pretended to be "kind of interested", but keener on "that eight bedroom place" we'd just explored. Afterwards we came back to my flat, aglow from the finery. Those great marble fireplaces, enormous conservatories, acres of land, feeling the connection between us strengthened by this conspiracy only we knew about.

I kissed the contoured whorl of her ear, half wanting the girl to wake as I enfolded her in my arms. Whenever we shared a time and place, aspects of our different lives, it felt inexpressibly *right*. Having her there made me unapologetically masculine, a protector against forces which might seek to hurt this sweet girl. It was a role I fulfilled easily, keeping Kathleen cosy and safe. I couldn't remember when I'd last felt this smitten, or even if it had ever been this way. Over the past two months we came to recognise the extent of our compatibility, how we slotted together like two pieces of the same jigsaw. As I got to know Kathleen her desirability increased, all thoughts of *type* forgotten as I saw beyond appearance. Even when we laid side by side I was kept awake, excited by thoughts of her, of our future together. And when we were apart I anticipated our next meeting, struggling to retain my self-control against an urge to phone her at work or in the middle of the night, forcing myself to count bears until I fell asleep whereupon I'd dream of her. The next day we would meet up again and my heart leapt, some mixture of chemical euphoriants inspiring me. Saying, *be attentive Monty, be an exemplary boyfriend to this girl*.

Sometimes I'd be walking along, to or from work, and I'd see a young woman in the street whose similarity to Kathleen caused me to catch my breath, fooled into believing it was her for

133

the briefest of moments, confused by some physical characteristic or nuance of manner. Then I'd look again, see how this stranger was nothing like my girl, Kathleen was unique. I spotted connections everywhere, unknown commuters reminding me of bar staff at the club, stories she told me of her family would feel like they'd befallen my own relatives, and every similarity of background or outlook we uncovered made our relationship seem more magical and destined. Thanks to Kathleen a change came over me as the year raced to a close, everybody said so. Suddenly I was full of energy despite my lack of sleep, people glancing at me strangely as I realised I was singing out loud in the rush hour crush, or at my desk for the whole office to hear. I'd never sung in public before, at least not while sober, but I was young and optimistic, full of vim and affection, able to stay up all night talking with her, then put in hours on the play or *Bears!Bears!Bears!* the next morning.

Most of my friends were pleased for me. Monty was back in the loop, had fallen for the idea of being part of a couple once more. I received a merciless ribbing from the guys in the band though, Si amused to see me walking around with a stupid smile on my face and Tosspot observing how "dopey" I was in her presence. Late November saw *The Airborne Toxic Event's* support slot for the washed-up Britpopper, interest having grown exponentially thanks to my laudatory fanzine article a few weeks before. The band's short set went down well by all accounts and they certainly sounded passable. But since I was at the back helping to sell their 4-Track demo ('*These Are My Pants, Show Me Yours*'), I couldn't see much of it.

The foursome were galvanized afterwards, celebrating long into the night and enlisting me for the next stage of what Giles called "the masterplan". All through December I sent out copies of my feature with their demo CD, targeting record companies I thought might be sympathetic to the melodic racket. The disc was accompanied by a flyer advertising the band's first headline show this coming Friday, and I'd even managed to wangle a few sentences of boxed hype under a photo of Tosspot looking suitably deranged in *Plectrum Abuser*, their show named 'gig of the week'. The start of the year was traditionally a quiet time for the music industry, journos had little to write about with successful acts still on holiday. Hopefully A&R men would have recovered from their New Year hangovers in time to check out some rowdy young tykes. If *The A.T.E.* could live up to their billing there was a good chance of record label interest after the show.

This Friday would also be the first time Kathleen had seen them so I told the boys they had to fulfil her high expectations, Giles and Tosspot responding with a battery of put-downs. Looking to Si for support, I saw only the pity he reserved for those lost from what he called 'the bachelor gang', a club of which he was once again an honorary member, having dumped Lettice after one unfunny rom-com too many. I didn't care what they thought, the importance of that girl in my arms overwhelmed any ridicule.

She rolled onto her back and looked up at me. I greeted Kathleen with a kiss, tasting last night and the hours of sleep in her mouth. The girl smiled and pulled away, out into the hall without bothering to dress. Fergal was away for his annual festive trip to Ireland, dodging the arrows of an authoritarian father and suppressing his character around four siblings who fought like professional wrestlers. Not that Kathleen would have worried about had my flatmate been around, she often wandered around in her underwear now she knew Fergal was *that way inclined.* In fact, the two of them had built up quite a friendship since she'd begun to stay over. Fergal warmed to her far more than my previous girlfriends and often talked to Kathleen for longer than me. My girl was cultured enough to be familiar with many of the authors and playwrights Fergal loved, and they could spend hours discussing the lives of Joe Orton and Oscar Wilde, speculating which movie stars were gay or who was the best looking actor on TV. I liked the two of them getting on, and tried not to feel excluded by these conversations. This friendship was the one upside to Fergal's recent existence. My flatmate hadn't committed anything to video tape for months now, and rarely went outdoors, ballooning in weight even as he got through a packet of cigarettes every day. Wandering from bedroom to lounge as if he'd forgotten there was a world beyond our front door.

Asking Fergal what was wrong would do no good, he simply deflected the query, changing the subject to my own routine or some odd story in the newspaper. For a while I racked my brains, wondering what could cause such a go-getting character to give up and spend his days under a patina of melancholy, only pretending to be upbeat when we were around. In the end it was Kathleen, able to extract personal details if his guard was down, who put her finger on the problem.

"He needs a man." She said.

Clearly the girl had some sympathy for Fergal's situation, having experienced something similar in a way I had not. We thought about trying to set him up with someone, like friends do, but it quickly became apparent the only gay guys I'd met lately were through Fergal, and as a heterosexual man I hadn't stayed in touch with the homos I knew at university. Kathleen said there were a couple of men on her course who were quite effeminate, but she had no proof they were *light on their feet* and wouldn't feel comfortable asking outright. So we were left with no gay leads and a man who'd grown tired of the facile young himbos bars and clubs threw up for his delectation.

The unmistakeable voice of Dr. Who's stair-avoiding enemy came through from the hallway. "Would-you-like-a-nice-cup-of-tea?" Fizzed the robot voice.

"Daleks don't offer hot beverages!" I shouted back, imagining a laughing girl bent over the voice box. "You're supposed to say 'ex-ter-min-ate' or something."

"Per-haps-you-fan-cy-a-scone?" Responded the dalek.

"It's pronounced scon!" I said, as she reappeared in the doorway.

"Scone!" Kathleen maintained, jumping on top of me before I could argue further.

The Tibbits' home was a short taxi ride from Purley train station. A semi-detached property, surrounded this afternoon by the remains of a cool December mist. I paid the driver and steeled myself to meet the relatives. Kathleen strode up and rang the bell, even though she lived there. How odd, I thought as I joined her.

The door was opened by a curvaceous blonde girl in a tight white top with the words *New York* on it.

"Monty, this is my sister Kate."

"Hi Monty, I've totally heard about you." Kate looked me up and down, a knowing glint in her eye. Then she turned and led us into the house. "Mum's way into the cooking thing right now, best not disturb. We'll go say 'hi' real quick."

The place was spacious, both tasteful and classically furnished. We passed a lounge full of comfortable sofas and I guessed Mrs. Tibbits was able to afford this house thanks to her divorce settlement. No wonder Kathleen was still living here at the age of twenty three, although since passing her M.A. my girl had promised herself she would start the year with a new career and place of her own. Our short walk to the kitchen was punctuated by a series of framed photographs lining the walls. In them the two daughters grew from tiny girls in matching pink dresses, through stilted school photos, to their respective graduations. With the advances of age the younger sister gradually became the more glamorous, Kate's bust swelling as she took to plastering that teenage face with blusher and eye shadow.

I was so caught up in this wall-mounted slide show, the movement of two sisters into womanhood, I walked straight into an unlatched cupboard door the others managed to avoid.

"Ouch." A woman in early middle age, crow's feet crinkling away from her tired eyes, looked up from the pastry she flattened with a rolling pin.

"Mum, hi. This is Monty, Kathleen's, ah, friend." And with that Kate disappeared, leaving the two of us standing before this woman, like two court jesters hoping for laughter from the queen.

"Hello." I rubbed my head, that door had given me a nasty crack. Mrs. Tibbits looked at me and something passed over her face, some emotion I couldn't really decode, but it certainly wasn't positive. It felt like a failed marriage and the onset of spinsterhood had tarnished her attitude to my gender.

"Good day to you Monty." She said without friendliness. "You'll have to excuse me Kathleen, there's a terrible amount to do before dinner so I need peace and quiet. Why don't you show your *friend* around?"

"Sure mum." Something clear barrelled into the kitchen at ankle level, whacked into a table leg, then changed direction and sped toward the dishwasher.

"Put Ethel back in her cage! Your sister's always letting them roll around like that, it's simply not safe!"

"I'll do it." Kathleen collected the plastic ball which was jiggling with frustration at being trapped between cooker and washing machine. I followed the girl back into her lounge.

"What the hell's in there?"

"Ethel, see?" She held the sphere up to the light so I could peer through the patchwork of windows. Inside the ball a brown rodent was frantically trying to gain purchase on its vessel.

"Is that a hamster?"

"We've got two, Ethel and Elsie." Up on the bureau I saw a multi-storey cage containing a veritable assault course of tubes and wheels. Kathleen opened the latch and coaxed the creature out.

"This is the crazy one." The hamster clambered from one hand to the other and was passed to me, immediately taking a crap in my palm.

"Great." Ethel finished and sniffed my skin. "You know, I don't think your mother likes me."

"Mum doesn't even know you yet, she's just absorbed by her roast." Kathleen took Ethel away and opened the wire cage door. "Here you are babe, go and join your sis." I wiped the black pellet of turd from my hand with a tissue.

"If mum tries to concentrate on more than one thing at once she gets all panicky and has a *crisis.*" Kathleen sat down and took my other hand. "That's just the way it is. One tiny thing goes wrong and she overreacts badly. Me and Kate keep everything smooth and we try to obey her at all times, that keeps mum relatively calm. She's got a huge heart my mother, but she lives her life in italics."

"What do you mean?"

"Everything that happens to her has *huge implications* and *potentially life-altering consequences.* Stuff normal people take with

138

a pinch of salt, like a friend being in a bad mood or someone not calling, or even like in there." She gestured to the kitchen. "If she burns something today there'll be hair-tearing and recriminations; *they think I'm a terrible mother, no one will ever come and visit us ever again!*"

"Blimey." Now I was terrified of the catastrophes I might initiate.

"Don't worry about it." Kathleen was reading my mind. "Come on, I'll show you my *boudoir.*"

We visited every room except Kate's, and I took special care to memorise the location of the toilet for later. Finally we ended up on Kathleen's single bed, from where I tried to mock her and failed. My girlfriend's room was nowhere near as teenage in its preoccupations as the one my mother kept for me. Kathleen had taken great delight in ridiculing my belongings during those days we'd spent in Basingstoke over Christmas (*"Spiderwoman? Fighting fantasy? Motor racing cards?"*) but clearly she'd redecorated this space to reflect her adult status. The room was simple and mature; a portable television, dressing table, photos of friends tacked up on the wall. Wherever the cuddly toys and posters of long-forgotten boy bands were hidden, it was far away from my derisive gaze.

I laid down and watched Kathleen go through her wardrobe. She assessed the suitability of various clothes, occasionally asking for my opinion on an outfit, some flowing dress or sparkly t-shirt. After I responded positively she would put the item on, me noting the colour of her underwear, that grace with which she moved between possible party costumes. Kathleen said her mother would only be around for dinner, a family affair I should feel privileged to be a part of, whatever the downsides. Mrs. Tibbits was leaving after we'd all eaten, off to see the new year in with her sister, leaving the girls free run of her house. Kathleen's mother was a querulous woman, apparently affected by all kinds of trivial matters, from the arrival in her house of an unknown male to the deaths of public figures (Kathleen told me she cried for a week when Diana died). But putting up with her for a few hours was the least I could do after my girl endured three Christmas days with the

Sandersons. Mum and dad did their usual relay dance of antipathy, never in the same room for longer than was absolutely necessary, embarrassing me in front of Kathleen. I'd told her about the situation in advance, that oppressive atmosphere, my mother's cooking, the increasingly odd behaviour of my father, but she'd remained insistent. It was only fair she spent some time with my family Kathleen argued, she wanted to help me through this Yuletide visit which, she sensed, was something of an annual burden to me. And despite the warnings she actually wanted to meet my parents.

In fact Kathleen got along terrifically well with both of them, easy-going girl that she is, although she had to meet them as two separate entities obviously. I knew my mother would welcome her, mum was relieved at any evidence I hadn't "gone queer", but more surprising was my father's response. Dad was very hospitable in his withdrawn way, showing my girl around his newly-insulated shed, inviting her to come back "any time" and thankfully refraining from any further advice regarding matters of the heart.

The two of us spent those festive days walking the collies around greener patches of Basingstoke and talking of the past, how our personalities were shaped by those who raised us and where we thought they'd gone wrong. For fifteen years Kathleen's stepfather brought the girls up as his own and the pair loved him dearly for it, the whole family taking their surname from kind-hearted Basil Tibbits. Kathleen didn't blame him for leaving, it was amazing to her that he'd put up with their mother's moodswings for so long. Basil would come home from a day at the office to a self-created maelstrom of histrionics, amid which his wife was always the victim of numerous disasters precipitated by others; a daughter, Basil himself, the world at large. Their stepfather struggled valiantly through these stressful situations, but the inevitable happened, Basil began to see someone from work, someone who would listen to him, who wasn't self-obsessed or insecure. The divorce became final a couple of years ago, but Kathleen still visited him often. Basil was content with his new love, and that made her happy. As for her biological father, he was some anonymous figure existing in her memory only as a hazy shape, absent since she was a few years old and rarely present prior to that. Mrs. Tibbits had made it a point of principle to erase every trace of this man a long time ago, and whenever Kathleen attempted to quiz her mother, the elder woman would glare at her and practically spit on the ground, making it clear he was not a suitable subject for discussion.

In response to this convoluted history I told Kathleen what I knew of my own folks, two people similarly tight-lipped about their pasts but doing the best they could, even as they grew further apart. After exchanging the information I felt we'd become closer, expressing thoughts I'd never said out loud making me want Kathleen even more.

But whatever the positives I was glad when Christmas was over. This year I had the additional responsibility of getting through the New Year period without making a spectacle of myself, but we were coping so far. From somewhere in the house a bell rang, followed by a cry of "I'll get it". Soon Kate knocked on the door to announce dinner and we joined the older generation downstairs, Kathleen's aunt and her bespectacled husband greeting us while Mrs. Tibbits retrieved food from the oven and pans, conducting a running commentary as she did so.

"Bring that out there, a bit overdone but it'll have to do, drain that away. Hope everybody's hungry? Those beans look a bit stringy, where are the potatoes? *My God, I've lost the potatoes!* Oh no, there they are. Who's going to carve? Come on!"

We ate in a whirl of motion and compliments. I made sure I consumed a portion of everything, including the parsnip and sprouts, both of which I normally avoided like Cleethorpes. Mrs. Tibbits' eyes were on me and avoiding those vegetables might have implied they were something less than delicious. I ended up bloated as a binge drinker.

After coffee Kathleen implored her mother to leave the tidying up to us; the elders should get a start on the lengthy drive to her auntie's place she argued. When her brother-in-law eventually managed to lead Kathleen's mother away I scrubbed pots and pans while the sisters set about organising the house for their guests. They brought out booze and nibbles, giggled at some joke I wasn't privy to, then rushed upstairs for final touches to their appearance before the party got underway.

141

People began to arrive at nine, fresh-faced young women and unsure guys whose alcohol I packed into the fridge. These were friends of Kate and Kathleen, tempted to Purley from around London and greeted with an exuberant sense of past fraternity. I teed up the music, a few of *Plectrum Abuser*'s albums of the year, records from which many of these twentysomethings would recognise songs.

After a few beers the party became a blur. I was introduced to strangers, Kathleen telling me a few details about each one, information which I soon forgot. At one point Kate transferred Ethel and Elsie to their exercise balls, releasing the hamsters to roll around the lounge at pace. They knocked over several cans of lager before Kathleen put the pets away, half-heartedly scolding her sister who only laughed at the chaos she'd caused. Shortly before eleven I felt that build-up begin, the atmosphere becoming charged as we entered the final hours of the year. I settled into one of the sofas and watched the sisters interact with their guests, wondering who would be Kate's target for her midnight kiss. She could have any of the single men present, those irresistible curves accentuated by the tight ankle-length skirt and Yankophile top. Kate saw me watching her and decided the time had come to talk, she slid away from the crowd and folded both knees underneath her beside me.

"Hey Monty, you having a good time?"

"Sure."

"I heard about you and Kathleen like, dating? I didn't think it was gonna work out, rilly. But she likes you, it's good?"

Her way of speaking made every statement sound like a question. "Yes it is, thanks. What about you?"

She rolled her eyes. "I don't need the hassle of trad dates. It's like, I can pick up any guy who's cool and looks good just by hanging round the right places and wearing something like this, ya know?" Kate gestured to the outfit she wore, it certainly highlighted her physical appeal. "I don't see the point of all that, like, effort? Why go on a date if there's no one to televise it, I mean rilly."

"Okay, fine." I sipped my beer while Kate held her drink and regarded me with interest, one arm up on the back of the sofa.

142

"Ya know Monty, Kath and me have this thing when we talk to each other about guys. We have to describe them in, like, three words. You wanna know what my sis said about you?"

"Go on."

"She called you *genuine, confused* and *uncircumcised.*"

I thought about it. "That's pretty good, if a little intimate." Before us the lounge turned into an impromptu dancefloor, people cavorting and stumbling.

Kate smiled. "Way cool."

At this point one of the merrier guests smashed against the sofa, jolting us fiercely. Kate struggled to keep a grip on her can of lager, the liquid sloshing over her legs and my side.

We stood up. "Oh damn!" She laughed. "My skirt's soaked."

I looked at the dark patches decorating my shirt, a garment Kathleen had just bought me in the sales. "I'm pretty damp myself."

"Come on." Kate urged. "I've got a hair dryer in my room."

I followed her through the crowd, pointing to the mess as I passed Kathleen. Kate's round behind led me up the stairs so I followed it into her room, unbuttoning the shirt as I went. Once there the girl threw open the wardrobe, searching through her massed clothing until she found a hair dryer and lobbed it my way. I plugged in the device and switched it to the highest setting. A powerful blast of hot air swiftly dried my stains as I sat on the bed with Kate facing away from me. The girl unzipped her sodden skirt then removed her underwear, tossing black knickers toward the laundry basket. She had a mole on the side of her right buttock. I turned away and switched off the hair dryer, laying the warm shirt over one arm as I moved to leave. But when I made my way out the half-dressed girl blocked my path. Suddenly she was up against me. *"She won't ever know"* whispered Kate, forcing her tongue down my throat.

It took me a second to register what was happening, then a moment longer to realise nothing good could come of it, except maybe some amazing sex with a hot girl. Stepping back, I hit the bed and lost my balance. Kate stood there before me, a burnt ochre triangle below that white t-shirt, the only item she had on. Looking up, the girl's face was expectant and enticing. I can't express how difficult it was to refuse the temptation before me, but anyone who knows senseless lust can understand my agony. All at once I felt victimized and aroused and caddish.

"I'm suh-sorry Kate." I stammered, pathetically. "You're really great and everything, but I can't, I-I..." What did I want to say? Something which might make her leave me alone. But it had to be truthful.

"I.... I think I'm in love with your sister."

Kate nodded. "Good." She said.

The girl turned back to the mess of her wardrobe and extracted some jeans. Not bothering with underwear she climbed into them. "I reckon you might be worthy of her."

"What?"

Kate buckled her trousers and came over to the bed. "Sorry about that Monty, but me and my sister are like, *rilly* close. She's been going on about you so much, it all got a bit dullsville? I wanted to make sure you were all that. For her." The girl ruffled my hair, a mischievous gleam in her eyes. "I thought I'd give you like, a little test? I couldn't lose, either you and my big sis were meant to be or I got a shag out of ya." She rose. "Glad it worked out this way."

Then she was gone, out the door with a flutter of fingers. I remained on her bed, unable to get a grip on events. After a couple of minutes the situation sank in and I decided to get the hell out of Kate's room. Mercifully the bathroom was free so I splashed water onto my face until I was back in control. Then I returned to the party, being met in the hallway by a smiling Kathleen.

"All dry?"

"Erm, yeah, great." I patted my side, wondering if she could see the guilt on my face.

"Kate's been singing your praises." From a group of circling males I saw my girlfriend's sister shake her yellow hair, moving that body as if the music were coursing through her. "She says I'm right about you."

"Oh yeah?" One moment of weakness and I'd have lost everything, everything in my life that was good. I looked at Kathleen. "Describe your sister to me in three words."

"Ooh, that's a good one. Never done that before." Those brown eyes shot upwards as she considered her answer. "I'd say, flirtatious, loyal... maybe a little shallow."

"I'd agree with you on the last one."

"You only say that 'cause you fancy her."

"I don't."

"Be honest, it doesn't matter." My girlfriend watched Kate revel in the attention of men around her. "Everyone digs my sis, I'm used to it by now. Come on, admit she's attractive."

"Only on a very, very, *very* superficial level. I couldn't spend serious time with her, she talks like a fictional American in some TV high school." I impersonated her voice. *"Like, what's that all about?"*

Kathleen put her drink down and pulled me forwards, lips against mine and fingers in my hair. The next track came on, a Jackson Five number.

"Oooh, I love this one. Come and dance!"

I was dragged into the throng, next to Kathleen as she frugged, wondering if this was the right time to explain my disorder, how the path between music reaching Monty's ears and his body responding was strewn with obstacles, unfortunate inhibitions and a terminal self-consciousness. But the music was too loud for chatter, and as this song built to the chorus something very strange happened. The rhythmic movements of my girlfriend, this woman I was only just beginning to understand the depth of my feeling for, proved contagious. Something inside me attuned to the seventies classic and now my limbs began to jerk, a barely perceptible movement in that room of undisciplined dancers, but I felt it. The enthusiasm had infected me and there was nothing to fear by joining in. Not now I'd gone so far as admitting I could, quite feasibly, maybe, if you added up all the evidence, be in love with Kathleen. I moved my feet back and forth, head shaking. This crowd of people didn't have to overthink it, their energy was deployed in the simple pursuit of a good time. And I was dancing with them, with her, Kathleen had brought something out of me I never knew was there.

Then the television was on and the chimes of Big Ben rang through the house. There were cheers and yells of exultation. People let off streamers and held each other, caught up in the hopes of another year. The party lasted until well after midnight, Kathleen eventually thanking each guest for coming and saying her goodbyes. The two of us spent the small hours clearing up and by the time Kathleen deemed the place ready for her mother's easily-freaked senses we were too tired to do anything but fall asleep.

The next morning I left her in bed, bidding farewell with as much affection as my hangover allowed. Mrs. Tibbits had returned and was stand-offish like before, greeting me cursorily in the kitchen before continuing to describe how inadequately she'd been treated at her sister's place. Kate wasn't really listening to her mother, instead she watched me with that knowing gaze. I helped myself to coffee, then offered up gratitude for the hospitality, something the older woman dismissed out of hand.

"I always look out for *friends* of my girls." She announced coldly.

I didn't hang around there long, in fact I was back home by early afternoon, bumping into Mrs. Winterbottom outside her house. She wished me a happy new year and inquired after the girl she'd seen coming out of our flat. I tried to explain that Kathleen and I were seeing each other, but the old lady seemed unable to comprehend that a man who lived with a homosexual could also have a girlfriend. Eventually I gave up and said that Kathleen was a guest, some relative who was staying with us for a while. This seemed to satisfy the old lady and she allowed me to retreat indoors where I spent that first day of the year in a semi-vegetative state. Unlike Fergal or Kathleen my holiday was over. The agency would be open for business on January the second. I had to go in for what we all expected to be an utterly pointless working day.

As it turned out I couldn't have been more wrong, although events didn't turn out to be valuable in exactly the way Martin envisaged. Early on Friday morning the boss issued a 'high importance' email announcing that someone "a bit special" would

146

be talking to us today. All part of his plan to inspire us, get our team ready for the *challenges* of the new year. Speculation from the blondes went on all morning, interrupted only by Justin saying how much of a mess he was after an all-nighter at the *Fleece* superclub where he had to queue for six hours to get his coat. During an appropriate interval I ducked away from the moronic talk to hand Martin my version of *Too Beautiful*. As predicted, the boss was taken aback by how slim the play had become, but he accepted it with good grace. Soon the team were ushered into Mart's office which he'd rearranged to resemble a miniature auditorium. I took a seat in the front row, between Lettice and one of the other girls, when a man who looked as if he'd been hewn from rock came in.

"Good afternoon." Boomed the enormous figure in a southern U.S. accent. "My name is Travis Hurtdabees. I'm here today at the request of my friend Martin Landry..." Mart nodded from behind his desk. "....to tell my story. A story which, I hope, will make you believe that anything is possible."

There was some whispering amongst the blondes about his size, then they quietened down to listen. "I was sixteen and working as a gold prospector in British Columbia when I first got attacked by a grizzly. As you can see I survived to tell my tale." The American held up a scarred forearm, the marks looked like they'd been made by claws. Girls around me made ooh noises. "I was badly hurt that day the bear mauled me, but as I grew up I came to think of it as the most exhilarating day of my life." I looked around the rest of this audience, all watching the speaker dutifully. Nobody seemed to share in my belief; this man was a nut.

Travis continued. "Through my twenties and thirties I worked as a scrap metal dealer and all that time I thought of a dream I'd been having. My ambition was to become what I called a *close-quarter bear researcher.*" He paused for effect. "To achieve this I would have to risk my life again by wrestling a grizzly. It wouldn't be easy. No special equipment existed for that kind of thing, in those days few people shared my dream. I was forced to design the protective clothing myself. It took fifteen years and half a million dollars to assemble the right mixture of steel, chain mail and titanium, but it was worth it. My name went into the Guinness

Book of Records as the creator of the most expensive research suit in history, but more importantly I was ready. This film picks up the story of my quest."

Martin got the lights while Travis fiddled with the video, bringing up a credit sequence for a National Film Board presentation entitled *The Grizzly Project*. The documentary consisted of highlights from several years in the life of Hurtdabees as he worked on various incarnations of what he'd christened *The Ursus Bear Suit*.

The film was certainly entertaining, although I couldn't tell whether the hero intended his life's work to be quite so comedic. On the TV friends and relatives tested Travis's armour by attacking it with pickaxes, throwing logs at his head and knocking him over with a truck. The intrepid researcher emerged from these assaults unscathed, although the suit took a bit of a battering. In-between clips the onscreen Hurtdabees talked of his hopes for the upcoming encounter and, at one point, even picked up a research prize from the Ig Noble awards.

At last Travis was satisfied. The Mark VI bear suit apparently offered enough protection for his work, although it didn't look too solid to me. The thing was covered in duct tape and so unwieldy Hurtdabees couldn't move more than a few yards without falling over. Despite this state of affairs he remained resolutely upbeat as the documentary neared its climax. Somewhere in Canada Travis met up with a wrangler and his bear, the latter of which was very far from being tame. After driving his charge into a state of frenzy with the smell of raw meat, the enormous grizzly was released from its pen by the handler, whereupon it raced over to Hurtdabees. Travis appeared to lose his nerve at this point, confronted with what must have been a male (it looked about three times as big as Poppy), he attempted to run away. A futile action, since the suit rendered even walking difficult. The grizzly knocked him to the ground and started battering the armoured man around like one of those freshwater fish bears pull from rivers. Next to me the blondes made noises of alarm as Travis tried in vain to fulfil his aim of actually wrestling this great mammal. The bear responding to his movements by shredding Travis's suit like it was tinfoil

148

The ordeal ended when the bear wrangler managed to distract his charge with the promise of food that didn't require a can opener. The grizzly abandoned his prey and returned to the pen where a raw salmon dinner awaited him. Once the creature was locked away research assistants rushed to remove the titanium helmet from their motionless employer. Inside his outfit Hurtdabees was out of breath and bruised, but not seriously hurt. Actually the man was exultant, calling for a close-up as he told the camera crew the experience was everything he'd hoped it would be. Travis raised an arm and gave us a thumbs up, then he passed out.

The tape stopped and Hurtdabees addressed the room once more. "I hope that gives you some idea of how much can be achieved with just a little determination and the will to succeed. In the eighteen months since that film came out I've travelled the world with my story and thanks to the goodwill of my public I'm close to completing *The Ursus Mark VII Bear Suit*. I want to thank you all for helping realise the dream by inviting me here today and I wish y'all the very best for your year ahead. I'm sure it'll offer up an exciting set of new challenges. Does anyone have a question for me?"

I raised my hand. "Are bears Catholic?"

"We can't confirm that at the moment." Beside Travis my boss glared at me. "Any others? No? Then I'll leave you by saying that the work you do here at *Bears!Bears!Bears!* impresses me very much. With some of the spirit and teamwork that took me into the record books I'm sure you can make this place even more of a success. I'm Travis Hurtdabees. Be true to yourselves and be true to the bears. Thank you, thank you very much."

The applause died away and Mart rose to offer a more jaundiced motivational talk. Our boss said it was shaping up into a difficult year for the business, but he believed we were the best people to help his agency through these uncertain times. I sat there wondering how much Hurtabees had been paid for his brief talk and longing for caffeine. When at last we were dismissed I was first out the door, halfway to the kitchen before I noticed the ringing phone on my desk.

"Hello?"

"Hi, it's reception, we have a man here to see you."

Oh great. "On my way."

Standing at the front desk was a bristly figure, fortyish with plenty of surplus meat around his middle. The man extended a hairy hand. "Randall Axelrod."

"Monty Sanderson."

"Good to meet you at last." I had no idea who he was. "I'm the bear." Said Randall, by way of explanation.

"The what?" Was there no end to the insane Americans lurking here today?

"The one looking for work?" Randall regarded me hopefully, he was about my height, with a cultured way about him. "You received some emails from me."

"Oh right, those." Had I responded? I suppose I might have in a bored moment, playing along with the joke: *Well done Mr. Bear, if you're ever in the neighbourhood just drop by the office and we'll see what we can do....* "I thought that was a wind up."

"A what?"

"Look, there's not really anywhere to talk here." The blonde receptionist was checking the sheen on her nails while the rest of my agency went back about their business, Mart discussing something with Travis near the entrance. "Tell you what Randall, let me buy you a coffee."

Axelrod added milk and sugar to his decaf mocha. "I'd just got out of a bad relationship and wanted to get as far away from the situation as I could. My sister lives over here and it was just a month's vacation at first, but I found myself liking England, I'm trying to find a reason to stick around." He stirred the drink for longer than was strictly necessary. "I've tried most of the acting agencies but they haven't turned anything up so I thought I'd give *Bears!Bears!Bears!* a go." The American looked at me. "I figured you might find work for people like me, your website makes the business look diverse and open-minded. But I guess you don't deal in man-bears."

"Not really." What the hell was a man-bear? "We mainly use pure ursines, actual animals or commercial projects relating to them." I sipped my drink. "You say you're a bear, what does that mean exactly?"

The bearded man took one look at my questioning face and burst out laughing, a strangely effete sound for one so doughty. "Have you really no idea?" Randall pulled a handkerchief from the pocket of his well-worn suit. "Oh, my dear fellow, do forgive me. I felt sure our little subculture had penetrated your world." I shook my head. "In the USA a bear is one who has facial hair and a little to spare." The American pointed to his belly. "He is, what do you Brits call it? A raiser of the shirt?"

"Shirtlifter."

"Shirtlifter, yes." The penny dropped. Now I knew Randall was gay his mannerisms made a lot more sense. "Of course, there's a lot more to bearness than just being fat, bearded and gay. I could spend hours explaining our philosophy and community, how we meet to support each other rather than pursuing the sexual." He tasted the mocha. "But I suspect I may bore you."

"Possibly not, I have an interest in homosexuality." A persuasive idea was beginning to germinate in my head. "Unfortunately as I've said my agency doesn't deal with actors, we wouldn't know where to start. Sorry I can't be more helpful, but it's best if I'm honest with you Randall. I wouldn't want to waste any more of your time."

"Not at all young fellow, time is the one thing I have plenty of at present. I'm sure something will turn up when things take their due course. You Brits are pioneers of gay drama, I've watched and enjoyed many of your televisual exports and it seems a point of honour that you deal with the gay experience frankly. I only hope some casting director needs a bear soon." He finished the drink. "In the interim I'm not short of funds. I've been enjoying this quaint city of yours at my leisure, although sadly there appears to be nowhere us man-bears can congregate and relax. From what you say I suspect such an oasis does not exist. Gay bars can be fun, but those places rarely play host to my kind of man." I got my first glimpse of the disappointment Randall must have been feeling then, a vague sense of melancholy about the tubby yank hunched over his empty cup.

"Are you free tonight?" I asked him.

Randall looked up. "Yes, but I'm afraid you're not my type Monty. Besides, you're straight. Any moron could see that."

"Thanks Randall, I appreciate it."

"It's quite obvious."

"But that wasn't my point." I smiled at the American. "You see, there's this friend of mine I want you to meet."

Chapter Twelve

We came out of the restaurant and onto the packed streets of Camden. The junction separating roads leading to and from parts of North London bustled. I saw teenagers with pierced faces, minor rock stars and their blonde girlfriends, groups of young males in sagging trousers who sported tattoos on their arms, girls in PVC trousers with spiky backpacks of a fluorescent pink matching their lip gloss, all the bubbling youth of Saturday night. Kathleen took my arm, staying close as we waited for the green man to show, then negotiated the tribes which congregated around the tube station, those punks and goths, metallers and skate-kids, drug dealers muttering of their wares, visitors meeting friends amidst the hordes. All of them sauntered along, some taking advantage of the unseasonably mild January to flaunt legs or midriff, an exhibitionism refusing to be censored by the elements.

I was happy and full, pleased with myself for booking a table earlier today. I'd guessed Kathleen might want to eat out, and she'd been delighted when I told her we were having Indian food, the girl's second favourite after sushi (out of bounds now, and she accepted that). When I picked up our bill I felt moneyed and masculine, a provider. This was where I'd always excelled, second-guessing a girlfriend, paying attention to her likes and dislikes. When my girl least expected it I would show I had been listening all along, spring on her a gift or night out she'd never explicitly asked for but ended up loving. Kathleen was no different from past partners, now we knew each other well I understood what she longed for during the day and how to make her weekend satisfying. I interpreted her flighty impulses or responded to fluctuating moods, from silent pouting to eager seductress. My success at sustaining a relationship was on a par only with my uselessness at dating, once I passed that initial hurdle I came into my own. Beyond the stress of meeting someone who saw me as awkward or sex-crazed at first came the capable Monty..

What I had now with Kathleen, that day to day exchange of affection, felt so much more natural than endless casual encounters. We learnt each other's faults and came to accept them, I en-

153

couraged her through uncertainty and she joked of my hyper-unsureness and clumsy traits. In fact I barely missed the exciting strangeness of being with somebody new, that irreversible loss as you come to know a lover better than anyone. The thrill of a plunge into the unknown may disappear, but in return comes mutual commitment, your lives entwined. I found joy in a romantic routine that left me a girl to share every weekend, liked the ritual of caring deeply about someone. As our honeymoon period wore off, Kathleen and I failed to tire of each other. Odd, because if we'd filled out dating agency forms we would never have been matched. When I was single and agonising over it I didn't look for a skinny blonde with a dirty laugh, rarefied taste in film and a gleaming pink gum appearing below her upper lip when she smiled (*God, how I always used to hate that*). Our profiles simply weren't compatible, but none of that superficial nonsense mattered, the fuzz and bluster of interests with which everyone surrounds their lives. In our souls and hearts Kathleen and I were in harmony, and that was where it counted. This girl was unique, indescribably lovely, and I wouldn't have learnt that by shouting at her in a club, trading banter by email or spending three minutes gabbling in that Godless Babel of speed dating. Beyond novelty and alcohol you have to really get to know a girl, be tolerant and understanding of any failings, give her a chance to overcome false impressions. Then a guy might fall into happiness, just as I had.

The two of us joined music fans in line for *The Alternative Club*, chatting about *The Airborne Toxic Event*'s chances tonight as I felt myself growing nervous. For my friends, of course, but part of the uneasiness was nothing to do with the band. This was the first time I'd been with Kathleen since evading the attentions of her sister and admitting how I felt. Now that I knew the recent upturn to my life, that sense of infinite opportunity which came with every new day, was down to being in love and over the past few days I'd moved from the clarity of an impulse; to tell Kathleen how I felt and thereby move us onto the next level, to the usual fears. What if my love had come too soon? Did she feel the same way? Would announcing I loved her sound desperate and pathetic? If the girl didn't return my sentiment it changed our dynamic, put undue pressure on Kathleen to admit something she didn't feel. What we had was good enough already, if I went charging in with *'I love you'* was I only asking for trouble?

And so my mind went on, a centripetal whirl that couldn't decide what to do. But still I felt the charged need for confession building up inside, these feelings wanted to get out, my heart ready to leap onto my sleeve for Kathleen to crush or embrace at will. She looked at me now and smiled warmly. My girlfriend had sensed some kind of emotional turbulence tonight while we were eating, but I'd claimed the unsettled vibe was down to the heat of my curry and drank two pints of water to prove it.

We reached the front of the queue and I told the simian bloke behind his Plexiglas screen 'Monty Sanderson and one other' would be on the guest list. He gave an ugly grunt and shuffled in his booth for a while, taking long minutes to discover the paperwork that had my name on it. Eventually the illiterate ape gave us permission to enter this L-shaped venue with a seated area just through the entrance. Beyond that lay the stage, a bar running away from the performers against which punters would stand to watch. Giles and Tosspot were gathered at one of the tables, bickering over something or other, while acquaintances of a similar age chattered nearby. Away from this scene the other two members of *The A.T.E.* ordered drinks at the bar.

"Alright kids. Hello Kathleen." Si kissed my girl on the cheek. "What do you want? He's getting them in."

The bassist turned to me. "Couldn't hold it in, eh, Brett?"

"...."

"Well, if you insist. Two bottles would be good, cheers."

Si collected his pint. "What's happening Monty? How's the homo?"

"Waiting for your call Simon, as ever."

Actually on Friday afternoon I'd returned from work to find Fergal still in his bathrobe, flicking through television channels in a listless fashion.

"Put some clothes on mate, we've company on the way."

"Don't worry about me." Fergal glanced up, he hadn't shaved for a couple of days. "I'll just go to my room."

155

"No you won't. He's coming to meet you." I tidied away the magazines and dishes littering our lounge. Ever since Fergal stopped leaving the flat he'd lost interest in keeping it clean, an irritating paradox which meant I was doing more housework than ever before, although Kathleen took charge whenever I convinced her to stay. "Our guest is a very interesting homo I met through work. He's new to the London scene and needs someone to show him the best places to go cruising, or whatever it is you perverts get up to."

"Oh my God, don't tell me you've fetched up some naive Spanish chicken. I've told you before Montgomery, I'm not interested in a man simply because he shares my sexual disposition."

"No, he's a very interesting American, and you'd better show him a good time because I spent a long time talking you up when I should have been working." I opened a window to let out the mustiness. "It's time you got back in the mix Cofaigh."

"Bloody hell Montgomery, whatever's happened to you?" He rose from the armchair. "Before Kathy came along you wouldn't say boo to a gay."

"Just get dressed."

By the time Randall Axelrod arrived, descending on our little flat like a patriarch returning to the family ranch, Fergal had dressed in varieties of tweed and consented to give the visitor a tour of his favourite haunts. Randall was funny and charming, complimenting my flatmate on his taste in artists before being singularly impressed by Dennis. The American inspected that six foot hamster from many angles before declaring it "the stuff of Richard Gere's nightmares.".

By the time they left Fergal had overcome any trepidation at returning to the social whirl. He was somewhat taken aback by Axelrod's certainty we would warm to him, but my flatmate couldn't fail to be impressed by Randall's buoyant talk, his knowledge of their shared interests. It was a good thing Fergal had the advantage of home turf, because for once he was in the presence of somebody more charismatic and worldly than himself. Just as I'd suspected, Randall was more than a match for my flatmate, and I reckoned their differing cultures could provide excellent topics for conversation. Indeed, Randall left the flat talking of the quarter Irish in him, while Fergal was growing more and more intrigued by man-bears. Smugly observing them disappear, I realised I still had it. Monty Sanderson remained a master of social matchmaking and after describing the scenario at length to Kathleen on the phone I had a quiet night in

Waking up on Saturday morning I initially felt disappointment when Fergal rose by himself, having slept alone. But the American proved the only subject matter that Saturday, my flatmate so enamoured he took it upon himself to reinstate our breakfast chats, a tradition that had vanished over the months as Cofaigh's downbeat mood left me preparing my own toast.

"I'm going to let it grow out." Fergal rubbed his stubble, shaking a frying pan with the other hand. "What do you think?"

"I think if you leave it long enough you'll have a beard."

"Thank you Montgomery, very helpful." He dropped eggs onto our plates. "Did Randall tell you about man-bears?"

"He did."

"You know, I can't believe I'd never heard of them before. All that gay literature of mine and no mention of 'bears' anywhere." He set breakfast before us. "Randall recommended some American authors to me, apparently his creed regard a beard as a kind of mystery on the face. He's a fascinating individual that man, lived in all sorts of places. I took Randall down *The Pink Oboe* and the gang absolutely loved him. They were quite jealous of me. Derek came out with a load of guff, how he detested American imperialism and the genocide of the Indians, but Randall's acutely aware of the problems in his country, he grew up there after all. Randall asked Derek why he was wearing American brand clothes if he was so against the USA and that completely threw the silly boy, I felt quite giddy."

"Uh-huh." I had no idea who Derek was. "So you're glad I brought him round?"

Fergal's eyes met mine. "I won't forget this Montgomery. Everyone was enormously pleased to see me and when they met Randall the gang all thought I'd been having a better time without them. I felt like a Sherpa returning from a mission out in the wilderness with some strange, charming yeti. We gathered round and listened to Randall's stories for hours, and that was when I had what you might call an epiphany."

"Oh yeah?"

"Yes. I've been wasting time my friend. I'm sure you knew this already, but I simply hadn't seen it." He impaled a piece of bread on his fork and mopped up oozing yolk. "If a man loses faith in the life he's always had what is he to do? He can't simply give up. But that's what I did for a while, much as it pains me to admit it. Last night I saw the answer at last. One doesn't stop, it's just a question of changing the ol' priorities." Fergal set his cutlery down and began to flick through the paper.

"Did you see this? Scientists have attached video cameras to cockroaches. They've tiny microphones too. Once more my mind is well and truly boggled."

"That's interesting." I finished my coffee and went to make more. "Are you seeing Randy again?"

"Please refrain from calling him Randy, he hates that." Fergal checked the clock. "I'd better get away now, I'm meeting the good Mr. Axelrod in less than an hour. We've arranged to go shopping."

"Shopping?"

"Yes, Randall needs some things and he doesn't know where to go...." Fergal tailed off, I'm sure his face had reddened. "You should know Montgomery, nothing has occurred between us. I'm not even sure I want him that way. The man is old enough to be my father."

"No he's not."

"Almost, he almost is." My flatmate gathered up our dishes and put them in the sink. "The point is, I'm not letting this year slip away like the last one. Now, if you'll excuse me I'd best be on my way. I take it you won't object to dealing with the washing up?"

"Erm, okay."

Then Fergal was gone, off to the boutiques and outfitters of central London with his new friend, and he hadn't returned when I left to meet my girl, shortly after the football results.

In the club Kathleen thanked Brett for her drink and we stayed at the bar to watch the support act, a female-fronted twee-pop outfit who used cardboard boxes as percussion. The rest of *The Airborne Toxic Event* joined us, extricating themselves from hangers-on, those friends and relatives induced along tonight through emails, garish flyers and accusations of disloyalty. Tosspot extended a slim arm for an ostentatious handshake, drowning out the mimsy acoustic strumming with his talk.

"You think the record companies are here?"

I glanced around the venue. "Could be. Anyone over thirty and dressed like someone's dad is usually from A&R."

Simon cut in. "I rang round yesterday with the info you gave me and a couple of labels said they'd already arranged to send someone down. I tried to persuade everyone else by quoting from *Plectrum Abuser.*" He clapped me on the back. "Sending that article with the demo really did the trick."

"Yeah, well. It's up to you now."

Tosspot handed me a creased piece of paper. "Here's the set-list, what d'you think?"

I glanced down at the song titles, all scrawled childishly in felt pen. "*Mensa Bimbo* second? Yeah, that's good. What's *The Antipope?*"

"That's our new title for the anti-Catholic number, Giles thought it up." The drummer nodded, satisfied with his work. Their list was grouped into two sets of four split by an 'Interlude'.

"Looks fine to me." They'd clearly put some thought into the sequencing for once. "What time you on?"

"Ten." Tosspot addressed his bandmates. "And we're not getting drunk before then, *are we?*"

The other three shook their heads, they were taking this seriously. I joined Kathleen who was enjoying whimsical ditties from the support act. It must have been pleasurable for her to watch a female singer in the ever-masculine world of the independent scene.

Ever since filing my copy for *The Pop Shots'* show I'd refused gig offers from *Plectrum Abuser's* editorial desk, telling those velvet-voiced girls who phoned me at work how "personal matters" and "prior commitments" prevented me from reviewing bands for the immediate future. My excuses were proximate to the truth, I *was* preoccupied, although it was more to do with my girlfriend than any tricky private issues. Kathleen saw enough uninteresting bands during her four shifts a week at the *5 Easy Pieces*, so she was reluctant to spend precious nights off having her eardrums assaulted by more no-hopers around London's scummier clubs. I'd heard it all before too and preferred to use my free time for endeavours I believed in, like the publicity campaign for this gig. When I wasn't hassling contacts in the music business on behalf of *The A.T.E.* I redrafted Martin's play, rehearsals for which began in a few weeks with Kathleen in the now-pivotal role of Jo, the lead character's sometime lover.

That jangling support band left the stage, then immediately returned to pack away their equipment and several squashed boxes. I put both arms around Kathleen's waist, my hands directly below hers, joining in with the applause. She turned in my embrace, smiling.

"Enjoying yourself?"

"I am."

"They're going to be good you know." The declaration was mainly to convince myself.

"I'm sure they are." She wriggled free. "Come on, let's get a seat."

We spent the next half hour talking with acquaintances, people who'd attached themselves to the band's entourage. I saw Kathleen chatting to a girl with profoundly red hair who could only have been Tosspot's sister, showing all the friendly gregariousness I adored in her. A guy I vaguely recognised was standing nearby and when I introduced myself he turned out to be a fellow freelancer for the music press whose coverage of tonight's gig would appear in next week's *Plectrum Abuser*. I talked up the headliners and their role as ground-breakers of some spurious movement I made up on the spot, *the new loud or the return of the rock* or something. After my briefing the journo went off to a dark corner by the mixing desk and started scribbling away. I looked forward to seeing some of my words under his by-line.

The club got busy, that few hundred capacity close to being met as it became more difficult to get served at the bar. A number of people gathered at the front while a soundman made sure the vocals were audible through a trio of microphones lined up onstage. Three seemed inexplicable to me since they'd only ever rehearsed with one, although I think Si added backing vocals on a couple of the demo tracks. I collected Kathleen from the seated area and squeezed through, others following us to the front. By the time the DJ faded his music down our crowd had filled the space.

Those who knew Brett and Si made hooting noises when the pair came out and plugged in their guitars, a swift tune up conducted with the minimum of fuss. Giles was next to appear, wearing a pair of dark glasses which made him look a bit like Stevie Wonder the drummer took his place at the rear. Then the lanky frame of Tosspot came from the wings carrying a bottle of water and the set list. The singer put stuff down on either side of the microphone stand and used a hand to shield his eyes, squinting out at the audience as if he couldn't quite believe its size.

"Evenin'." Cries of *whoo* floated up. "We're *The Airborne Toxic Event* and this is *Copacetic.*"

From behind the drums Giles yelled *"1-2-3-4"* and the band crashed in like the initial shock of an earthquake. It's difficult to convey quite how high the volume was, but those people standing to the sides, inches away from the speakers, came to resemble astronauts under the influence of G-Force. The band were tight as well as deafening, Simon's choppy guitar lines pulling us in while the rhythm section provided a forceful undertow. This was an attention-grabbing start, abrasive and uncompromising, Tosspot half-yelling and half-singing the lyrics.

"Well fed! Contented! Work 'til you drop!
Keep our country going! Don't let you ever stop!"

The power kept building, guitarwork threatening to spiral out of control as Tosspot's voice grew hoarse, repeating the words *well fed* over and over again. I felt certain something had to give, an amp blowing under the pressure or maybe a string would break, but they managed to end it together. Silence for a split second, then the band segued into *Mensa Bimbo*. Here was their trump card, an

161

ability to switch from ferocious to tuneful in an instant, the singer's voice clear and strong.

"I tried to fit into your life, but somehow there wasn't time,
I'm the letters L-A-N-D, fallen from your Hollywood sign."

Simon provided backing vocals as they hit the chorus, emphasizing the song's hook while a pocket of dancing broke out, some of the more inebriated crowd members shuffling around gracelessly. The song ended in *ba-ba-bahs* and we erupted in applause.

"Thanks everyone, cheers for turning up tonight." Tosspot took a swig of water while the musicians glanced at each other, eyes making sure there weren't any technical problems. There weren't. "This is our *Anthem For Groomed Youth*."

Another catchy track which kept our heads nodding, this song was inspired by Tosspot's discovery of a 'hair-restoring' shampoo in his local supermarket, a miraculous product which he believed to have been specially formulated by wizards. After the warm reception to their opening the singer had lost his inhibitions, Tosspot jerked and twitched in that signature way of his now, a restless ball of movement. I was surprised by how much power dual vocals gave to the chorus until I looked right and realised Brett was adding his voice to the mix. Amazing, how they discovered the bassist had a singing voice I'd no idea but it was a masterstroke. Brett's deep growl filled out the sound, took their 'anthem' to a whole new level.

The band followed this song with the mathematically precise stop-start dynamics of *Archipelago*, bringing the first half to a brooding conclusion. The crowd lapped it up, cheering through the unexpected twist this performance now took. At the back Giles replaced his sticks with brushes while Si and Brett turned to face one another and play a series of apparently improvised notes.

"This is your intermission." Behind the singer *The A.T.E.* worked it out. "If you need to get a drink now's the time to do it."

Tosspot went to the side of the stage where someone passed him a bottle of lager and a towel. The rest of the group were having great time, looking to each other for cues, Si making his guitar sound like a toy piano while behind the kit Giles sat bolt upright, holding the rhythm like he could do this in his sleep. Their frontman sat on one of the speakers and watched them play for a couple of minutes, sipping his beer and leading the applause when the jazz-funk interlude reached its conclusion.

"Thanks, hope you enjoyed that one. We call it '*If You Don't Like My Potatoes, Why Do You Dig So Deep?*'" Laughter from the crowd. "It won't be our next single, in fact I doubt we'll even remember it tomorrow so you're very privileged." Tosspot checked the set list. "Right, we ready? Good. This one's for anybody who's ever been touched up by a priest."

They launched into *The Antipope* with a fury which came as a surprise after the instrumental. This was their fastest track and possibly the most hummable, like some punk classic updated to soundtrack the twenty first century. The song reinvigorated the crowd, some even jumping up and down, caught in the energy of it all. Their animation continued through the next number which was close to wordless. The only sounds Tosspot made during *Kinetic* were a series of yelps and shrieks as he threw himself around the stage, this movement matching the track's title. Spotlights flashed on the band as they built up a rock face of sound, stopping all of a sudden to leave the frontman on his knees, groaning into the microphone.

"Thanks, thanks a lot." Tosspot struggled to his feet. "Two more to go. We having a good time?"

"*Rearh!!*"

"Cool. We're gonna do *A Town Called Bastard* for you people now." The singer ran a hand through his matted ginger hair. "It's about being trapped. Uh, we hope you enjoy it...."

Another potential single, this one was written after the band watched the film of the same name and featured an off-kilter guitar solo combined with a chant-along chorus, Brett joining in on the *"yeah, yeah, yeahs"*.

The crowd lapped up this most conventionally pop moment of their set, were left breathless as the track ended, either due to over-enthusiastic dancing or sheer awe. I sensed the audience wondering how they were going to top that but sensibly the band

163

didn't even try. Instead they seamlessly switched gears into closing number *Contrail*, a song which began and ended with the drone of Si's guitar. In-between Tosspot crooned of a final departure by a loved one, off to some faraway, conflict-ridden land. After his story ended the singer dropped out while the rest of his band raised both volume and pace, building up to an ear-splitting maelstrom of noise. Giles rose into the air each time he whacked the drums and Simon's fingers were a blur on the guitar strings, sustaining this molten intensity for longer than I thought possible, then slowly easing back into that incessant sound which started the piece. At this point Tosspot abandoned his place onstage and jumped down beside Kathleen and me, watching the band play from our viewpoint. After a minute or so Brett dropped out leaving only guitar and drums, then Giles fell away and we were left with just the drone, a noise which went on and on until, boredom threatening to intervene, Simon cut it out.

Their set was over, it had been a triumph. Tosspot leapt up to the microphone and thanked everyone, his voice drowned out by hollering from the crowd.

"They were good." Shouted Kathleen.

"I know."

The applause should have died away in the traditional manner, but just as I was expecting the DJ to put a record on the clapping was replaced by a duller noise. A hundred pairs of feet stamped the floor in unison, people chanting all the while.

"More! Mooore!"

The band re-emerged looking a little sheepish. Tosspot stepped up to address us.

"Thanks everyone, you've been great. As have we." From behind the drums Giles threw a sweaty rag at his head. "They say there's time for one more." A cheer. "But, uh, we didn't plan for this, so it'll have to be a cover."

"The cheeky song!" Yelled one wag.

Tosspot smiled indulgently. "Maybe next time sir. This one's for our good friend Monty, without whom, etcetera, etcetera...."

"Whoo!" Kathleen bounced up and down.

"Yeah, whatever." The lead singer looked a little embarrassed, he wasn't good at sincerity. "This is a *Tripmaster Monkey* song."

Si cranked out the intro to *Shutter's Closed* and the band kicked in, cutting a swathe through this familiar melody, the best track from one of my favourite LPs. All of a sudden I was back in the teenage years, a sensation inside the same one I felt when discovering loud guitars, girls, booze, freedom. Tosspot's singing was pitch-perfect and now even Kathleen joined in with the movement, people taking their last chance to dance along on this pivotal night. I watched my girlfriend move, feeling overcome by it all, by her beauty and the day, by everything that was happening. That buzz inside my head and a warmth in my heart, all emanating from my friends and this girl and the song.

Then it was over, the crowd dispersed and I was left with Kathleen in my arms. "You did very well tonight." She said.

Up on the stage Brett began unplugging equipment as a soundman dismantled the drums. I looked around for the rest of the band and found them at the bar, deep in conversation with a man in his late thirties wearing a beige shirt tucked into stone-washed jeans. Bingo. Several other music-biz types flitted around waiting for their chance, frustrated but determined, like balding male groupies. *The A.T.E.* would secure a record deal on the strength of this performance, I felt sure of it.

"Thank you for coming my dear." I kissed Kathleen on her forehead. "I'd never have enjoyed it as much without you by my side."

"Every time I give you a compliment you give me one back, why is that?"

"I have to flatter you in return, I see it more like a challenge than a rule."

Kathleen placed a hand on the back of my neck and brought my mouth to hers. We kissed and then I stood there, in the middle of a Camden club smelling of sweat and coarse tobacco, with plastic glasses rolling around on the sticky floor, and told Kathleen I loved her.

The girl held my gaze. "I love you too Monty." She smiled. "You want to say goodbye to your friends now?"

I don't remember leaving *The Alternative Club*, or boarding the tube home. Nor do I recall walking from the station or even going up the stairs to my flat. I was lost in her eyes the whole time, thinking about what had happened, letting myself be convinced that, yes, she did love me as intensely as I loved her. What we had was real and mutual and ours.

That talk of chastity on our first date had been misleading, just as Fergal suggested. My girlfriend wasn't abstinent, not by any means. But then again, neither had we explored each other like we did that night. I mean, sure, there was satisfaction in the past, as our relationship grew in stature so the sexual side of what we had became more powerful, a gradual development which kept me enthralled and wanting more. But when we got back to my bed that night all those boundaries we'd once observed were gone. We came together as never before, soaking the sheets with sweat in spite of the January freeze, Kathleen responding to my touch with a directness and hunger that was new to me. Because now we knew how big this thing was, we'd confessed the deepest of all feelings, a shared love written on our hearts but never deciphered until now. Those words passing between us added an extra dimension to the night, left us destined and free. When I eventually fell asleep in the early hours I was utterly spent, barely able to move. Exhausted from explorations on this new level, the passion and symbiosis, I passed gratefully into dreamless sleep.

Late Sunday morning the phone rang in our lounge. Unsure whether Fergal was in or not I struggled out of Kathleen's embrace but the shrill sounds had ended by the time I threw on a dressing gown and made it to the living room. Randall Axelrod was there, holding the receiver to his ear.

"Uh-huh. Yep, he's here." The American wore a pair of my flatmate's pyjamas. He handed me the phone. "For you."

"Hello?"

"Hello Monty," said mum. "Your father died last night."

Chapter Thirteen

In August 1982, four months after winning his only Oscar (for *On Golden Pond*) Henry Fonda succumbed to a long bout of heart disease. On that balmy summers day Jane hurried to her father's side to say goodbye, so preoccupied she left her car in gear outside the hospital entrance. Thanks to the swift actions of an orderly who jumped into the unlocked vehicle as it rolled down the driveway to apply the handbrake, no damage was done, but leaving her car like this gives us some indication of how desperate Jane was. She needed to see her father one last time, share whatever private thoughts the two of them failed to mention in less emotionally fraught times. Only when catastrophe hits do true feelings make themselves known, bubbling to the surface as the normal junk and noise recedes into the background.

Maybe Jane would have burst into the room and absolved her father, forgiven all the times he unwittingly hurt her, those off-hand remarks which led to a father-daughter dialogue often conducted through the gutter press. Forgiven the emotional distance, that coldness and disapproval he exuded all his life. Maybe Henry would have let his daughter know how much he cared, how proud he was to see her grow up successful and strong. Perhaps he'd have spoken of his contentment at the end of this full and varied life, there may even have been gratitude, for buying the rights to *On Golden Pond* especially for him. We'll never know. Henry was dead by the time Jane got to him.

My father's death wasn't like Henry Fonda's, his came fast and unexpectedly. Within minutes of feeling a pain in his chest dad was gone. One seismic shock of coronary thrombosis was enough for his heart to give up, that muscle ruptured horribly, as if a wild horse had kicked him in the thorax. Dad collapsed last Saturday, during one of his brief forays into the house and entirely without warning if my mother is to be believed. One minute he was reading a paper while she watched television the next there came a low whine, like someone letting helium out of a balloon. He fell to the floor and the dogs rushed to his prone form, licking my father's hand as if to revive him. It was no use. I'd been back three days and only now was it registering, how I'd never see dad again.

Up in the attic I sorted through boxes of his papers, trying to separate the relevant from the disposable, having difficulty concentrating on what I was doing as dust motes circled the dim bulb above. This space still held his smell, that scent of rain-sodden jackets and day-old aftershave which dad carried with him wherever he went. I was never conscious of this odour before but now I'd registered it the smell hit me everywhere I went.

When I wasn't lapsing into thoughts of him, memories triggered by objects and fragrance, I worked mechanically, taking each crate of detritus and sorting it into three piles. There was 'obvious rubbish', 'needs to be kept' and 'ask mum'. The first heap was by far the largest, Dad appeared to have kept every piece of paperwork he'd ever received, from decade old bank statements to unopened junk mail. I found items his office had thrown out years ago that "might come in handy one day"; keyboards and mousemats and floppy disks pulled from skips around the industrial estates. The scale of my task was monumental, there was a tonne of stuff up here, but sorting through it gave me something to do. Whenever I'd accumulated a carload of rubbish I made a trip to the dump, driving a family car I wasn't insured on, and propelled dad's belongings into the enormous metal containers. And all the time I was really somewhere else, my body vacant as an abandoned building.

In the lounge my mother sorted through his clothes, decided which items might be suitable for the charity shops, disposed of older belongings which were tattered and frayed from years of wear. Mum was quicker to come to terms with the situation than me, on Monday morning she was up at dawn, ready to eradicate every trace of her dead husband from the house. Whether it came from strength of character or that same unfeeling quality which saw dad banished to the shed during his lifetime I couldn't tell. Up until today I'd been unable to help her, instead I slumped on the sofa watching bad TV, my mind returning to those years growing up in his company, what he'd given me, how life would differ from now on.

I arrived in Basingstoke on Sunday afternoon after two hours of agony, pretending nothing was wrong until Kathleen had left my flat. Catching a train, I trekked half a mile in heavy rain from the station, mum holding me for long minutes while she wept. My close family suddenly felt very tiny, just myself and this stricken woman versus a world ready to drop disaster on our heads without a qualm. Mum told me I was the man of the house now, the only one left in her life, and she needed me now if we were going to get through this. I remembered what my mother was like during the last years of his life and felt bothered by her hypocrisy, wondering if his heart attack had been exacerbated by that self-imposed exile in the shed. Whether she could have been more understanding, helped reduce the stress dad must have suffered.

Over the next few days mum picked herself up, put the histrionics of grief aside and prepared herself for the unknown textures of this new life. I barely managed to rouse myself from the sofa, only rising for meals or to walk the dogs through frostbitten fields. Sheba and Betty absorbed the despondency at one remove, sloping around the house as if unwell or anaesthetized. It's impossible to tell whether an animal feels grief or loss, their countenance gives too little away, but even if the collies failed to notice dad's absence, were only responding to the negative atmosphere left behind, their behaviour touched me. The dogs refrained from jubilance and there was little boisterous canine play. Rather than battling energetically for some ephemeral object, some stick or ball, the collies joined me in front of the TV, nuzzling up or laying a head on my feet, offering what consolation they could for this strange human matter which beleaguered me.

In the end I spent most of Sunday and Monday watching football, the F.A. Cup third round, normally my favourite soccer weekend of the year when part-timers from obscure hamlets take on the most sought after players in the world. A time of the underdog, when an unemployed pipe-fitter could tussle with Europe's most expensive forward, or a tree surgeon from Nantwich might put one past the England goalkeeper. This year the matches failed to stimulate, I was uninterested in the drama, those big days out when half the inhabitants of a town travel to the gigantic stadium of their

Premiership opponents. My mind was elsewhere, numb inside and distracted further whenever my mother took a break from her efforts. Then she would take up her ever-developing monologue while I sat nearby in silence.

"I knew this would happen, it's always those left behind who deal with the mess. Did he ever think about who would deal with all that rubbish when he brought it home? We'll be at it for weeks. But that was your father all over, always assuming he'd live forever. I remember how he looked at me when I told him to get a life insurance policy back when you were little. It was unbelievable to him anything could happen. I was working on Brian for months and we argued for hours, but without it I'd have been left with no one to provide for us. He said it was a waste of money, but then we moved here and he finally got one and thank God he kept it up. Touch wood we'll have enough to pay off the mortgage, that's one less thing to worry about. I don't know what benefits I'll get but it won't be enough, that's for sure, I'll have to get a part-time job I suppose. There's no inheritance either so don't go fooling yourself, I'm not. He didn't earn enough to put any away, I know that for a fact....."

And so on, until it became a blessing to wake up this morning and feel like helping out at last. In his car or shed I could escape these speeches, opinions I didn't want to hear or anxieties I couldn't cure. To me our loss rendered petty concerns like money and work irrelevant. They'd be resolved in the fullness of time, but the man who taught me about life was gone. My father's legacy didn't seem huge, but he'd been an important figure in my ongoing attempts to be a man, and without his efforts we'd never have got off that noisy council estate.

My mother stayed in the house every day during this period. She wanted to be there for calls from colleagues and friends who rang to offer condolences or ask about the service. Journeys into the outside world were left to me. Even that short walk to the shed was beyond my mother, she "couldn't bear to face" what was inside. So I bagged up the clothes and bedding dad stored there, studying his tools and utensils with a scrap dealer's asperity. Everything which wasn't essential to the everyday maintenance of the garden went outside to be removed later.

I threw out corrugated steel and cracked plant pots, wooden runners and plastic sheeting, broken shovels and bent metal trays. Inside one of dad's many jars of miscellany, in amongst the screws and used batteries, I found the gold-plated bicycle clips I'd bought him as a birthday present one year when I was a kid. Sitting on the cot, the gas heater alight beside me, I turned the gilded fasteners over in my hands. Each bore the inscription 'dad', engraved by a local jeweller. They must have come from that period when my father was briefly between cars and elected to cycle to work, a routine only lasting a few weeks one summer. During that time my father would come home drenched in sweat and full of criticism for drivers who had "no respect". Studying the clips now, a lump came to my throat. What if he'd stuck at it? Taken that extra hour of exercise every day. Might dad have stayed strong? Would his heart still beat now?

The evening of my father's death an ambulance took more than thirty minutes to arrive. Dad had the misfortune to be taken ill just as Saturday night kicked in. At that time the emergency services are preoccupied by the high street, called to bars and pubs as they stitch up brawlers or deal with underage girls whose stomachs need pumping. The doctors told my mother that it wouldn't have mattered. Even if the medical crew had arrived in minutes, even if she knew first aid and pressurized his chest with her hands, my father still wouldn't have survived.

I watched the dogs sniff areas of the garden, inspecting plants and shrubs with their wet noses. Dad envied these animals their freedom, an utter lack of interest in legacies, the dislocation from posterity or commitment. I wonder if he also wished for their lack of emotional attachment. Possessions didn't cast a nostalgic hold over creatures the way they did us humans. How foolish it was to hoard things we'd never use again.

I pocketed the clips and left that shed for my room. Once there I pulled everything which reminded me of childhood out of the cupboards and drawers, packing items into crates. A kid somewhere might enjoy this parcel of action figures, comic books, cartoon playing cards, but I was beyond it all. The Montgomery of my past wasn't the man I'd grown into, I would never return to those days when toys and games filled my life. These hobbies were part of growing up, and my adolescence was over. To keep this stuff was just another symptom of my unwillingness to let go. It was time to let go.

After clearing the shelves and drawers I lay on the bed and turned on my mobile. This was the first time I'd checked the phone since coming back, as I expected the voicemail symbol flashed up.

"Hi Monty, it's Mart. Listen mate, sorry to hear about your dad. Don't worry about coming in, take as long as you want, Justin seems to have everything under control...." I allowed myself a smile. "....and I know how much needs sorting at times like this. It's not like there's anything pressing here so have a couple of weeks, whatever it takes. Give me a call when you're ready to come back, just so we know. Okay mate, look after yourself. Oh, and thanks for the work you did on the play, very imaginative. Liked it."

I thought about the work he mentioned. During my research into *Too Beautiful* I came to realise why Richey Edwards was an iconoclastic figure to so many. Unlike most pop stars he had a coherent philosophy and was better read than his fans, the man full of quotable aphorisms. Richey once said a conventional career was nothing more than "thirty years of slow death". He'd been right in dad's case. Each year sapped a little more from my father until he finally slipped away, ashen-faced and old before his time.

The second and final person to leave me a message had a faint but distinctive Irish accent.

"Montgomery, where are you laddo? You can't just switch off and disappear without a word for goodness sakes. I've had that young lady of yours on the phone and you can imagine what it was like. Speak to her will you? Personally I couldn't care less what you're up to, but young Kathy thinks your vanishing act is connected to whatever went on last Saturday. She said you were acting very oddly the next day, so I told her that was par for the course, but she wouldn't be mollified. Whatever craic it is you're on, explain it to her. Got that? Good. I'm going to hang up now, but I hope to see you soon. Randall was a little worried but I told him you were a big boy. Not as big as me of course, but that goes without saying." He paused. "Oh yes, and about Randall, I'll just say *thanks* and leave it at that. He's exactly what I needed." Another brief silence, then the sarcasm returned. "Right then, better go before I burst into tears like the big ol' fairy I am. Goodbye my friend."

I deleted the messages and switched off my phone. Kathleen and Fergal had abseiled into my thoughts many times since skipping the capital, but I still didn't feel like talking with either of them, and I wasn't about to burden others with my loss. These negative feelings, that gnawing grief which dictated my days, it was best kept to myself. All that supposedly regenerative talk, poking and prodding the pain like a fascinating blemish you won't allow to heal, that was the way of the charlatan psychoanalyst, the self-obsessed fool. Englishmen kept their emotions inside. We didn't inflict tragic matters on anyone else because, despite shows of sympathy, they didn't need all that misery. Fergal was happy with his new man, he shouldn't be brought to earth with talk of fathers and death. And Kathleen? Well, Kathleen I loved, and when you love someone you want to spare them unhappiness. I was doing the right thing, protecting her from this situation, but Fergal was right too. She deserved better than being kept in the dark. Since I didn't trust myself to keep control if I spoke to her, I decided to send my girlfriend a text message later that evening. Tell Kathleen I was alright, how she shouldn't worry, end by expressing my love, let her know I'd be in touch soon.

My father knew the importance of protecting others from these harsh truths, dad always kept his feelings locked away, hidden behind a barrier of affability and habit. The British were often criticised for their collective character, that stiff upper lip which enabled us to get on with routines where lesser mortals might crumble. But next to someone like Kathleen's mother, a woman with no screen between how she felt and expressing it, dad's repression seemed kind of noble. The man had his bad days, for sure, but he never complained, just like he never discussed the past. The time before my memories started was something of a mystery, I knew little of his life before me. Now I'd lost my chance to learn more first-hand.

Perhaps a sentimental guy would have felt sorrow about that fact, but it wasn't sensible to dwell on what might have been. Regretting dad's failure to share locked-off aspects of his life was to wish on him a whole different personality. As Jane Fonda said of Henry: *"We've never been intimate. My dad is simply not an intimate person. But that doesn't mean there isn't love."* I could have asked Brian questions while he was alive but I wouldn't have got any answers. Whenever I talked of anything personal my father just looked at me strangely and glossed over the subject. That's what happened when I was a blundering kid, asking how he and mum met, why they'd fallen in love. Had dad lived to be a contented nonagenarian I refuse to believe I'd have learnt anything more.

I carried the crates downstairs and told mum about my toys, how they were going to Save The Children with the rest of our donations. Mum mentioned who had telephoned today and what they'd said, how she played the dutiful wife for casual acquaintances, people who still believed my parents' marriage was a success. In the *Basingstoke Advertiser* I checked the death announcements but there were no local names sharing my grief. The newspaper only contained a report of negligence at an undertaking firm, staff accidentally cremating a man who should have been buried. Then they tried to cover up the mistake by putting an old woman and some bricks inside his coffin. What the culprits didn't foresee was that this man would be exhumed a year later, and his family were now suing the company for a huge sum. The story depressed me, it added a farcical element to the tragedy of death, robbed the ceremonies we cling to of their palliative powers.

My mother brought two plates of chilli con carne to the table and we ate. For several days I'd possessed little appetite, forcing the food down as a service to my mother without satisfaction, but today my hunger was back. Unfortunately with the hunger came my sense of taste, a mixed blessing with mum's cooking, and it only took a few bites of the spicy meal before my eyes began to water. As if there hadn't been enough tears shed around here of late. After plenty of water to counteract the burning I ploughed on, eventually excusing myself when five hours of prime-time television in my mother's company seemed less enticing than the prospect of continuing the work.

I plugged in the attic light and set a metal ladder against the wall, clambering back up into the dull clutter of that roofspace. So far I'd worked from the entrance backwards, but now I decided to sort through some of the junk piled around the edges, items the Sandersons brought with them from Montgomery Road and hadn't looked at since. With some difficulty I navigated a path through the beams and obstacles, lifting dusty boxes into the space I'd created. I knocked my head on the swinging bulb, whacked an elbow against a wooden support, swore twice, then got down to it.

Much was the same as before, detritus and trash. Evidently dad had been hoarding used chequebooks and old travel brochures all his life. Things only got interesting at the bottom of a nondescript box where I found half a dozen envelopes of the kind used to store photographs. As far as I knew dad had no pictures of his own, all the photos from his marriage were mounted in my mother's family album, a depressing book depicting the erosion of smiles and face-lines deepening as the years passed. Of the six envelopes, five were empty of photographs and negatives, but the last contained one print, a snap I'd seen somewhere before. In the picture a pair of pretty girls, sisters aged about three and five, wore pink dresses and smiled for the camera. The younger of the two had a ribbon in her hair, while the elder's lips were wide apart, revealing a pink upper gum and the Arthenian mishmash of disintegrating baby teeth.

I stared at the photograph for a long time, unable to work out how a smaller version of the photograph in Kathleen's hallway had ended up with my father's belongings. There was no explanation I could think of which made sense. Dad wasn't the kind of man to lech over little girls. If he had been there would surely be more evidence than a single snapshot, hidden away in that morass of dreck and untouched for years.

So I continued to look at the picture of my girlfriend and her sister without understanding what it meant. That is, until a possible reason occurred to me, an explanation so horrendous and implausible I knew, somewhere amongst the fear and nausea engulfing my being, that it had to be true.

Chapter Fourteen

Grey and black clouds rolled across the sky, like furies hurrying to punish wrongdoers. They gave the lie to those who assured me there'd be no rain today. My father's associates had all seen the meteorological reports, the prognosis was cold and dry according to these men stood with us at the graveside. They were my fellow pallbearers, dad's boss and his colleagues from the office, middle-aged men Brian socialised with standing beside friends of my mother who knew Brian through her. Our heads were bowed, the vicar reciting his sermon, talk of the dead man's journey into the Lord's kingdom, Brian Sanderson's qualities as a husband and father, how he'd be welcomed into the next world.

This speech would have meant nothing to dad. Religion, heaven, the sympathy of a beneficent God, such considerations came well below the football pools and his income tax returns on my father's list of priorities. I stole a glance at the mourners, each swaddled in black and lost in a private world, places where Brian evoked memories, images of the dead man. None of these people really knew my father. He let them into aspects of his life but the overall picture was absent. Brian Sanderson had been an employee or a neighbour or a mate and other sides got closed off, shut away, withdrawn. They never knew good old Brian's marriage was a sham. How his wife, sick of that distant nature and with a long memory for accumulated slights, had effectively banished him from the family home. Nobody suspected the couple were estranged, even as they lived in the same house, just as I never suspected dad was living a double life throughout my childhood. While I spent my days at playgroup or primary school, linking sticklebricks and throwing straw at the other children, my father was in London, cheating on mum and fathering two baby girls.

It took several days of steady persuasion to get the full story from my mother. I confronted her with the photograph of Kathleen and Kate, keeping a lid on my anger as I made it clear to her that I needed to know what this meant. At first she gave the barest of outlines; dad had another woman, back when I was too young to understand. My mother had been careful to hide this situation from

177

me after she discovered the betrayal, waiting it out instead, confident dad would return to her. She was right, but when he came back the trust was gone. Dad would never cheat on her again, but as soon as his infidelity came to light their marriage was locked in a downward trajectory, a curve descending like some colourless rainbow over the next twenty years.

"I was so stupid back then." Mum admitted. "He had his new job and I believed Brian when he talked about regular conferences and team-building activities. Your father was very clever, he'd only stay away one weekend a month and I never cottoned on. Or maybe I did, somewhere deep down, but I just couldn't face it. When you're young and you can't face something you just pretend it isn't true and put it to the back of your mind."

"How could you keep it to yourself for so long? How could you never tell me I had sisters?"

She sighed. "I never saw it as my place. You have to understand Monty, I didn't want anything to do with that woman. I couldn't have cared less what was happening to his bit on the side, I just wanted him back. If anyone should have told you it was your father but nothing ever got said. Besides, I doubt the girls would have welcomed you. From what I heard, the mother went mad when he ended it. She threw things at him, lashed out, even talked about getting a restraining order. He came back from her that last time with a black eye and cuts all over his arms so I fixed him up and we talked for a long time. Then we just got on with it ."

"How old was I then?"

"You must have been five or six."

I thought back to that time, unable to remember my dad with a damaged face. But the memories were fragmentary and illusive, there were nights when I'd barely seen my father. His absences weren't keenly felt, dad spent time with me on Sundays and I felt lucky compared to many of my playmates. A number of kids in the old neighbourhood had fathers working on oil rigs or posted overseas by the army. Other men were absent altogether due to criminality or selfishness. These children relied on harassed single women to raise them on government benefits, generally disliked around the area because of this *free ride*.

"I can't believe he acted like that." I said to mum the next day, after my shock had turned to shame.

"You don't know what he was like before we married. I saw Brian on and off for years before I accepted his proposal. Your father used to have three or four girls on the go at once when he was your age. Oh yes, a real man about town. But I stuck it out, and when the others fell away I thought I'd tamed him. He used to tell me I was the only one and like a fool I believed him."

That plain fellow I called dad was once a renowned ladies man? A silver-tongued charmer working his magic around the south east of England? It was inconceivable to me, his son had only known a dull and defeated figure. "So you agreed to get married in the end."

"He promised me there was no one else and in the beginning there wasn't. Brian spent all his time with me, he didn't even get drunk with his cronies anymore. They probably thought I trapped him but it was me under his spell. Not that I was any kind of a victim, don't go thinking that. No, when we walked up that aisle I was the envy of quite a few women. Rightly so, those first years were good. We didn't have much money to spare, but I had my job in the cafe and he got work at the coach company, I honestly believed things were looking up."

"Then I came along."

She looked at me, sorrowful. "You were exactly what I wanted Monty, don't ever think any different. But things can be hard with a little one. We didn't plan for you and Brian thought I'd tricked him into it. Not true, I was as surprised as him when I started getting sick. I took the test and there I was, pregnant, and I knew immediately I wanted it. To me you were a happy accident, but your father didn't see things that way. He only saw the difficulties of another mouth to feed and he was right, without me working things did get tough. I didn't have time for Brian like I used to, you took up too much of my strength. I suppose the affair was a way of getting his own back.

"God knows, I'm the last person to stick up for his behaviour, but I knew your father better than anyone and when I found out about the other woman I understood how he acted, even if I could never bring myself to forgive him. Brian always had such a lot of attention from women, that was what he thrived on, it made him who he was in a way. When I couldn't supply it your father went looking somewhere else."

That was all she would say for a long time and it left me sitting up at night, unable to consider sleep and wishing there was liquor to block out the agony. But I knew my mother never kept alcohol in this house, the only drug she condoned was her television.

Had these been normal circumstances I might be surprised at this story of my father's faithlessness, maybe even shocked to learn of my parents' fallibility, how these omniscient adults turned out to have more weaknesses than my own generation, but none of this would have felt like a big deal. Instead the past was destroying my present, through an unlikely combination of circumstances, one chance encounter and a coincidence worthy of the most contrived of soap operas, everything good in my life had disintegrated.

Every waking moment questions churned through my brain, but I forced myself to wait, choose a time when my mother was receptive and tolerant. I couldn't tell her why I needed to know more and she was reluctant to dredge up the painful past. The situation called for tact and delicacy, neither of which was easy to come by in my emotionally heightened state.

Finally I could hold it back no longer. "How did you find out?" I ventured.

Mum groaned. "She rang up, back when we were in Montgomery Road. I tell you Monty, that woman was absolutely hysterical. She'd found out she was expecting for a second time and she didn't have a clue what to do. Your father wasn't happy when she bore one child, now she'd forgotten to take her pill and got herself knocked up again! I told her he wasn't home and tried to calm her down. Of course, I wasn't feeling too happy myself at that point, and I ended up telling the woman to pull herself together. Well, that just set off the waterworks, and I had to put the phone down. When Brian got home he confirmed it all, every one of my worst fears. He said every time he tried to end it she screamed and wept and clung to him, after speaking to her I believed him."

I nodded, thinking of Kathleen's mother and her penchant for melodrama.

She went on. "Had it been someone else I might have felt sorry for her, but this woman was out to break up my family. I gave your father an ultimatum, her or me, and Brian did what I hoped he would, he chose us. Maybe if I'd been a stronger person I'd have kicked him out there and then, but I had no desire to be a single mother and I knew how much losing him would hurt you.

"Your father did a good job. It took a while, but he convinced me I was the one he loved. To his credit Brian never wandered again, but I was still frightened. That woman had two children by him, what if she came after his money? We were struggling enough as it was. Luckily the child support people were a lot worse in those days and they didn't bother tracking absent fathers, not if the mother didn't raise a fuss. Thank God that woman found someone with a bit of money as soon as your father left her."

"She did?"

"Yes, I read one of the letters she sent, after her second girl was born. That's how Brian got that photo you found. She kept writing for years, spiteful pieces of work if the one I read was anything to go by. I never looked at them after that, one was enough to reassure me that woman hated Brian as much as I hated her."

"Did dad never try and contact her?" I found it hard to believe any man, even my father, would willingly miss out on the lives of his only daughters.

"You know what your father was like, he didn't understand kids. I told him it wasn't worth the risk, also I think he was scared. She could have come looking for money, and the more time that passed the better those child support people got. If they proved he was the father they'd hound him for back payments so why make a nuisance? No, after we got the mortgage on this place Brian was content to count his blessings and live quietly with us. I don't think he even gave her the forwarding address when we moved. None of those horrible spidery letters ever came here, I know that much."

By the time mum finished explaining I was empty inside, unable to even feel anger at my father for his thoughtless behaviour. Through the younger years dad had no concern for the consequences of his actions, was only out to gratify his own needs. As a direct, if unforeseeable, result of this irresponsibility, I was in love with one of my half-sisters and had almost been seduced by the other one. There were laws against what Kathleen and I had been doing, and our ignorance was no defence in court. Worse than the legal implications though was that sickness, an overpowering revulsion for what I'd done. Somehow the prospect of prison was more inviting than facing up to what had happened. Locked up I wouldn't have to struggle through the days and pretend I wasn't dying inside. The hardship of incarceration was nothing when set against the sadness attacking my heart and mind.

The vicar droned on, a passage from the bible offering some consolation for those lapsed Christians in attendance, weeping and shivering as the freezing winter air blew through them. Earlier we'd waited for the limousines to arrive, cars partially paid for by the coach company which had taken out a policy on my father's life, apparently without his knowledge. The mourners congregated around my mother then, offering their solace: *"Lived life to the full"* and *"at least he didn't suffer"*. Women I didn't recognise told me how much I reminded them of Brian, what a cheerful and happy-go-lucky fellow we'd all lost. I got an insight into dad's masks then, the different guises worn around people he knew. Members of his family would paint pictures of Brian which contrasted wildly with the ones a friend, acquaintance or Kathleen's mother might describe. Mrs. Tibbits would never recognise the friendly saint of these words, this man everyone believed was a decent human being, now venerated in death. How easy it was to speak well of a man when you no longer had to cope with his flaws. When the limos finally appeared they interrupted these fiftysomething men, widowers, the divorced or separated, who offered support to my mother, happy to help if she needed anything. They knew how difficult it would be, with Brian gone and no man to rely on. The thought of mum accepting one of these propositions, taking up with a new man, it would have outraged me if I could have been any more upset. In the event I felt only annoyance, parting the huddle of figures in suits to take mum by the arm and lead her away, the two of us walking toward the vicar who now ended his eulogy with talk of Brian Sanderson's "place in the community". How he was "a family man of the highest order".

We asked that dad rest in peace, then I took up a spade and began shovelling earth into the hole as my mother and a few others gathered some dirt to sprinkle on the wooden box, offering up their own silent prayers.

Specks of rain landed on the back of my neck, the presage to a downpour. I didn't quicken my pace, instead I welcomed this wetness. At least it reminded me I was still alive, despite bereavement and a broken heart. Ever since my mother told me the truth, more even than the pain and nausea, I'd experienced a dreadful and overweening sense of self-hatred. In the house of my teens, a place built on mendacity and funded by lies, I thought of Kathleen's innocence. How one horrific situation could kill our love, as surely as dad's life force had been extinguished by his heart failing.

Funny, funny peculiar. I'd never been one who experienced the vagaries of synchronicity before. Others talked of bumping into old school-friends among millions of Londoners or travelling around the planet to find acquaintances holidaying in the same resort and exclaim *"small world!"* but such congruities never happened to me. I couldn't recall ever finding familiar people in unexpected places or seeing someone I knew amidst the random multitudes. Now the Gods of coincidence had caught up with Monty Sanderson in the most spectacular manner. Unbeknownst to us, me and that girl I'd fallen head over heels for both possessed the same father.

Drops mixed with the sweat which poured from my skin, left me damp inside and out. The rest of the cortege began to drift away, back to their hired vehicles, none of them interfering with my work. Kathleen had phoned the Sanderson home a couple of days before having found things out from Mart at her first rehearsal. I suppose I should have seen it coming, but my mind was preoccupied with larger matters and I didn't think Martin would pass on my emergency contact number. Fortunately I was out when she rang, walking the dogs outside town, but mum and Kathleen must have discussed my erratic behaviour because when I turned on my mobile that evening there was a message waiting.

"Monty, it's Kathleen. Your mum told me about Brian and how hard you've taken it." The girl sounded plaintive, if only she knew. What befell the old man was sad, sure, but that wasn't the reason for my silence. "I wanted you to know that I understand, about you taking off like that. I know it's an awful thing and I'm not mad, just a bit worried that's all. I wish I could help you through whatever it is you're feeling but if you don't think you can share these things with me then what does that say about us?" She paused. "You're not alone Monty, I want you to know that. I'm not just here for the good stuff, that's not what love's about. And I do love you, you know that right?" I knew. But what good is love when you come from the same Y chromosome? "So call me when you get this message and come back soon, I miss you. Whatever's wrong, we can make it better."

Thinking about her words tears joined the rain, rolling down my face and into that rectangular hole in the earth. To be in love now felt like a flaw, a shared weakness, an Achilles heel that could only lead to our downfall. The sympathy and compassion in Kathleen's voice had brought my incestuous tendencies to the surface, I thought about her smile, that body I knew so well and what had once been arousal was now repulsion. I could only ever right my wrong by keeping the two of us apart. But however much thoughts of sex disgusted me love wasn't something I could put aside when it became inconvenient. I hated to admit it, but a part of me longed to see her again. Take Kathleen in my arms and never mention that what we had was sick and wrong. I resolved to myself then and there, grimly laying my father to his final resting place, that I would resist this loathsome urge. No more secrets and denial, I knew the truth. There was no excuse.

The thought was almost too much to bear, the prospect of never seeing those brown eyes again, never stroking her skin, never sharing Kathleen's joy or listening to that bawdy laughter, it shook me bodily. Overwhelmed and feeling faint, I ended my work and rammed the spade into muddied earth. All my life I'd been indoctrinated by the platitudes and clichés, a belief that love made the world go round, could conquer all, ought to be my priority above all else. But when a love comes along that's defective or inappropriate and still moves with the force of a juggernaut those sayings are shown up for the lies they are. So what then? Love isn't always mutual or legal or right, and when love is wrong there's no saving grace, no redemption to nullify the heartache. Just the numbness of melancholy, a vacuum engulfing every vicissitude of existence. This was a malignancy my everyday victories, those things which make up the goodness of life, simply couldn't cure.

I looked down into the grave one final time, my father's coffin completely covered by wet, black soil. Goodbye dad. I thought I knew you, but now I guess I never will. Maybe I can understand enough to realise you never meant any harm. The pain came from you being you and I don't know how easily I can forgive that. So if you're watching over us, looking down on me and mum and my hurt, know that I'm not bitter. Just take a good look at our plight, at my suffering and tears, and perhaps then you'll feel the smallest pang of remorse.

"I'll visit." I told the headstone, covered in flowers and wreaths, wilting now under the force of great raindrops. Then I turned away and took a path between the graves, alone and sodden as I traipsed up to that elongated black vehicle, the one limousine which remained, parked at the roadside.

Part Three:
Overcome By
Ambivalence

Chapter Fifteen

Fergal was awake early today, he'd been up before me every day since I got back but since I hadn't been rising before noon that wasn't difficult. I didn't expect to see him this morning though, today was my first back at the office and it wasn't even eight o'clock yet. But there he was, cooking the most important meal of the day.

"I'm doing bacon laddo, did you want hash browns as well?"

"Not too much."

My appetite was never strong at this time of day and recently I'd barely been eating at all. The trouble was that Fergal always went to plenty of effort with breakfast, like some kind of supportive man-wife, so I couldn't really refuse. I'd told him everything on my return from Basingstoke of course, we talked for long hours that first night while I drank endless whisky sours and he got through half a bottle of gin. Fergal appreciated unlikely events and had an acute sense of the absurd, but even he was appalled to hear of my misfortune. Since then he'd tried to do what he could, when Randall wasn't around my flatmate would make misguided attempts to cheer me up or suggest entertainment which might pull me out of my malaise. He cooked food after finding out I hadn't eaten all day, and even looked into what he referred to as "my condition". Fergal's research continued now as he came to the table with our food, a book under one arm.

"Just as I thought Monty, what happened to you isn't at all unprecedented. This woman founded an adoption agency after giving up her child years before." He pointed to the picture of a plump authoress on the back cover. "When Barbara here was reunited with her son she immediately wanted to boink him. It took her twelve years to get over those feelings, and that's when she started looking into the reasons."

"Uh-huh."

"Apparently it's quite common, when people from the same family are kept apart as babies and become reunited in adulthood. Chances are they'll fancy each other, she calls it *Genetic Sexual Attraction*."

"The whole thing makes me queasy. Can we just drop it?"

Fergal closed the book. "All I'm saying my friend, is that you're not alone. Barbara says it happens to half opposite-sex siblings when they meet for the first time as adults. Whenever you and Kathleen bumped into each other there would have been the same result, and the odds of that happening aren't as long as you might think. You live in the same city, remember? It was unfortunate you had to get acquainted with her, but once that occurred no one was to blame."

"Yeah, well, I still say its worse luck than I've ever heard. Millions of eligible women in this country and I fall for one of the two who can make me a criminal. Not only that, I almost knew her sister in the Biblical sense as well."

"Really?"

I nodded. Here he was, dredging up everything I wanted to put behind me and my temper was rising. "Whether it's an actual medical condition or not, all this feels like to me is sadness and misery. If there's no way of curing it I'd rather we talked about something else."

"Alright old man, I get the message." Fergal drank coffee and stroked his beard. It had filled out in the time I'd been away, progressing from scrappy patches to the full bush and I could tell he was pleased by the growth. Regrettably his natural hair colour was dark brown so the light catching it in a certain way had the effect of making his chin look ginger.

I gave up on breakfast and left my food half-eaten, leafing through a tabloid while Fergal read his broadsheet. Much to my flatmate's consternation I'd begun taking *The Daily Class* on a regular basis. Not only was the newspaper middlebrow and easy to read, it's editorial philosophy tied in with the opinions I'd nurtured since finding out about my sisters. The grinding hopelessness of the situation led to a movement of mindset, from somewhere on the left wing to what I called *dis-compassionate conservatism*. Life was hard, ordinary blokes like me didn't get the breaks, and everyone was only out for themselves. In these circumstances a guy didn't expect any favours, all he could do was survive as comfortably as possible. Maybe make some money and live out a pleasurable life. I could take or leave the paper's other obsessions, house prices, the filth on TV, drug-addled kids running amok in our streets, but I agreed with its stance on morality and values in the home. If my family had been nuclear and stuck together, not fragmented into a miasma of adultery and extreme emotions, I'd never be deep in a depression, that place where each week held not promise or hope, but the gloom of loneliness. A time when I chose to hide from the world inside our flat.

Fergal interrupted my thoughts. "Is there anything in that rag of yours on the latest crimes by fat people?"

"Not that I can see."

"It seems there's a gang of them. Five obese men, a pregnant woman and a young urchin who does the getaway sprint. They've been lurking on tubes looking for rich people or tourists. The woman asks if she can have a seat, and when the victim gives it up the fat boys appear and surround their target, taking any valuables. So far two Englishmen, an Italian and a Spaniard have been robbed. It says here no one really sees the crime because their views are blocked by blubber. Then the kid takes the haul and runs off while the rest of them get out at the next station as if nothing's amiss. I quote: *'The fat men are so loud and obnoxious the victim has no idea what's happening until it's too late. So far they've escaped every time and the police have no leads.'*

"There's a picture here of someone waddling through the ticket barriers but it's too grainy to make out." Fergal pointed to the photograph, all I could see was a dark shape. "Better watch out for elephantine criminals when you go out there Monty."

"As if I didn't have enough to worry about."

"Oh well, at least you don't have to bother with dear Justin anymore."

"He didn't die while I was away Fergal, let's get that straight."

My flatmate lit a cigarette. "I have it on good authority our feather-brained associate was listening to his iPod while texting his girlfriend and cycling down the centre of a main road." He exhaled a cloud of smoke. "An act of mercy I'd say. The driver took one look at the pinhead he'd knocked down and backed over him to make sure. For the sake of everyone who knew Just-in I think he made the right decision." Fergal took another drag. "Poor Yohanna's the one I feel sorry for. All we have to remember him by is half a sentence, saved for posterity on her mobile; *am cycling in road...* then it cuts off."

"I've asked you before to stop putting the rumour round he's died." My flatmate's face fell, he inhaled again on the fag. "And can't you stop that stinking habit? You started smoking because life sucked, now it's all sweetness and man-bears, shouldn't you just stop?"

Fergal put his cigarette out, crestfallen. "Sorry Montgomery." He mumbled.

"That's another thing, don't call me Montgomery, okay? No one calls me Montgomery any more except my mother. The name's Monty, got it?" I rose from the table. "Look, I've got to get going, I know you're only trying to cheer me up but you really shouldn't bother. It's not going to work."

I collected my coat and left for the station, unhappy at having sounded Fergal out, but the prospect of facing the office after weeks away was getting to me. I shouldn't have taken the frustration out on him I guess, my flatmate didn't mean any harm, but his attempts to cheer me up were sorely misguided. I wanted to be left alone with my unhappiness, ever since the truth came out other people had given me no pleasure. Banter, socialising, friends, they all seemed like so many pointless distractions. A craving for others was meaningless to me. You came to rely on it only when the good stuff ended, when love and romance and optimism were gone. No one I knew could help me get over Kathleen so what was the point?

I dodged the birds which flew down at me, pigeons passing over both shoulders as I weaved away from their flight paths. Arriving at the end of the road, I bought a travel pass from the newsstand and entered the tube station.

The circumstances in our flat had switched since Christmas. Now it was Fergal who enjoyed a rewarding relationship while I moped and dawdled and couldn't have cared less. When the Irishman was around he moved from bouts of seriousness, remembering that downbeat state of mind he'd only recently left, and being un-

192

able to contain his joy. I was treated to regular updates on Randall, how rewarding it was to be with a real man. This worldly, experienced gay who cared little for mirrors. Only yesterday Fergal came in full of the clips they'd filmed together, my flatmate delighted by Axelrod's ideas, his fresh approach to pratfalls and trickery. The two of them used the American's charm on the English public, persuading an old man to stand in front of a sprinkler so it looked as if the jets of water were coming out of his ears, or making young mothers read out silly statements on camera for a possible TV show pitch. Cofaigh's new man was supportive and inspired, Fergal quoting Charles Boyer when he talked of Jane Fonda, how the actor said of his female co-star; "she is compassionate, and concerned about more things than her hair". Wasn't that what we all wanted in someone, he asked. For them to be special and caring and interested in the deeper things? These were certainly the qualities Fergal prized most highly, he simply hadn't realised it until Randall came along.

The Irishman caught himself then, saw who he was talking to and apologised. I told him not to worry, it was good someone could find happiness, had moved away from that stagnant lifestyle which left Fergal so empty. Maybe my flatmate felt like he was chiding me with his joy, but I was hardly going to be envious of a couple of homos. It was strange though, seeing Fergal as the submissive male. Previously he'd always dominated an affair by force of personality, but the American showed Fergal fresh opportunities, mentored him in the ways of man-bears and opened Cofaigh's eyes to a wealth of previously unknown philosophies. Randall was unassailably the senior partner.

Thankfully they kept a lid on physical affection in my presence, although I did once walk into the lounge and find them entwined on the sofa, a great mound of flesh and hair, the pair stroking each other's beards and comparing tummies. I blew my nose and they stopped instantly, moving apart in embarrassment. It was one thing not to begrudge the romance, quite another to have the pair petting in my house.

"Monty, Kathleen. You haven't got back to me so I don't have a clue what you're thinking. Who does? I tried offering to be with you and it didn't work so now I'm telling you my side. You know, it's not right, leaving me on the dangle like this. I've been thinking a lot, but I still can't understand why you'd behave this way. It scares me Monty, I thought I knew you as well as I know myself. The whole thing with your dad, it was sad and unexpected and I liked him, I really did, but it doesn't explain why you haven't got in touch. I mean, you haven't cut yourself off completely have you? I know you spoke to Martin, and you've been with your mum all this time. But I haven't heard anything for weeks and I don't know what to do. It's been hard for me too you know. Kate's been helping me, but mum makes everything worse and the only thing I can think of is that you might have met someone else. Now I've said that the whole thing sounds crazy. Where would you meet her? At the funeral? In Basingstoke? It's all too weird.

"I don't know, my mind's been going round in circles. I can't sleep and there's no one here to sort me out. Just let me know what's going on Monty, please. I'm sorry for rambling on but I really can't help it. I miss you and I love you. That's all I wanted to say."

I got off the tube at Tottenham Court Road and joined passengers struggling through the bottleneck, that single escalator which led up to the interchange area. Once away from the North-ern Line people peeled off, leaving me with space to breathe. I stood on the moving metal steps as men barged past, late and thoughtless, knocking the side of my body while I made myself small. A freakish-looking woman with a huge barrel chest glared down at me from the escalator opposite, small breasts sticking out from her enormous thorax, like two mushrooms on a compost heap. I stared at them for a while until she disappeared from view, wondering how I was going to explain things to my boss.

Mart phoned the flat yesterday and moved from civility to a controlled rant in seconds. He said I was taking liberties, I'd been told to keep him updated and hadn't, plus he wasn't happy with the way I was treating Kathleen. My boss left me with the impres-sion that he wouldn't be sympathetic to a continuation of paid leave if I didn't make it in today, so I forced myself to rise early and get back in the perpetual bustle. I suppose my days away had turned into weeks, but I didn't notice. After the funeral I'd somehow managed to catch a cold despite consorting with no one except my resolutely healthy mother, and retired to bed for a couple of days. That recuperative period delayed the organisation of dad's affairs, and by the time I finished and got back to London even thinking about *Bears!Bears!Bears!* was enough to induce a bout of catalepsy. But Martin was right, I couldn't blame illness for my long weeks of absence, it was more fraudulent than that. Had my boss not rung with his ultimatum I might never have gone back.

I cut across a deserted Soho Square and turned right towards my office. Under the steps Bernard huddled in so many blankets he looked like a furry pod-person. I couldn't make out a face under the material but I assumed it was him and tossed a pound his way. The coin clinked down into Fergal's niche, to be discovered later. Our receptionist let me in the building and I wandered through to where the single blondes discussed men they'd met over the weekend, while attached girls talked of their boyfriends' newest failings. They noticed me and said hello, Lettice offered sympathy for my loss which I accepted with good grace. She made me feel awkward and fraudulent, the grief I felt for my father had been comparatively fleeting, it was losing a future with Kathleen that really choked me up.

Justin wasn't there so nobody pestered me as I settled in to be confronted by scores of unread emails. Many were disregarded immediately, but one message from Si caught my eye. He said the man from *Whelmed & Naughty Records* had made the band an offer they couldn't refuse and they would now be taking a short hiatus from gigging, this company paying *The Airborne Toxic Event* a flat wage while they set about recording an album. I was vaguely familiar with *W&N*, one of many subsidiaries belonging to a well-known multinational. The label was specifically dedicated to left-field or experimental acts and their roster was well thought of in the industry. The romantic in me would have preferred *The A.T.E.* to sign with a true independent, but I guess that would have meant limited backing and the foursome keeping their day jobs.

I'd just begun to cut text from a press release on London Zoo's latest acquisitions, ready to paste the details onto our website, when Justin turned up.

"Hi Monty, how's it going?" My colleague wore leather chaps, an ironic *Iron Maiden* t-shirt and a baseball cap.

"I'm busy, as you can see."

"You want coffee?"

"What do you think?"

For a few minutes all was peaceful. I played around with the information until Justin brought me my drink, arriving at about the same time as the first email of the day, a terse request from Martin to step into his office *now*. Why he didn't just tell me in person I'd no idea, but I tried to finish the work at hand before walking the ten paces to his door.

"You know anything about baby pandas Just, the ones at London Zoo?"

"Yeah, we went on a day trip to see them a few weeks back."

"Anything strike you?"

"Not really, they were sleeping. I liked the monkeys."

"Monkeys, great. How's that going to help me with a feature on red pandas?"

"Don't know." Justin swivelled in his chair. "Whee!! Hey, Monty, d'you wanna come up *The Manqué Bar* tonight? DJ Nutsac's playing a set."

"*DJ Nutsac?*"

"He's really good. I thought you might want to get out and about again. It's mainly soft house and nu-skool cheese, but if you request some phat-hop he'll play that too."

"Justin, you know I hate that sort of shit. The last time you convinced me to come out with you we ended up speed dating." My colleague opened his mouth to speak but I didn't let him. "So you're saying nothing's happened while I've been away? No agency business you want to update me on?" Justin looked blank as a spotless domino. "Fine, then there's no point delaying the inevitable."

I left Justin spinning in his chair and knocked firmly on the door of Mart's office. Landry told me to enter and requested I take a seat. My boss looked tired and drawn, dark patches encircling his eyes.

"Good morning Monty, I trust you're feeling better."

"Much, thanks." I sniffled. "Still a bit clogged."

"There's a lot of it about." Mart pushed at the bridge of his glasses. "I'll get to the point straight away. I can't afford you going missing in action like that. As a number two Justin proved an utterly inadequate replacement."

"You don't say."

Mart's expression told me this was no time for insolence. "We lost the *Venustra* biscuit contract last month, they decided to go with ocelots instead. It doesn't look as if we've any campaigns coming up to replace it, those were key clients."

"Things are bad aren't they?"

"Yes they are. Bears don't possess the market power they once had. We may have to look at other streams of revenue to keep the business going." I wondered what he meant by that. "Not a word to anyone, understand? It won't help *Bears!Bears!Bears!* if the team think their jobs are at risk."

"Okay."

"The financial climate's responsible for this of course, but not having anyone to rely on while I'm organising the play doesn't help. You weren't to blame for Justin's failings, but it would have been nice if you could have trained him to be capable."

"I didn't realise that was part of my job." *You employed him Martin, if anyone should have put Justin through a competency test it was you.*

"Well it's part of your job now." Mart nudged at his specs. "Barry was in touch this morning, he wanted to know if we had any work for his *girls*. I told Justin to explain the situation weeks ago but clearly that hasn't happened." So the wrangler still didn't know he was out of favour. "Here's Barry's number, that's priority number one." I took the note he passed across. "Your second priority is talking with those clients we have left. Make sure all their needs are being attended to. Everything."

"Fine."

Martin leant back in his chair. "On a different matter, I don't condone the way you've behaved with Kathleen. I know I'm the last man who should be preaching to you." Damn right, in his younger days Mart had a considerable reputation for seducing and abandoning young girls. "But to get Kathy a part in my play and then ditch her without a word, it's a bit beyond the pale don't you think?"

"That's personal."

"Of course it is and I'm not about to interfere. But everything I do is connected with the business in some way, which brings me to priority number three." Martin took some papers and a guide to London out of his desk drawer. "The first performance of *Too Beautiful* is next Friday and you'll be there supporting us. Not only that, you're going to make sure it's packed out. I want you to call up every music magazine, theatre critic and *Manic Street Preachers* fan club there is. Get emails off to websites on Richey Edwards, meet people in person if need be, as long as you sell the thing right. I want the opening night packed out, and if you have to work overtime or canvas goths in the street then so be it. I'm putting you in charge of this publicity campaign because I've enough on my hands with the cast and crew. Don't see it as a hardship, this is more of a challenge. We both have a vested interest in making my play a success." Mart smiled, he'd pulled a good one on me alright.

"Is that it?"

"Yep, go and get on with it."

I slunk out.

"Monty, me again. I just spoke to Fergal and he was really sweet, I miss him. It still doesn't make a whole lot of sense though. He said there were *clandestine facts I wasn't privy to*, and that he couldn't tell me more. You're back, I know that much, but Fergal can't force you to talk. It's not his place and I understand that, but it shouldn't be like this Monty, you know? What's so terrible you can't even pick up the phone and speak to me? I know you've still got your mobile and I honestly believe you're thinking of me, but I'm beginning to think you're weak Monty, weak and spineless. I can't go on like this any longer so I'm giving you one last chance to prove me wrong. Call me this week and explain yourself. I'll be reasonable, we can forget all the trouble you've caused me and you can have your say. I don't want anything more than your voice on the phone. We don't even have to see each other, and you don't have to apologise. God, you don't even have to love me anymore. Just give me some answers and I'll leave you alone, I promise. You've got until midnight Sunday to think it over, that's three full days. If I don't hear from you by then I'm going to do what everyone says I should do and put you behind me, once and for all.

"Was it really such a bad thing for me to fall in love with you? I never thought I'd regret it, but I'm starting to. You've got 'til the end of the week to set me straight. I know how good you are with deadlines Monty so make sure you observe this one. That's all, bye."

Barry could have taken the news better.

"You London folk, sittin' there in yer fookin' climate-controlled offices, thinkin' up yer fancy ads and usin' Poppy like a piece of meat. You don't know what it's like. Bears have feelins too."

"I'm very sorry Barry, but you know what happened as well as I do. We simply can't take that sort of risk."

"I know what yer thinkin', you think...." At this point the keeper adopted a higher pitch, his impersonation of a woman. *"Ooh! Bears are nice aren't they? Bears are lovely, I like those bears. I think I'll buy some chocolate if I get to meet the bear. Then I'll buy a big TV. Look how big the bears are on my TV. Ooh, I say!"* Back to his normal voice. "You southerners 'aven't a clue what it's really like! You never 'ad to go out in the wilderness, yer too soft to shove a thermometer up a brown bear's arse, you've never seen yer dad torn limb from limb by a rogue grizzly!"

"Neither have you Barry, your father's a mechanic."

"They won't be tamed, them bears are smarter than you think. They don't like the way you ponces treat 'em and they don't like the fookin' stuff you rope 'em into sellin' neither."

"Look, I don't actually have to take this. We're only letting you know out of common courtesy, I can speak to the zoo's management just as easily."

"That a threat? You threatenin' me yer little gobshite? Well, we'll see. I'm gettin' me a lawyer, then you'll be sorry. With what I know about that place I could blow the whole thing wide open."

"Barry, we're an advertising agency, not the mafia. Anyway half the incidents we've had to keep quiet were your fault."

"Fookin' nonces, wait 'til I get down there......."

"Okay, I'm putting the phone down now. Thanks for all the work you've done for us Barry. If you're seen in the vicinity of this office I'll call the police. Thank you, goodbye."

I didn't leave work until after six that day, by which time the building was deserted apart from cleaners and the distant sound of that poker game, drifting through from the smoking room. When I did get out there were problems on the underground, all of us subject to delays, a couple of the lines closed as fleets of stock were checked and repaired. There'd been a number of derailments since the year began and twice trains had failed between stations, skidding against walls to injure passengers. No one was seriously hurt, but the problems combined with constant bad-mouthing and the talked-up possibility of chemical attacks to leave commuters jittery. I felt it myself, standing there amidst the crush of the platform. All of a sudden trains pulling in were no longer futuristic metal capsules, full of wide-eyed girls who might catch my glance and hold it a second, but a deadly threat to my well-being and that of everyone on board. A madman could push me in front of the approaching train, cause a gory sight which left everyone stranded. Or beggars moving from carriage to carriage might slip and fall on the line, be splattered beside the track. Or there could be a sarin-wielding fundamentalist at the next station, ready to condemn us all to grisly death.

Leery and fatigued, I boarded the train, allowing the forceful to push in ahead. That was when I realised my fellow passengers weren't tense and scared like me, the horrors of the world couldn't have been further from their thoughts. Commuters carried Hallmark bags and wrapped gifts because today was St. Valentine's Day. Sentimentality provided a backdrop for them, people with gold chocolate hearts or snuggly love teddies. Today they would return to loved ones, dress for an expensive meal booked months in advance, drown wives in affection and clichés. Nearby a woman sold red roses from a wicker basket, forcing her way through the crowd. After a day concentrating on the theatrical or ursine, love returned to my mind. No matter how much I tried to keep her out of my thoughts, Kathleen was back, there now, the way that girl instinctively understood when I needed reassurance or flattery. As insecurity and fear encroached, Kathleen knew how to fend it off, like no girl I'd known before. Had she been here the girl would have talked me round, cured me with a touch, pulled Monty out of his mental rut until I felt good about my life again. Kathleen protected and emboldened, coaxed me into happiness and asked only for love in return. But those times were gone. The girl was gone now, gone from my life. Whether as a lover or a sister, I could never know her again.

"Look, I know its late, but I guessed your phone wouldn't be on so what's it matter? Whatever the time is we've passed my deadline so I guess that's it. I've got to put you behind me and there's nothing more to say. I'm not going to mention how much I've come to hate you these past weeks Monty, I don't think it would do any good, I need to move past that and get on with my life. You might think it strange, but the one thing I want to say is *well done*. You had me fooled Monty, you know? I never thought you'd be one to duck out, but I suppose I'm just as naive as those lovesick girls I used to look down on. You know the ones, they wait by the phone all night for him to call and you just want to say; *give it up*, because he's out there doing something better. Or some*one* better.

"So I'm looking to the future. You've become a very good reason for me to make a new start, you know? I'm going to do it too, so I want you to let me be, this is something I have to make happen myself. On present form you probably won't, but if you do suddenly decide to get back in touch, do me a favour and don't bother. Don't feel you have to come to the play either. If Martin makes you, don't try to catch my attention or speak to me. I've waited in vain for an explanation and now at least I'm managing not to care, I don't want to start again. I'm sure I'll soon be happy about being free so don't concern yourself. Worry about Monty, I'm sure that's what you're doing anyway. Goodbye Sanderson. We had fun, but please forget it ever happened. I'm going to forget about you, don't doubt it." *<click>*

Chapter Sixteen

The sound of stagehands grappling with scenery was overwhelmed by the chatter of people. They walked the aisles, gregarious and self-possessed, peering at the numbers on rows to find their seats. I watched the theatre fill from the shadows of its rear, Kate arriving with some guy, Fergal and Randall squeezing past, Justin and Yohanna talking loudly at one another, blondes from the office mixing with diehard *Manic Street Preachers* fans in leopardskin and eyeliner. By the time the show was due to start this auditorium looked about two thirds full, not bad considering the four hundred capacity. I'd been giving away tickets around Soho all afternoon, descending upon Londoners who sat in cafes or browsed through record shops, a last-ditch attempt to meet the producer's demands. It meant box office receipts were unlikely to be as high as Mart might have expected, but at least the opening night was busy.

The lights went down and an expectant hush enshrouded us, then a primitive guitar riff filled the house and the velvet barrier was raised upon a scene of violence. Four young men in stencilled t-shirts mimed to the hurtling music while from the side an unseen audience threw bottles which smashed at the band's feet to form a carpet of broken glass.

This was the first I'd seen of *Too Beautiful*. I skipped the rehearsals, not just because I wanted to avoid Kathleen, I was still suffering from that general apathy which had come to characterise my days. Now came my chance to see the actors playing this band and the foursome certainly looked the part. The bassist was almost seven feet tall while both singer/guitarist and drummer looked stumpy as gnomes and that kid playing Richey appeared suitably emaciated. The front three did star jumps and pulled rock star poses in-between kicking the missiles back at their offstage audience. As an opening it was action-packed and succinct, everything that needed to be said about the band's battling early gigs, but when the backing music ended my heart sank.

The second scene came after the performance, the band attempting to get drunk and confront their aggressors. Richey talked them into leaving instead, he had to drive back to Wales

(*"Come on boys, my dad needs the van first thing and Sean's got to work...."*). Next he appeared alone on the proscenium, delivering a monologue on the early nineties music scene, how the Manic Street Preachers' intended to generate controversy, put the intelligence and glamour back into rock.

Richey's speech went on for a while, accompanied by the faint sound of scenery being shifted and a bad feeling in my gut. There were two immediately obvious problems with this as I saw it. First off, Martin had his actors speaking in entirely unconvincing Welsh accents. Now, I've nothing against Wales, it can be a land of beauty and freedom. Male voice choirs have their place and poetry delivered in that booming tone holds a certain gravitas. Unfortunately the actors playing the band were obviously not Welshmen and their shaky delivery removed all dignity from this accent. I kept expecting them to lapse into *boyo* or *there's lovely* or some equally silly verbal tic. These were Englishmen attempting to sound Welsh, not good for a story that was part tragedy. The actor playing Richey was particularly bad, explaining his plan to combine the political awareness of black rappers with the sledgehammer tunes of heavy metal in a speech regularly tinctured by his natural Liverpudlian.

That was the first negative point, one which could be cured by making the cast avoid their stereotype impressions during future performances. *The Manic Street Preachers* never sounded Welsh on record, and they were always more interested in the bigger picture than jingoism. More troublesome was the knowledge that they weren't using my script. I'd deliberately exorcised all of Martin's early monologues and here they were, being delivered to us. But this wasn't the first draft my boss had shown me either. As the play wore on it became clear that this *Too Beautiful* was some strange hybrid of Mart's original work, a few of my changes, and additional scenes never seen before. This had the troublesome effect of returning all the flaws I'd painstakingly unpicked; the inordinate length, that lack of cogency, some really stupid bits from Richey's life we could have done without. All that work tightening up the damn thing, making this play work, all for nothing. The time was a quarter to eight and there was no telling how long this performance would drag on for.

Lights went up on that bedroom in which the band members congregated throughout their teens. The friends swapped ideas, quoted from the existentialists and situationism while Richey glued together a collage featuring his favourite celebrities. Then a Welsh woman called them all to tea and the action moved onto the night-time streets of their small town, the celebration for Edwards' birthday ending with these young men branded *faggots* and beaten up for the way they looked.

"We've got to get out of this town." Observed the future singer as they lay in crumpled heaps.

"We will, I promise you that." Said Richey.

Another monologue followed, our hero reflecting on his identity and the intolerance they worked so hard to escape. He explained how the band gained a following, publicising themselves around the country. They wrote letters to people connected with the music business and travelled to London repeatedly, their buzz created by a manifesto which promised a *coup d'etat* on the lifeless entertainment industry. I could feel the audience growing restless during this exposition, so it was a relief when the lights came up on a packed dressing room somewhere in the capital.

A music journalist interviewed Richey who sat in a corner biting his fingernails while the rest of the band cavorted drunkenly in the background.

"You have a very strong political message, yet you use such bludgeoningly simple music to get it across. Why is that?"

The musician answered in that faux-Welsh drawl. "We want nothing less than revolution and revolution only comes from the kind of art the working classes can understand."

"I'm very interested in your image." The journo inspected Richey's make-up and his home-made t-shirt with the words *Death Sentence Heritage* spray-painted on it. "Is it true that all your mothers are hairdressers?"

But Richey was ignoring him, distracted by the arrival of a blonde girl in a short denim skirt, knee-high leather boots and a cut-off t-shirt. Kathleen playing Jo. "Hi," she said. "Loved the show."

A twinge inside me, but of what I couldn't be sure. Recognition - yes, affection - maybe, desire - certainly, she looked fabulous, but there was also that nausea which came with fancying your own sister. Maybe some jealousy there too, Kathleen was hanging around artistic types, exploring herself wearing costumes like that. They were bound to be hitting on her. I forced myself to ignore this thought, if she couldn't be my girlfriend it didn't matter who was interested in her.

Watching Jo seduce the rapt hero I came to feel something beyond the pain, a pride at the way Kathleen held herself. There was confidence and magnetism here, Jo making it entirely plausible Richey would fall for her then and there as the plot needed us to believe. What Kathleen had wasn't exactly star presence, and she'd an unfair advantage over the others by retaining her normal accent, but she was still the best thing about *Too Beautiful.* A natural in the role of Richey's companion, assertive yet vulnerable, just as she was in real life. Every time Jo left the stage Mart's production lost several notches of class.

Suddenly we were back in Wales, the nascent *Manic Street Preachers* excitedly sharing press reports describing their 'incendiary' live shows. Then another gig, the sound crisper and nothing hurled from the floor but cheers and declarations of love. Unfortunately the percussionist was miming a little too enthusiastically and occasionally we heard an out of time *thump* as he followed through and hit a drum. Now more interviews and Richey took one belligerent reporter aside to prove he was '4 Real', carving the characters into his arm with a Stanley knife. The more squeamish elements of the audience hid their faces and squealed, mainly blonde females in truth, although I think Justin might have contributed to the noise. This violence looked entirely unconvincing to me, the knife was clearly a prop and Richey barely touched his arm, but there he was, dripping fake blood from a rag wrapped around his wrist. The actor moved centre stage and delivered a laborious speech on converting non-believers to his message, while in the background came the sound of an ambulance, a sound effect I knew to be factually inaccurate. The scrawny man collapsed in the spotlight and there was a musical interlude while everyone prepared for act two.

I looked at those seated before me, whispering into the ears of friends. A couple of older men I took to be critics made notes in their PowerBooks. I tried not to think about what was appearing on those electronic screens. Some people went to visit the bathroom and I saw Kate about to pass my seat, just feet away. I slouched down, the thought of Mart coming up here at any moment was the only factor keeping me there. Every instinct cried out for me to slip away, avoid the consequences of mediocrity and reclaim the rest of my evening from this half-baked play I'd spent so long trying to make work. But I stayed, a certain fascination with Kathleen's performance the only aspect keeping me interested. After all those weeks away I felt a little of the old compulsion, to watch and admire her, even as I hated myself for ever loving this girl.

The second act began with a projected montage of real headlines, all culled from music press articles or pieces on the band in national dailies. Photographs showed Richey scarred or bleeding, lurid externalisations of his inner turmoil making good copy. The actor who played Edwards came into the spotlight and talked of his success, how it never filled the emptiness inside. Then we moved to the band's tour bus where *The Manic Street Preachers* were playing video games, Richey swigging from a bottle of vodka, as bored by the routine as I was becoming of this narrative. Following some pointless dialogue we switched back to Richey's family home where our hero was distraught over the death of his childhood pet.

"Snoopy! Snoopy! What'll I do without you?" Cried the actor, as the overwrought soundtrack swelled up, like something from a fifties melodrama. Richey's mum did his washing and expressed concern over her son's well-being, seeing the fact that he took a bottle of vodka to bed as a bad sign. The next thing I knew Richey was in rehab, inside a room at the clinic where the recovering alcoholic was visited by his sometime companion. Kathleen came on, the very picture of the debauched model attempting to look respectable, entering The Priory in dark glasses and a long, plastic coat. With anguished pleas Jo made Richey promise he would stop poisoning his body

Richey: "I'm going to beat it, I swear."

207

Jo: "I believe in you baby."

Richey: "It's not easy in here, it's like a prison in here. The Prozac did nothing."

Jo: "What about the twelve steps? A friend of mine said they really help."

Richey: "I can't do that either, you have to believe in God."

Jo: "Don't you believe in God baby?"

Richey: "If God doesn't exist then I am God."

Jo: "Oh baby, I love you."

Richey (*Looking panicked*): "..."

Kathleen held him close and begin to cry. I felt sorry for the girl, she was putting her heart and soul into this spurious nonsense. If Richey Edwards were dead we defiled his memory with this play and I felt guilty just being a part of it, sorry for getting my poor half-sister mixed up in this claptrap. The lead actor came back into the light, wearing pyjamas which made him look like the inmate of some Russian Gulag. Richey said he was tired of being in a band, the endless tours were getting to him. As someone who could barely play a note he loathed the neverending emphasis on musicianship, found himself sick of groupies and adulation, hated those people who wanted his soul and wasn't sure who he was anymore. At this point it occurred to me how *Too Beautiful* was just another vehicle profiting from Edwards' despair. It took one man's unhappiness and attendant symptoms, self-abuse and eating disorders and the inability to express love, and turned them into entertainment for the warped. I felt a wave of remorse, wanted to apologise endlessly, but I didn't know who to. It would have been futile anyway, maybe I should just get drunk until the urge went away.

The story moved to the evening of Richey's final gig, our hero in camouflage gear as he applied military-style make-up inside the great cargo net which took up most of his dressing room. Flashforward to the end of the concert, Richey trashing his (obviously wooden) guitar, stood before us in a Christlike pose while the band break their cheap props. Then Richey picks up the microphone stand and begins to smash himself in the face with it. The rest of the band fade away as Richey comes forward, still hitting himself. The spotlight follows him while feedback squalls through the theatre and Richey is before us now, shouting a slogan between each thwack.

"WE ARE THE SPECTATORS OF SUICIDE!" *<crack!>* "ALL IS VANITY!" *<thud!>* "NEVER LIVE PAST THE AGE OF THIRTEEN!" *<smack!>* "STAY BEAUTIFUL!" *<wallop!>*

The lights went out and we were left in silence. This was our intermission, the halfway point eighty six minutes into the performance. A portion of the audience dashed to the bar, including Randall who galumphed up the steps. I squirmed to the end of the empty row, laying across several seats so as not to be seen.

"Pssst!".

"Monty dear boy!" Axelrod puffed. "Whatever are you doing down there?"

"It's complicated." I passed a banknote to him. "Could you get me a beer?"

"Surely I will, no need to insult me with that." He waved the money away. "I'm getting two bottles for Fergal and two for myself, I've a feeling we're going to need them."

"Two sounds good."

The American wasn't the only one abandoning the auditorium. Groups of people slid into their coats and pulled on scarves, hastening toward the exits. Attendance would be well down in the second half and I felt sad for the actors, looking out from the stage onto a reduced audience. Then I realised what a hypocrite I was, I'd be out that door if I could.

Randall returned with half a dozen beers, holding the bottlenecks between his podgy fingers. I took a pair of the drinks and set one down for later.

The second half of *Too Beautiful* opened on a reporter who looked suspiciously like the band's drummer. He stood before the Severn Bridge, informing imaginary viewers of the facts in the case of Richey Edwards' disappearance. The man had vanished at the start of February, abandoning clothes, passport and anti-depressants at his Cardiff flat before driving to the motorway services on the England/Wales border. Police conjectured that, once there, the musician lived out of his car for a number of days before killing himself by jumping in the river. An extremely tall police officer who bore more than a passing resemblance to the *Manic Street Preachers'* bassist was interviewed, explaining how a man's body could be washed into the Bristol Channel and then on to the Atlantic Ocean without ever being found.

The officer appealed for calm from impressionable sections of the British public. "To those people who follow the philosophies of this troubled young man, particularly teenage girls who base their lives around duplicating Mr. Edwards' every action, I ask you not to run away from home or try anything drastic. Talk to your parents, seek help if they think you need it. We do not expect to recover Mr. Edwards any time soon."

That photo of the bridge was replaced by a pub interior where the band's singer, Jo, and Richey's mum, responded to the official verdict. Richey was in good spirits before the disappearance and he'd withdrawn two hundred pounds a day during his last two weeks in London, weren't these the actions of someone planning a trip? The singer said a man with Richey's intelligence could easily vanish into thin air, but even he couldn't answer the mother's question of *why?* Then Kathleen rose from the table and faced the audience to deliver a familiar speech. I knew these words, I'd written some of them.

"Why would he go? I can think of a hundred reasons that he talked of during those times we used to sit up at night, when he'd end up crying in my arms. Richey was tired of the pressure, that's true, sick of obsessive fans looking up to him as an example. Can you imagine? He didn't want any part of their American tour either, Richey knew his demons could rise to the surface over there and nothing cured him of those horrors. Medicine didn't work, and he was terrified the mental institutions would take his identity away. They wanted to get rid of Richey's talent as well as his problems, remove what made him unique. Treatment like that would leave my love an average man, unable to express himself or feel much of anything. He might as well have been dead.

"Maybe escape was the only option, leaving behind everyone he loved for the sake of his sanity. But there are times when I

210

wonder if the police are right. In my darker moments I ask myself if he took the permanent way out. So many of Richey's heroes joined that stupid club, might he have followed them? That's what the officials decided, even if they didn't have a note to prove it. What I mean is, he never admitted to killing himself. There was a message left behind, one written just for me. Something he'd never been able to say when we were together: *I love you.*"

By the time Kathleen reached the end there were tears in my eyes. I couldn't help it, her delivery was so emotional, spoken with such feeling, it broke my heart all over again. Rubbing my sockets, I didn't see much of what happened next, I only heard the policeman say they were ending their search for Mr. Edwards. Then Richey's friends and relatives stood in the spotlight and recited some of his lyrics, the voices expressing his alienation and despair. Unfortunately the lines were delivered in such a hackneyed manner, straining for poignancy and meaning, that by the time they'd finished talking of *removables* and *finely-tuned jealousy*, my visceral reaction to Kathleen's speech was a distant memory.

I'd calmed down by the start of that final act, settled enough to open my second bottle of beer. The conclusion of *Too Beautiful* was a new low, beginning with a backdrop of some sunkissed paradise. Richey appeared in shorts, playing volleyball with some unseen beach bums. He mimed the sport for a while then turned to us, laughing at some of the more outlandish theories about his disappearance. Those suggestions he'd joined a monastery or moved to a deserted island and was living like a castaway. The black-clad trio from the pub appeared as well, far off at the back of the stage, spotlighted as they shouted questions to Richey.

How could you do this to us? Why didn't you call? Are you happy now?

The lead answered them, saying he went to Goa in the hope of understanding life more precisely. Maybe he would return to friends and family one day, but for now Richey was happier than ever, at ease with his body and the world. Surely his interrogators would rather he stayed sane, left behind those who yearned for his downfall?

Soon Richey had argued down his girlfriend, mother and best friend. The actor moved back to the proscenium and delivered a final address, more Scouse than Welsh valleys, by which time I was experiencing a wide variety of cramps and a need to piss that was almost transcendental. The story ended with Edwards asking us not to regard him as a martyr, to think for ourselves instead and challenge the system. Then he backed away, toward a passing car stopping nearby to reveal a group of hippies inside. They waved Richey over and offered him a ride to the talukas. He accepted and disappeared, whereupon the noise of the departing vehicle was replaced by a *Manic Street Preachers* riff. The play was over. We were plunged into darkness for an instant before the house lights came up. A smattering of people, probably relations of the cast, gave the production a standing ovation while the rest of us clapped along half-heartedly.

The actors appeared for their curtain call, acknowledged our applause and bowed formally. My contribution to the noise was meant for Kathleen alone, that girl who looked like a diplomat boarding the last flight out of a war zone. Finishing my beer, I made for the door. That was when Mart appeared, bounding up the stairs toward me.

"Congratulations."

"Thanks Monty, shame we couldn't get a few more people in, but that's the way it goes."

"I'm sure word will spread." I noticed he was covered in some kind of white dust. "What did you want exactly?"

"We'll talk later. Wait for me at the bar and I'll buy you a drink."

"Alright."

He jogged off and I slipped away, absconding before Justin or Fergal or anyone else could spot me. At the empty bar I purchased a beer, positioning my table behind a pillar in such a way that that people couldn't see me on their way out. From this vantage point I watched them all leave, critics and music fans first, moving lethargically after three hours cooped up. Then came the friends and families, upbeat in their personal conversations, like inconvenienced travellers whose permission to fly has finally come, all forced cheeriness in an unfortunate situation.

After the crowd dispersed into the freezing night I visited the toilet at last. There was no sign of Mart when I got back so I bought another drink to pass the time. The barmaid opened my bottle and took payment, then she moved to serve someone who'd just arrived nearby.

"Double vodka and lemonade." Specified a female voice I knew well.

"Hello Kathleen."

She still wore Jo's final costume, that long black dress which made me think of repression and death. Up close her stage make-up altered the girl's appearance, made Kathleen paler than usual with incongruously red lips, like rose petals in the snow. Mart must have played another trick on me, trapping us like this. The girl fiddled with her purse and counted the coins inside, she hadn't looked at me once.

"I thought you were great."

"Thank you, everyone was very sweet." Kathleen drank half the vodka in one gulp. "It was good to see people again. Fergal was nice, he told me even Jane Fonda felt like apologising to the audience when she first got up onstage. I think he understood what I went through."

"It wasn't *that* bad."

"Yeah, well, you don't have to perform it for six weeks. You know what I wish? I wish Martin used your version. I'm not saying it was any better, but at least we'd have got it over with quickly." She finished the drink.

"You want another?"

"No, I only needed one to calm me down."

"Maybe it'll get better the more you do it."

Kathleen looked at me. Here was that girl I'd tried to forget, as lovely as ever but her eyes gave away how she really felt.

"Just drop it, okay? I don't want to talk about the fucking play. Tell you what Monty, let's talk about you." She folded her arms. "What are *you* doing here tonight? After I specifically told you not to come."

213

"Mart wouldn't let me stay away, I tried to keep out of sight..."

"Fuck all that, we're here now. Mutual pals have brought us together to communicate, so let's communicate."

"Kathleen, I...."

"What's going on Monty? Been enjoying yourself have you? Got other girls now?" Her anger made me sad. What I was about to do made me sadder.

I opened my wallet and took out an old photograph I'd been keeping there since the funeral. "I found this in my dad's things."

Kathleen studied the picture. "That's me and Kate."

"Yes."

"But it doesn't make any sense."

"My father is your father Kathleen. Kate's too." I felt unwell as the words came out. "I know it sounds unlikely but that's the truth."

No sound for long seconds. I could hear us breathing. "It can't be. No, it can't."

"Ask your mother if you want confirmation." I put the photograph away. "We could have gone to prison you know."

"No."

"We've the same genes Kathleen. I had to stop it, don't you see?" The tears were on their way again, I could feel them coming.

"No, no I don't see." She broke my stare and backed away. "I think you're making it up to excuse your behaviour, but what I don't know is why. Pretty sick to say something like that Monty, *sick*, you understand?"

And with that she stormed away. I wiped my face and wondered if it would be only right and proper to dash in the opposite direction, out onto those unwelcoming streets where I might find antagonists, some mugger who might redeem my spirit by breaking my body, pass out the punishment I deserved. But suddenly I found I couldn't move at all, speaking to Kathleen had rendered me immobile.

There was movement close by and the barmaid looked up at me.

"Another drink?" She said.

Chapter Seventeen

"I don't really understand what you're offering me. It's not a thing anyone here wants or needs. Look, I'm a realist, I have to be. I come from a generation with red where the whites of their eyes should be, we're bloodshot through overwork and lack of sleep and the drink we use to make life bearable and we don't come together like people used to. Because, when you get right down to it, no one's really *like* anyone else. None of us *needs* anybody to go on living. A warm body at night is nice, but anyone'll do for that. We're programmed to go on existing and everybody else is just surplus to that need. Believing your lover or child or deity is somehow *special, chosen, destined.* It's the way of the fool if you ask me. They say no man's an island, but that's a load of crap. Some people simply don't need the facade of company, some people *want to be alone.*"

At this point the Jehovah's Witnesses backed away from our door and moved to the next flat along.

Fergal had been listening from the hallway. "Was there any need to vivisect their beliefs like that, I ask myself."

"I'm late for work."

"Don't you want breakfast?"

I grabbed gloves and a coat. "Not really no."

Winter started late this year, but now it seemed the bad weather was never going to end. All across Europe the elderly were succumbing to this ongoing cold snap, and when I opened my curtains this morning snow had fallen in the night. The calendar said early April but this city was frozen. I trudged along, compacting the white stuff with my shoes, my breath forming speech bubbles of mist with every exhalation.

Too Beautiful didn't last anywhere near six weeks. Despite my best efforts the play was wound up after eight performances. I'd spread the word as far as I reasonably could, but none of the reviews had a good word to say about our piece. Even the internet fan-sites roasted it, citing a number of factual inaccuracies as their justification. With promotional material the normal tactic was to use some quotes out of context, but that became difficult when the critics were unrelentingly negative. They said things like "amateurish", "inept on every level" and "utterly failing to convey what made Richey special". After that first weekend audiences dwindled away to nothing with Mart forced to write off the production. My boss must have taken a big hit on his play and the rumours abounded, how he was desperately trying to recoup the losses with dodgy deals and unsavoury practices. During March various women I didn't recognise would hang around the office, usually dressed in some combination of stilettos, miniscule skirt with a g-string or gaudy boobkerchief. These floozies distracted Justin and made the blondes nervous, but Mart said he was only dabbling in the modelling business, claimed every time a woman was sent out in response to a call it was for a magazine or catalogue assignment. I had to wonder

He gave up the experiment a month later when one exceptionally voluptuous hussy stormed into his office and walloped Landry in the face after some kind of disagreement about money. Sadly their argument was too muffled for those of us with an ear up against the outer wall to make out, but speculation was rife as to what strange scheme our boss would attempt next in a bid to increase his "revenue streams". My vague fears were realised this very morning, arriving at the agency, red-faced and irritated and scraping slush off my shoes, to discover Mart had struck up a deal with Leon. The latest idea was to capitalise on and expand those gambling opportunities generated by the smoking room. I'd popped in after logging on, hoping to enjoy a swift game of cards before the day got started, finding instead a couple of blondes shivering as they tried to have a fag. The back door was open, so I looked around the yard and saw Justin clearing a patch of ground. He shovelled snow into a pile while Mart, Leon and the long haired guy from the record shop stood watching.

"Morning Monty." Said my boss.

"Alright?" Both Leon and the other guy had a fat ball of feathers under one of their arms. "What's going on here?"

"We've arranged a cockfight."

"A cockfight?" I took a closer look at the feathered balls. "Mart, those are chickens."

Leon was apologetic. "I couldn't get roosters anywhere so some anti-capitalists I know went down the battery farm and liberated these hens. It's all poultry isn't it?"

Before us Justin arranged some bricks to form a rudimentary pit, Mart observed him thoughtfully. "Yes Leon, it's all poultry. Unfortunately there's a world of difference between the trained gamecocks you promised me and those things." The hens were set down in the ring to lurch around contentedly, occasionally pecking at the concrete.

"Maybe we could dope 'em up or something?" Suggested the long haired guy.

"What about if we only put down enough seed for one? That'd annoy them."

"Justin, the great fights of the past featured cocks specially bred for their ferocity and fitted with razor-sharp spurs." Mart sighed. "I don't think this is going to be up there in terms of spectacle if we rely on them being *a bit hungry.*"

One of the chickens looked up at us quizzically, it was quite sweet. "Isn't this illegal?" I asked.

"Well, veggies might say this is a nasty business, but I don't think it's any worse than slaughtering one for your Sunday dinner. This way they get a chance of glory." Mart gave one of the birds a nudge with his foot. "It's a moot point if we can't make them attack each other. I told everyone this started at noon, did you sort out the weapons Just?"

"Um, I've got a penknife. We could sellotape that to one of them."

"Good grief."

The long haired guy bent down and cooed at one of the hens, grabbing hold of the bird and bringing it upwards so the chicken's head faced him. Then he squeezed the body of the bird with some force. The hen squawked in pain and surprise as a great spurt of excrement flew out of its anus and hit Justin in the face.

"Yeoww!!!"

"Ha ha!"

"I've always wanted to do that." Said the long haired guy, placing the traumatised bird back in the circle.

If that was the best moneymaking idea my boss could come up with I couldn't see our agency overcoming the financial trouble any time soon. For much of the day I stayed at my desk, drinking cup after cup of coffee and forcing myself to read emails which contained only bad news. Clients wrote to me saying: *"I'm afraid we're scaling back our advertising at this time...."* Or: *"In the current climate we simply can't afford to initiate new campaigns...".* Or even: *"Yes, we like your bears, but our beauty products have traditionally been associated with humans...."*

Justin returned after lunch, still smelling faintly of chickenshit. I asked my colleague whether the work situation ever worried him, if he noticed we were never busy like before, how little post arrived and the phones didn't ring. My co-worker wasn't concerned, Justin said I should enjoy the relaxed atmosphere while it lasted, a head buried deep in the sand. His blasé attitude irritated me, adding to the anger I felt when I thought of all the money Mart had wasted this year; the vanity project, those pointless talks, the wasteful outings. It made me madder still.

I checked the news sites and discovered a teenage popster online, a celebrity girl famous for her Lolitaesque hit singles and perfectly preserved hymen. The star offered to be an agony aunt for anyone who wanted to email in so I asked her why I felt the urge to attack complete strangers and rip their throats out with my teeth. A few minutes later I got my answer. Apparently the problem could be solved by purchasing a copy of her latest album on the compact disc format (with free DVD). I turned off my computer and went home early.

On my way back to the flat I picked up a copy of *The Daily Class* to read on the tube. There was a report on a woman who'd murdered her husband's lover but otherwise the paper contained little about family values. Instead the tabloid reported several further robberies by the so-called *Fat Family* and led with a series of stories on the apocalyptic threat to this nation's well-being posed by asylum seekers. Apparently they were flooding the country, wave after wave of dark-skinned corruption heading our way.

This story might have found an audience among rural folk, but to Londoners such scaremongering cut little ice. Few people here had been born and raised in this city. All of us were immigrants to some degree, arrivals seeking out the best lovers, careers, social scenes. That multiplicity of choice which came with England's capital.

As with other first world cities, thousands rushed to London after growing up in foreign lands or suburban towns, faraway islands and isolated hamlets. From New Zealand to Basingstoke we all came, happy to be a part of those opportunities the capital offered, a place where it was difficult to find peace or feel at home but easy to lose yourself in the speed of passing days. We were mixed up and confused under the skyline, wondering whether to live somewhere safer, friendlier, smaller. But something kept us around, some aspect of the material life, some Darwinism or impetuosity which meant we did what was necessary to stay. Some falsified paperwork or entered marriages of convenience with naive Englishmen, others took out loans or stayed in jobs they hated, biting the bullet and getting past the bad stuff. In spite of the pollution, the stress and crime and noise, those council estates and bench-ridden madmen, despite thugs with blunt knives prowling the streets at night or tourists blocking your way through the daytimes, this city won out over the negatives. Whatever it was London had we wanted it. And so I stayed, unable see of anywhere else as the centre of my pitiless universe. I became isolated during these months, unable to assuage my loneliness, that single man's pain worse than ever during nights secluded in my room.

The weeks passed and my habits become more solitary and eccentric. I checked my bank balance twice a day and paid in cash, knowing how much money I had at any given moment, right down to the last few pence. I dug out six books from my teens and reread them, starting five more I'd bought but never got round to when those were finished. At weekends I took to wandering frosty parks, trying to remember how the world looked, watching mothers with children, staring at mallards and swans, wondering if the great white birds suspected they belonged to our monarch. On the tube I looked at the scrolling words, hoping for guidance, then realised what I was doing and glanced away. Nothing ever came up anyway, even the spirit of the message board had forsaken me. Back at the flat I would go through my old tapes, albums I'd once borrowed as a penniless student, finding songs to encapsulate my mood. Listening to *Palace* and *The Velvet Underground* and *Wheat* I filled spare evenings, kept myself distracted, almost forgetting my behaviour was like that of a prisoner marking time. Except I had no release date to look forward to.

The only memorable day during this period came when I hesitantly accepted an invitation from Tosspot O'Reilly. *The Airborne Toxic Event* were putting the final touches to their album; *'Close Your Legs Girl, You Sit Like A Harlot'*, and I was welcome at the studio. In reality the band weren't even close to finishing the record and I came upon a charged situation. The singer wasn't happy with Simon complicating his guitar parts, Giles wasn't happy with the way the drums sounded, Si wasn't happy with Tosspot's attitude, no one could tell whether Brett was happy or not and the producer was losing his rag with all of them. Sitting behind the mixing desk I watched Simon take another shot at the guitar line for *Copacetic*.

"Can you put some more reverb on that Larry?" The producer did as he was told.

"Don't listen to him." Tosspot was sitting with us, behind the glass screen. "You're too crackly. Turn the distortion down, it's not gonna fit with the vocals."

"Sounds alright to me."

"Can we please get something down?"

The guitarist began to play once more, it sounded very wrong.

"Stop, stop!"

"What?"

"I thought I told you to leave the echo alone?" Tosspot rounded on their producer. "We're going to end up sounding like a goth bar band."

"I like the way it sounds."

"What do you think Brett?"

"..."

"Monty?"

"I'm not getting involved."

Arguments abounded, the song impossible to complete to everyone's satisfaction. They abandoned the guitar and Giles tried again to nail one of his drum parts. If this was the level of perfectionism at the recording I dreaded to think how the band would get on when they tried to get the right mix. In the end my fears went unrealised. *Whelmed & Naughty Records* decided they'd spent enough money on this unknown band with their limited commercial potential. Representatives came to the studio after the band were gone and took the master tapes away. The songs were mixed without the players' involvement.

I saw *The Airborne Toxic Event* once more after that, and it was clear they were a group on the verge of disintegrating. The songs remained as strong as ever, but something was missing, one of those unfeigned elements which made a band so compelling, passion or soul or maybe chemistry. Si didn't even look at his bandmates for much of the set, while Tosspot made the group cover *The Flaming Lips' Halloween On The Barbary Coast*, apparently so he could sing the line *"Boy, you still got shit for a brain"* into the unhappy guitarist's ear. Never would I see a clearer image of a formerly close-knit band breaking down, the dissolution of that gang mentality plain to see.

Even partisan sections of the crowd knew something was wrong. This gig was supposed to be a celebration, the band out of the studio and back in that live arena where they belonged. But the fault-lines within *The A.T.E.* were horribly apparent, between songs Tosspot talked bitterly of the label taking their album away, made snide remarks at the expense of his fellow musicians and indulged in ill-conceived attempts to whip the crowd into a frenzy, cajoling and mouthing off like a dying comedian. I think some of us suspected we were watching the band's swansong, and perhaps our negative vibes bounced back onto Tosspot, made the singer believe he had to attempt something outlandish and theatrical to win us back round. After the last song but before what turned out to be a very short encore, O'Reilly squirted lighter fluid on his trainers and set light to them. That final number was performed while his feet were on fire, Tosspot jumping around the stage as the flames licked at his shoes.

The singer cut an intimidating figure, gave the whole spectacle a pointless degree of peril and self-abasement. They were halfway through the track when he began to yell out. Tosspot tried to put the fire out as the rest of the band played on, ignoring his screams of pain. Eventually a roadie ran onstage with a fire extinguisher, but by then it was too late. O'Reilly was kept in hospital overnight with second degree burns to both feet.

While the doctors examined him I made my way home, feeling even more heartsick than usual. Alcohol had combined with the violence of the spectacle to leave me in a hazardous state of mind. The tube wasn't packed, but it was a time when people stumbled home after an evening of heavy drinking and my carriage had its share of casualties. The drowsy and incoherent sat below loud twentysomethings who joked and fell against the doors when we creaked into motion. I was at the end of the row, one of those seats given up for mothers with children or the physically impaired. It was strange no one had taken this plumb spot, but I soon discovered why.

An extremely ill woman floundered to my left, holding her stomach as if an alien were about to burst out of it. She leant leftwards, across the next seat along, and proceeded to vomit onto the worn material, a repulsive combination of sound and smell I had to turn away from. A city type in a suit sat opposite, a guy beside him who'd clearly spent the day on a building site, his clothes covered in dust and grime. Both men pretended there wasn't a woman puking her guts up in front of them, indeed the businessman seemed to take these splashing heaves as his cue to start up a conversation.

"Construction worker eh?" The suit was exuberantly drunk, speaking slowly and with the boom of a solvent alpha male. I hated him instantly.

"Uh, yeah." Replied the builder, bemused.

"Excellent, excellent. I've been wanting to meet one. One of those people my taxes subsidise. I don't suppose the government takes any of your money does it?" He stubbed a fleshy finger into the builder's spattered trouser leg. The worker looked away, trying to ignore this man addressing him like some kind of peasant, spittle flying from his fat mouth. I felt that fury I'd been suppressing rise up, triggered by this combination of circumstances, my bad night, the effect of that woman's vomit, a hatred of the world, the way it was for unfortunates like myself and the builder.

"Excuse me." I spoke loudly to get the businessman's attention.

"Ye-es?"

"I was just wondering if you knew how obnoxious you were being?"

"Now see here, I was having a very pleasant chat with this fellow."

"No you weren't, you were being condescending and pathetic. Those are telltale signs of sexual impotence, did you know that?"

"Now.... see here." He said again.

"You're looking down on us as if we're pieces of crap, but you're the only scum I can see. Do you really think you're better than us because you earn more money? I hope you get taxed so hard you can't sit down for a month."

"I don't have to take this." He stood up, turning out to have a height advantage over me of several inches.

I rose to meet him, we were face to face now. "How many people did you screw over to get where you are today, huh? How much arse did you slurp? Now you expect everyone to do the same for you 'cause you're the big man, yeah? Well fuck you, you tragic wanker."

The suit placed both hands on my chest and pushed me down, a playground bully dismissing the weaker child. I don't recall deciding to do what I did next so it must have been something instinctive. After landing next to the hacking woman, I instantly got back on my feet and put everything I had into a right hook, My fist landed squarely on the businessman's chin and he went down like a felled tree, the other passengers withdrawing their feet as his body landed in the aisle, on top of that puddle of vomit which had dripped down from the seat.

I looked at the other passengers but nobody was reaching for the emergency alarm. In fact no one was even watching, all eyes were averted. To these people I was just one more nutter, looking my way might redirect the ire. The man on the floor moaned and tried to get up as the tube pulled into a station. I got off and changed lines, working out a complicated route home in case someone had alerted staff and they were out looking out for me.

The extended journey provided me with plenty of time to sober up and I started wondering what had gone so wrong. I'd never displayed aggressive tendencies like this before, always thought of myself as placid and easygoing. Normally I let idiots be as offensive as they liked rather than intervene, but something had changed inside me this year. Getting into a stupid fight on the tube was another result of my current state of mind and I began to consider seeking some kind of psychiatric help, because if this continued I'd end up in traction.

The next week *'Close Your Legs Girl, You Sit Like A Harlot'* was given a desultory launch by *Whelmed & Naughty*, trickling into stores with the minimum of support and vanishing amongst less interesting releases. A couple of reviews were generally positive, but the label had effectively given up on their charges and the promotional machine was noticeable only by its absence. I bought a copy because I wanted the songs, however imperfectly done, but it turned out to be expenditure I could ill afford. The following Monday my boss called his team together for an announcement I'd been half-expecting for months.

"Hello everyone. Some of you may have had your suspicions for a while, so I've decided to get this over with." From behind his spectacles Mart scanned the pensive faces. "There's no easy way to say this I'm afraid, but *Bears!Bears!Bears!* will cease trading at the end of this week. I'm very sorry, we've tried as hard as we can. Believe me when I say this hits me as hard as it does you, this is my dream that's died here today." Shocked mutterings from the blondes. "Sometimes you just have to do the decent thing and admit defeat. There's no sign of the business picking up any time soon and we're currently operating at a big loss. If I don't liquidate now we'll only go bankrupt in the summer so I'm afraid it's the only way. If anyone needs a reference I'll be willing to give you all excellent write-ups." Landry adjusted his glasses, I felt like I was trapped in a plummeting lift.

"It's not all doom and gloom though." The boss smiled. "We've enough petty cash to pay for a night out this Friday."

"Yay!" Cheered Justin as the girls regarded him with scorn.

"I'll send out details of the location later on. Entry and drinks will be on me all night. It's not much, just my way of saying thanks to each and every one of you for the hard work you've put in over the years."

Outside the girls comforted each other, serious in their shared loss, like ocean-goers relegated to the lifeboat. Lettice was tearing up and accepted my hug gratefully.

"Shush, don't worry." I patted her sweet-smelling head. "You'll be fine, they always need blondes in this industry. I reckon you can do better."

The girl pulled away, gave me a sad smile. "But what will you do babes? I can't imagine Monty without bears in his life."

I chuckled. "Sometimes it's good to expand your horizons, I've been getting quite into chipmunks lately."

We spent much of that week clearing our workstations. I destroyed great piles of ursine memorabilia, packed stationery and computer accessories away with my personal effects. Files and mousemats and staplers I'd never use but took home anyway, reimbursing myself for the time I'd lost on Martin's dream. He sent through details of the bash and I took one look at the dress code for our celebration of imminent joblessness (*school uniform?*) and wondered how I could weasel out of it. Justin's reaction was at the other end of the spectrum, my soon-to-be-ex colleague predictably excited by the prospect.

"Ever been to *'Teacher's Pet'* before Monty?"

"Can't say I have."

"You'll love it. They play classic Eighties pop and there's loads of women dressed like schoolgirls, it's totally fab."

"Sounds it." I wondered whether I'd miss his silly little face when we no longer worked together. "You don't seem too upset at losing your job."

"Nah, this is just the push I needed. I've been wanting to try something different. This way we get a good night out, that's more than you normally get with the sack." He turned to me, serious now. "You are gonna come Friday aren't you?"

Yes, I agreed that I would. However horrible the club might be, there was no way it could hold a candle to speed dating. Besides, it was only right to tap Mart for as much free beer as possible.

Each day of my last week I spent an hour or two tying up loose ends, cancelling ads or informing contacts of the company's dissolution, before checking the paper for jobs, hanging out with Bernard or playing a few hands of poker. Leon had returned the smoking room to its former set-up and dealt me in happily, although he was tight-lipped about what had happened to the chickens.

In the evenings I went home and talked to Fergal about my worries. The loss of livelihood brought me out of myself a little, gave me a more immediate concern than the unremitting melancholy which had characterised past months. We started hanging out again, and I think the Irishman was a little concerned at how thin I'd become while he wasn't paying attention. True, I often skipped dinner, preferring to go without food rather than expend the effort required to get some, but I was only a few pounds underweight, although compared to Fergal that was positively anorexic. He was still on a quest to become more bearish and maintained an impressive belly, helped by Randall who took pity on my gastronomic impoverishment. The American started coming over regularly to share his love for Mexican food. We ate burritos and tacos smothered in all kinds of appetising sauces, accompanied by fresh salads and sometimes I felt like a cub being fattened up by mummy and daddy bear, although I had no idea which was which. To be looked after was pleasant though, as was the opportunity to explain how I felt, it was good to let out some of the angst and fear.

"You won't have any problem getting work my friend." The three of us were eating beef-filled tortillas a couple of nights after Mart's announcement. "Think of it as graylisting."

"What's graylisting?"

"A kind of limbo, it's how the film industry ostracised Jane Fonda when she came out against the war in Vietnam. They wouldn't distribute Jane's movies or send her scripts for consideration. One studio boss said: *That bitch will never be allowed inside my gates again.* Jane didn't make a movie in four years." Fergal swallowed a lettuce leaf. "Of course, she had the last laugh. Not only was Jane right politically but she went on to win a cornucopia of Oscars."

Randall put his cutlery down. "Ferg, I know you mean well, but when will you learn? Jane Fonda's life doesn't have some catch-all moral you can apply whenever people need advice. The plight of this poor boy has nothing to do with an actress who doesn't act anymore."

"Precisely." I felt vindicated for once. "Thank you very much Randall."

"Harumph." In the past no one was fearless or smart enough to cut Fergal down to size, now he had to accept these home truths if he wanted to be Axelrod's significant other.

The American continued. "Monty needs practical advice to help him through this. We ought to be capable of figuring something out."

"It's good of you gays to rally round like this, really. I just need to find a job, and it doesn't look like that's going to be easy. There aren't too many organisations looking for someone with an encyclopaedic knowledge of koalas or experience fighting off brown bears."

"Unemployment isn't the real problem my friend, you know that as well as I do."

"No. No I don't actually." I looked to Randall. "What's he talking about?" A shrug.

"What I'm talking about laddo, is the way you've been acting. You mope around in your own world, walling yourself off from everybody, and it's because you're still in love. Like the other night when you struck that businessman. It happened because you're not over Kathleen, a blind man could see that."

"You really think so? You as well Randall?"

"It does sound like lovesickness Monty. Tell me, does everything in your life seem irrelevant and meaningless since she left?"

"Well, yeah."

"And you've been walking around in a daze, feeling like a hollow shell of a man?"

"Uh-huh."

"Then Ferg's probably right and something must be done." Randall scratched his lush beard. "The question is, what?"

"I take it you've heard everything that happened between her and me?"

"Enough."

"Then you know I can't ever be with Kathleen the way I want to be." I wasn't sure whether I believed this pair. That anger I bottled up, the jaded wanderings of my existence, it felt like a normal response to an unkind world, a loss of faith in the pursuit of happiness. Could they be on to something? Was that which ailed me smaller than I thought? "I've been away from Kathleen for months now. If you're right, if I haven't recovered and there's no sign that I will, then tell me. How the hell do I get over her?"

"Maybe you don't have to."

"In my book Barbara says Genetic Sexual Attraction is a normal response to an abnormal situation."

"Exactly. Sometimes the morality of the masses is not the morality that's best for the individual." Axelrod pointed to his lover. "Not so many years ago young Fergal and I would've been persecuted for what we have."

"He's right."

"I'm not sure Randall, I still get queasy when I think about my sister."

"Goddamn Monty, I'm not saying the two of you should go off and screw like marmosets." My flatmate was about to light a cigarette but Axelrod cut him a forbidding glance. "You're brother and sister for crying out loud. You can't deny that kind of attachment then expect your mind and heart to retain their equilibria."

"Erm, I suppose not." There was a brief silence. Fergal put his cigarettes away.

"You know what dwarf tossing is Monty?"

"Some other homosexual group? Are they affiliated with man-bears?"

"No, dwarf tossing is a very popular sport in my country." I nodded. "A while back several states banned it because the kind of folks who live behind white picket fences got upset, they thought it was cruel. Bills were passed under the auspices of protecting public order to stop it and the middle classes were happy. But then it was the dwarves who were lobbying their senator. They'd lost their jobs you see, there was no way for them to make ends meet if the sport was outlawed."

I pondered his story. "Are you saying I'm like the dwarf or the tosser?"

"All I'm saying is sometimes you have to look at things from a slightly different angle if you want to see the true picture. Everyone thought those little men were hard done by, but they weren't victims until the do-gooders came along. The concerned citizens eased their consciences by taking away the work and it made no sense to those midgets. They didn't want what we thought they wanted, us regular size people thought the job was dangerous and demeaning, but being tossed was one of the few ways a dwarf could earn a living and feel proud doing it. If we really respected the dwarves as people we'd have let them be."

We ruminated on the moral of this for a while. "There's nothing like being thrown around by big lads," observed Fergal, disappearing outside for a smoke.

Chapter Eighteen

We stood behind the velvet rope as the bouncers guarded the entrance, men exuding tranquillity, they had all the time in the world. The night air chilled those of us waiting, this country hadn't entered springtime yet, although the snow and ice had gone from the roads. We were wrapped in thick coats but it wasn't enough, the blondes shivering as the breeze sought out their bare legs. Worse off were those groups of girls who clambered out of rented stretch limousines at regular intervals. They rose to the kerb, hands on black microskirts, pulling faces of dismay when they saw the doors weren't open. Walking to the end of the line, these women were treated to cries of *"'ray!"*, *"mate!"* and *"hubba hubba!"* from the male elements in the queue, they wore white shirts unbuttoned to the cleavage or knotted to reveal flat stomachs, perfect flesh exposed to this night and goosepimpling before our eyes. The cheers those girls elicited were egalitarian, every scantily-clad arrival brought shouts, but when the most striking went past it was almost as if the blokes became *Merry Melodies* cartoons. Eyes popped out on stalks and tongues unrolled along the pavement to a honking sound effect which turned out to be coming from the traffic.

I enjoyed staring at these bodies as much as anyone, but I was more entertained by the way Justin pretended not to be interested. His girlfriend hadn't exactly been chuffed to learn that he was coming here tonight. Thanks to a prior engagement Yohanna had to give her flatmate the responsibility of supervising Justin, Lettice making sure he didn't get up to anything untoward with some intoxicated bimbo. My colleague was dressed in an official *Teacher's Pet* souvenir tie and dark shorts exposing bony white legs. Constantly aware of Lettice's eagle eyes, every time Justin caught himself watching a girl his face would contort in horror and look to see if she was noting his lechery.

On my other side, and already one sheet to the wind, stood Martin. He was talking to anyone who would listen about what he might attempt next, how his time with bears had served as inspiration. Perhaps he'd devote his time to conservationism, work with environmentalists to expose illegal trappers around game reserves or

231

campaign against the extinction of threatened species. Or maybe Mart would start selling cut-price snowboards. Whatever he decided, Landry saw it as a sweet relief, this trying something new. I half-listened to him, wondering if I was the only one there pessimistic about the turn of events, that solitary team member who didn't see impending unemployment as my chance to explore wonderfully unlimited opportunities.

I'd miss *Bears!Bears!Bears!*, that was the honest truth. The realisation had really hit home this morning when Martin joined us for a while to chew the fat. Over the years my job provided the closest thing I had to security while I moved from house to house, experiencing problems with women or my family. Whatever happened, I always knew that when the week began I'd be commuting to a job I didn't hate, working with a group of people who weren't objectionable. That was more than most people had. There'd been a few difficulties lately, sure, as the work became unrewarding and colleagues got my back up, but when we sat there this morning and laughed over our memories, the good times came back with renewed clarity.

We reminisced about the celebrations every time a panda was born into captivity and I spoke of seeing a black bear climb a tree, scooting up the trunk like an enormous furry squirrel, the creature's agility belying its weight. Then there were the amusing anecdotes, like the time Mart's house was infested with mice and none of the cats he tried seemed to be any use. In the end we convinced a wrangler to take his spectacled bear in after it had finished filming one day. The mice never came back after that. Despite the bear causing a fair bit of damage, Mart said it was worth it just to see the look on his neighbours' faces. We led that great animal with the yellow-ringed eyes through his front door as if it were the most natural method of pest control in the world.

These conversations continued for much of the afternoon and it was fun, but afterwards I felt little better. Nostalgia makes the past bearable by fooling us into believing we haven't wasted our lives, but it's a dangerous way of thinking when the present sucks. Everything was drifting away from me. I lost my job like I lost my dad, and the band, and Kathleen. Kathleen. The girl had been back in my thoughts after that conversation with Randall last night. I stuck around this morning for a leisurely breakfast with Fergal, Axelrod having left to supply the voice of a waltzing potato for a TV commercial. That left the pair of us at our table, eating scrambled eggs and trying to figure it all out.

"Do you think Randall's right?" I asked him. "Is it worth getting in touch with her?"

"That all depends on whether you're over your guilt."

I pondered. "I still think what we did was wrong."

"That's because you're poisoning your mind with this rubbish." Fergal picked up today's Class, the front page describing how some violent film posed a threat to the infrastructure of humanity, and tossed it in the bin. "If you believe some people then we've all acted immorally at one point or another. Randall's right, it depends on how you look at it. There's no higher authority than God, and according to the propaganda he's not too fond of the way I conduct myself. So do I suppress the way I am to avoid a fiery fate? Simply because the Good Book reflects the prejudices of some straights who found the way men make love to men distasteful? Of course I don't."

"Having sex with your half-sister is icky though, you've got to admit that."

"Which is why you must be strong. Spend time with her and the attraction will still be there. I told you what Barbara says, GSA takes years to go away. As long as you're prepared for that *frisson* I say go and see her. You need to resolve this for the sake of your mental stability. That'll never happen if you deny you've even got a sister."

I didn't know whether I could stay strong though, there was a knot in my stomach and it tightened every time I thought of meeting Kathleen.

A nudge in my back and I turned to see Lettice, breasts outlined beautifully under her pristine shirt, urging me onwards. At the front those bouncers ripped up tickets, letting clubbers in a few at a time. I moved along and gazed at the shaven-headed men with black jackets unzipped to the waist. Did they have dilemmas like mine? Maybe their lives were just one long sequence of base instinct followed by immediate action. Like children, or polar bears.

Soon we were through the barrier, checking our coats before moving to the main arena. At the bar bottles of lager were on sale at four times the price of the shop down the road, but Mart had instructed the bar staff to set up a tab for the agency so I got three for nothing. We'd arrived early enough to secure a table, separated from the dancefloor by a wooden partition and I took the cushioned seat which offered the best view of arriving women as the blondes gathered round, talking amongst themselves.

Justin wriggled in beside me. "All those yours?" He pointed at the trio of bottles lined up before me, I nodded. "Nice one."

The DJ played a few hits from recent months but the bulk of the evening's soundtrack came from songs made famous during the eighties and nineties, addictive tracks which stopped just the right side of irritating, from *Video Killed The Radio Star* to *Pop Musik*. The bar got busy and a few pockets of girls took the floor, tiptoeing around handbags in time to the music.

Justin leant over. "You know Monty, the other day this friend of Yohanna's started telling her how sad it was about my death, and there's a guy I kind of know around Soho who hugged me in the street last week and said *thank God you're alright.*"

"I'm sorry Justin, I did ask him to stop."

"It's not your fault, I'm just fed up with people thinking I'm dead. My girlfriend got an email last week asking how people could get in touch with my mother to offer condolences. Imagine if someone had got through."

"I'll tell Fergal again, I promise." The prank wasn't my doing, but I knew how often I'd let it slide in the past, even laughing along with my flatmate when he thought up particularly outlandish death scenarios. I felt guilty, Justin was a harmless guy and he didn't deserve to be picked on this way. Fergal just found it easier to think of my colleague as a fashionista fool rather than a rounded human being with thoughts and feelings of his own. Hell, I'd done it myself for long enough.

My change of heart had happened earlier that day. We both arrived late and in school uniform, neither of us willing to go home before beginning our session on the beer. Insecure at my own appearance, I'd mocked his shorts, but Justin maintained that the drunken ladies at *Teacher's Pet* would adore his knees. The outfit made him stand out from those other guys and Justin offered a kind of unity with girls who were compelled to flaunt their legs (he said this when Lettice was out of earshot). Was it worth going the whole hog and shaving them too I asked. Then I went on to express envy that those shorts were only available in child sizes so there weren't any to fit me.

He brushed away my sarcasm and we drank coffee, talking out the rest of the day before leaving early. Justin had some kind of errand to run and I didn't want to get stuck in the centre of London alone while wearing school uniform. As well as marking me out as the kind of person who attended ludicrous club nights, these clothes weren't meant for daylight. There were permanent sweat marks around the collar of my only white shirt and suspicious-looking creamy stains on the back of the trousers which no amount of scrubbing could remove.

The two of us travelled east on the Central Line and I speculated that the chore involved some kind of chapeau shop, Justin returning an item of clothing because it wasn't in any more. I couldn't have been more wrong.

"I might wait out here." I said when we got to the retirement home, a Victorian building somewhere outside Stepney Green.

"Come on Monty, it's cold and I could be ages." He opened the glass-panelled door. "There's nothing to worry about, everyone's tame in here."

I lurked in the reception area while Justin chatted to the girl on the desk, timidly following when he was allowed through. I'd never been inside a nursing home before and it was unnervingly quiet there after the hubbub of central London. We walked past a huge window looking out on rocks and shrubs and I noticed the faint smell of disinfectant, an odour undercut by something musty and ancient. The atmosphere made me nervous, at a time of the week when people my age were eager for the weekend, putting another working week behind them and maybe sinking a few bevvies,

I was inside a private building which felt like a library. A library with the upbeat undertow of knowledge and learning replaced by the harsh reality of this mortal coil.

The passageway opened out onto a room containing a mishmash of easy chairs and tables, jigsaws and board games strewn across the surfaces. Various grey-haired men and women reclined in their seats, some moving wrinkled fingers or misshapen lips to no obvious purpose, the tics of physical disrepair. Adjoining this space was another room where elderly folk congregated, from it came the faint sound of a quiz show. That was where the more alert inhabitants relaxed of an afternoon, enjoying their favourite programmes before dinner. My instincts told me to go in and watch the TV until Justin was done, but it wasn't to be. He approached a woman with permed white hair and a glazed look in her eyes.

"Grandma, hi." Justin kissed the woman on her cheek. Something, possibly recognition, flickered across her face, but it was gone by the next breath. "I brought a friend."

He got two chairs and we sat either side of the old woman. She looked to her grandson but gave no response when he spoke, no evidence of understanding. Justin talked about his mother and the rest of their family, how he'd be heading for a new job very soon. Knowing the names of the other residents, Justin mentioned some, all the time encouraging this elderly lady to speak, words which never came.

"Does she say anything?" I asked after one protracted longueur.

"Not anymore, she's worse this year. It's in the later stages now."

"What is?"

"Old age, forgetfulness, Parkinson's. They don't know how much time granma's got but no one expects her to last very long." He must have seen the look on my face then. "Don't worry Monty, she can't understand what we're saying. The doctors say a familiar face does her good, but I only talk to put myself at ease. We could be going on about bears for all she knows."

"Do you come here regularly?"

"Once a week, sometimes more. I like to make sure she's okay and getting the best care. Wouldn't want my money going to waste."

"Your money?"

"Yep, I pay for this." He brushed a curl from the old woman's forehead. "Eats up half my wages every month but it's worth it. You should see the state of the council homes they offered us."

"I saw a documentary once."

"Then maybe you've some idea." A tremor shot through her arm, as if the old lady had seen a bug on it, I felt humbled by Justin's sacrifice.

"Shouldn't she be your parents' responsibility?"

"They can't afford to keep her here, there's a mortgage to pay off. My dad was quite happy to keep her with the council. She's just the mother-in-law to him, you know? But granma was always really good to me, I couldn't let that happen. Me and mum struck up a deal. I stay on at the house rent-free and I pay for this in return, however long it takes." Justin patted his grandmother's hand. "I've given up a bit of freedom and I can't buy as much stuff as I'd like, but when I'm here that doesn't seem to matter much."

Across the room one of the nurses assisted an old man as he struggled out of his chair, intent on walking despite failing legs.

"I know what you mean." I watched the man make slow progress. "When life and death come along everything else seems a bit small. It happened to me a while ago."

"Your dad, yeah, that must have been terrible. At least I kind of know when granma's gonna go."

"I don't know, I think this might be worse." I glanced back at the oblivious woman. "Watching someone deteriorate and being powerless to stop it, my mum went through that with her parents. She knew their time was ending but it still hit her hard. You can grieve a person before they're gone, but however much your defences try and protect you it still hurts. Our minds put sandbags up against grief until the pain of losing someone overwhelms them. It's like a flash-flood."

Justin used a handkerchief to dab the corner of his grandmother's mouth and I thought about life. You thought you had a handle on people, then they pulled something like this. For the first time since I'd known him I realised Justin could teach me a thing or two, about loyalty and selflessness.

"You're right, I won't be ready. Even if I prepare myself."

"How do you prepare yourself Justin?"

"Me? I don't know, it's difficult. Sometimes I like to think of her as an ice sculpture. Granma's here now, but one day she'll melt away to nothing, and when that happens I'll just have my memories. I wish she was around to watch over me forever, but she won't be. You have to appreciate loved ones while they're here, there's no secret to it." He kissed her on the cheek. "Goodbye granma. C'mon Monty, let's go."

The dancefloor filled, girls getting up on a podium before the DJ's platform, shaking their lithe bodies. I sat and watched, thinking about the transience of us all, how opportunities were lost forever when we failed to grab them. Yet there was also that capacity in people to overturn your expectations. This afternoon Justin proved to me he existed in three dimensions. For a long time I'd dismissed my team-mate as facile and easily led, someone who thought of his appearance above all else. That was one side of him, sure, the flash-in-the-pan clothes and immaculately coiffed chin. But beyond my caricature existed a loving man, working to make sure his grandmother had the best possible care. He'd turned around everything I believed today, made me feel like the small one.

I leant against the partition and scanned the club. Guys with shirts untucked and ties askew drank their way through bottle after bottle. In the seated area one girl had overreached herself already. She flopped around, legs waving to reveal skimpy underwear every time they opened. The people from the agency decided to get up and dance, giving up on their attempts to persuade me. Lettice and the blondes took a spot near the front while Mart and Justin slipped alongside, pumping their fists as they strutted beneath that podium. It was easy to see why *Teacher's Pet* had become such a hit, this night combined the two elements girls look for in a club (music they recognise and a chance to dress up), with the one thing guys want (attractive chicks in revealing clothing).

At the table I was joined by three teenage girls who set about comparing recent piercings, pulling up tops to reveal gold or silver studs in the loose skin around belly buttons. One had some kind of bejewelled incision in her chest too, a glittering ruby adornment which punctured the top of her cleavage, going in and out of the flesh just as the breasts began to separate. Her friends cooed enviously over this mutilation while I wondered if my gaze was that of a desirable older man; someone to take these girls under his wing and excite them with new experiences, or whether I'd crossed the line to lecherous old duffer, ogling unsuspecting teens as they innocently compared piercings. Whichever, it didn't really matter. If I wanted to pull any of these females I'd have to carry out some kind of impressive dance routine and even if I managed what was clearly beyond me, I'd probably become irritated by their immature fixations.

I looked away, to Mart who climbed up on that raised dais in a bout of drunken excitement. He joined the podium dancers who thrust their bodies in time to the music, followed by Justin as the two of them shuffled on the rostrum until a security guard had a quiet word in Mart's ear and they got down. I ordered another beer and walked away from the bar, past girls flapper-dancing on chairs and guys staring at them, on into the toilets.

After I'd pissed a black hand appeared at the sink, turning the taps on and offering me a paper towel.

"I can do that myself."

"Just trying to be helpful sir." The attendant was a smart man, about my height with obsidian skin and a consummately clean uniform. Near him was a counter of powerful aftershaves and liquid soaps beside a holder containing a variety of colourful lollipops.

I peered down at the confectionery. "How much?"

"Our system is donation-based sir, give whatever you can spare."

"I'll take two." I sorted through my change and passed the attendant a two-pound coin. "There you go."

"Thank you sir, very generous."

"Don't worry about it, I'll be flat broke soon enough." I leant against the counter. "Mind if I stay here to eat?"

"Not at all."

I unwrapped one of the sweets and popped it in my gob. "What's your name mate?"

"Leroy."

"Leroy, I'm Monty." We shook hands. "Don't call me sir Leroy, it makes me feel like you pick cotton on my land or something."

"Fine, good to meet you Monty. Excuse me a moment." The attendant squirted some fragrant goo onto another pair of hands and was rewarded with a silver coin. Something about these toilet transactions made me kind of uneasy, but I stuck around.

"Isn't this a bit demeaning for you Leroy? I mean, you seem like an educated guy."

"It is much more demeaning to be at home and unemployed. This work helps me to complete my university course. You would be surprised Monty, how much can be made from the drunk and happy."

"I guess." A thick-set man stumbled past and fell into one of the cubicles. "At least you don't have to deal with girl bands punching you in the gents."

"No, it is not all sweetness and roses though." Leroy grinned, his teeth gleaming under the electric light. "Sometimes I feel the urge to push a head down the toilet bowl."

"Really?"

"The aristocrats are the worst. They show me what they have done." He adopted a braying upper class accent. *"Boy, look. I have passed a plop plop, see? Flush for me boy."* Leroy tutted. "And they leave without a tip. I dread it when the posh ones come in."

"Bummer." The stocky man came out of the stall before staggering away, when I turned back the attendant was looking at me curiously.

"Let me ask you this." He ventured. "You have paid for a ticket, yes? Why then are you here talking to me when you could be out there feeling the women?"

"Well, Leroy, it's like this..."

I told him my story, all the way from meeting Kathleen to giving her up. We were interrupted by visitors several times and Leroy didn't believe the more outlandish aspects so I had to repeat them. By the time I'd finished my bottle of lager was empty and I needed to piss again. "What do you think?"

"I think I am glad to have a job which does not involve bears."

"Yes, but what about the girl?"

"I am not sure I'm the one you should be asking."

"Your opinion's as good as the next man Leroy. Hell, at least I know you're not a hallucination. I used to get my advice from information boards in tube stations."

"Hummm..." The attendant considered my plight. "I think perhaps the batty boys you speak of are correct, you must talk with her once more."

"You don't think that's asking for trouble?"

"A man is worth nothing without a little trouble. Perhaps one day I will tell you the story of my trouble." He wiped the counter. "You must reach some agreement with this Kathleen, like adults. Just do not make her with the child, it may have more than ten fingers."

"Or webbed feet."

"Perhaps just the one eyebrow."

"And not on its face."

"Hum, yes. Do not worry about the past Monty, it is nothing. My family came here from Africa when I was a teenager and we settled in Somerset, I do not know why. One of the men I went to school with married a horse."

"That's not true Leroy, is it?" The worker chuckled to himself and returned to his duties. I urinated, grateful for his help and the chance to laugh at my life. Then I paid a pound for one last lollipop and left the bright bathroom.

241

The dancefloor was a seething mass of bodies now, all try-ing to move in time with songs from the *Grease* soundtrack. I got a couple more bottles and stayed near the bar, reluctant to force my way through. Watching these guys and girls carouse, sweaty flesh squashed together as they allowed bodies to jump and sashay, I felt that familiar pang of someone stuck on the outside. With Kathleen gone I was sidelined once more, left to play the wallflower as I stayed apart from joyous cavortings. Whatever that girl's love had freed me from, it was back to oppress my nights once more.

Time passed and I got through more beer. The shirts of some of the girls came undone, leaving them in a costume of mini-skirt, wonderbra and school tie. Others turned around in surprise as men groped behinds or pushed hard-ons into backs, culprits adopt-ing the expression of a naughty boy caught with a pea-shooter, as if they couldn't be expected to resist this temptation. The whole scene became less about fun and more orgiastic, marauding guys sticking their hands up skirts or pawing at the breasts of girls too drunk to know what was happening. Some females fell down in corners or attached themselves to those they liked, grabbing hold of guys who had difficulty escaping their attention due to the mass of bodies.

As the event lost its restraint those uniforms we wore struck me as having a sinister aspect. The clothes rendered each clubber anonymous, removed our individuality and made it easy to see every girl, from repressed virgin to engaged librarian, as sexually-adventurous sluts, all out for the casual lay. The look of this place, that overindulgence and simple music, it was all designed to let us regress to a level where civilization could be abandoned. These sur-roundings encouraged indiscriminate groping, *Teacher's Pet* a ha-ven for casually threatening males, men committing acts they might have been arrested for in another context.

I pushed my way through the drunkards, found a dry chair near my colleagues and waited for the evening to end. Justin and Mart were so intoxicated by now they could barely stand, escorted to a seat by two burly security men after stumbling into several peo-ple. The blondes soon joined us, tired of stabbing erections and busy hands as they tried to boogie. When someone suggested we get our coats there were no objections.

Outside I kissed each of the girls in turn, wishing them all the luck in the world. Mart shook my hand and said he'd be in touch while a glassy-eyed Justin demanded I give back his car keys.

"What?"

"Just give me the keys, I'm fine to drive."

"What keys? You don't have a car Justin."

"Let me drive, I'm fine."

"Nobody here has a car, they're all getting taxis."

"Give me the keys. Go on."

"The only keys I have are for my house." I showed him. "Are you going to drive a block of flats?"

But Justin had stopped listening to me. He was swaying down the street, getting the lyrics to a Kylie Minogue track wrong at the top of his voice.

Lettice reassured me. "Don't worry, I'll make sure he gets back to Yohanna in one piece. You gonna be okay?"

"I hope so, I've a vague idea what to do next."

"Good." She gave me a final hug.

Everyone I spoke to agreed, I couldn't leave the situation as it was. Tomorrow I'd have to go up to that house, knock on Kathleen's door and be confronted by whatever the Tibbits had to throw at me. In retrospect I probably should have thought my intentions through better, but at the time calling to see what would happen felt like forward planning enough.

Part Four:
A Big Hollywood
Ending
(For The
Romantically Inept)

Chapter Nineteen

Of course, when I woke up the morning after *Teacher's Pet* I had less resolve about the action to be taken, suffering as I was from a throbbing hangover and confused as to why we didn't keep paracetamol in the flat. Actually, my first thought, on waking from an extremely vivid dream where I was back in a CDT lesson to look at the clothes I'd slept in, was that I must be late for school. Then I stared at the sickly man in the bathroom mirror and slowly it dawned on me. Although I'd passed out wearing a uniform, I shouldn't worry, today was Saturday. Besides, I didn't go to school any more.

I drank half a gallon of coffee and watched a couple of idiotic TV programmes before the promise I'd made to myself felt achievable. Time to fulfil my destiny, whatever that was. Probably I should have waited until my thought processes were functioning properly, I spent an awfully long time trying to lace up my shoes. Then I practiced talking out loud for a bit. Soon I sounded almost coherent. There was no putting it off any longer.

An hour later my train pulled into Purley station and an hour after that I finally managed to find the right house. I'd decided to save money by avoiding taxis and this turned out to cost me more in the long run, since I ended up buying something in each of the shops where I asked for directions, it was only polite. Thankfully this was a nice day on which to be lost, clear and with the warmth of Spring in the air, but I was buckling from exhaustion by the time I reached that place, following a mile-long stroll through the suburbs. I looked at the door for a while, straining to hear movement inside the house. A few minutes passed and I realised someone was watching me from across the street. Smiling at the man who tended to his garden, I swore to myself then pushed the button. The bell rang and someone came down the hall. Kathleen's mother looked as if she was neither surprised nor pleased to see me. I imagined this was the same face she used on political canvassers and trick-or-treating kids.

"Monty."

"Mrs. Tibbits." She went on staring. "Erm, is Kathleen in?"

"She doesn't live here anymore." The woman glanced over the road where that man had paused to watch us. "You might as well come in."

I followed her down the passageway, ignoring those framed photographs which appeared in my peripheral vision. Taking a seat at the kitchen table, I accepted this aloof woman's offer of tea and watched her move between kettle and fridge and cupboards. Mrs. Tibbits' physiognomy was similar to Kathleen's, although she carried those extra pounds which come with age and children. Her lined eyes were just as brown, but the mother's hair was curlier, a few dashes of grey in the tumbling locks. The person she reminded me of most, in physical terms, was my own mother. Both were fairly slim with dark tresses and high cheekbones. I saw now what my father looked for in a women.

A mug was set before me. "Kathleen's got a new life now." She declared. "I don't think she wants to see you."

"I guess you've told her everything."

"After what you said to her at that awful play I had to, she was terribly upset." Outside birds twittered above the sound of distant lawnmowers. Mrs. Tibbits held her drink with both hands. "I was sorry to hear about your father Monty."

"Thank you." There was another silence. I'd no idea what to say and the hangover wasn't helping. The possibility that Kathleen didn't live here had never occurred to me.

"I don't know why you've come." Kathleen's mother was becoming slightly fraught. "I thought you put the whole thing behind you. My daughter certainly has. Now you turn up on our doorstep...."

The emotion was beginning to overtake her again, my presence an unwanted strain. I expected her to start blaming me for something any minute, in fact I'm sure she would have ranted at my expense had we not been interrupted by the doorbell.

"My God! It's like Piccadilly Circus here today."

Kathleen's mother went to get the door. I heard another female voice, this one breathless and harried, my ears catching a few snatches of the visitor's talk.

"Car broken down....mobile needed charging....husband working today...at my wit's end."

Stretching to glimpse this arrival I saw a woman in her thirties, smartly dressed in a trouser suit and with a red face from some recent exertion. Mrs. Tibbits said something I couldn't make out and allowed the woman inside. Then they both turned right, into the lounge.

I sipped the tea and tried to place that niggle in my thoughts. Something was familiar about this turn of events but my brain was moving at the pace of a paraplegic tortoise today. It was a while before I remembered that email warning, one I'd read the same day Poppy went on her rampage.

Jumping to my feet, I reached the lounge in eight strides. The 'businesswoman' was at the phone, having dialled what she'd have told Kathleen's mother was her husband's office number.

"Hello, can I speak to....." But that was as far as she got. I cut her off, hitting the button to leave her with nothing but a ring tone.

"Hey!"

"Monty, what in God's name are you doing?"

I turned to the squawking woman. "Block the way out Mrs. Tibbits, this person isn't who she claims to be." The female visitor stayed where she was. "You've tried this trick once too often lady, sit yourself down."

The woman did as she was told. Kathleen's mother stood before the door with her arms folded. "You'd better explain yourself." She demanded.

I pulled up an armchair and sat opposite the interloper, trapping her in "This isn't some damsel in distress Mrs. Tibbits, and she wasn't about to call her husband. That line she just dialled is one she's set up herself." I turned to the woman. "How much does it cost? Twenty five pounds a minute?"

"Bloody hell." Kathleen's mother exhaled. The conwoman glared at me

"There isn't any broken down car is there? You just say that to win over trusting householders like Mrs. Tibbits here."

"Please Monty, call me Val."

249

I nodded. "You play on the goodness of their hearts, Val wouldn't have known anything was wrong until she got the bill and one of the calls cost several hundred pounds. Just those few seconds before I cut you off probably add up to several quid." I gestured to the woman's flashy handbag. "You going to reimburse her?"

The woman moved slowly, plucking money from her purse while I watched. In the background I heard Kathleen's mother breathing heavily, her body's response to the commotion. A five pound note was thrown at me.

"Good. Now we have to decide what to do, now that we've got you trapped."

"Should I call the police?"

The woman exuded disgust. "They won't be able to do anything." She spat.

"That can't be right."

"It is Val, I'm afraid she hasn't committed any crime. You gave her permission to enter the house so they can't get her for trespassing and it's the phone companies' responsibility to crack down on overpriced lines. They don't though, that might cut into profits." I tried to invest my grin with some malevolence. "All the police could do is hold her for a while and we can do that just as well."

A feigned madness in my stare and voice, the latter pitched somewhere between evil genius and Peter Lorre. The combination must have got to this con-artist, for the first time there came some understanding of her position. "You can't do this, it-it's kidnapping."

"What do you think Val?" I kept my eyes fixed on our detainee. "Should we tie her up?"

"My husband's behind the whole thing. He'll be out looking for me."

"But he'll never find you will he?" I placed a finger on the woman's face and ran it slowly over her cheek and lips. "We can do whatever we want with you."

The woman shuddered and tried to shrink back. I was laying the depravity on a bit thick but it was working, she looked genuinely scared. I might be a serial killer for all she knew.

250

Val stayed in front of the door as the conwoman reached into her bag once more. "Here, I've got cash." Panicky now, she was grasping at straws. "There's a mobile if you can use it, and make-up. Take what you want."

"Take what I want eh?" Leaning over that carefully-styled bouffant, I came so close that my stale breath made her recoil. She flinched as I stayed close. "You got a camera in the house Val?"

"I do."

"Good." I sniffed the woman's skin like a dog, or maybe a cannibal. "Shall we take some pictures?"

Several hours later that man over the road was clearing up the mess he'd made trimming the hedge when the front door of the Tibbits' house opened on a strange sight. Emerging into the early evening was a woman in her thirties, dressed like a scarecrow but without any hair. As the man watched, slack-jawed, the figure looked both ways and swung a handbag over one shoulder of her moth-eaten jumper, stained fingers marking the wool as she did so. The woman hurried off down the street while Val and I watched from the lounge, Kathleen's mother hooting with laughter all the while.

"Did you see the look on her face?" Val grabbed one of my arms for support, bent double with mirth. "Absolutely priceless!" Around us were scattered the instruments of our revenge. Clippers had shorn those soft locks which lay on the floor, all what was left of the woman's expensive hairstyle. Her trouser suit was left across a chair (Kathleen's mother reckoned it might fit Kate) beside the pad of paper on which we'd done some rudimentary fingerprinting to go with the mug shots, just in case we needed to inform the authorities.

Val straightened up and wiped the tears of mirth from her eyes, looking at me now with an odd expression that changed from pleasure to anguish. I guessed she was remembering why I'd come here. Kathleen's mother requested I join her in the kitchen where she would make us dinner, a very timely plate of spaghetti after which Val said it was time I heard her side of the story. The full truth was laid out in that exaggerated manner of hers, the forty-something woman growing apologetic as the extent of her deception became apparent.

"I felt it the first time I saw you. Now you know why I wasn't very welcoming. Something in me suspected you straight away, even before I heard your name was Sanderson. When you turned up at New Year I remembered he had a son and I saw him in you. There were a thousand little things in common and they all made me want to keep you away from my daughter. I know, I know, it's not a nice thing to say. But what if you were just like him inside too? Kathleen would have experienced what I went through all over again." She paused. "You don't sleep around do you Monty?"

"No."

"Good. Yes, I can see it now, you were just one more victim of his ways. It can't have been easy, having Brian as a father."

"He did okay."

"I wanted to kill myself when he left. *Oh God*, you can't imagine it. The pain never stopped. I came to terms with it eventually, but I never forgave him for walking out on me. That's what left me in this condition, the problems with my back and stomach. The doctors say it's all in my mind, but what do they know? I think you have to forgive because the alternative isn't healthy. Don't you agree?"

"I guess."

"You must forgive, otherwise it'll stay inside you and cause more damage. I hope Kathleen finds it in her heart to forgive you, after what's happened today you deserve it, talk about my hero." She smiled and touched my arm. "I'd never have been able to pay the bill that nasty woman rang up. Thank you Monty."

"That's alright." I wondered why she hadn't mentioned how disgusting it was, the half-siblings being lovers. Maybe Val was squeamish, preferring to gloss over that sort of thing. At least I had her blessing now. She was happy for me to know my sisters.

"So, yes. I'll put in a good word for you with Kathleen the next time I see her. If I tell my daughter what you did it might help her forgive you for running away."

"Thanks."

252

"Now you have to forgive me in return."

"Forgive *you?*" That tickle of foreboding was back in my stomach. "For what?"

"I shouldn't have let you go on believing your mother's story but I did. How was I to know you weren't bad too? You might have inherited the things I hated about Brian, God rest his soul. I didn't want those traits inflicted on my little girls, safer if you thought they were both your sisters,."

"What?"

Val looked up, her dark brown eyes in need of redemption. "I'm not proud of it, my God of course I'm not. To think what I was like back then. By the time Kate came along there was only Brian in my life, but with Kathleen, well..." Val trailed off, she was distant now, staying calm and collected, something I'd never have thought possible. This was turning into a weekend of people pulling the rug out from under me. Val's self-control in delivering her news contrasted wildly with the tumult in my heart.

"Let's just say, I was single, those were liberated times and I felt a bit insecure. More than a bit I suppose. I needed a lot of love and support Monty, don't we all? So I looked for it everywhere I could, but none of them came close to your father. Those other men just led me astray and let me go. I didn't think he was like that, so when I found out he was, it hurt me. Really hurt, right here."

Kathleen's mother clutched both hands to her breast. I wasn't about to tolerate any more theatrics. "Just tell me Val."

She gazed at the young man before her, a guy who didn't want any more nonsense. Then Val laid it out as plainly as she could. "Brian and I both have the same blood group. Kate has it as well." She paused. "Kathleen doesn't."

A sound rose out of me, something low and whimpery which wasn't too far away from "Aargh!". Whether it emanated from distress or relief I had no idea.

"Kate's your sister but Kathleen isn't. There it is." Val studied my reaction. "I'll make some tea." Yes, tea. Tea would make it all better. "You don't know Kathleen's father, no one does, I haven't a clue where he is. He was younger than me and what we had didn't last. He's probably got other girls in trouble since then. It's best if she doesn't go looking for him and Kathy agrees with me, she can see no good would come of it."

Val washed our mugs and took out two more teabags. I wanted a pill or a shot, some kind of pentobarbitone which might knock me out for fifteen hours so I could wake up and work things out with a clear head. The *if onlys* were racking up in my mind. *If only* this woman had sent dad a picture of Kate on her own. *If only* mum hadn't assumed they were both his children. *If only* my father had put her right.

So that was why dad extended his affair with Val after Kathleen was born, she wasn't his. Damn this generation before me, damn their sexual meanderings and convoluted love lives. *The Daily Class* was right, liberation only caused trouble. Here we were, the young, the next crop, weighed down by having to deal with the shambles they'd left behind. Everything was too complicated and immoral and it *hurt*. What a waste.

Who was at fault? I could blame Val for not telling me the truth months back, my mother for not caring enough to explain my family tree long ago, my father for his infidelities. But that kind of thinking felt useless and empty. The buck stopped with me. If I'd investigated further, hadn't jumped to conclusions or hidden myself away, I could have avoided all this sadness. I'd broken my own heart without knowing it, sent away the girl I loved, been insensitive and presupposed. Maybe it wasn't too late to put things right, what Val told me could be wonderful news. The thought of Kathleen as a lover no longer made me feel ill all of a sudden. In theory there was nothing to stop us becoming a couple again, but in practice I suspected nothing would be easy.

Val brought the tea over. "Does Kathleen know she's not related to me?"

"I told her after that first time she did the play." The woman sipped her tea. "I wouldn't keep the truth from her, not if she wants to know."

But Kathleen kept the truth from me, never left a message or put me straight. She hadn't been in touch since that night we ran into each other in the theatre bar.

Mrs. Tibbits smiled at me, sympathetic. "Are you alright?"

"Yeah." I was numb and confused and directionless but yes, generally alright. Val went to the kitchen drawer and took out a pen and paper.

"Here, let me give you her address. The phone number's changed too."

"Thanks."

She ripped the page out and handed it to me. "I've learnt a lot over the years Monty. That's one good thing about getting older, you gain wisdom. I consider myself a good judge of character and you've convinced me you're a genuine boy. I'm sorry about everything that's happened."

"It's not your fault."

"You came here because you care about Kathleen, that much is obvious. I want you to know that if the two of you get back together you've my blessing." She took my hand in hers and gave it a squeeze.

"Thanks Val, it means a lot."

The front door banged and a girlish voice filled the air. "Hi mum, sorry I'm late, we lost track of time at the store. You'll never guess what I bought." A pause. "Hey, what's been goin' on here. Whose hair's this? Got yourself a little sideline do you ma? Looks like a holding pen for convicts in here..."

Val let go of my fingers, a twinkle in her eye. "Why don't you say hello?"

In the lounge Kate wiped stray follicles from the clippers we used earlier. The girl wore a long sleeved cream top with a short silver skirt. Seen in profile like that the shape of her nose was unmistakeable. It was my father's. Our father's.

"Hey Kate."

"*Whoooo!* Hiya bruv!" The girl threw her arms around me. "Good to seeya!"

"Likewise."

Kate withdrew, staring at me. I think it was only just sinking in for both of us. "Ohmigod, you're here. I've got, like, a brother?" She pulled me down onto the sofa. "This is *sooooo* cool. We have to do loadsa stuff together you know?"

We talked a while, Val tidying the lounge and reflecting on the extent of the mess. I told Kate about my life, about Fergal and being unemployed and small-time bands. Then I spoke of dad, how reliable and strong he could be. When her mother went away I explained to that girl with the lipgloss and the hoop earrings how she should never be ashamed of her father. There were worse than him on this planet.

In the end I agreed to meet Kate's friends and hang out sometime, maybe even accompany them on a night out should I feel the urge. My sister made a promise to come and visit dad's grave, pay her respects with me and harbour no grudge. Hard feelings would only eat away at that pretty face in the years to come. Those two people who made her, Val and Brian, they couldn't live together, so Kate's family turned out this way. No point feeling hard done by.

After bidding farewell to Val her daughter joined me at the door, speaking in a whisper now. "Listen bruv, I just wanted to say thanks. You know, for not shagging me?"

"That seems a long time ago now."

"Yeah, but I was *soooo* stupid. If you weren't strong about it we'd have been, like.... ugh!" Kate pulled a face. "I don't even wanna think about it."

"I guess no good comes from screwing other peoples' boyfriends."

"I've learned my lesson, rilly. Thanks Monty."

"Hey, no problem. It's only right I look out for my little sis."

She embraced me then, on that doorstep at twilight, and I thought back to all the times I'd been by myself as a child. How much I wished for a sibling to relieve the boredom. Now I had one, a funny girl who talked in pidgin Yank, knew about those feminine mysteries which so confused me as a teenager. Hell, they confused me still.

Suddenly my family was extended and for the first time I felt good about that, happy to belong to more people than ever before. I felt protective, although clearly Kate could look after herself, and I felt nervous because her breasts and groin were pushed right up against me. I thought of bears then; dog bears, short-faced bears, honey bears, and somehow I managed to stay flaccid. Patting Kate on the back I pulled away from her arms, kissed my sister on the cheek and walked off into the night.

Chapter Twenty

The address Val gave me was in W1, toward the centre of London, but by the time my train got back it was close to eight on a Saturday night. If I went round Kathleen's now the likelihood of anyone being there to see me wasn't good. Not that I was in any state to speak to her, and turning up on another doorstep without knowing what I was going to say would be pushing my luck a little. I decided to give Kathleen a call instead and got off the tube at Embankment to get a signal, passing a trackside notice which said: *'Please don't feed the mice, the rats eat the mice'.* Under which some joker with a felt pen had added: *'And the lions eat the rats'.*

Through the barriers and out the exit, I found a side street which was shielded from the traffic noise and didn't appear to contain any collapsed drunks. Pulling out that piece of paper I tapped in the number, praying I could read Val's spidery handwriting in the semi-darkness. I got her voicemail.

"Hi, this is Kathleen. Either I'm not available at the moment or I can't find my phone. Whatever, please leave a message."

The recording made me smile. It was a long time since I'd heard the girl's voice, that sound filling me with gladness. The knowing quality, both light and musical, the scattiness implied by her words, the deadpan delivery. Kathleen was welcoming and hilarious and by the time the tone came I knew I was still in love with her. Shame she didn't answer really, but probably for the best. I didn't know what I wanted to tell Kathleen, and those days when I could charm the girl into ringing me straight back were long gone. I hung up on the beep.

At the end of the alleyway laughing couples walked along Victoria Embankment, toward lights promising alcohol and entertainment, enjoyed a riverside stroll on this dry May evening. Hope had reappeared in my life and it left me wired, Kathleen wasn't my sister after all and I needed to talk about that. I rang the flat but no one picked up so I tried Fergal's mobile.

"Hel-lo good sir."

"Evening mate. What you up to?"

"Myself and the good man-bear are on what you might call *the scene.* Yourself?"

I looked around. "I'm up a back street near Charing Cross."

"Ah, taken round the back, I know how you feel." Laughter from somewhere near him. "Tell me my friend, if I wanted to buy you a drink would you accept?"

"Does the pope shit in the woods?"

"Er...."

"Yes I'll have a drink."

"And a good thing too. Come and join us on Wardour Street."

The Pink Oboe - Licensed Bar & Sauna was a prosaic building sandwiched between a noodle house and a piercing studio in the centre of Soho. The place felt like an exclusive club from the outside but Fergal assured me membership wasn't required. I hoped being a bumboy wasn't required either. The plaque on the outside wall read; *Pleasing Gentlemen Of Refinement Since 1870* and the doorman gave me a nod as I passed by. I descended the stairway which was given a crimson tinge by the lamps fixed to the walls, slowing several times as I went down. On each occasion I persevered, the need to purge my soul greater than my straight boy's fear of entering a homosexual area.

When I walked into the bar several dozen male heads turned at once. I felt exposed and fraudulent, like a failed arctic explorer. That is, until Fergal raised himself from the table he was sharing with Randall and a couple of others, greeting me in his customary, all-encompassing manner.

"Monty my good man! What are you having? I wholeheartedly recommend the vermouth, Sydney here mixes a mean drink." The serving gay grinned.

"A beer would be fine."

"How uncouth! Well, you heard the man Sidney. A pint of your finest wifebeater it is. Do come and join us Monty." I followed Fergal to the table where Randall had instructed one of the others to fetch a chair for me. "This is Derek, and you remember

Roland." I acknowledged the tanned poofs. "Now, do share with us your reasons for this inaugural visit to our establishment."

I looked around the group, all four of them waiting for me to speak. No doubt my flatmate and the American generally did most of the talking, but tonight they'd seen fit to give me the floor. The table waited for me to divulge, why a man like me, well-known for being heterosexual and bellicose about it, should venture into this world. I described everything Val had told me, filling in the background for Randall who needed to know it all.

"I'm confused." Derek admitted, he was a young homo with a peroxide head. "You're saying you thought she was your sister, but now she's not?"

"That's exactly what he's saying Derek lad." Fergal beamed. "This is splendid news."

"Yeah, maybe. But how exactly do I go about getting her back?"

Randall stroked his beard. "That could take a while. The first step would be to open up a mutually-supportive dialogue."

"Forget all that self-help balderdash, what you need is a grand gesture. Something she won't be able to resist. Why don't you hire a pilot to write her name in the sky?"

"I'd like to higher a pilot." Derek was all a-quiver. "I do so adore flyboys."

"Fergal's such a romantic." Confided Roland.

"You've seen too many movies dear fellow." Axelrod turned to me. "The very last thing you should do is try to sweep this girl off her feet."

"Harumph." Complained my flatmate, and left for the bathroom.

Seizing the opportunity, I asked Randall to have a word, see if he could stop Fergal picking on Justin. He promised to do so and Axelrod must have been successful, because whenever I subsequently met up with my ex-colleague he never again complained of people mistaking him for a corpse.

The rest of the night was spent drinking obscure cocktails and feeling fortunate none of the gays around me were out to cruise. Derek and Roland were obviously a couple too, and together with the others they formed a kind of sodomite shield for the token heterosexual in their company.

I learnt how Roland continued his love/hate relationship with Carshalton and Derek described his job, how being a document controller was "a lot like working in a rodeo, only with bits of paper instead of horses". Meanwhile Fergal recited some of the juicier stories regarding *The Pink Oboe*'s clientele. He pointed out a man who accidentally started a fire in Buckingham Palace during the Golden Jubilee celebrations after some camp courtiers invited him up to freebase, then the West End producer about to put on an all-male alternative to *The Vagina Monologues,* entitled *The Scrotal Conversations.* There came cattiness and bitching from the younger pair, some queer who possessed "the brain of a mollusc and a face like a slapped bus" or the once rampant queen rendered celibate thanks to genital unreliability, although in Fergal's opinion "a bad workman blames his trowel". Randall told me about the offers of employment starting to come his way after the potato voiceover, bit parts and ad work which kept him in gourmet food. Then the American mentioned one of the gays at the bar was asking after me, how he'd said I was already spoken for having recently married a Mountie in Ontario. I asked Randall why he didn't just say I was straight, but the tubby man shook his head and impersonated John Wayne.

"A man gets run outta town for that sorta thing round these parts."

I was quite relaxed by then and only became apprehensive whenever men wrapped in towels wandered into the bar. When this happened the drinkers would pause in their conversations to stare at the unclothed fellow who was talking with the barman about sauna facilities and suchlike. Each time I followed their eyes and unwittingly caught a glimpse I had to look away in horror when it became apparent what I was ogling.

But all in all it was a most agreeable evening, I experienced none of those vaguely-imagined horrors I'd always associated with the gay scene. There were no narcissistic bodybuilders aggressively trying to turn a straight boy or overly-keen poofters discussing whether to take me by force. I was enlightened, and despite what my mother might assume I didn't walk out of that bar with the urge to buy a feather boa and join the cast of *Rent*. No, all I could think about on my way home was how much I wanted to see Kathleen.

The next morning I snapped awake with none of the usual Sunday lethargy, made coffee and gobbled a slice of toast before going out the door. Giving Mrs. Winterbottom a quick wave, the old woman at her kitchen sink handwashing some bathmats, I bolted down the stairs. Outside our block the sky was clear and there was a purpose to my life, an unfamiliar feeling which filled me with energy even as it left my actions erratic. That's why I decided to jog up the street without thinking about what might be flying down, my first mistake of the day. I was racing along the pavement, between churchgoers and the returning casualties of Saturday night, when I failed to see the pigeon soaring down towards my face. *Smash!* The bird's beak connected with the centre of my forehead, its feathery body slamming into my skull. We fell to the ground.

All was dark for a moment, then I opened one eye cautiously. An old man in a long coat and pork-pie hat stood over me shaking his head.

"Bloody vermin." He muttered and bent down. I thought the old guy was about to give me a hand, help up this injured person spread-eagled in the street. Instead he picked up the pigeon, its neck obviously broken by the impact, and put the dead bird into his carrier bag. The man shuffled off, leaving me momentarily glad the pigeon hadn't suffered. Then I got to my feet, before some stray dog or passing nutcase decided to investigate my prone form.

I made it onto the tube and checked my reflection in the carriage window. There was a nasty crimson welt in the centre of my forehead and a larger bruise around it. I got dizzy then and had to sit down. At Notting Hill Gate I changed lines and disembarked at Marble Arch, turning right out of the station. My intention was to walk up the Edgware Road to Kathleen's street, but it was at this point I ran into my second hitch of the day.

Turning into the junction I found myself slap bang in the middle of some kind of protest march. Thousands milled around these roads which had been closed off for the demonstration. Actually it was more like tens of thousands, the main body of people moving down the A5 toward me, walking in the opposite direction from where I wanted to go.

I touched my sore head, withdrawing the fingers as pain shot through my cranium. The ache was exacerbated by these chanting multitudes who waved placards and whistled in a general show of dissent. The marchers were certainly unhappy about something, these travellers and students, older men with sideboards and their strident wives, the academics and left-wingers, minorities beside anti-establishment types. A great swathe of signs became visible above the sea of individuals walking along, they called the Prime Minister a liar, demanded an end to globalisation and the capitalist society, clamoured for the legalisation of marijuana, freedom for Palestine, an end to racism and empire building, peace in the middle east, opposition to GM foods and poverty. I had no way of telling how long this would take to pass, and standing there observing it all I felt like the polar bear beside the blowhole, not knowing his prey would surface.

Without that arctic-dweller's patience I eventually concluded I would have to force my way against the tide, passing an anarchist collective and dodging union speakers as I walked up the road. I was forced to move to the left while the procession came at me, plunging into crowds who watched from the pavement, a struggle through the curious and supportive. The audience was there to encourage marchers, people who didn't feel strongly enough to complete the walk themselves. Or maybe they were supporting everything the protestors were against. I definitely heard a few shouts of *"rubbish!"*, *"shut up!"* and *"crusties!"* as I moved along the Edgware Road, swerving between shopkeepers and local people drawn outdoors by the demonstration. One diminutive fellow slow-clapped the walkers, but I couldn't tell whether this meant he was in favour of the protest or against it.

I made steady progress, the main problem now was that my A-Z showed Kathleen's street on the other side of this thoroughfare. I looked to my right but there was no way across. It was long minutes before a slight gap appeared in the stream of people, the space coming before a group of anti-nuclear types who played instruments. As I raced over the main road I almost collided with an enormous African man who had a bass drum strapped to his chest. He waved the beater at me in a threatening manner while I reached the kerb.

There it was, her avenue. I found number 8a and wondered how Kathleen could afford to live in such an exclusive neighbourhood, trying not to dwell on the possibilities of rich boyfriends or, even worse, some kind of sugar daddy. Her block was only a few yards along the byway and many of the marchers spilled along here, breaking free of the squeeze in Edgware Road. Youngsters smoked joints and talked to each other in the excited tones of the nascent agitator while one raggedy bloke pissed the morning's cider into a gutter. I gave the stream of urine a wide berth and ventured up a flight of stone steps.

"Yes?" A female voice answered my buzz.

"Is Kathleen there?"

"Who is it?"

"Monty, Monty Sanderson." Long seconds passed. I watched more marchers go by, the carnival atmosphere continuing on the main road.

"She's coming down to meet you." Said the girl, probably a female flatmate. That was good, at least Kathleen wasn't cohabiting with some posh yahoo in his London love nest.

Time elapsed, the seconds turning to minutes, and now I was back at the blowhole, wondering exactly how long before the seal showed itself. I examined my coat, scuffed where that bird had knocked me over, and there was dirt on my trousers. Not bad though, not compared to the injury which damaged my face. I touched that bruise again and immediately wished I hadn't.

"Ow!" I screamed. The door opened and there she was, Kathleen's presence hitting me as forcefully as that damn pigeon (R.I.P.). She looked the same, gracile and pretty like always, but the hair was thoroughly blonde now, all the way down to her roots, and there was a weary expression in those brown eyes. We stood there for a while, looking at each other.

"What happened to your face?"

"It's not important." I cupped a hand over my forehead. "Hello Kathleen, how are things?"

"Not bad, I work in the city now."

"I like your flat. This area's very swanky."

"My friend lets me stay for less than she should, her parents own the place. Still not cheap but... you know."

"Yeah, I know." You do what you have to, that went unsaid. Cheers and shouts came from the passing parade. "I only found out yesterday, about Kate being my sister and..."

"So now you know." Kathleen remained impassive. "What's the point of coming here?"

"Well, uh, now that we're not related, I thought..." Shit, I was turning into Hugh Grant again. "Erm, maybe you'd like to...."

She cut me off. "You want to rekindle the old fire, is that it? Now everything's above board you want what? To start dating again? *Puh!*"

"Why not?" The situation, that pounding in my head, her attitude, it caused me pain. "You got a new bloke? Is that it? Some broker you met through work?" Her face fell. "Come on Kathleen, can't we at least talk?"

"You really don't get it do you?" The girl looked up to her flat, a couple of windows open in response to this mild day. "Come on Monty, let's take a walk. I don't want my flatmates hearing this."

I followed her down the steps, about to suggest we went left, towards the relatively peaceful district of Marylebone. Before I could say anything Kathleen had turned right and headed for the march. I caught up with her at the crossroads, the girl watching those demonstrators passing by, costumed men pumping the air with their fists, insurrectionary clowns on unicycles.

"First of all, there's no one else. I'm off men for a while funnily enough. Although you don't seem to be able to understand that."

"I'm trying, but..." I guess the flame of hope must still have burned and Kathleen saw it flicker. When she spoke next the words came out bitter and facetious.

"I know exactly what you thought. You thought you'd come here and get your happy reunion and big Hollywood ending and off we'd go, the same as before." She laughed. "Well it's not going to happen, *mate*. I drop my guard once, just the once, allow a guy into my life, and what does he do? Lets me down. It really screwed me up Monty, you know that? I asked you not to just turn up but here you are, as if you don't realise what you did was wrong. But your actions have consequences Monty, really fucking painful consequences."

"I know, I messed up." Down in the gutter a crumpled purple tin rolled past. "Give me a chance to say sorry Kathleen, please."

"You think words can put everything right?" She sighed. "I thought you were different Monty. I let myself fall in love with you because you weren't like those other mongoloids, the ones who'd wander off and abandon me without a second thought when they got turned on by someone else. Do you know how many times people have walked away from me?"

"It's not been easy, I know that much."

"You have no idea. And my worst fears came true thanks to you. Off you trot, away forever, breaking my heart. What was that about?"

"Christ Kathleen, everything was impossible. My dad died and I tried to grieve alone and get over it but then my whole world came crashing in."

The tail end of the march passed us now, that human mass thinning out as observers drifted away.

Kathleen's voice was calmer now, but the emotion behind it remained. "I'll never understand what you did, not letting me know about your loss. How could you do that? I thought we were soulmates. You never got in touch, you never supported me through that damn play *you* got me into. Worst of all you didn't come to me when you heard about your sisters, and now you want to talk?"

"I was trying to spare you the pain."

"Yeah, great. Brilliantly done. You know what? I never cared much if you were related to me. Sex isn't the most important thing, I don't think so anyway. What killed me was the way you shut yourself off. Instead of helping me figure things out you lay it all on me and vanish again. By the time mum told us that Kate and me didn't have the same father I wasn't interested in you any more. By then you were just someone I had to get over. Because it's patently obvious you don't have what I look for in a man."

"How can you say that?" I sidestepped and turned to face her, my back to the road. "What we had was amazing. If you find it in your heart to forgive me anything's possible. Let's start from scratch. I'll tell you everything about me, forever. I swear. Please Kathleen, I'm not part of it all without you and I've changed, can't you see that?"

"I don't believe you, people don't change." Kathleen moved closer. "Listen to me Monty. It's over. You're nothing I want in a man. I don't go for selfish and uncommunicative and cowardly. I'm very sorry about your dad, but I'm sorry for Kate too. I don't want you in my life and I definitely don't want you trying to see me with my family." She was belligerent now, angry. My natural instinct was to back away so I took a step off the kerb. "You went round mum's house didn't you? I suppose I can't stop you from seeing Kate but I don't want you hanging around when I'm there. You got that? I want nothing more to do with you."

I nodded, terrified she was about to leave. "This isn't fair Kathleen. You say I'm uncommunicative but I'm trying to communicate right now. I still care about you, can't you see that?" The girl looked at me, this guy stood in the gutter, then away. I thought I might have finally roused her compassion, but when Kathleen glanced back there was no change to her flinty expression.

"This conversation is over."

"No it's not, you're still talking." An edge of panic in my voice. "Now *I'm* still talking, and we need to keep talking. No one says *'this conversation is over'* in real life. Don't you believe me when I say I love you?" I blurted it out in desperation, trying to elicit some kind of reaction. Kathleen's eyes flicked to the right.

"Watch out for the horse." She said.

I looked into the snorting nostrils of a policeman's steed. The animal took me by surprise and I leapt backwards, barging into

267

a uniformed officer who brought up the rear of the march. He grabbed me.

"Cool it sonny Jim, why aren't you with the rest of your buddies down there?" The policeman nodded towards Marble Arch.

"I'm not part of the demonstration. Can you let me go please?"

"Are you resisting me? What's that on your face son? Been in a fight have we?"

"A pigeon did it."

"A likely story."

"It's true, I swear." I looked to Kathleen, she was watching events unfold.

"Excuse me madam, are you *with* this gentleman?"

The girl delivered her line with all the conviction of a seasoned actress. "Never seen him before in my life officer."

Then the policeman ignored my protestations of innocence and dragged me off to join the fading parade while Kathleen turned away from my struggle and disappeared.

Chapter Twenty One

And so began what I would come to look back on as my fortnight of defeatism, a time when each day was about the same. I rose around ten resolving to find employment, then showered and went out to buy newspapers featuring media job opportunities. These I would scour for about fifteen minutes, by which time I was in a kind of trance, the tedium of endless ads for work I didn't want or wasn't qualified to do, getting to me. Disillusioned, I flicked through the rest of these papers, reading transfer speculation in the sport pages or the latest dawn raid on a batch of clinically obese suspects as police continued their faltering attempts to apprehend *The Fat Family*.

If the weather was fine and Fergal was in I might wander the city with him, seeking out slapstick to film. Otherwise I tended to slump in front of the television, enduring live curling on BBC2 or the Channel 5 film for kids. My favourite from this time concerned the adventures of an animatronic squirrel who was also a genius at backgammon. He had to pluckily overcome the prejudices of humans to reach the Olympic qualifiers in Washington. The hours passed well enough, but the longer my stasis continued the more I worried, about my bank balance and what might happen should I fail to find work.

Fergal tried to help, offering to pay the rent until I got back on my feet. Although I refused the loan I was happy to let him and Randall cook food for me when they were around. Over dinner the gays would discuss their day, what tomorrow might bring, events occurring out in the world. Remaining tactful at all times, the pair didn't ask me about finding work or mention Kathleen. Sometimes Fergal would elucidate a reprehensible aspect of *The Daily Class*; the paper's hateful attitude toward Jewish asylum seekers before the second world war or the lie, published back in the eighties, that Jane Fonda had suffered a heart attack. His tales wore me down and I eventually stopped buying the tabloid. Fergal took this as a good sign, maybe I was over my flirtation with mainstream morality.

After we ate the male couple had usually prepared some kind of appetising dessert, and during second helpings of trifle or spotted dick they would ask if I wanted to spend the evening in Randall's spare room. Apparently the American had a "most marvellous" collection of Pooh figurines and ornaments I really ought to see. I declined every time, told them I was past bears, happier by myself. They should go have fun together, three being a crowd and all that.

That left me alone in the flat so I cracked open a couple of beers or my faithful bottle of scotch and turned on the nightly TV top one hundred. These thematically connected clips were counted down as I drank, my mind floating away to Kathleen as I tried thinking of reasons why she should give me another chance. In my mind I rebuffed her accusations, convinced the girl to listen to me. If only reality were that simple

Sometimes I would get exceptionally hammered and think about calling her up, giving Kathleen the case for the defence which had been evolving all night. Everything seemed so coherent in my head, but some logic which refused to be muffled by alcohol told me not to bother, I'd only regret it. That is until one night, during the top hundred most arousing TV moments, I was thinking about my love life as a montage of skimpily-dressed *Dr. Who* assistants flashed by. Against the backdrop of a sidekick barely contained by her tiny bikini (Peri running away from a dalek not unlike the one in our hallway), I dwelt on my father's failings, aligning them with my own mistakes. I found understanding then, melded this into the arguments formulated over my nights. The whole swelled up to an irrepressible urge and I grabbed the phone. That recording again, but this time I left a message.

"Kathleen, Monty. Sorry about this, but I couldn't go on without giving you my side of the story, I owe myself that much. I'm not going to blame anyone else for the way I treated you, I just wanted to let you know some good has come of all the pain I caused. I've knowledge now, of myself, what I'm like. You see, I'd been following the example my dad set me, messing up just like him. For as long as he lived Brian never saw it, dad never knew what he was like, but I've done better than him Kathleen. And maybe understanding is the first step to righting my wrongs.

"You were right, I didn't see how it looked from your side, back when you cared about me. It was like my dad keeping several women on the go. Us kids, me and Kate, we found ourselves scattered around, not knowing each other, not until now that is. My father caused that, just by being who he was. I followed in his footsteps and lost the only good thing I ever had, but I've changed my outlook Kathleen, really I have. I'm learning to see the world from others' point of view, and I'm trying to feel what they're feeling. Right now I reckon you're annoyed at me for leaving this message, maybe wondering whether I'm full of crap or not. What I say is true, I don't intend to bottle everything up any more. I'm going to let it all out, *share*. It's not easy, putting your emotions in the hands of someone else, it goes against the way I was brought up. Hell, sometimes I think any emotion goes against the whole idea of Britishness. But screw the stiff upper lip, from now on I'm gonna let people know how I feel. I'm working on it Kathleen, working really hard, this is just the start...."

A couple more like that, left late at night, after the beep. Me vowing to be more receptive, show sensitivity and wisdom. I think that's what I said anyway, I was very pissed at the time and despite managing to remain semi-articulate, I'd wake up the following morning unable to remember if I'd got my point across.

Kathleen wouldn't call me back, I knew that. Mine was just another voice rambling in the darkness, the wittering of one more inebriated soul, like that drunk who shouts profanities at the moon. Still I clung to my hopes, however frail they might seem, spending my days sat beside our landline with the mobile on, just in case. It happened Monday, the start of my third week as one of the unemployed. I was in my armchair, staring at a pile of newspapers I'd bought but hadn't opened, when the telephone rang. I fell upon it like a European bear on a beehive. It wasn't her.

"Hello?"

"Morning mate, how's it all going?" Martin Landry.

How *was* it all going? I was becoming knowledgeable about local news stories and eating a lot of blancmange. Those were positives. "It's going okay, sort of."

"Found work yet?"

"Nothing definite, I'm still weighing up the options." Option number one; get a job sharpish. Alternatively go and live with Bernard under some steps. "How come?"

"I've been busy Monty, very busy. We settled the concept last week and backers haven't been slow coming in. Remember when I lost the *Venustra* contract near the end of *Bears!Bears!Bears!*"

"Ocelots wasn't it?"

"Yes, ocelots. We didn't have the experience to cover what that company wanted and you know Monty, when I finally got some time to myself I started thinking about those ocelots."

"Oh yeah?"

"We set our sights too narrowly in the last agency. Today's climate demands a flexible marketing industry. I suppose what I'm saying is this; a man cannot live by bears alone." He sounded confident and enthusiastic, just like the old days. "Then it came to me, I've the experience and the contacts, why not broaden my horizons and employ different animals? I could apply about we learnt from ursines across the board. You know yourself how some products don't suit bears. Tea for instance, or condoms."

"I guess it could work."

"Could work? It *will* work mate, I've financing for the start-up and everyone knows my name in the ad world. The real coup was getting London Zoo on board, they're going to be our sole supplier of exotic animals so we don't have to worry about drunk northerners anymore."

That was an achievement. "How come?"

"They were sick of different agencies ringing up to rent a hippo for the afternoon or whatever so the zoo's management agreed gave me exclusive rights to represent their creatures. That's major selling potential, right there."

"Bloody hell." Landry had pulled all kinds of entrepreneurial stunts before but this was impressive, even by his standards.

"But why are you talking to me Mart? I know sod all about most of their animals. It was always bears or nothing. You'd have to understand a tapir inside out if you wanted to use it for a campaign, use it effectively I mean."

"Exactly, and that's where you come in. What are you doing at the moment?"

I glanced at the television. On the screen Terry Wogan was receiving a makeover against his will. "Not too much."

"You've got time for some research before starting with us then?"

"You want me to work for you again, just like that?"

"There has to be an interview first but it's just a formality. I'll tell you what to say, the decision's been made anyway, I just have to get official confirmation from our backers."

"Tell me when and I'll be there."

"Wednesday morning, back in Soho, Martin's new office on Old Compton Street." When he hung up I stared blankly at Wogan as he ran out of the studio pursued by a vengeful mob of make-up artists. Then I switched the TV off and got organised.

Over the next two days I didn't touch a drop of drink and I certainly didn't make any more pointless calls to Kathleen. Instead I spent hours at the internet cafe looking up the inmates of London Zoo. Then I went and got my increasingly fluffy hair under control, looking forward to an attractive woman running her fingers through that unkempt black mass. Unfortunately the only free chair in the salon turned out to belong to an intense-looking Russian and he didn't take my hints, how I wanted to wait for the girl hairdresser instead. He yanked my head all over the place but at least I looked tidy by the end of my Soviet ordeal. Back home I dusted off my work clothes, selected my newest tie, ironed a shirt and even found my library card. I took to the reference section, reading up on every caged beast the zoo possessed. By the time my interview rolled around I felt more than adequately prepared.

On Wednesday I rose earlier than usual and found that the year had somehow moved into June. Leaving my coat at home I walked to the station, past cars with sunroofs left open overnight, a symptom of the early summer warmth. Tube trains were running normally and I absorbed a *National Geographic* article about meer-kats until I arrived at Tottenham Court Road. Once there I took an indirect route into Soho, greeting Bernard who was out from his crawlspace to revel in the sunshine. The tramp greeted me with a protracted bout of coughing, wished me luck at the interview and agreed to join me for a power lunch soon.

Mart's new office was situated on the first floor above a wine shop. I waited as the trio of interviewers readied themselves, men pretending there was more than one candidate for this job. Eventually Martin ushered me inside where I was confronted by a corpulent fellow in his mid-fifties, a man called George who, de-spite his good humour, clearly suffered no nonsense. Across from him sat Keith, a thin, grey individual in a double-breasted suit who represented the bank. Meanwhile Martin Landry, friend, former boss, hopefully future employer, positioned himself in the middle to get proceedings underway, posing a series of questions which were little more than paraphrased accounts of our past successes, designed to give the older men an insight into how capable I'd been at *Bears!Bears!Bears!*. For example:

Martin: "So, as well as maintaining the website, writing copy and dealing with clients, you were also responsible for assess-ing the workloads of other staff?"

Me: "That's correct, yes."

Martin: "This might seem like a lot of responsibility to some, but it's possible I may ask you to take on a similar schedule in your new role. How would you feel about that?"

Me: "In all honesty I can say that I've always hankered after opportunities to show what I can do. I absolutely *thrive* on a chal-lenge."

And similar fakery. Questions from the others proved more taxing, but thanks to my advance planning I was able to field them effectively. The banker asked me what I'd learnt in business terms from my time at the last agency, so I babbled on about niche mar-keting and how it was a double-edged sword or the importance of opening yourself to new *revenue streams*. I didn't mention the real maxims I intended to observe at this new organisation, like employing competent people or keeping turnover out of the boss' ill-starred creative projects. Vague as they were, my answers seemed to satisfy the moneyman. I guess it wasn't my place to think much about accounts or profit margins so as long as I didn't come over as a dunce everything went positively.

The evaluation continued, George asking his questions. That was when I got the pleasant feeling this interview was becoming a walkover. Here are a couple of the highlights:

George: "How would you deal with a moaning zookeeper if he didn't want to wake a leopard in time for its photo shoot?"

Me: "You ask him why he scheduled the animal's appearance at a time when it would be asleep. Then you talk to his boss, which I believe would be you George."

George: Are you willing to commit to the kind of research that enables you to know, for example, the diet required when filming commercials with a capybara?

Me: "Ah, the capybara. A member of the rodent family if memory serves, although actually it's about the size of a pig. Your zoo currently has three of them and I believe they mainly eat grasses and melon." *<pause for effect>* "Research isn't a problem George, I enjoy learning....".

The firm and friendly handshake at the end told me all I needed to know about George's opinion of me. I left with his compliments resounding through my brain and Mart soon rang my mobile to say the banker had also been impressed. The job was officially mine, although Martin was careful to stress that now the real work was about to start. I had to return to his office the next day and pick up some zoological literature my once and future boss expected me to digest over the weekend before reporting to work on Monday.

On my way home I tried to think of a way to celebrate. Maybe I'd call Si, see if he wanted to come out on the razzle. Or I could go for a good meal and fine conversation with Fergal and Axelrod. The city was my playpen.

Unfortunately the merrymaking ideas became null and void as soon as I got in and Fergal announced, with inappropriate levity, that, "Kathleen, rang while you were out."

"Whaaaat?" Whatever did this mean? Had she sought legal action following our altercation? Was I now required to keep a certain distance away? So? What, what, *what?* "What did she want?"

"That girl got on my ass because I couldn't find your ass. For the sake of this ass get that ass where her ass can see it." Fergal smiled. "Otherwise my friend, her ass will kick your ass over to my ass and we won't see her ass again, then who's the ass? Huh?"

I groaned, flopping into a chair. "Why do I get the feeling you're spending too much time with Americans? Look *Ferg*, stop being so damn flippant and tell me what she said."

"Make some tea and I might just do that."

Apparently Kathleen had spent last night at her mother's where they had a long talk. About me, about Kate, about what was going on in my head and why I put Kathleen through so much. Given a new perspective by that most unlikely of sources, Kathleen went back to W1 and listened to my messages for the first time.

"Kathy thinks she's been slightly harsh." Fergal spooned sugar into his tea. "I told her not to think like that, whatever she did you deserved it."

"Oh, thanks."

"But you know what that girl's like, far too lenient. Kathleen's worried about your mental health. She asked me whether you'd been taken into custody at the protest march, any idea what she meant?"

"Don't ask."

"I told her I hadn't heard anything, but you weren't acting like someone on the run. Then she expressed the opinion that you were drinking too much. Is this true?"

"Erm, uh...."

"We'll leave that for the moment, I'm in no position to lecture you on the importance of moderation." He moved beside the window and lit a cigarette. "What intrigued me was when she alluded to speeches you left in the dead of night, ones where you despair at not being able to dance without her then break down and start blubbing."

"Oh Christ, I don't remember that."

"Sounds suitably tragic to me, however something in your impersonation of a reckless sociopath must have touched her. Kathleen's softened her opinion of you, I could hear it in her voice."

"Really?" I sat down. The fronds of some comforting but unfamiliar plant were wrapping themselves around my heart. A tree called hope. "What do I do?"

"That's where your kindly Uncle Cofaigh comes into the equation." He flicked the lit cigarette butt out of our window. From somewhere below there came a cry of pain. "APOLOGIES SIR!" Fergal brought his head back inside. "Where was I? Oh yes. Kathleen agreed to give you one last chance, she'll be outside Embankment station at six thirty."

"Aargh!" I leapt to my feet. "Nyeuuur!" Walking in circles now. "What do I do? What do I say? *Eurgh! Eurgh! Eurgh!*"

"Dear God, the man's having some kind of attack. Sit down Sanderson, you'll do yourself a mischief."

At that moment, as if in tribute to Fergal's powers of prophecy, I slipped on an old copy of *The Class* and fell against the doorpost.

"Ouch."

"I told you no good would come of that rag. Maybe you'll settle down now. Good God man, do you want me to call the men with the butterfly nets?" Fergal helped me up. "Where would Jane Fonda be if she'd responded to the Hanoi thing like that? I'll tell you where, damaging herself inside some asylum like her mother. But no, she saw it out and came back stronger. History will be kind to her."

I rubbed my forehead. That swelling caused by the incident with the pigeon had only just gone down and now this. "Eh?" I said.

"You need a plan."

"Um, okay." We sat there. "What about, I turn up, tell Kathleen the truth, and we take it from there?"

"A little vague, what's the truth?"

277

"That I'm not the same person without her. That on my own I get stuck at the fringes, away from everyone else, without happiness or pleasure or feeling fulfilled. My world looks monochrome when Kathleen isn't in it. Without her I feel like there's no reason to get through the day. What we had was brilliant and shining, it changed my life forever and every relationship before her seems like a schoolboy crush now. I'd do anything to get her back."

"Hmmm, why do I suspect that instead of saying that you're just going to see her and have another seizure?" Fergal scratched his beard. "I understand what you're going through my friend, really I do. If Randall were giving me one last chance I'd be panic stricken too."

"You really love him don't you?"

"I want to be with him forever, I know that much. If you consider that a valid definition of love, then yes, I love him." Outside our window the white triangle of an aeroplane descended on Heathrow. "But as wonderful as it feels to admit that and know it's reciprocated, we're not talking about me, or whether I share your plight. Perhaps Randall does make all those other boys I've known look like dry runs for the real thing, but what we need to do is stick to the point and make sure there are no cock-ups when you meet that dear girl. I fear the only way to ensure that is if I'm with you."

"Really?"

"Indeed, and I'm minded to bring this along." Fergal lifted up the video camera. "If all goes well we'll want something for posterity."

Chapter Twenty Two

Through the glass I saw a couple dressed in black. He wore a long coat and heavy boots while she had on several tops and a thick skirt. They scurried across the road, finding shelter from the sun under a doorway awning.

"Bad weather for goths this. There's nothing light in the wardrobe so they end up wilting in the heat." Fergal shook his head. "Sad. Another cuppa?"

I concurred. We were in a coffee house opposite the Embankment Place entrance to the tube, sat at the table which gave the best view. Actually it was more of a bakery than a cafe since behind a counter assistants sold bread and pastries, but there was also a small area for those who wished to relax with a beverage. I watched the station, observing the numerous ways that homeward urge expressed itself through rush hour London, from men hailing taxis to women with impractical footwear who tottered down the paved roadway.

On the table in front of us lay a bunch of begonias I'd bought on a whim from a nearby flower stall, much to Fergal's disapproval. He didn't think Kathleen would even be interested in apologies, let alone flowers. I agreed, but I'd no other way to say sorry, so I bought them. Kathleen was living with another girl, I'm sure they'd enjoy aesthetically pleasing plants around the house.

The Irishman brought me another mug of coffee and I checked my watch again. The time was close. We'd been over what I needed to say several times. No grand proclamations or lovelorn entreaties, just a simple and respectful request; *Kathleen, allow me back in your life.* As swiftly or as slowly as you can handle, keeping me close or at arm's length, it didn't matter as long as I was there. Now I yearned for her to appear so I could say my piece, all that caffeine making me wired, one foot tapping out the rhythm to an *Airborne Toxic Event* song on the floor.

"There she is!" The girl appeared under the archway and moved to one side, glancing at those who milled around with something like suspicion, the fruit sellers and Big Issue men, women offering free magazines or travelcards at knocked-down prices.

279

Fergal had his video camera up on the table and manoeuvred the lens to get Kathleen in shot. After a moment he looked up from the eyepiece.

"Well laddo, what are you waiting for?"

I snatched the begonias and left the shop, circumventing a delivery van before cutting back. As I walked towards her I got a good look at Kathleen's new image. This was an aspiring career girl, young executive, trainee banker, share-vixen. Whatever the hell she was it seemed to call for enhanced presentation, more elaborate special effects than I'd seen on her before. The girl's face possessed an unnatural sheen, colour layered on lips and eyes and those emphatic cheekbones. She wore a dark skirt and frilly white blouse under her black suit-jacket, something about this get-up having the effect of artificially enhancing her bosom, Kathleen's modest breasts appearing more prominent than they actually were. Then there were the objects decorating areas of exposed flesh, bejewelled bracelets, a golden necklace, silvery earrings. I wasn't sure I liked this look, the style she adopted for financial types, high-powered brokers visiting her desk at every opportunity to slaver over their female colleague. I wasn't particularly enamoured of the expression she held either, that of the dutiful citizen forced to perform some unpleasant task, like a pop star doing community service.

Her face didn't change when she saw me. "Monty."

"Hello Kathleen, I got you these." She took my flowers and turned them downwards, pointing the begonias to a grimy pavement.

"Okay, whatever. Look, I don't know if I'm up to this so let's keep it short, I've had a terrible day at work."

"Yeah, right." I looked at her outfit once more. "Is it really worth it? I mean, how long does it take to get ready? Then you have undo it all at night. Must be hours and you don't need it."

From uninterested Kathleen's demeanour moved to affronted. "It's my life Monty." There was vehemence in her voice, I was in the wrong again. We stood and watched the passers-by for a while.

Kathleen said, "I read a story that reminded me of you the other day. There was this bit in it about polar bears."

"Yeah?"

"One character described how male and females aren't loyal to each other. They fuck once a year and then the guy bear runs away, like he's terrified. He never sees the girl bear again. Remind you of anyone?"

I gazed at her, saddened. "That's not fair Kathleen, I thought you were going to give me a chance." What a professional appearance she had, that pure blonde hair, the wizardry of blusher and lipstick. "You look lovely today, really beautiful."

"More words, useless compliments. That all you can offer, words and flowers? What do they prove?" In amongst the commuters and consumers there was a young woman pulling a toddler, she looked like she hadn't slept in a month. Kathleen offered her the begonias. "Would you like these love? Here you go, I've no use for them." The young woman looked dubious but after a few seconds she realised there was no catch and took the flowers, muttering a *thanks* before dragging her child away.

"Great."

"What? She'll appreciate them more than me." Kathleen's astringency defeated my positive approach. This wasn't going at all like I imagined. "So Monty, that last chance. What do you have to offer? What's so great I'd be missing out if I never saw you again?" Clouds rushed to block out the sun. "Come on boy, your messages said how important this was and Fergal assured me it was worth hearing you out. How exactly are you going to convince me?"

I'd no idea. Whatever it was I'd come here to say had dribbled away, out of my brain and through my ears like some kind of aural phlegm. This was very bad, I felt like an autistic kid before his teacher, unable to answer the simplest of sums.

"Can't you just come over the road for a bit?" I played for time. "We'll get a cup of tea and talk properly."

Before she could respond the pavement was engulfed by a wave of people. Some trains must have unloaded down in the station and now the rush and clatter of these travellers made further conversation impossible. Kathleen watched them go, becoming more sharply-defined somehow, as if she'd awoken from hypnosis. When the street cleared my ex-girlfriend moved to the entrance.

"Look Monty I'm sorry, this was a bad idea. I haven't been sleeping, my job makes me feel crappy and I just want to get home." Kathleen passed through the archway. "I'll call Fergal okay?"

Then I was alone, alone and thinking of all the times she'd disappeared before, wondering if I'd ever see her again. A London Underground worker was having a smoke nearby and when he looked at me I realised I was partially blocking the exit. Unwilling to quietly accept my fate, I made a decision. If Kathleen was upset I hadn't spoken to her after the funeral surely it was hypocritical to give me the silent treatment now? Come on Monty, *act*.

I shoved my ticket into the machine and ran down the escalator. Stupid, bloody stupid, going on about her appearance like that. If Kathleen didn't make the effort for work she'd feel bad about herself, colleagues making snide comments because the girl didn't present herself well enough. That way for the Northern Line. Okay, get out the way missus, the northbound platform I guess. All Kathleen's accoutrements meant nothing to those who loved her, it was the girl underneath we cared about. Whether she was looking her worst or all dolled up, that shape and perfume and clothes and lipstick were all just garnish. Forget the visual stuff, what I needed was her inner beauty, her personality, Kathleen's heart and soul. Now, where was she? I hope a train hasn't just gone. Mind out fella! Yes, there she is.

"Kathleen, I..."

"Jesus, nine minutes 'til the next train and the platform's crowded already. It's gonna be a nightmare." She turned to me. "I can't believe you followed me here Monty. Get it into your head won't you? Now's not the right time. Maybe we'll hook up again when I'm not feeling so crabby. I can't seem to keep a thought in my head at the moment."

"Right, well, um...."

"And I definitely don't need you crushed up against me on the tube. It isn't even your line. Sodding delays..."

I stared up at the scrolling message.

"Delays to all Northern Line destinations due to an earlier defective train at Mornington Crescent. Let her be Monty Sanderson, leave the girl and go."

Great, even the ghost in the LED machine was against me. Thoroughly defeated, I trudged outside, the ache in my heart becoming more pronounced with every step away from her.

At street level I avoided the station worker and a couple of exceptionally wide men in baseball caps to cross Embankment Place. The sky was opening and drops of water landed on my tidy hair as I entered the bakery. The shop was busier now, possibly because of the rain, or maybe it just seemed that way. Two of the customers took up quite a lot of space, an obese man and the heavily pregnant woman with him.

I sat beside Fergal. "How'd it go?"

"Isn't here is she?"

We drank coffee and watched the downpour. From behind us I heard the pregnant woman harangue her elephantine associate for not knowing what to buy.

"Look, it's pissin' it down! I told you this was stupid. Hurry up wouldya?"

"Fucking hell woman, keep your shirt on. Yes love, I'll have two of your meat pies and a cream horn."

"We shouldn't even be in 'ere like this."

"Cheers love. Right then moaning minnie, I'm with you now." The overweight guy bit into one of the pies and waddled out, following the woman who held her bulge too tightly. That can't be the way to deal with an unborn child I thought while watching them walk across the roadway. That man really was enormous, the kind of overfed character who has folds of flesh hanging from his chin and armpits. When they reached Embankment the two fat men in baseball caps appeared to nod to them. Then they all went inside.

"Anything I can get you?" Asked Fergal with some concern.

"Eh?" After two and two come together hindsight makes everything seem so straightforward. Usually I was someone who could never find the numbers in the first place, but not this time. "Yes, actually. Grab your stuff and follow me."

"I meant about Kath... wait a second Monty!"

There was no time to waste, I dodged between parked cars and entered the station. Running as fast as rush hour would allow, I'd almost caught up with *The Fat Family* when I reached the escalators.

There were five of them on the moving stairs, standing at intervals so nobody suspected they were a group. The other two must have been waiting somewhere near the ticket machines because now they were all here. People walking past had to turn sideways, such was the girth of these males, and I tried to think what I might do when we got to the platforms. Inspiration didn't come, I'd run on gut feeling so far, hopefully that would serve me again as I blew the whistle on these criminals.

We got to the bottom, the fat family merging with that crowd heading for the Northern Line. They weren't very swift so I waited at the foot of the moving staircase until I saw Fergal hurrying down. Catching his eye, I silently communicated my route, then zigzagged between commuters and caught up with the gang.

The men turned onto the northbound platform and I followed. There hadn't been a train in ten minutes so the area was packed, the display board saying one more minute to go. The fat gang barged their way through and took up a position two thirds along, near that place where Kathleen had given me the brush off not so long ago. I couldn't get to her now, there was too much flab in the way. The men huddled to talk while their female cohort pulled at her lump and I stretched to look the other way, seeing a raised video camera above the sea of heads. As Fergal came towards me I raised a hand and urged him on, which was when the next service pulled in.

"Please allow passengers off the train first!" Pleaded the announcer as people toppled out. I saw Kathleen go through the double doors seconds before the fat boys. No one gave the strange group a second glance, they were all too concerned by getting on the only train for six more minutes. I made it through the single entrance at the carriage's end and moved into the aisleway, a few feet away from those mountainous men.

Kathleen had found a seat and was reading a copy of *Glamor* monthly, oblivious to those around her. The train started to move and that supposedly expectant mother tapped the girl on her shoulder. I couldn't hear what passed between the two women but it ended with Kathleen giving up her seat. Forced to stand, the readjustment of passengers caused her to drift away from me and toward the fat men. All five were gleeful at this point, belching and sniffing, the one I'd seen earlier sucking cream from his fingers in a disgusting manner.

The train pulled into Charing Cross and there was a bit of argy-bargy behind me as people got on and off. I took this opportunity to push nearer the men, spotting a skinny youth standing close by, his eyes flicking around the carriage. To my left one of the arrivees turned out to be Fergal with the video camera. He looked at me so I mouthed the word "fat" and jerked a thumb at the porkers. In response Fergal checked the viewfinder, then used his superior height to film above the other passengers.

Turning back, I noticed something barely perceptible pass between the criminals. They began to shuffle about, those on board shrinking back each time a flabby individual got too close. Quickly it became clear what they were trying to do. While emitting a series of unsavoury grunts and snorts the men attempted to encircle Kathleen.

I shoved past a man with a briefcase and a sweaty metalhead but I was too late, within seconds the fat family had surrounded my horrified ex-girlfriend. Half a minute to the next station and their hands were moving fast, more nimble than seemed possible for such monstrously overweight men. I couldn't see the girl among them and the gang were drowning out most of her cries with their vile noises, but from what I did hear it became clear Kathleen was very frightened.

Rocking back, I took a one-step run up, screamed an obscenity at the top of my lungs and threw myself into the melee. Somehow my momentum carried me between a couple of podgy shoulders and I grabbed Kathleen, slapping away those sausage fingers which grasped at her belongings. With a superhuman effort I pulled us both out, giving the terrified girl a hard shove that sent her away from the robbers and down the aisle, commuters making half-hearted cries of *Oy!* and *Hey!* as she collided with them.

Panting from the exertion, I gripped a pole to support me. The pregnant woman rose from her seat, pulled the padding out from under her top and smashed me in the face with it. I sprawled backwards, hitting something soft and spongiform, something which smelt of sewage and rancid meat and iced buns. It was a fat man. The quintet closed around me, blocking out any hope of escape. Our train slowed, approaching the next stop as the four mammothlike men came closer and closer. In desperation I shouted for Cofaigh.

"Fergal, pull the emergency alarm!" A high-pitched whine spread through the train while five enormous bellies crushed my chest. "It's the fat family!" I hollered to no one in particular. "Block the doors!"

My larynx was squashed, their combined weight leaving me unable to breathe. Ten porcine eyes glared at me, their fetid breath and glabrous faces convincing me I wasn't getting out. The train came to a halt and I felt my legs give way. About to black out, I tried to scream but there came no sound. So this is how I'd die, asphyxiated on the Northern Line by a bunch of bloated fuckers. What a bloody stupid way to go. I closed my eyes and saw light, divine light, white light, a benevolent figure with a beard (and a strangely ginger beard at that) drawing me towards him. I'm coming Father, holy Jesus, I hear you....

"Ow!"

"Gerroff!"

"Don't do that, y'bugger!"

The pressure on my body eased and I dropped to the floor. The men were forced away, my surroundings coming into view as they backed off. My fellow passengers had grasped the situation and were clawing, pinching and twisting great handfuls of flesh. Gasping, I took in air and looked around. Six other passengers, including that businessman and metalhead, had arranged themselves to block the doorway, arms linked as they trapped the criminals. Unable to push their way out, the fat family had begun to argue among themselves, trying to bribe people with the contents of Kathleen's handbag while the youth and woman denied any involvement. Meanwhile the man who engineered my escape and also choreographed this entrapment stood over me, a great, hairy figure, backlit and cheery, who offered me his hand. I took it and rose shakily.

"Wouldn't let you down now would I?" Said Fergal.

Leicester Square station was closed for the rest of the evening while police took their suspects away in a series of specially reinforced paddy wagons. The station staff gave me oxygen at trackside and while I felt like I'd been badly winded after a short rest everything was fine. Once the travellers from our carriage had given their statements the train was taken out of action and services became non-stopping. I watched them whiz past, hundreds of faces peering out at officers and forensic experts as they worked, wondering if this might be covered on the local news when they got in, whatever it was. Close by a policewoman finished jotting down Fergal's version of events, probably a verbose and grandiloquent take on the story. My flatmate came away and sat with me, still holding his video camera.

"We've got it all here my friend, this footage will be the talk of the town. The fuzz wanted my cassette but they're not getting it until I've made a copy."

"Um-hum." To my left another female officer talked with Kathleen, the girl wrapped in a blanket brought down from the supervisor's office. Another train zoomed past causing me to glance up at the electronic board above.

"Delays to all destinations due to a police investigation at Leicester Square. Go to her Monty."

When I looked back down Fergal was staring at me. "Well? What are you waiting for?"

Slowly, unsteadily, feeling my way along, I walked up to Kathleen. The policewoman smiled, gave her a reassuring pat on the hand and came to meet me.

"Mild shock but she'll be fine. It's understandable to be a bit shaken up, those are formidable thieves. You were extremely brave."

"Thank you."

The underground was warm this June night but Kathleen still shivered. I took a seat beside her and looked into those brown eyes, all fear and wariness now.

"Hey."

"Hey."

"How's it going?" I stroked some matted hair away from her face. "You okay?"

"I'll be fine, they gave me my stuff back." She spoke softly. "Monty?"

"I'm here."

"Don't get the wrong idea but....." Kathleen looked to the floor, then back at me. "Can I stay at yours tonight?"

"Sure."

"It's just, my housemate's away, and I really don't want to be on my own. Does that sound silly?"

"Not at all, I'll sleep on the sofa."

"Thanks, I knew you'd be a gentleman about it." And with that the girl in the scratchy grey blanket, the girl I loved, snuggled up close to me.

I put an arm around her, holding Kathleen while staff and police cleaned the platform, understanding how right she'd been. Sometimes words aren't necessary.

Chapter Twenty Three

I came out of the building and onto Old Compton Street, blue skies and a swollen sun giving Soho an almost spiritual ambience. Inside my bag were books about our new suppliers along with the guidelines drawn up by Mart and George explaining our rates, conditions and percentages. The boss had also passed me photocopied documents covering everything from the dietary habits of pelicans to amateur otter psychology, but the paperwork could wait. I had a long weekend to read up on these creatures before my first day at *The London Animal Hire Company* next week. This morning was a time for visiting old friends, letting them know I was back in the neighbourhood for good.

Yet when I got to my old workplace Bernard was nowhere to be seen. I expected him to be sunbathing again but a brief search proved he wasn't around. Worried the new occupants might have tired of a tramp living under their staircase and moved him on, I went inside to make inquiries.

"Monty Sanderson! As I live and breathe!"

Leon welcomed me to the smoking room like a prodigal son, introducing me to poker players I didn't recognise then dealing me in, a few hands during which I bet modestly and talked of Mart's new agency.

"Where's Bernard? I couldn't see him outside."

"Working."

"Working?"

"Yup, two for Nigel there and dealer takes three." Leon put down his deck. "Bernard got a day's employment as an extra for something the BBC are filming over the square. They said he had the authentic vagrant *look* they were after." The dealer's turn to bet. "Alright big shot, I'll see your ten and raise you five."

Intrigued, I folded with three nines which might well have won the pot and told Leon I'd be back regularly as of next week. Outside I decided to give Kathleen a call and looked for a quiet doorway. I'd disturbed her before leaving this morning to get an office number which she blearily recited before going back to sleep. The girl was snoozing again by the time I rang her boss, peaceful under my duvet. I explained to him that Kathleen had suffered an accident and the nurses were instructing her to rest. The man at the other end sounding like he had other priorities so didn't question this tenuous excuse which was lucky, because if I had started going into specifics I'm sure he wouldn't have believed me.

Except he'd have had to, there was evidence everywhere you looked. The apprehension of *The Fat Family* was big news today; the front of the *London Metro*, page five in the *Class*, mentions inside other dailies, all of which I'd bought on my way in to meet Mart. None of the witnesses to the arrest were mentioned by name so I didn't get any credit but to me that was a relief. The prospect of recognition for thwarting those villains wasn't what thrilled me about last night, the important thing was Kathleen's safety. She held me tight all the way home while I cradled and comforted. Then I tucked her up in my bed, leaving Kathleen safe and sound and snug with a light kiss on the forehead garnering one sweet smile in return.

She answered my call. "Hey."

"You're up then. How you feeling today?"

"Not so bad, a bit dislocated. What you up to?"

"On my way to Soho Square. Bernard's got some kind of job there, if you can believe that."

"The homeless guy?"

"Yup, they're filming a programme for TV."

"Hey, wait a minute, I think Fergal might have texted me about that." A pause. "Yeah, I got it just now. You stay put, I'll come straight over."

"Okay."

I'd skipped breakfast earlier so went for elevenses, a baguette which looked green and appetising but turned out to contain just rocket and fennel in wholemeal bread. Certain the wrapper said it consisted of some meat or fish, I checked the packaging again. No, this was effectively a cabbage sandwich. Chucking it to the birds, I strolled over to the busy square where extras, technicians and the rest of the film crew fussed around, checking light and sound levels. I spotted Bernard on one of the benches watching proceedings with fascination.

"Good morning young man."

"Alright Bernard, what's going on here then?"

"A documentary my boy, the life and times of a lady movie star."

"Oh yeah?"

A man with a megaphone, evidently one of the director's minions, announced they were ready to begin.

"Better assume the position, see you soon Monty." Bernard went to linger at the edge of shooting range while a mysterious woman in large sunglasses appeared, walking up to the suited individual with the clipboard who would pose the questions. Careful to keep out of view, I crept behind the cameramen for a better view, drifting in closer until I could make out what was being said.

There was something about this actress about to be interviewed, some radiation of elegance or savoir faire, an efflorescence which meant the eyes of bystanders gravitated towards her. The woman was middle-aged and not much over five feet, but her charisma was undeniable. When she removed her shades to reveal brilliant blue eyes I understood why I felt such star presence.

"Aaaand action!"

Facing his subject against the central London backdrop, the interviewer read out his first question. "Jane Fonda, for much of the sixties you were married to the film director Roger Vadim and lived with him in France. What was your relationship with England at that time?"

"We tried to get over here as much as we could, everyone knew London was *swinging*, and I was young so I wanted to be a part of it. As I grew up I came to appreciate the other things you have, like the marvellous culture and history of these islands. And of course I love coming here to shop." She laughed. "It's nice to be back, I always get such a warm welcome in Britain. Over the years I've come to feel at home in any number of countries, much more than I do in America in some ways. Europeans tend to be more sympathetic to my worldview. You don't suffer so much from that terrible anti-intellectualism which afflicts our culture and only seems to get worse as time goes on."

A shadow crossed Jane's face, but she brightened when asked about her experiences working on *Barbarella*. It was at this point my attention was interrupted.

"Hey." Said Kathleen under her breath, the girl having joined me near the crew members.

"Hey." She looked fresh and clean, dressed in one of my shirts. I wondered whether she'd borrowed my underwear as well. Together we watched the actress talk about her *feminist space movie*.

"I can't believe she's here." I whispered. "Where's Fergal? He should see this."

"His text made it sound like he was here already."

"*Aaaaand cut*. Right, let's break for lunch people."

The crowd dispersed, crew members lining up in one corner of the square where a catering company dispensed cool drinks and buffet food. Fonda walked in the opposite direction, chatting informally with the presenter.

"There he is, look." I followed the angle of Kathleen's finger and saw Fergal holding some kind of garment. As Jane broke away he opened out the coat and helped her into it.

I watched with an open mouth, only brought out of my comatose state by Kathleen tugging at my sleeve. "Come on, let's go say hi."

"Erm...." And before I knew it she'd dragged me over.

"Monty, Kathleen, come and meet Jane!" Fergal beamed, the cat left a network of dairies in someone's will. He didn't have to worry about not getting *the cream*.

"Are these the couple I've heard so much about?" Jane Fonda shook my hand. *Jane Fonda*.

"..."

"Hello my dear."

"Hi." Said Kathleen.

"N-nice to meet you." I burbled. The deterioration of age was pretty much absent in her. The woman had medium length brown hair and a beatific smile. Jane's skin had been left a little uneven by the passing years, a few wrinkles blemishing her neck, but the strong chin and piercing eyes kept Fonda looking youthful.

"You all hungry? Shall we get something to eat."

"Yes, we must."

Jane led the way, side by side with Fergal who seemed to have installed himself as her unofficial assistant. Star power enabled us to jump the queue and get our cold cuts, my flatmate bringing chairs up to a bench so we could all sit together.

"Great to meet you Ms. Fonda, you're a big inspiration to girls like me." Kathleen was enthusiastic. "How did you and this big lunk hit it off?"

"Lunk?" Fergal regarded her with mock outrage.

"He just turned up and introduced himself this morning. There were so many people buzzing around; doing my hair, suggesting clothes, all that. I was barely awake so I didn't bat an eyelid when some sophisticated young gentleman came over and started paying me compliments. By the time I figured out he was just a fan Fergal had made me laugh so much I simply had to take up his offer of a tour. We're going to visit some places around the city after my work's done."

Her voice was rich and mellifluous, just a trace of California in the accent (or so Fergal maintained later). Sitting there then, eating our lunch, I wondered if my flatmate was planning to be the toast of *The Pink Oboe* tonight or whether he'd take Jane somewhere less gay.

"I simply couldn't let the opportunity pass me by." Said Fergal between bites of meat. "When the grapevine told me Jane was in town I resolved to meet her, however much stealth or persuasion it took."

"He is your number one fan." I confirmed, adding hurriedly. "That doesn't mean he's a stalker or anything."

Kathleen set her plate down. "You said Fergal mentioned Monty and me."

"Oh yes." Jane touched his knee then, the Irishman blushing for about the fifth time in his life. "We were talking about me of course, but I get so tired of myself sometimes so I said to Fergal, tell me about yourself instead. Well, he's too wily for that, so I got this incredible story about a couple of his friends."

"It is weird isn't it?"

293

Jane smiled at Kathleen, her mouth a dazzle of white, teeth from a Hollywood dynasty. "Love will always be unusual my dear, you can be sure of it. If anyone knows that it's me."

"Any advice for them Ms. Fonda?" All of a sudden Fergal was reticent, shy as a load of coconuts and about as hairy.

"Yes you did ask. Well, if you're willing to take advice from someone with three divorces behind her." Jane replaced her sunglasses. With Kathleen listening attentively I remained quiet, this was turning into a very odd week.

"You know what I tell my children? Don't be afraid to make mistakes, I never was. I paid for it a few times, but you get a sense of pride learning like that, by living it. The two of you are young and from what Ferg tells me you've had more than your share of bad luck, but you're still together. Looking at you now I think the two of you will look back on the choices you made and see they were right; for the best, for a reason. To me regret is something we suffer when we're untrue to ourselves. I've never felt regret, everyone I've loved has contributed something to my life and I wouldn't want to erase any of them, my past is a part of who I am. The truth of it is that sometimes people in love want different things from life, that's when it gets difficult. Somehow I don't think that's true of you two." Kathleen held my hand. "We change as we grow, but whenever I'm with someone and we're trying to make it work I always think of what Saint Exupery said: *Love does not consist in gazing deeply at each other, but in looking outward together in the same direction.*"

An autograph hunter encroached then, breaking the spell Jane had cast upon the three of us. She inscribed his book while Kathleen pulled me down, the two of us sitting on the grass now.

"Let's gaze deeply at each other."

I couldn't help but laugh. "Sleep alright last night?"

"Yep, you?"

"Bit nervous when I woke up, I was in the middle of this dream where I had a lion for a pet. Damn dangerous, nearly took my arm off."

"Funny, I dreamt about fat people falling into mincing machines."

I adopted a scholarly air. "There are two schools of thought on a dream like that as you may be aware. It's either fallout from your unconscious mind trying to cope with the events of yesterday or, to take a more Freudian interpretation, it shows the transposition of hidden lust into apparently unrelated events. In this case a burning desire to sleep with me as soon as possible. In my opinion the latter diagnosis seems far more likely. What are you doing tonight?"

"Careful boy." She wagged a finger. "*You're* still on probation."

I reclined in the sun, watching people come and go from my supine position. A few feet above us Fergal quizzed his screen heroine. I closed my eyes and listened to their conversation.

"So Ms. Fonda, what do you think of the incumbent president?"

"God Fergal, aren't you comfortable calling me Jane yet? I hope you don't refer to me as *Ms. Fonda* when we're out on the town."

"Indeed no, apologies."

"As for the president, you must know my politics. Any reasonable human being would say he's the embodiment of everything wrong with my country."

"Someone told him you were placed in the top hundred women of the twentieth century and he said, *she wouldn't be on my list.*"

Laughter. "Figures."

"But Jane, who *would* be on the list if he was compiling it? My mind boggles. I could only think of his mother."

"Farrah Fawcett, no doubt about it."

"You've beliefs in common with the president haven't you? You're both Christians for one."

"Hey, I thought I was on a break! What is this, some kind of interrogation?"

"Please, I don't mean to offend. You must understand Jane, this is likely to be my only chance." A brief silence. "Did you find God? You can tell me."

"*Find God?* You make Him sound like a sock. I hadn't *lost* Him." She paused. "Don't you ever feel like there's something bigger than yourself?"

The familiar sound of Fergal patting his belly. "There's not many bigger than me."

More laughter. "I noticed. Remind me to send you one of my workout videos."

"I can't get thin!" Horrified. "My boyfriend likes it this way...."

They talked for a long time, about the memoirs Jane was writing and her solar house in New Mexico, the millions she gave to charity and what Fonda had learned during her decades of celebrity, a time when everyone, from the friendly to the hostile, thought they knew her intimately. Despite Jane's utter lack of superiority I was still overawed, although that wasn't why I failed to join in. No, despite being within touching distance of a film star for the first time in my life, granted access to this woman I'd come to respect through Fergal's biographies and obsession, my thoughts were elsewhere. Even though a multiple Oscar-winner and world-famous activist chatted to my flatmate, I felt like the priority sat before me, cross-legged on the grass.

I opened my eyes and took Kathleen's hand. "So, what do you think of Jane's advice? Reckon we can make it?"

"Maybe. Depends on what we've learnt I suppose."

"And what we're after. Do we want the same things?"

"Tell me what you want Monty."

I thought about it. "Remember those months we were together? Remember how it was back then?"

"Sure, that's why it got hard. What we had was so good."

"Not just good, *magical.*" I squeezed her slender fingers. "All I want is some of that magic back."

Eventually Jane was called away, off for the rigmarole of questions and retakes. This afternoon's session took her beyond these gardens, out onto the streets of Soho where she dropped by stores, checked out retro fashions and the merchandise from her movies. Randall Axelrod joined Fergal then, the pair of them following the shoot as it proceeded, going on to accompany Jane for

296

the rest of her day. We let them go, taking this opportunity to laze in the first serious heat of the year.

I'd just positioned myself to massage Kathleen's shoulders when she asked me the question. "Will it work Monty? Can we get that magic back, like the old days?"

"It'll be even better, you'll see. Whatever this world throws at us now can't be that bad. Not after all we've been through."

"You could find someone else."

Ever so gently I encouraged the girl to twist round. She was facing me now. "I'll do you a deal, okay? You catch your insecurities and don't say ridiculous stuff like that, and I'll try to stop being such an insensitive male." She nodded. "You promise?"

"I promise."

I touched her arm. "I know it's all part of the fun, but sometimes knowing I'll never understand women gets me down." Looking into Kathleen's eyes now. "Why don't you get it? Why don't you believe me when I say you're the sweetest, funniest, most lovely girl I've ever met?" She blinked. "Doesn't matter though, I'm happy to spend the rest of my life convincing you it's true."

Kathleen raised a hand to stroke my cheek. In response I came closer and when we kissed I could see our embrace from above. Even as I felt her lips upon mine my picture of us became smaller, as if from a space-bound camera zipping upwards, and soon we were just a couple of anonymous people on that isolated patch of green. Then up and up, nothing more than two specks in the square, the byways of Soho coming into view, intersecting lines and the movement of vehicles. Higher and higher I went, the whole city appearing, millions of people and buildings, the River Thames like a twisting blue snake cutting through this metropolis.

And I accelerated, rising even faster now. I could look down on all of England, the verdant greens and lush pastels, this waterlogged country of farms and landowners. The whole of Britain was there, two great land masses surrounded by roiling seas, but that wasn't all. There's Europe as well! And we're leaving the continent behind, flying at supersonic speeds. Still I rose, into the troposphere, the shape of the planet visible between clouds. And even that's not the end, because now we leave Earth behind, that planet which so beguiles us. Then I'm watching the globe become just another dot in space, part of a whole solar system, of asteroids and comets and stars. A place where love can seem like such a tiny concern, or the most important thing in the cosmos.

Epilogue

Sorry, but I can't end it there. If I leave everything like that you'll think Kathleen and me had some kind of fairytale ending and from then on life was perfect. Nothing's ever perfect, you should know that by now. Despite the incredible effort us *homo sapiens* put in, all that preparation and striving, everyone gets caught by surprise sometimes. That's how existence works, we're subject to uncertainty and flux, no matter how predictable some days feel. If life always conformed to our expectations we'd be disappointed. When events progress as we imagined, the results never diminished or surpassed, well, that's not really living is it? Especially when it comes to affairs of the heart. Love isn't about accuracy or completeness, and relationships are only perfect in Hollywood or the heads of teenage pop stars. Kathleen and I had to compromise and give in, fight a host of daily battles, improvise our way through pitfalls and booby traps. But it worked, we made it work.

Sometimes when I'm exhausted and fed up with selflessness, I remember how much easier life was when I only thought for one. I'm sure Kathleen occasionally feels that way too, but it soon passes. We know how cold and curtailed this world can seem when experienced alone. So she supports me and I care for her needs, I'd do anything and everything to keep hold of what we have, she knows that, even if she can't quite bring herself to believe it. And Kathleen's got me thinking she feels the same way. It's good, but I take nothing for granted nowadays.

What's that? What happened to everyone else? They're doing pretty well I think. Justin sells strange clothing to jazz aficionados out of a Chelsea basement. I see him sometimes and if I'm not careful he tells me about it. Apparently they do a nice line in smoking jackets.

My job's going well. It's challenging, you know? I enjoy having a friend as my immediate superior and working with animals so I guess I've got it made. Kathleen earns more than me now but she's talking about giving it up for another shot at acting, auditions and whatnot. That might make me the breadwinner again which would be good for my masculinity, if not our finances.

Fergal used his media contacts to sell that footage around the world, calling it "a daring apprehension of nefarious miscreants

'The Fat Family' by courageous members of the general public".
He'll be living off the royalties from that clip for the next decade,
I'm sure of it. Randall still puts up with him and Fergal's promised
to give up cigarettes, although I'm sure he'll still sneak one when
nobody's looking. They've been talking about living together across
the pond, and if that happens I guess the next step is for me to
move in with Kathleen. What would happen then? Marriage? Joint
bank accounts? *Kids?* God, I hope our mothers never meet each
other. What a living nightmare that would be. But I'm getting
ahead of myself, I've no idea what's going to take place. Another
lesson I've learnt is never to analyse too much, at least not before
the event.

What I can be sure of is one moral you won't hear from all
those other romcoms. *Love is work.* We're never let in on all the
hours of concentration and effort when we watch Hugh and his
latest squeeze on the big screen. How couples pay as much attention to the menial duties as those isolated moments of explosive
passion. There are good times and there are bad times, but when
love is worth it you're enriched and never complain.

I guess that's why I told you this story in the first place, to
help people like me understand what they've got. If something's
troubling you or your lover, some set of circumstances threatening
to damage the relationship, take a step back and realise it's not a big
deal. Don't believe me? Okay. Have you just found out you and
your girl are directly related? And when that turned out not to be
true, did you screw up so badly she wouldn't even talk to you? Was
your optimism killed stone-dead by the lack of an honourable way
out? Do you keep getting attacked by bears? No? Well then, your
life's not really that bad is it? Your love ought to be easy to fix. The
two of you just need to communicate and understand each other.
Because what you've got is too precious to throw away.

Right, sermon over. I've got to go and negotiate rental
terms for our number one gorilla now. Some yogurt manufacturer
wants to teach him to hang-glide and send the monkey over Ched-
dar Gorge, don't ask me why. This isn't goodbye though, I'll be
around. Keep your eyes open for that average guy, out on the
dancefloor shaking his hip, it might be Monty Sanderson. You'll

know the one. He's sealed from disapproval and embarrassment by the presence of a skinny blonde girl dancing alongside him. And at first glance she might not look beautiful, but she is. She is.

Acknowledgements

The epigraph in this book is taken from *City Life*, a story featured in Donald Bathelme's collection 'Sixty Stories', the most recent version of which is published in the UK by Penguin Classics.

For research purposes, Simon Price's excellent study of the Manic Street Preachers, 'Everything' (published by Virgin), was invaluable.

There are many terrific books on bears and I strongly recommend you try reading all of them.

For more information on how you can help some of the creatures featured in this story, visit www.animalsasia.org.

Tripmaster Monkey's debut album 'Goodbye Race' was released on Sire/Reprise in 1994.

Thanks to Metaller for the cover art and Jane Fonda for the movies.

Alan Devey is the Co-Creator and Editor of Home Defence, a satirical webzine (www.homedefenceuk.com).

Lightning Source UK Ltd.
Milton Keynes UK
30 June 2010

156317UK00001B/18/A

9 781905 006014